"HAVE YOU EVER ATTENDED A TORTURE PARTY?" AUGUST ASKED.

Kolet faced August. "Many. 'Cutters' we call them, because knives are the usual method— although some people prefer fire, burns." He reached into the medic bag and removed a small steel knife. It gleamed in the light.

Kolet held his left hand up, palm facing August. A patternless network of thin scars from long-healed wounds crisscrossed his hand. Carefully, like an experienced surgeon, he pressed. The blade cut into skin, leaving a trail of blood and open flesh.

BECOMING HUMAN

VALERIE J. FREIREICH

BECOMING HUMAN

A ROC BOOK

ROC
Published by the Penguin Group
Penguin Books USA Inc., 375 Hudson Street,
New York, New York 10014, U.S.A.
Penguin Books Ltd, 27 Wrights Lane,
London W8 5TZ, England
Penguin Books Australia Ltd, Ringwood,
Victoria, Australia
Penguin Books Canada Ltd, 10 Alcorn Avenue,
Toronto, Ontario, Canada M4V 3B2
Penguin Books (N.Z.) Ltd, 182–190 Wairau Road,
Auckland 10, New Zealand

Penguin Books Ltd, Registered Offices:
Harmondsworth, Middlesex, England

First published by Roc, an imprint of Dutton Signet,
a division of Penguin Books USA Inc.

First Printing, January, 1995
10 9 8 7 6 5 4 3 2 1

ACKNOWLEDGMENTS
"Do Not Go Gentle Into That Good Night," Dylan Thomas: *Poems of Dylan Thomas*.
Copyright 1952 by Dylan Thomas. Reprinted by permission of New Directions Pub-
lishing Corp.; and Dylan Thomas: *The Poems*. Copyright 1978 by Dylan Thomas.
Reprinted by permission of David Higham Associates.

The first three chapters of this book, in altered form, appeared in *Tomorrow Specula-
tive Fiction*, Volume 1, Number 2, March 1993, as "The Toolman."

Printed in the United States of America

To my husband,
Jordan

PART ONE

•

CENTER

A Dying Toolman

Chapter 1

Alexander Greeneyes was hungry, but he wanted to live. Those conflicting desires made him hesitate outside the toolman entrance to Sanda Brauna's apartment. Her security routines would be watching, together with Center's automatic monitoring system, routinely evaluating even this slight hesitation. Eventually he would no longer be able to hide his hunger, but he kept his head high, smiled, and touched the panel, opening the door; the time when he would be put down for flare approached, but it hadn't yet arrived.

Ting Wheeling, Sanda's latest acquisition from the toolman farm, stepped smartly down from the guardian station as Alexander entered the apartment. "I'll escort you," he said, his high-pitched voice rendering him deceptively nonthreatening despite the obvious power of the bulky physique inside the slick black guardian uniform. "Elector Brauna is in the sunroom." He spoke Sanda's name as if it, and she, were holy.

Alexander bowed in mock solemnity and followed, without protesting the officious escort through the entirely familiar apartment. Their footsteps were the only sound, except for the low, eternal, background hum of Center. "How is she today?" Alexander asked, to break the silence.

Ting turned around. His plain face was made graceful by its strength in the careful aesthetic of toolmen/guardians; wide-set eyes gave him an air of innocence. He observed Alexander warily, as though the comment might precede a wild attack. "Elector Brauna is anxious to see you, probe."

"Wonderful." Perhaps Sanda was watching, so Alexander said nothing more as they resumed their course. Lately, she watched him compulsively. He restrained a frown, knowing only one reason for such a change.

Ting led the way through the apartment, his gait as precise

as on a parade ground, each heavy footfall brushing fanciful flowers sculpted into the carpet's thick weave. His right hand rested on his gun as he passed each internal door—generally closed; presumably the empty rooms of Sanda's apartment needed privacy—as if hoping for an enemy ambush. Guardians were not usually so anxious. Offhandedly recognizing the likely cause, Alexander said, "I don't encroach on your duties. Why do you dislike me?"

Ting stiffened further, but didn't respond. Dull, like all guardians, Alexander thought: a sub with muscles. They reached the oversize bronze doors to the sunroom without exchanging another word.

Ting signaled the doors open and moved aside for Alexander, but stayed inside the sunroom. The steamy heat oppressed Alexander as he walked the earthen path to Sanda, who was reclining on a lounger in the central clearing. After the temperate atmosphere maintained throughout the rest of Center, it was like visiting the tropics.

The immense sunroom was a hothouse—glass-walled except for the single wall shared with the rest of Center. Sanda's apartment was on a high outer rim of the Center complex, so no part of the great, enclosed, floating city was visible through the windows. The sunroom was an isolated garden hanging far above Sucre—high enough that the dull gray, surface town of Sucre-semp, grown up to support Center with power stations, transit points, cheap human labor, and illicit entertainments, appeared distantly charming. The rich odor of the damp soil floor and the fragrance of the profuse vegetation were a stimulating change from the olfactory sameness of Center, particularly because the room had just been watered. Sanda kept two toolmen/subs whose sole duty was to maintain the foliage, under her supervision—her route to the Electors' red robes had been through botany. Occasionally she still dirtied her hands planting an interesting specimen.

She was viewing a replay of his meeting with the Neulanders, an obvious clue to their coming discussion. As always, it was a shock to see himself—hanging in midair and much reduced in size—on a replay display. He seemed a shell, not a real man. Sanda ordered the replay off. "Come here," she said imperiously.

In addition to her lounger, the clearing contained a table with four chairs and a multipurpose desk set belonging to her assistant; nevertheless, Sanda indicated the ground beside her. The bare dirt floor was hard-packed along the path and in the clearing, where nothing was planted, but it was still wet from being watered, and always uneven underfoot. Alexander sat awkwardly on the moist soil with his raised knees between him and the lounger. It was necessary to look up at Sanda.

Her white hair shone like a halo in the dappled sunlight coming through the walls. Its color did not suggest age; her rich dark skin was entirely unlined; her brown eyes were clear. Sanda looked just past adolescence, although no one could have risen to her exalted position and been truly young. As a result of the Electors' special medical attention, she appeared younger than Alexander, but she'd entered the long middle age of standard humans before his birth. The thought was bitter.

"Do you like what you're seeing?" she asked sharply.

"As always." He didn't avert his eyes, though she disliked being surveyed. Unusual, for a beautiful woman.

"Smile when you compliment me. Haven't I taught you anything at all?"

"I'm too distraught," he said, smiling brightly. "Are you going to have me put down for talking to the Neulanders? Am I being returned to general services? Will Ting Wheeling shoot me in the back? Have mercy, Elector. I seek some guidance here."

She laughed, but the sound was sour. "Sometimes, Alex, I suspect that I keep your service more for your clever talk than your skill as a probe." She sighed and leaned back in the lounger. "Report."

Alexander moved his gaze sideways to where Ting Wheeling guarded the door, then back. Sanda's lips tightened, but she did not order Ting outside, so Alexander began. "Delegate Huana was in conversation with the two aspirants from Neuland. He noticed me and asked me to join them."

Elector Brauna raised her hand. Alexander immediately stopped speaking, bowing his head in the conventional probe-waiting posture. "I won't bother to ask why you approached Huana's group to begin with, knowing how likely he is to include you in a discussion," she said sternly, "but after you were there, you used your genetically enhanced abilities as a probe to predict that the Republic of Neuland won't be admitted to the Harmony." She leaned forward. "Alex, was this a facilitation?"

"No." He drained tension from his voice before continuing. "I would never perform a facilitation without orders, Elector Brauna. While a transcript recital might give that appearance, in context, considering the audience with whom I was interacting, this was *not* a facilitation. Neuland's admission to the Polite Harmony of Worlds was neither promoted nor otherwise affected. Truly." He looked into her eyes and nodded slightly, encouraging belief.

She studied him. He smiled and cursed the hunger that had driven him to stretch toolman/probe proprieties in order to distract himself from his appetite. He should have stood inconspicuously against a wall, a living statue eavesdropping on the Delegates' conversations, not joined them.

She decided, then leaned back, stretching her fine body, catlike, to ease its tension.

She believed him. He glanced away, immensely relieved. Sucre's cloudless sky spread far beyond the clear sunroom walls, but its light reached even to the sunroom's mucky soil. Shadows of the taller sunroom vegetation fell like irregular bars across Sanda's body. The shadow-pattern wouldn't shift for hours. Center kept a counterfeit twenty-four-hour clock-day schedule, but Sucre, the world above which Center was suspended, had a daylight cycle 136 hours long. Sucre's sun hung in the sky like something broken, and Sanda's sunroom was one of the rare places in Center where that reality was apparent. In making an artificial city on an Extreme world the capital of the Polite Harmony of Worlds, the planners had removed nature. Center had sun-stones, not sunlight, corridors but not streets, flowers and no weeds; it wasn't true. Alexander disliked the sunroom for its ersatz return to nature; it was Sanda's favorite place.

"What do you think of the Neulanders?" she asked.

"They're odd." He shrugged. "Arrogant and crude. Perhaps because they're Altered humans, and pain-free." The compacted soil made an uncomfortable seat, and his long legs were in the way, but Sanda hadn't offered him a chair. "Talia Kaviscu is in charge, not the man, Pavel Havic. She's the more intelligent of the pair; she was made anxious by my presence. It's an open secret that probes survey the Grand Assembly's deliberations for the Electors." Alexander reviewed the conversation with his eidetic memory, like mental replay tape, trying to find the best justification for his faux pas. "The Neulanders are hiding something, Elector. That's unexceptional in Center, however I suspect their secret is larger than usual. It might have something to do with outsiders—they mentioned the Bril several times. Both Kaviscu and Havic were sincere; the Republic of Neuland wants to join the Harmony. Unfortunately that desire doesn't carry over into recognition of the role of Electors in determining the proper philosophical and scientific course of society. Neuland will remain adamant in its refusal to allow the establishment of Jonist Academies, claiming their local style of Jonism is ideal." He paused, to add emphasis, then continued. "What surprised me is their depth of belief in Neuland's ultimate success being admitted to the Harmony. My forecast of a defeat in the Grand Assembly voting had no effect on them." He showed his empty palms. "I have no explanation."

She smiled. "But you'd like one. I respect your intuition, Alex, and I'm interested in the Neuland situation. Focus on those Neulanders. I'll have Ahman Grass assign you as their protocol aide. Watch tape from the mechanical snoops for the periods when you can't be present—make them a special project. Discover what they're hiding."

"It would help me considerably if I knew the Electors' position." Alexander was curious. "Do the six of you favor admitting Neuland?"

She waved a hand in the air. "You don't need that information. Besides, you talk much too freely with your Andian friend, Huana. Look what you did today."

"Understood, Elector." He moved slightly, signaling an uncompleted readiness to rise to his feet.

"No." She placed her hand on his knee and looked to where Ting Wheeling was visible through the greenery. "You can leave," she told the guardian. "Return to your post. Alexander will stay with me."

Ting acquiesced, but let his heavy steps echo resentfully as he left the sunroom.

"He's jealous of me."

Sanda's smile widened. "I know. I rather enjoy it. Too bad I haven't been able to make you jealous of him."

"I *am* jealous of him."

"But for the wrong reasons. You wish you were twenty-two again, or were a guardian instead of a probe, but not that you spent all your time here, protecting my body." He performed an appropriate grin, which she missed as she brought her legs around so her feet were flat on the ground beside him. She ruffled his close-cut hair, then rested her hand on his shoulder. "Alex, are you . . . well?"

He worried instantly that she knew his secret, but she couldn't—she had just given him an ongoing assignment. Sanda wasn't so cruel as to tease a dying toolman. He forced a chuckle. "Only tired, Elector. There has been a great deal of activity since the Neulander aspirants arrived. I've watched more replay than usual."

Sanda touched his chin. On cue, he looked up into her eyes. "You've lost four pounds in the last two weeks, Alex, according to my sensors, although you're eating more, too. Your attitude has become noticeably more reckless—witness this business today. You were thirty-three on your last nameday. I think you're in flare, and trying to hide it from me."

He didn't say anything.

"Well?"

"Was there a question, Elector Brauna?"

She slapped him.

He touched his stinging cheek. She'd never struck him before. It felt peculiarly pleasant, a measure of her emotion.

"I've never liked that mask toolmen are trained to wear around humans, and it's much too late for you to begin using one with me," she said. She scrutinized a mass of inconsequential red flowers bordering the clearing, then turned directly to him, her face flushed with strain. "Just tell me—are you in flare?"

"Yes," he whispered, bewildered by his inability to speak at normal volume. He had expected a measure of relief to accompany the admission, but he felt none. It only brought his nightmares into the light. Alexander imagined his traitor body collapsing as his metabolism became increasingly erratic, until he could no longer consume enough calories to sustain himself, even eating constantly. Rumors in probe quarters said there would be a slow shriveling of his flesh as his body ate its muscles, accompanied by fever, an alternating restlessness and lethargy, then continual and increasing pain.

"I'm sorry," she said. "Alex, I am sorry." She slid onto

her knees and embraced him as a mother does an injured child.

He wanted her comfort and for once didn't inspect it for flaws or insincerity. He leaned against her, breathing in her violet-scented flesh, feeling the fabric of her embroidered gown against his cheek, gathering new courage to face his fear from this simplest of human contacts. The shadows from the foliage over her shoulder were motionless; there were no breezes here without her order. The sunroom was a universe that obeyed her will. "Are you going to have me put down to the farm now that you know?" he asked, steeling himself to accept an affirmative, without futile protests.

She shook her head, and moved back to observe him. "I should. That's proper. But if you wish, you can stay in the apartment with me. Flare can extend for six or eight months. Here, you can eat as much as you like, and keep working as long as you're able." She pretended to scan the sunroom, never quite meeting his eyes. "I'll miss your work, Alexander Greeneyes. You're the best analyst I've ever had." She sighed. "Fifteen years is a considerable time, even for me. I wish they designed you probes for longer service, like guardians and subs."

Balanced between a humiliating gratitude and despairing fury, he said nothing. He stood, wiping off the pants of his black matte probe uniform as she watched.

"The rules say no medical treatment for flare," she added apologetically.

The anger burst from him, making his low voice ragged. "You're an Elector. You and the other five make the rules; you decide the proper interpretation of Jon Hsu's *General Principles*. You decide which research advances order, who is human and who is not, when a toolman can be made, and at what age he has to die. So don't say 'rules' to me. I know better. And don't say you're sorry—you're the ones who ordered my death."

Her face had become the public mask of Elector Sanda Brauna. "I'll ignore that. Once." Her tone had no softness. She stood, frowning as if at an untidy mess. "Are you staying with me or not?"

He thought of the quick decline and painless death granted at the toolman farm, and the slower, longer one she offered. There was no real choice. "I'll stay."

Her smile was hollow. "Good. But no more outbursts. Absolutely none."

Poetry was her favorite hobby, the best means of communicating emotion to her. Alexander had heard, and therefore memorized, many poems and found meaning in some. He quoted,

> "Do not go gentle into that good night.
> Rage, rage against the dying of the light."

She hesitated, then laughed and placed her hands high on his upper arms. "I'll miss you, Alex, and not only for your work. I understand the policy that keeps probes from a longer life. I agree with it. It isn't fair, but it's necessary, if we're to make even the few probes we do. But in this case, I am sorry."

"Yes, Elector." He surveyed her, barely conscious of doing so. Her regret was real and more intense than a superficial inspection showed, but he found it gave no meaning to his impending death, and didn't ease the grief or violent indignation he was not allowed to show. "Thank you."

Her hands slid down his arms. "Was the Neulander woman attractive?"

"Attractive, but not exciting." Alexander placed his hands carefully at her waist. She was familiar and comfortable. In whatever way was possible between a toolman—the product of genetic manipulations of the human genome that yielded useful substitute men—and an Elector—one of the most powerful humans inside the Polite Harmony of Worlds—perhaps she even loved him. At her slight nod, he pulled closer, wanting her warmth despite the overheated atmosphere of the sunroom, enjoying her violet fragrance mixed with the rich, damp hothouse scent.

"Those Neulanders might be interesting. Pain-free ..." She sighed as he kissed her neck, the overture she liked best. "But then, pain is a most sincere form of pleasure."

Alexander gorged himself the next morning, only slowing the urgent pace of his breakfast as he began his third over-size helping of cheese-filled rolls and eggs. By then, even Elector Lee's two probes, who kept to themselves, were staring openly.

"Another long night with Elector Brauna, eh, Greeneyes?"

Katryn Friendly asked, using Alexander's use-name with hearty, if fraudulent, familiarity.

Alexander shrugged. He didn't often play at one-upmanship—he didn't have to, being at the apex of the tool-man hierarchy. "I'm in flare," he said quietly, and gestured at the food.

Katryn nearly choked. The entire room quieted, not with compassion, but like wild animals, Alexander thought, waiting for their companion to fall so they could tear into him. The Electors' Ahmen discouraged friendships in favor of competition among probes.

"When do you leave quarters?" David Runner called, insultingly loud, implying Alexander was deaf as well as dying. Flare was a convenient death, giving a probe time to complete assignments and, for those dozen or so in personal service with an Elector, a period of general indulgence before being put down to the toolman farm to await a kind, neat death.

"Don't mind him," Katryn said quickly. "He thinks Sanda Brauna will take his personal service next."

Alexander smiled with perfect condescending disbelief and turned to David, a dark, intense young man he'd had a hand in training. "I leave today." David's eagerness was transparent. Alexander's smile became innocent, the better to enhance delivery of his final thrust. "Elector Brauna wants me moved into her apartment this afternoon."

They were stunned. Toolmen lived in toolmen quarters. He finished the meal and returned his plate to a sub attendant while the probes whispered. It was the first time in weeks he'd felt satiated; perhaps it would be the last, too. From the doorway, he surveyed the contrived grandeur of the dining room, where he'd taken most meals since age fifteen, the subtle gradations of position, the harsh brightness of color against the black uniforms, the sensors throughout the room, measuring. He despised the place. His voice had an edge as he said, ostensibly only to Katryn Friendly, "You know, I was eighteen when Elector Brauna took my service. I've been with her longer than any other probe. Maybe I should make a recommendation as to my successor." He watched, cynically noting who displayed visible remorse; David Runner even began to stand, gathering his resources for the charade of synthetic regrets. Alexander stopped him with direct, hard attention, glancingly applied, and a brief shake of his head directed at all of them. He was ashamed: of probes for being so much less than they could have been, and of himself for indulging in such pettiness. A true man, a man like Esteban Huana, would have resisted the temptation. Alexander nodded and left, but with so many eyes upon him, he didn't take an extra roll, as he had planned.

Only a privileged few probes in personal service to an Elector were given freedom to roam Center at will. Alexander, due to the nature of his assignments from Elector Brauna, generally ranged beyond the Jonist Academy, the Electors' domain, and into the heart of Center—the Grand Assembly. It had been several weeks since he had entered the probe tape study room.

It was already crowded with junior probes reviewing data for the daily political report they prepared for the Electors and the Electors' senior officers, the Ahmen. Unlike most overdecorated probe areas, tape study was utilitarian, the only significant color coming from the recorded images dancing in fast-forward as data from the mechanical snoops—sensors and monitors—was reviewed. Alexander remembered such work as tedious and dreary; it was delegated to the youngest probes, just up from the farm, to refine their surveying patterns and analytical skills. Some designed their own search programs. Alexander had been released from tape study after only eight months; he'd modified the basic searcher program to highlight certain types of body language, not only words, and for his initiative he'd been sent among senior probes, to man a post: first inside the Academy, watching Jonism's scientific researchers do their work, then at seventeen, he had been one of the youngest posted to the Grand Assembly's Great Hall. It was then that he'd realized that probes were not merely the eyes and ears of the Electors; they had another purpose, less direct. Probes—toolmen generally—discreetly displayed the Electors' power to do what was forbidden to others. Only the Electors could create persons so ostensibly different from standard humans that they were not accorded human rights; only the Electors could possess such beings, their toolmen, and even so, only at Center; only the Electors had the ability to declare who was human and who was not, to define the differences between standard humans, adjusted humans—accorded full citizenship rights—and noncitizen Altereds.

And then Sanda Brauna had chosen him.

Alexander walked past the two toolmen/guardians ostensibly protecting their fellow toolmen/probes from unauthorized contact with the world, directly to Daniel Oldest, the tape study librarian, and asked for a displayer position. "I need references to Neuland—general references, not this latest Petition," Alexander said quietly, over the tumult of attenuated voices from the multitude of displayers. "I want information on their technology, society, and current problems. I could use a helper to sort through the material, if you've got a competent spare. One other thing. I'd like to review old tape on the Bril, particularly anything with a Neulander connection."

Daniel stopped and tilted his head to the side. "Odd request." He scanned his indexes, his fingers dancing over the keyboard much faster than anyone could coherently speak. "Nothing much. Neuland cooperated in the Last War, of course. Even the crossmen did. One Bril ship crashed on Neuland." He shrugged. "A few minor items."

"Whatever you have."

Daniel nodded. "Becky!" he called, as his quick fingers raced his eyes through the requests. His was the lone screen in the room, able to sort through the vast archives. Alexander wished he could index for himself, but only the probe librarian had access to more than current material.

"Before I see that," Alexander said, "I'll replay a portion of yesterday's tape from the lobby of the Grand Assembly."

Daniel looked up. "Your infamous interaction with the Neulanders?"

Alexander smiled. "Is it already in the reports?"

Daniel laughed. "You? You're constantly watched. Have you forgotten how it is to be ambitious?"

Alexander didn't answer; the juniors had been awaiting his flare. He walked to his assigned place, and the replay he'd requested was already registered on his displayer. He scanned until he found the proper spot, then slowed and watched.

His own voice, speaking to Huana, said, *"I estimate that the vote, if taken today, would be nineteen worlds against admitting Neuland to the Harmony, five abstentions, and twelve in favor."*

"You see?" Esteban Huana crowed to the Neulanders. *"Altered humans aren't wanted in the Harmony!"*

"What does this imitation man know! He's not human, according to your own Electors." Pavel Havic seemed to step to the front of the group as the replay automatically shifted the monitor displaying the scene in order to focus on a different speaker. The other Neulander, Talia Kaviscu, nodded.

"We're Jonists, too," she said. She tossed her auburn hair behind her back with a well-chosen gesture that seemed artificial on replay, but in person had been exactly right. She was a handsome woman. She, as well as Havic, had reeked of perfume. The status line on the sensor replay noted the scent and, unless such strong odors were a Neulander custom, Alexander supposed they were attempting to disguise their emotions from mechanical sensors and probes. *"We aren't crossmen or alans,"* Kaviscu continued, *"and we are not Altereds! Your real difficulty isn't that we've modified our genetic makeup—you do the same, though you don't admit it—but the fact that we follow the teachings of Jon Hsu in our own way and don't consent to a shadow government by so-called Electors of Order. The Harmony's Jonism is practically a religion!"*

Alexander stopped the replay. Frozen, Talia Kaviscu stood in mid-gesture, the polished black band of her medical condition monitor glittering on her left wrist like a bracelet instead of the badge of genetic inadequacy that it should have been. Alexander skipped ahead and chose a different, more distant view. The replay continued.

Huana shrugged, turning to Kaviscu. *"I wonder if your inability to feel pain affects your attitudes. I've heard disquieting things about Neuland."*

Kaviscu touched Havic's wrist, stopping him from speaking. From his demeanor, he would have been bellicose. Then she raised her arms in a theatrically imploring gesture. *"Quickships travel constantly between Neuland and the Harmony. Trade benefits us both. Neuland is ahead of you in some medical arts. As Jonists, the pursuit of knowledge should lead you to us because of what we can contribute to that search."* She smiled in the direction of Delegate Huana, though she averted her eyes from him and showed signs of strain. *"We need you, too. Alans and crossmen from the Emirates have attacked us before, and they're growing stronger. They wouldn't dare bother a member of your Jonist confederation. And who knows? There may be more hostile aliens waiting for us out in the dark, like the Bril. I am as human as you are. Please, Delegates, keep open minds."*

"I'll listen," Huana said. "We all want to be fair." He glanced sideways at Alexander, frowning. "What do you think, Alex? Are Neulanders human?"

Alexander remembered noticing the corrosive hunger that meant he was too old to bother being coy. He hadn't wanted to contradict his ... friend, but their unlikely relationship was based on honesty and mutual respect. *"The Electors have not spoken directly and explicitly on this issue,"* he said slowly on the replay. *"As to my own opinion, based on my skills as a probe, I would say yes, Neulanders are human."*

The Neulanders smiled grimly, no doubt uncertain whether they wanted approval from a toolman.

"Why?" Delegate Huana looked troubled.

Alexander's image bowed. "I've seen old tape of the Bril, from the Last War. I couldn't analyze their behavior or anticipate their reactions. They were alien. But Neulanders have only minor differences from standard Harmony patterns, well within normal cultural variation."

Huana nodded thoughtfully. "I see. Clearly, your definition of humanity is useless for the Grand Assembly. You would consider most Altereds to be fully human, and probably all crossmen and alans. Interesting, however."

"And what is the Harmony's criteria?" Kaviscu smiled icily. "The Electors' pronouncement?"

Real-time, Alexander stopped the replay. Are you human, Alex? he thought. Hunger burned in his gut, flaring suddenly like a fire raging out of his control, despite the huge breakfast.

Becky, called Longlegs, arrived a moment later with a printout list of the additional materials Daniel had made available at Alexander's station. Alexander remembered to smile; Becky was young enough to require encouragement. "Go back. Ask Daniel for anything we have on contacts between Andia and Neuland: trade agreements, historical references, anything."

Deep hunger reawakened Alexander to the passage of time several hours later. An afterimage of hissing Bril obscured his vision for a moment, then he focused on Becky. "What else?"

"You've seen everything Daniel pulled, except what we

discarded. You really take it fast! There's more Neuland tape, Daniel said."

"No, that's all I want to assimilate now. I need some real-time work. Except, where's the Andian material?"

"There was none, per Daniel. No treaties or paperwork between them, and trade is minimal. No direct commercial routes. No co-history, except through the Harmony generally. He said that if you know of a connection, tell him so he can search for it, but nothing came up on his indexes." She displayed a tad of skepticism at Daniel's failure.

Alexander got up, stretching. "Daniel Oldest is an excellent librarian. If he says there's nothing, I believe him."

She stood, too. "Was that a facilitation yesterday or were you just buttering up your usual Andian? Everyone wonders."

Alexander laughed and closed the carrel. "It wasn't a facilitation, but it was close. Don't try anything like it until you're as old as I am." He glanced at her, a pretty girl of fifteen, just up from the farm. There was an unusual degree of residual rapport between them from the teamwork; he enjoyed the sensation. "Will you have lunch with me?"

She was unable to hide her embarrassment, or didn't bother. "No," she said ungraciously. Her eyes were cold. "*I'm* not hungry."

"Flare's not contagious," Alexander said. He purposely let strong irritation show as he added, "Too bad. Elector Brauna always sets a good table, and she'll need another probe in her personal service soon." He left before Becky could try to rectify her error.

No Grand Assembly session was scheduled for the afternoon, only public committee meetings for the Deputy Delegates, so there were no Delegates in the Assembly lobby. Alexander rarely bothered personally surveying anything, like the meetings, that would be summarized on the daily reports. He started toward the Andian delegation offices to discuss Neuland with Delegate Huana, then met Huana in the main corridor, striding toward the shared offices of the delegations from Chan and Co-Chan. Alexander made a pretense of probe reticence, but, as usual, Huana ignored it.

"Alex!" Delegate Huana extended his hand, but Alexander smoothly moved aside so as to prevent Huana from thoughtlessly embarrassing himself. Huana's chubby, dark face beamed good-naturedly at him, accepting while seeming to disdain such caution. It was difficult not to respond to such an affable reception, so he scanned Huana like a stranger, noting his big ears and small white teeth—not an ugly man, but more interesting than handsome. He wore a mix of Center-formal and native Andian clothing—like his colorful headgear—although most Delegates from worlds with strong traditional dress abandoned their native clothes for Center's banal suits.

"Delegate Huana?" Alexander bowed deeply and took pains to keep warmth from his voice, though he avoided probe monotone.

"I hear you're assigned as protocol aide to the Neuland aspirants. Is this a signal from the Electors? Tell the truth now, Alex, not some harmless probe cliché."

Alexander couldn't prevent a smile. "No signal intended, Delegate Huana. Attention from the Electors isn't necessarily approval."

Huana laughed cheerfully. "Good. I wish everything wasn't so subtle here on Center. Those hidden meanings! Remember how you had to help me when I was new on Andia's delegation, what, ten years ago?"

"Thirteen standard," Alexander corrected him.

Huana stood quite still. He stared at Alexander, alarm in his dark eyes. "How old are you now, Alex?"

Alexander felt the rumbling of his stomach, as though it was pain, and heard it as the ticking of an alarm clock. "Thirty-three."

"I'm sorry, Alex." Huana's voice was a whisper. "Are you still well?"

"Yes, of course, Delegate," he said briskly. "I'm fine." He hoped no one was monitoring, since the lie was an embarrassing acknowledgment of emotional weakness. He didn't want pity, but mostly he dreaded an indifferent acceptance of his death from Huana. He used posture to disengage from Huana, feigning urgency, but felt Huana's eyes following him as he hurried away past the Andian delegation offices as if they hadn't been his goal.

Two aides of Delegate Valeron Panet of Flute went by.

". . . Says they can cure anything," one said. "That Rapid Healing Function makes them invulnerable to cuts and burns. And those medical monitors!"

"Yes." The other nodded vigorously. "Are they for sale?"

Alexander registered the words in memory while his thoughts wandered back to that morning. Sanda never slept long, and Alexander had awakened very early, as she'd left the bed. *"Why are you restless?"* he had asked her, still half-asleep.

Sanda had returned and sat beside him on the edge of the bed. "Neuland." She brushed her hand across his cheek. *"It's a dilemma. Jeroen Lee says they really are ahead in certain aspects of human biological studies, and he's the only Elector with the competence to evaluate their claim himself. He favors admitting them, but his opinions are eccentric."*

"The orthodox Delegates will vote however you rule."

She had smiled and kissed his forehead. "You're not on duty. Relax and get some rest."

"I haven't time enough left to spend it relaxing."

She stood. "I've warned you, Alex, no outbursts and no whining." She smiled gently, however, and said:

> *"The boast of heraldry, the pomp of power,*
> *And all that beauty, all that wealth e'er gave,*
> *Awaits alike th'inevitable hour:—*
> *The paths of glory lead but to the grave."*

"Please, Elector, not an Elegy so early in the day."

She laughed, enjoying his identification of the poem. "My favorite part is the reference to someone named 'Hampden,' as if we're supposed to know the name."

He had sat up in the bed and began fiercely to recite:

> *"No! I am not Prince Hamlet, nor was meant to be;*
> *Am an attendant lord, one that will do*
> *To swell a progress, start a scene or two,*
> *Advise the prince; no doubt, an easy tool,*
> *Deferential, glad to be of use,*
> *Politic, cautious, and meticulous;*
> *Full of high sentence, but a bit obtuse;*
> *At times, indeed, almost ridiculous—*
> *Almost, at times, the Fool."*

Sanda's eyes widened. "You're no fool, Alexander Greeneyes."

He'd kicked off the covers, but still felt warm. "Elector.

It's only that I've seen the moment of my greatness flicker, and been afraid."

He had nothing to fear anymore. Alexander looked down the gently curving corridor—it circled the Grand Assembly—and slowed his pace. It was a seemingly endless succession of dull, heroic murals, uninspired pastoral window screens and closed doors, interspersed with small seating arrangements in alcoves, a public space designed for doing business that now seemed pointless. He stopped at the cross corridor that led to the Assembly's guest suites, where the Neulanders were staying, and considered the massive medical problems of Neuland's population, most of whom couldn't sense the warning signals of pain. He did not know what created the runaway metabolism of a probe in flare, but suspected it could be easily corrected, with proper stimulus.

The security guards at the residential area's entrance were Harmony citizens—human men, not guardians—but they let him pass without a question, seeing only the uniform marking him as an Elector's toolman. These corridors were narrower and even less artistically decorated, though they still had regular monitors, being part of Center's systems. The corridors were color coded, all in slight variations of blue, which Alexander thought gave a sickly cast to the few people he passed. He almost hoped one of them would send him away. Opposite the Neulanders' door was a conspicuous monitor and sensor array. Alexander avoided staring into it, and knocked. A stranger—from the medical condition monitor he wore, a Neulander—opened the door.

"I've come on behalf of the Electors," Alexander said. He could explain to Sanda that this private meeting was direct research on her assignment. Perhaps she would believe him.

"Who is it?" he heard Talia Kaviscu ask.

"A toolman, by the uniform," the doorkeeper shouted, turning back into the suite.

Kaviscu came to the entrance. She wore a tight-fitting bodysuit, normal Neuland leisure wear, green and gold to highlight her eyes and hair; in the bluish light he noticed a delicate tracery of thin scars, like lace, on her right cheek. A medical condition monitor gleamed on her left wrist. "You're the one from yesterday. What do you want? We were promised there would be no surveillance within our own apartment."

"And you believed that?" Alexander smiled. Behind Kaviscu, the doorkeeper frowned, but the aspirant herself was imperturbable. Alexander hoped the same could be said for him. His palms were sweating and his stomach churned, not with hunger, but anxiety.

"Not particularly, but we've taken our own measures to enforce our right to freedom from 'information gathering' by the Electors of Order," she said, sneering the name. "If you enter, there's no telling what snoops you'll bring along."

He bowed. "I am deeply insulted, Aspirant Kaviscu," he said in the teasing tone he sometimes used with Sanda Brauna, but he pitched his voice to suggest some urgency. He had to get away from the monitors quickly. "I am in personal service to Elector Sanda Brauna. I wouldn't require mechanical aids to monitor you. In any event, I have been assigned as your protocol guide by the Electors, should you choose to accept me. Perhaps we could discuss the matter further? Inside?"

She studied him suspiciously. "What the hell? Come inside, probe, but only into the main hall."

He followed her into the suite, a pleasant one that, fortunately for him, had no true windows, only window screens. Sun-stones set into the ceiling were set for noon, out of synch with the rest of Center. The entry's floor was carpeted in a dark, thin fabric; the walls were tiled in the eccentric style of Rockland, without obvious symmetry or pattern, disturbing if one gave it much attention. He didn't, studying Talia Kaviscu as he closed the door. It all depended on her. Could she be bluffed?

"Well?" she asked.

Several more Neulanders came into the hall, including Pavel Havic. "That toolman? What does he want?" Havic asked Kaviscu, as if Alexander was a speechless cipher.

"The differences between adjusted humans, Altereds, and toolmen are a matter of power, legalities, and random distinctions," Alexander said, hoping she was curious enough to listen—betting his life on it. "It's not a question of degree of deviation from standard. Your rapid healing—RHF—makes Neulanders much more different genetically from standard humans than probes. Our senses are substantially enhanced, but RHF is new."

"Get out!" Havic pointed at the door, but Kaviscu smiled.

"What's your point?" she asked. She tapped her foot against the carpeted floor, keeping silent time with her impatience.

He took a deep breath. "I know about your plan. I'll help you get Neuland admitted to the Harmony at the vote next week if you help me." Before Kaviscu could protest, he held up a hand. "I'm in flare. That's the term they use for the metabolic changes in probes that precede death. I don't want to die, and I believe you can help me."

"What will you do for us?" Kaviscu asked scornfully. "You can, at best, help convince one Elector to support Neuland, and the extent of your influence over someone as intransigent as Sanda Brauna remains to be seen. If this arrangement backfired, Neuland would be at the center of a scandal. No, Alexander Greeneyes—you see, I know you— you'd best leave and hope I'm kind enough—and sufficiently trusting—not to turn you in."

He shook his head, concentrating on his hunger and not the feeling of being unclean, because he knew he had her; this woman would take risks. "I know about the Bril," he said.

Kaviscu stared too impassively at him; Havic moved threateningly close. The rest of the Neulanders had only puzzled reactions, but at Havic's hand signal, several stepped between Alexander and the door. He'd been right. There was something there, some plan that gave them the confidence to snub his offer.

"You know nothing. *What* about the Bril?" Havic asked.

"I know a plan exists. I know it involves the Bril somehow. That's all I need. I'll recognize it once it begins."

Havic walked between Alexander and the door. "You've just had a fatal accident."

"Don't underestimate my importance because I'm not a citizen—not legally human," Alexander said calmly. His fear of what he was doing far surpassed any threat these Neulanders could make. "I live with Sanda Brauna. Few probes have the confidence of an Elector as fully as I do. She'll be suspicious of any accident. I calculate my death after this visit would ensure Neuland is not admitted under any circumstances. No orthodox Delegate would vote you in, whatever your plan, if the Electors directly oppose you."

Talia Kaviscu shook her head at Havic. "I think he's genuine. We'll see if his medical condition is real. Brauna's personal toolman could be useful." She turned to Alexander. "Just what do you propose to do for us and how can we trust that you'll do it?"

He spoke rapidly, with force, like an Elector giving orders. "I'll promote Neuland's admittance to the Polite Harmony, and do so in a way that suggests the Electors want Neuland admitted, though my work will necessarily be quite discreet." He willed Kaviscu to believe that he could do that. He could.

"I need to leave your suite. The longer I'm here, the more difficult it will be to explain this visit—assuming you're correct and Elector Brauna isn't watching us at this moment. For now, accept me publicly as your protocol guide and stay away from other probes as much as possible. However you perfume yourselves or try to disguise your movements, you're as easy for a probe to survey as any human. Most importantly, to get my silence and my help, I want immediate treatment of my medical condition. I need you so I can live. Do you understand and agree?"

They stared at him, slow to absorb it all, and he ached for Sanda Brauna's quick understanding. Kaviscu said, "People will notice when you continue to survive."

"That's my problem; obviously I'll have to leave Sucre. Do you agree?" He looked at the door, hoping to hurry her.

She paced the entrance hall in an excess of nervous energy, then turned to Havic. He nodded curtly. "All right," she said.

He felt the pressure ease in his stomach, then tighten again. "Good. We'll pretend I am engaged in a sexual relationship with one of you. Aspirant Kaviscu is the most believable. Please kiss me for the sensors, Aspirant, then I'll leave."

"Kiss you? You ask a lot." She crossed her arms against her chest, grimacing with distaste.

"It's necessary, to excuse the length of this private visit. Meetings without monitors are always regarded with suspicion, but it's not unusual for a probe to be used in this way." He bowed, to emphasize the sham of their supposed relationship, but spoke bitterly. "You can close your eyes and pretend I'm not a toolman."

She glanced at the other Neulanders. "It's the traitor, not

the toolman, that I don't care to touch." Every gesture indicating profound disgust, she allowed him to embrace her. Her body was stiff, her lips were cold as death against his. A true Jonist, Alexander told himself, did not believe in omens.

Chapter 2

Alexander went directly to Sanda Brauna's apartment. Ting Wheeling was on duty. "She's furious," he said, stepping down from his post.

"So you can actually initiate a conversation." Alexander walked past him, engrossed in his own thoughts.

Ting caught up in one long stride, grabbed Alexander's shoulder, yanking the soft fabric of the uniform so it stretched along the shoulder seam, then shoved him roughly to the floor. Alexander broke his fall with his knees and hands and stared up at Ting, openmouthed. His palms stung, and his right knee was sending shattering lines of pain throughout his leg. The guardian glared down, unrepentant, his verbal frustration obvious in his twisted expression. "I apologize," Alexander said, and warily sat back on his heels. The knee hurt, but the pain was subsiding, and movement hadn't made it worse. "What did I do?"

"You think you're better than everyone."

Alexander shook his head. His neck ached. Sub, guardian, probe: to be a toolman meant to be dedicated to the Electors, still, there was a hierarchy drummed into them—at least drummed into probes. Subs were menials who cleaned and served; guardians were muscle, to protect the Electors and the Academy. And probes? Companions. Toolmen, but more, the Electors' trusted confidants. What he'd just done, betraying the Elector, was sickening. "You're right," Alexander said. "We're both nothing."

Ting scowled—apparently that wasn't what he had meant—but he helped Alexander to his feet, although with no sign of apology or remorse.

Alexander hoped Sanda hadn't watched the episode. His fingers ached, so he opened and closed them while Ting observed. The shirt had already partly reformed its shape; he hadn't time to change.

"Let's go," Ting said.

Alexander followed him to the sunroom, watching Ting's wide, muscular body through Ting's tight uniform. Some Ahmen, though none of the present Electors, liked guardian companions. Ugh. Bodywork with a bear.

Sanda was pacing the clearing between the table and her lounger. She stopped. "Leave us alone," she told Ting, then studied Alexander as Ting retreated from the room. As the bronze doors closed behind Ting, Alexander bowed low, holding the bow until she resumed pacing. Then he straightened.

His attention was unwillingly drawn, by the fragrance, to a box of chocolate candy open on the table, probably left by Ahman Young, who had a sweet tooth. He pressed his nails into his palms to distract himself.

"Sensors say you had intimate contact with that Neulander woman," Sanda Brauna said. She faced the tall, slim shape of one of her imported palm trees, where it rose through the fleshy underbrush of other exotic vegetation. Its leaves were drooping; palms did poorly in Sucre's light. She spun around. "I want to hear verbatim what happened inside that suite."

He sidestepped her order. "I did what you wanted, Elector Brauna." He came closer, smiling into her eyes. The sweet chocolate smell flooded his mouth with saliva; he swallowed it away through his constricted throat.

"What? Begin an affair with an Altered aspirant the day you move into my apartment?"

The Neulanders had been right: there were no working monitors inside their hall. He had a choice.

"Compassion is a dangerous emotion, toolman. It evaporates faster than mist in a desert once sympathy is strained. I can have you put down this instant, and what will your Neulander do for you then?"

Alexander surveyed her, dissecting each syllable she spoke, inspecting every movement, but scarcely conscious of the threat, absorbed by Sanda Brauna, woman, and Elector. She was dressed formally in her red Elector's robe, and the hard color emphasized her anger and authority, but her dark eyes were more injured than angry. He expanded his survey, examining the sunroom as a reflection of its owner's heart. The trunks, stems, leaves of the plants—only rarely was the green accented by flowers, and then modest ones—took on elusive meaning against an enclosing but remote sunshine that seemed brighter in comparison with this nearly monochromatic garden. The graceful vegetation nevertheless held its own secret elegance. The garden was a place for growing shapes and shadows as well as plants. Broad, flat leaves were a counterpoint to delicate ferns. Squat shapes balanced slender ones. Even the awkward dirt floor was a paean to exquisite simplicity. He didn't like the room, and yet its mystery was fascinating. Like the Elector.

"Answer me, Alex! Report!" She pounded her hand on the tabletop, making the chocolates jump in their box. Their curved, matte surfaces reminded him of the texture of a woman's skin. He looked back at Sanda Brauna; she was exactly the milky brown color of the candy. He ached to embrace her. She was a passion outside his conscious management, a loyalty beyond reason; she was the woman he craved. "I don't know, Elector. I'm not having an affair with Talia Kaviscu. The contact was only a disguise for my real purpose."

She stood motionless, reining in her emotions and becoming Elector Brauna, the red of her robe brilliant against the green foliage, a fire in the garden's heart. "Well?"

"I offered to perform a facilitation for Neuland and also not to disclose Neuland's plan to aid their entry into the Harmony in exchange for medical treatments to prolong my life."

She recovered quickly. "Why did you do that?" Her words were precisely controlled, but simultaneously she hand signaled for immediate security. Ting Wheeling, swiftly followed by two other guardians, burst into the sunroom, running. They skidded to a halt, raising a fine dust that smelled of decay and tickled Alexander's nose.

He was lucky she hadn't called for a more immediately lethal response. Alexander bowed and didn't rise. "I believed it was what the Electors wanted, Elector Brauna, and it seemed to me in the best interests of the Polite Harmony of Worlds." He stared at the brown dirt, unpleasantly reminded of the farm on Sucre.

"It seemed to *you*, probe? Explain."

He looked up.

She gestured at the guardians to hold their positions. Alexander sensed weapons trained on him. He didn't move. Sweat broke out on his forehead and back, its stink increasing his fear. Speaking quickly, but choosing his words with care, Alexander said, "Elector Brauna, it was clear to me that the Electors would favor having the Republic of Neuland join the Polite Harmony of Worlds but for the fact that Neulanders, while claiming they're Jonist, don't acknowledge the Electors of Order. Even so, it's obvious that Neuland would be an asset to the Harmony. It is an energetic, economically successful world. Jonism values knowledge, and Neuland is ahead of us in certain areas of scientific study, since they lack the Harmony prohibition on human experimentation. Furthermore, the Harmony has been expanding in that direction for two centuries, and Neuland is now at our border. Neuland's enemies are the same as our own—the alans, crossmen, and other groups who reject Jonism in favor of religious superstition—but Neuland won't be our buffer if it falls to them. Because Neuland's Jonism is different, the Electors cannot openly favor admitting Neuland. Strictly orthodox worlds won't vote in favor of Neuland because the Electors classify pain-free Neulanders as Altered humans—not proper citizens. It seemed to me that this impasse would be broken if the Electors gave only covert support to Neuland, support that could be disavowed at any time, particularly so if the Neulanders themselves were unaware of the source of that support."

"So you made a secret agreement to facilitate their admission solely to further the interests of the Harmony?"

"Neuland has a plan, Elector, and the aspirants believe it will win Neuland enough votes to become a member world of the Harmony. I don't know their plan, but I doubt they can ever obtain sufficient support without your help." He hesitated, and took her failure to interrupt as a good sign. "This furthers your interests, Elector, and incidentally mine. It was too excellent an opportunity to discard. I don't know that I would have been so reckless if I lacked a personal stake in the outcome, but whatever I may have done in other circumstances, the choice is now entirely yours. If you wish to proceed, then the plan is established. If you do not want Neuland in the Harmony, then you can publicly discover their secret manipulation of an Elector's toolman and shatter Neuland's chances of entry for a generation. If the Electors are still undecided, then you can put me down, and let events and Neuland's own plan take their course without me."

He hesitated. "However you decide, Elector Brauna, I see no advantage whatsoever in killing me just now."

She laughed and clapped her hands. "Stand down," she said to the guardians. "In fact, you can leave."

Alexander knew their departure was her judgment in his favor. "Elector," he said, nodding at the closing door, "do you ever wonder what they think of the bits and pieces they overhear?"

She chuckled at the odd notion, then seated herself in one of the chairs, drumming her long, red nails against the ceramic top of the table, very near the chocolates. "Tell me, why the physical contact with Kaviscu?"

"Entirely for your benefit, Elector. I took no pleasure in it. If you wish to run this maneuver without informing the other Electors, then, if they later discover it, my alleged involvement with Aspirant Kaviscu gives you the ability to appear personally uninvolved. It's obvious that you would not assent to my engaging in a sexual relationship with anyone but yourself."

She seemed to examine her garden again, then she nodded. "This is a truly beautiful plan, Alex. How much is extemporaneous rationalizing and how much did you work out before you met with the Neulanders?"

He spread his hands wide, in a broad style owing something to Delegate Huana. "I don't really know, Elector. My motives are so confused . . . I don't know. But I would never betray you."

"Then I won't ask why you didn't come to me first, before implementing the plan." She stood and walked to the edge of the clearing, peering through the greenery at Sucre's sky. "We can hardly pretend not to notice when, because of Neuland, you survive. What do you suggest?"

"I've always hoped to leave Sucre, Elector Brauna."

She laughed and turned back to him. "I'm not sure it would be wise to let you out of my sight. Well, something can be arranged." She came close and touched his arm. "I've had a macabre idea for several years. The farm sometimes clones toolmen who do exceptionally well. I considered commissioning a duplicate of you. It felt wrong. I didn't, but I might have succumbed to the temptation eventually." Her fingers traced a line along his forearm, and she took his hand in hers. "I'm pleased with a plan that includes your survival."

He smelled the nearby chocolates so intensely that, as relief allowed him to relax his guard, it was difficult to think of anything else. He kissed her, since her stance indicated the desire, and prolonged the kiss, to savor the chocolate he tasted in her mouth. His arms circled her back, drawing her against him, then she pushed him gently away, pleased by his ardor but uninterested, and began to pace restlessly again.

"I'll convene a special meeting of the Electors," she said. "You'll testify, but you'll say you've been acting under my direct orders all along. If pressed, that business with Kaviscu was solely to throw off her suspicions of Electors' involvement. Understand?"

"Yes." Alexander felt light-headed. He reached for the nearest chair and used its back to steady himself.

She stared. "Are you all right?"

"Elector, may I have some of this candy?"

Wordlessly, she slid the box to him, then looked away as, unable to control himself, he greedily stuffed several pieces into his mouth, one after another.

Alexander was asleep in one of the apartment's smaller guest rooms when she returned. "What are you doing here?" she demanded, shaking his shoulder. "This isn't my room."

Her subs had transferred his few possessions—uniforms, trinkets from various Delegates, worth no more than a few counts, except for an elaborate polychrome Andian vase, and Sanda Brauna's own occasional gifts of jewelry and hardbound books—from his cubicle in probe quarters to this room at the far end of a long, little-used hallway, at the edge of her apartment, so he had gone there. "I had no orders, Elector."

"Do you need orders? I thought you made your own, Alex." She lit the sun-stones with a gesture, and he squinted in the sudden glare. "Never mind. The meeting went well. Your plan is adopted, though they don't know it's yours." She smiled, as if reminiscing. "Get up and come to bed."

Yawning, he obediently kicked off the cover and swung his bare feet to the floor.

"Wait." She frowned, staring at him. "Just move over."

He had received many private kindnesses from Elector Brauna, but this unexpected consideration was extraordinary. Drowsily content, he watched her undress, admiring her slim figure, which was too often hidden by her bulky, formal robes. She prudishly still kept her back to him. Sex with her was unexceptional, but her power was its own aphrodisiac.

"Stop surveying me, Alex," she said.

"I like to look at you, Elector." He turned away, though, and moved to the far side of the bed.

She came to bed, but propped herself up with all but one of the pillows, almost to a sitting position, and looked at him. "Once you're well," she said, sending a shiver through him at the thought, "when the Neulanders cure your flare, you can't be a toolman any longer. When it's obvious you aren't dying, the effect on other probes would be catastrophic. Extremely irritating, anyway. Elector Rose suggested that we put you down once the Neuland vote is over."

He touched her bare thigh. She placed her hand over his and met his eyes.

"I opposed the idea quite vehemently. I used words like justice and generosity, concepts we Electors don't consider often enough. Jeroen Lee sided with me, and pointed out that you're our proof of the conspiracy, should the Electors need leverage against Neuland. Eventually, they all agreed to let you live, but only if you leave Sucre."

He kissed her cheek without awaiting permission. She flushed like a pleased child. "When did you become important?" she asked. "I thought you were only clever and comfortable, a useful companion; now suddenly I'm not entirely reasonable on this subject."

"I don't know, Elector, but I'm glad."

"I have a home on Flute, very private. You could stay there." She smiled shyly, charmingly, and reached out to cover his hand with her own.

"I'd like that."

Sanda tossed an extra pillow to the floor and settled into the bed. Alexander lay back with his arms beneath his head, and wondered how not being a toolman would feel, and if the other Electors would really let him live, whatever they told Sanda Brauna.

"I can protect you," she said, as if she had read his mind. She turned off the light.

He smelled her violet fragrance, and the clean, fresh starchiness of the linen sheets. Standard humans claimed they couldn't hear the hum of Center, but Alexander listened and found it comforting, like his own heartbeat. Her soft breathing said she was awake, no doubt planning their future and not disposed to be interrupted, but he asked, "Will I be human after this? Will I be your partner, Elector?" He was glad of the dark.

She hesitated, and he thought he'd pushed too far. "You're different from other toolmen, Alex, and always have been." She reached across to him, and unable to see well in the dark with her merely standard eyes, she grasped his side rather than his hand. "I find the thought of a partner quite appealing."

Pavel Havic approached Alexander openly early the next day. "If you are our protocol guide, probe," he said, "then there are matters to discuss. Talia is waiting for you in our suite."

"This could be handled in a meeting room," Alexander protested for the benefit of listening probes and monitors.

"Go to her, toolman. Do as you're told." He glared at Alexander, either a fine actor or a malicious man enjoying his power to command.

Alexander bowed, and went to the Neulander suite. Kaviscu answered the door herself. "About time," she said. "Come in."

He walked inside, and she shut the door behind him.

"This is Med. Stefan Janus." She indicated a tall, thin man holding a black case. "He needs a blood and tissue sample."

Janus stepped forward with a guardian's precision; all Neulanders moved carefully, like soldiers in a minefield, their most distinctive characteristic, since, unlike many worlds, Neuland lacked racial homogeneity. Janus removed a white, cuff-shape instrument from his case. "Roll up your sleeve and extend your arm."

Set at ease by the medic's professional manner, Alexander obeyed.

"What do you have for us?" Kaviscu demanded.

"I'll start with Huana," Alexander said. "I'll begin by . . ." He stopped, gasping and struggling not to jerk his arm away. "What are you doing?" No medic had ever hurt him before.

Kaviscu smiled, wet her lips, and came closer. Her eyes darted between Alexander's arm and face.

Janus glanced impersonally at him. "Is it unpleasant? I've never had a patient capable of experiencing pain. No damage occurs from the procedure." He glanced at a red display on the side of his instrument. "The sampling is completed." He removed the device carefully, watching Alexander's face. "There's pain after the procedure ends?"

Alexander grunted, gingerly touching the abused flesh of his upper arm. There was a line of blood in the incision site, but the medic hadn't covered it with a skinsack. Alexander wiped the blood away with his other hand while Med. Janus looked on curiously. "I suppose it *will* heal?" he asked. "How long does it take?"

"Never mind that. Whimpers do heal." Kaviscu nodded at the door. "Talk, probe."

More blood was oozing from the small wound, but less than before. Alexander had discounted the unsavory aspects of Neuland's culture mentioned in the materials he'd surveyed. Pain-free. Just how different did it make them? Kaviscu was waiting. "I'll begin the facilitation today, before the Assembly session. Don't approach me; I'll be with Delegate Huana. It's entirely plausible that any subtle message the Electors wanted to send to the Grand Assembly would pass to him through me. You already have Amacuro, don't you? Was it a bribe?"

She stared at him. "You do know your trade, toolman."

"When do I get the medicine?"

Janus looked up from his device. "I'm not familiar with your condition or physiology, so we'll do it in two treatments, with sampling between them."

Alexander surveyed and saw an honest intent to keep their bargain. So far. "Hold a reception for the Delegates," he ordered Kaviscu, beginning to roll down his sleeve. She watched attentively until the wound was covered by the black uniform. "Invite me here tomorrow to help you plan it." He reached for her. She moved hastily away. "Elector Brauna needs to think she knows what's going on."

"All right." Awkwardly, they embraced. "We're recording you, toolman," she said. "Don't try to change your mind."

"Aspirant Kaviscu, my goal is to survive." He bowed, glad to leave them.

As he returned to the Grand Assembly lobby, he considered Kaviscu's face when the medic hurt him, the look of a curious but unmoved child watching someone cry. Such innocence in the face of pain was disquieting.

* * *

Delegate Huana, smelling tantalizingly of onion and peppers from his lunch, approached Alexander in the Assembly lobby, as if he had been awaiting his arrival, but his steps were slow and his head was down. "Will Elector Brauna come today?" he asked. An Electors' visit to the Grand Assembly had been announced.

Alexander noted Huana's melancholy, but didn't comment. "I'm not certain, Delegate, but I'd project she will come. She wants to meet the Neulanders informally. She finds them interesting."

"Good," Huana said, inattentive to Alexander's facilitation. "It will save me the necessity of an appointment and formal petition." Strong emotion momentarily clouded Huana's ability to speak, then he said, "Alex, I'm going to ask her permission for you to visit Andia. I inquired this morning, and Ahman Young told me you were in flare. This is no place to . . . be."

Alexander gaped at him.

"Toolman or not, you are my friend," Delegate Huana said in a rush. "I know about that 'farm' on Sucre's surface. I'm confident I can convince Elector Brauna that you deserve better. You'll stay with my family. You've met my wife and daughters, of course, and Andia is only a week away by quickship; I'll try to visit."

"Delegate. This is not necessary."

"No, listen, Alex." He took a deep breath and clasped Alexander's arm, in full view of the watchers in the lobby. "It's the right thing; I won't do less."

Alexander struggled for a properly reserved self-control, and failed. There were tears in his eyes; he couldn't remember having cried before. He bowed low to Esteban Huana, surreptitiously wiping them away; when he straightened, only his training allowed him to calmly say, "Thank you, Delegate, but I don't believe Elector Brauna will agree."

"I'll insist. I won't contradict the Electors' ruling that toolmen are not human—I know your death is irrevocable— but you're still my friend. I won't let you die alone."

"Delegate, you misunderstand." It was difficult to continue. Affection between a probe and an Elector was embarrassing, and in the middle of the lobby of the Grand Assembly of Worlds, it seemed unreal, but Huana's own offer was equally incredible. "The Elector has asked me to

stay with her. She offered me the choice; it wasn't an order.
I'm living in her apartment now."

Delegate Huana smiled and clapped Alexander on the
back. "Good! She's seemed a cold, manipulative . . . Well, I
should have known you couldn't be so free if she hadn't allowed it. I'm glad, Alex, and it makes me feel better about
the Electors. Knowing you, I've had doubts about their
sophistry regarding toolmen. My offer is unimportant, then."

"Oh, no, Delegate! It's *wonderful* for me to learn I have
a friend." Alexander had maneuvered his way into survival
with the Elector, while Huana's offer came from his heart.
Tentatively, despite their public surroundings, Alexander
touched Huana's hand.

Huana embraced him, then stepped back. "Of course you
have a friend."

Ebullient, Alexander needed to focus on something else to
prevent his further overt expressions of pleasure. He scanned
the lobby. The two Neulanders were staring with hard, hostile, apprehensive eyes, eyes so cold that, in spite of Esteban
Huana's recent, warm embrace, Alexander shivered.

The procession—all six Electors, resplendent in their
shimmering red robes of office, progressing two by two
while flanked by a dozen black-clad toolmen/guardians and
preceded by eighteen yellow-robed Ahmen—came through
the Learning Arch, gateway between the Grand Assembly
complex and the Jonist Academy of Sucre/Center. Ahman
Young, Elector Brauna's personal assistant, seemed distracted, and she almost tripped on the hem of her long robe.
Ting Wheeling marched to the right of Elector Brauna, too
earnest for true dignity. Alexander smiled as Ting's eyes
briefly met his, but Ting did not acknowledge him. Despite
the snub, perhaps partially because of it, Alexander was
happy—he had a future, and Sanda's entourage was, in a
way, his family. He'd learned, from Delegate Huana's off-
hand remarks, that families were not always courteous.

Sanda Brauna, walking beside the handsome, enigmatic
Jeroen Lee, looked majestic, and Alexander was struck by
the contrasting memory of her nakedness. He wondered how
long he would live and if it would be long enough to see her
grow old. What was he, if he was not her toolman? What
might he become?

He knew Center, and politics, and something of Sucre, at

least in the Green, as the jungle was called on Sucre. He could read emotion in faces, and extrapolate a dynamic societal trend, but he had only vague ideas how ordinary citizens of the Harmony managed their lives. He knew little science or math—the lingua franca of the World Academies—and had never noticed in himself an inclination or talent for any art. Except for Huana's apartment on Center—and Alexander recognized that a World Delegate was not an average man, and that this apartment was not Huana's home—he had never seen a household run without subs.

But Alexander was unafraid. If he could survive, then he could manage the rest, too.

The Delegates, with those aides who happened to be in the lobby, all had bowed, and held the bow as the Electors' parade advanced into the room. The Neulanders had not. Talia Kaviscu had somewhat inclined her head, and kept her gaze steady and to the front, but Pavel Havic was upright, watching Alexander. Slowly, carefully, calculating the motion that would not be picked up on screening programs he had helped design, Alexander nodded soothingly at Havic, as if to say that everything was fine. Havic frowned and turned. Just then the Electors arrived at the front of the room; with a swishing of cloth, throat clearings, and sighs, the Delegates straightened.

Elector Jeroen Lee spoke, despite being the youngest and most junior, first polite nonsense to the Delegates, then a brief mention—Electors Xhasa Kin and Thomas Chen scowled—of the Assembly's Neulander "guests." Lee, by training a systems biologist and human medic, was the most liberal of the Electors, framing rulings in which others seldom joined, including one that Altered humans should be citizens. Alexander should have liked Lee for his opinions, but didn't. Lee had been Ahman of Sucre, in charge of toolmen, before his election, and Alexander remembered too well those culled children, vanished into the long nights of the farm, and the fear that he would be next.

Although they'd arrived formally and together, the Electors had no rulings to announce, and the Assembly session would not begin for half an hour, so the Electors dispersed, conversing casually with the Delegates; their guardians kept close, though more for the Electors' honor than their security.

Alexander surveyed the lobby generally. It was a monumental space, well designed to be impressive on broadcasts, but in person it made everyone look small. The Polite Harmony of Worlds had begun as a loose confederation united by Jonist philosophy, with its emphasis on knowledge and rejection of superstition, but over the six centuries from its founding, the Harmony had become centralized in administration and policy—thanks in some measure to the common recognition of the Electors, and their influence. The construction of a capital city—Center—and particularly the grandeur of its design, when combined with the successful gradual expansion of the number of worlds within the Harmony confederation (and those worlds' economic success), had created a consciousness of the Harmony as an entity above and not dependent upon the member worlds, a unity and not an agreement between sovereign provinces. Due to expansion of the Great Hall to accommodate the more than doubling of the member worlds since Center's initial construction, the lobby was too narrow for its height; that fault was often remarked on by Delegates with pride. It was dimmer than most of Center because, instead of sun-stones or a ceiling screen, the towering ceiling was painted. The work was famous, if not great: the *Mural of Worlds,* a pastiche of the sixteen original Jonist worlds, painted four hundred years earlier by Daniel Ert of Rockland.

The lobby floor was a place of shadows and light, purposely designed with secluded alcoves for meeting or negotiation, yet deceptively open in its center. A narrow balcony overlooked it on one side, but it was closed. This was a private session, with no visitors or press allowed. Alexander began a slow stroll to position himself better in the new dynamics of the bustling room. He avoided the Neulanders, not trusting their discretion and not liking their mood.

Jeroen Lee left the group of Delegates with whom he had been speaking; he intersected Alexander's course and paused. "Distasteful people," he said. "Your new friends."

Alexander hesitated, uncertain if Elector Lee was speaking to him, although no one else was nearby. Even Lee's guardian was across the room, watching. Alexander began a deep bow.

"No," Lee said immediately, stopping him. "I don't want this conversation monitored; be careful of your words." Lee glanced about the room, pretending to survey it as he stood just far enough away from Alexander that a monitoring program would find the two of them coincidentally juxtaposed, not interacting.

Alexander wanted to get away. Jeroen Lee was an enigma. The public, including the World Delegates, esteemed him as principled and candid because his rulings were apparently based on conscience, yet Lee was the most private—secretive, even—of the Electors, and arguably the most astute politician in all the World Academies. Sanda heeded him more than she did any other Elector, and resented that fact. Alexander had been privately interviewed twice by Jeroen Lee, before Lee's ascension to the Electorship: once on Alexander's nameday and once just after he had been sent up to Center. Neither had been a comfortable experience. Occasionally, he still sensed Lee's distant observation of him, but since Lee had become an Elector, giving up administration over toolmen to the new Ahman of Sucre, Ahman Grass, and, more importantly, because of Alexander's personal service with another Elector, Lee no longer had any supervisory control over him; Alexander was glad of it.

"This plan was your idea, not Sanda's," Lee said. "Don't bother to protest. I know how her mind works, and she isn't subtle enough to have conceived it, or bold enough to use a toolman as an independent agent."

"Sir," Alexander said, careful for the sake of monitors not to address Elector Lee directly, or to say the name "Neuland" aloud, "it's for the general good."

Briefly, Lee turned directly to Alexander, and fleetingly, he smiled. "I agree. I don't disapprove; I'm impressed." He stared out at the lobby and spoke from behind his hand as he pretended to yawn. "After the vote, after they cure you, if it happens you're bored with your other choice, as I guess will quickly be the case, I have a proposition. I maintain a residence on Co-Chan. The work would be challenging."

From no choice but death, Alexander was gathering them like medals at an exhibition, but he was suspicious of this one. Lee's tone was too intimate; his smile had been that of a collector, gathering a new piece. Besides, Electors didn't share or trade probes; toolmen knew too many secrets. That could be why Lee wanted him—to learn about Sanda. "I think there would be an objection," Alexander said, to be politic with his refusal.

"Decide when you are no longer hungry," Elector Lee

said. "Use your mind to decide where your loyalty is best spent. I am a patient man." He walked away.

Alexander forced himself not to gape at Lee, so as not to provoke the simplistic monitoring programs into reevaluating the disjointed conversation, and continued his circuit. He'd been moved by Huana's offer, but he had been flattered by Elector Lee's. It was good to be appreciated. He looked at Sanda, far across the room. She'd chosen him; he'd never had a choice before and could not imagine life without his loyalty to her, yet the concept of such freedom was exhilarating—then she happened to look up, notice him and smile. Improperly, he returned it, then went on about the room.

An alarm bellowed, one Alexander didn't recognize. The lobby vibrated with sound, and it echoed in his head. Sunstones in the walls flashed red and black. Men stared at each other in confusion.

The noise, the flashing lights, all stopped suddenly. "There has been an attack on the Harmony of Worlds!" The Marshall's voice trembled. "The Bril have returned!"

Chapter 3

Alexander looked for Elector Brauna, but she had vanished in the lobby's roiling confusion. Delegates struggled to use their closed callers in too close proximity to each other, and screamed their frustration when they could not. They became a shouting mob, scuffling and pushing, although they moved in no fixed direction. Alexander stood motionless, listening and waiting for order to develop, or for a clearer understanding of what the Marshall had said.

The Bril?

That bogeyman name was being spoken over and over around the lobby. The aliens had attacked a Harmony world. Andia.

And Alexander understood.

His stomach tightened. His understanding was intuitive, the logic and particulars not yet clear, but Alexander was frantic to report his sudden, horrible insight. He pushed through the crowd, forgetting they were Delegates, and human, and that he was not. Finally Alexander glimpsed Elector Brauna's red robe entering an alcove near the Arch, with Elector Lee. The other Electors, aided by their guardians and Ahmen, were joining Lee and Brauna as Alexander struggled closer. A buffer of empty space around their alcove had been created by the guardians.

The fear-sweat smell, in the Grand Assembly lobby, was terrifying and galvanized him to press Delegates out of his way. He ignored the dryness of his mouth, the coldness of his hands and the darting, fearful glances everywhere, becoming an automaton on a mission. Men turned and cursed, but he moved ahead.

"Elector!" he screamed when he was close enough. "Elector Brauna!" She didn't hear.

Still shouting, Alexander shoved through to the protective circle of guardians. Ting Wheeling grabbed his arm in a tight, firm grip. Twisting, Alexander kicked at the guardian. It was a mistake. Ting lifted him off his feet and thrust him back into the crowd in a smooth, easy movement that jolted hard those into whom he crashed. Alexander was too intent on reaching the Elector to feel anything. "No!" He scrambled up. "I need to see her! Ahman Young!"

Other guardians eyed him, but left him to Ting.

"Ahman Young!"

Riva Young glanced up as her name was called, saw Alexander, and beckoned him. Moving warily past Ting, Alexander came. The Electors noticed his arrival.

"What, Alex?" Ahman Young asked.

Sanda Brauna looked at him. He brushed past Ahman Young and stumbled into the midst of the six Electors.

Winded, it took him a moment to speak, and she began to frown. "Elector Brauna!" he panted. "This is it!" He looked back at the crowd, most of whom were still engrossed in the news a few were receiving on their callers. Elector Kurioso was on an open call, but there was a security field around their alcove.

"Report!" Elector Brauna snapped. "What do you mean?"

He lowered his voice, and turned away from the Ahmen. "Neuland planned this attack. It's their strategy to get into the Harmony—a common enemy. It must be Neuland; all the pieces fit."

They stared at him.

"Are you certain, Alexander?" Jeroen Lee sounded calm in the midst of the chaos. "It doesn't seem plausible. The report says Bril."

"Yes, Elector, I'm certain." Alexander felt sick as the meaning of Neuland's plan hit him. "One Bril ship crashed on Neuland in the Last War. They must have used it to engineer a false Bril attack. The reports I've overheard said there was a single Bril ship involved at Andia." He turned to Sanda Brauna. "That's why they were overconfident, why they had an odd reaction to the mention of the Bril. They were uncomfortable around Andians, too. Neuland guessed we would want them with us against a Bril attack. Our differences would seem trivial. It's a brilliant plan." He swallowed. "It's evil."

Elector Chen smiled grimly at Elector Lee.

"How was it done?" Elector Rose's aged voice was crisp.

"I don't know yet," Alexander replied. He looked at Sanda Brauna. "Do you have more information?"

She turned to Elector Ica Kurioso. "The quickship that brought the news has more complete data," he said, frowning at Alexander. "We're trying to move the World Delegates inside their Hall, so we can all view it together."

"What about the Neulanders? Shouldn't they be arrested?" Alexander shuddered, tasting again the vaguely medicinal flavor of Talia Kaviscu's lips.

Jeroen Lee crossed his arms against his chest and looked at each Elector in turn. "They only have one ship, then, according to Alexander. Probably, it has already been destroyed—by our forces or by Neuland, to get rid of the evidence. The advantages of admitting Neuland to the Harmony still exist if we can keep our knowledge of the plan secret."

"What a hold we'd have on them!" Elector Rose grinned savagely.

"We could force them to accept an Academy," Kurioso said.

Stunned, Alexander saw their decision. "They attacked the Harmony!"

"We are not the government of the Harmony," Elector Lee said impatiently, looking toward Elector Xhasa Kin. "We are not religious priests blathering about gods and morality. It furthers order to admit Neuland, even now, if it can be done without our explicit approval. Particularly so if we can establish an Academy on Neuland."

"Say nothing, Alex," Elector Brauna said. "You've done excellent work. It's for us to use it now. Go back to the Assembly. Talk to the Neulanders. Get more information."

He didn't recognize the woman hidden by the Electors' mask. "Yes, Elector Brauna." He hesitated, bowed to them all, dismissed and ignored once again, except that, leaving, he felt eyes on his back, and glanced around. Jeroen Lee was watching him. Alexander hurried away into the crowd.

The World Delegates were less agitated. Many had entered the Great Hall, and others, even aides normally not admitted, were moving toward the open doors. Alexander spotted the Neulanders and, because of his orders, went to them.

"You were with the Electors." Kaviscu's statement was an accusation.

"I work for Elector Brauna," Alexander said in probe monotone. "She ordered me to watch the Andians." He glanced around. The crowd was thinning, but there were monitors. "The Bril are quite . . . ingenious."

Havic grinned. Alexander's stomach churned with a combination of bile and sickening hunger.

"We'll have something for you soon, Stefan says." Kaviscu was watching him. "Unless you're too worried about Andia." Havic's hand hovered near Alexander's arm, ready to grab him.

He forced an easier smile and controlled an urge to recoil, relying on probe training in flat, innocuous behavior. "The Electors will appreciate Neuland's help during such a dangerous time." He had to convince them he was on their side. He stopped using probe monotone and said, "Perhaps I'll even be able to visit Neuland—I feel confident you'll be admitted, soon, with my help as protocol guide. There will be a great deal I can tell you about Center, then." Anything to cool their suspicions. "In the meantime, I have other work to do, aspirants. Please excuse me." He bowed, and hurried into the Great Hall with the rest.

The Great Hall was majestic, a half-circle amphitheater, not as large as even a simple Rangeball Arena in one of Sucre's minor cities, but gorgeous in its opulent decoration. The walls were of intertwined materials from member worlds: wood, shell, woven fibers, ceramic—whatever was beautiful and distinctive. Scenes from Jon Hsu's life—his training, his scientific work, his flight from a crossman jailing, the writing of the *General Principles,* and his martyrs death—were pictured in precious and semiprecious stones on panels, with the *General Principles* at the front, above the raised platform where the Marshall—selected from the world membership on an annual, rotating basis—presided and where designated speakers and sanctioned guests, such as the Electors, sat on throne-line chairs.

All six Electors were on the dais with the Marshall as Alexander entered. The chief Delegates of each world were in the boxed delegation areas, surrounded by the junior delegation members. Others crowded around the Hall's periphery, whispering, searching for answers. The probes on regular duty there looked glazed; their seniors, like Alexander, who'd followed the Delegates inside, were worse. Alexander moved to the side of the Great Hall, where he could see some of the delegations fully and had a profile of the rest. Hunger, exacerbated by stress, leaked through his self-control.

A low chime reverberated, and the room quieted. The Marshall, a Delegate from humble Surf, stood at the podium. "A quickship just arrived from Andia with the news you've heard. Andia has been attacked by a single Bril battleship; Andia's defenses were inadequate to prevent substantial damage. We'll replay visuals in a moment. The Bril destroyed without reference to military significance, but fortunately they didn't land. No human captives were taken." A sigh of relief swept the room. "The Bril ship was damaged after the first sweep by the heroic kamikaze attack of an Andian police cruiser. The Bril moved off after two sweeps, but Andia was unable to give chase. A Harmony fleet is searching for the ship, and any others."

Two sweeps. Alexander couldn't put off surveying the Andian delegation any longer. Delegate Huana was hunched in his chair like a dying man. His elbows rested on the desk; his head was in his hands. Other Andians were worse. Huana's aides, Pacha and Maria, were sobbing. Julio, his Deputy Delegate, stared blindly ahead.

Two sweeps. Alexander recalled what he knew of the battles of the Last War. A sweep could be anything from a few meters to ten kilometers in width, and could extend a short distance or the entire circumference of a planet. It depended on the type of ship, its orbit, intent, range, and the defenses. Surely the Neulanders hadn't done substantial damage. It would have been pointless pain.

The room darkened. In the air between the Delegates and the dais a choppy replay of space seen through planetary system monitors began. There was no narration; it seemed like a grade-B cyclone entertainment. The swooping panoramas meant nothing to Alexander, whose knowledge of Andia's planetary system was scant. The blip that was the Bril ship looked inconsequential. He relaxed, and noticed many Delegates do the same.

The picture changed focus and closed in on the gray-green world of Andia. A frightened voice began to explain. The first sweep had passed through relatively unpopulated areas, and the focus had been weak. Some people, inside substantial buildings, had survived. The second sweep was different.

A city was burning in the center of the Hall. From a distance it seemed almost pretty, like a bonfire against the dark. Only when the view tightened did the crumpled buildings and the wrecked towers make the scene ugly. In some places stonework had exploded from the heat. The ground had buckled. Except when the narrator spoke, there was total silence.

Alexander heard the name of the burning city, Ayacho, and recognized it with horror as the capital, Delegate Huana's home. He remembered a former member of the Andian delegation. She'd been homesick for Ayacho and had returned to Andia after only a year at Center. Like Huana, like all of the small Andian delegation, she'd treated him as a man when he'd visited the delegation offices, and not as a toolman. The view reached closer and closer to ground level. He saw grotesquely burned bodies, flesh melted into the stone, only the occasional bones giving the blackened things a shape. Drawn into the image by his horror, Alexander sensed heat still emanating from the charred surface of the world. It began to rain, and the ground sizzled and steamed, making the valley of Ayacho into a cauldron of human stew.

Alexander wondered if any of the corpses was that of Huana's aide. Or Huana's wife and children—the family with whom he'd been invited to stay by the husband and father who hadn't yet known they were already dead. He turned away from the images, unreasonably afraid of recognizing faces.

He imagined the burned meat odor of Ayacho and felt his hunger. He swallowed, disgusted that he could think of food. The narrator spoke of a glass plain ahead, where the sweep's intensity had strengthened. Alexander refused to see more. He walked out to the lobby. He was not alone; many people had crept away from the sight of the carnage. They whispered together, and he did his job, observing.

"We'll be able to provide medical help to the survivors," Talia Kaviscu was telling Delegate Purl in a low voice. "Neuland medicine can virtually rebuild a body. Our work is impressive."

Impressive. Could they raise the dead?

Eventually the remaining Delegates stumbled out of the Hall and silently returned to their offices and homes. Alexander stood motionless, unable to think of anything but his hunger and the impressive cost of its cure.

* * *

"She's back from her meeting with the Electors and wants to see you," Ting Wheeling said disapprovingly from the entrance to the gloomy sunroom. Sucre's sun was setting, casting long shadows across the clearing. The room smelled dank.

Alexander pushed the plate away, dismayed that he had eaten and that, although the fruit and cheese were gone, he was still hungry. "Do you understand what they're doing?" he asked Ting. "Andia means nothing. They're letting its murderers into the Harmony."

Ting's stolid expression didn't change. "You take too much on yourself. Toolmen obey. Come on. Elector Brauna is waiting."

Alexander followed him to a formal sitting room where Sanda Brauna was watching Sucre's public news. The press had limited access to political information since policy debates were the province of the Academies, not the populace. However, the "Bril" attack on Andia was being broken to the public—carefully. The Marshall was on the news describing the mobilization of Harmony resources to exterminate this final nest of Bril. Sanda looked up, her face aglow with excitement. "Do you think they actually constructed puppet Bril, or did they crew it with their own people and somehow transmit false readings? Their level of biological expertise would be extraordinary if they could manufacture credible aliens!"

"I don't know, Elector."

"Try to find out from the aspirants. Jeroen thinks we should open direct negotiations with them. They're obviously desperate to get into the Harmony—probably the alans at their backs are worse than we knew. We'll drop a few hints of our suspicions, and before long there will be an Ahman of Neuland. Too bad they're all Altered, though; it complicates matters."

"Neuland attacked one of our own worlds."

She turned and smiled. "You don't take the larger view. What's been done to Andia is *done;* it won't be repeated. We're not crossman priests, who tend a flock of superstitious sheep. We don't seek revenge—or punishment—where to do so would provoke blood feud and war. We are arbiters of order. Don't worry, we'll watch Neuland, but they only had one ship. These false Bril will vanish once they're admitted,

yet we'll always have a lever if they cause us trouble. The
fact they've done something," she stopped a moment, frowning, "contemptible, doesn't mean we can't use them in the
Harmony."

"Is it worth it, Elector?" he asked wistfully. "They make
my skin crawl."

"You're ridiculous," she said fondly. She signaled and the
news went off, dimming the room. She came close, gently
putting her hand against his chest. "My favorite reason to
continue with your plan is to have your flare cured."

"Perhaps Harmony medics could cure it?"

She shook her head. "No. The other Electors would never
agree. Don't feel guilty about survival. Admitting Neuland is
a political necessity. If you hadn't understood and grasped
this opportunity, the only difference is we wouldn't have
been aware of Neuland's scheming—and you'd be dead."

"Another probe would have realized the truth."

"None has so far. The other Electors—especially Jeroen—
are jealous that I have you. You're an expert at nuance and
outstanding at extrapolation. You're different from the rest."

"If you say so, Elector." He wished she didn't need to believe that in order to justify her feelings for a toolman. She
would have let him die to assuage that pride.

She patted him. "Go to the lobby; the emergency session
begins soon. All the Electors will attend." She laughed.
"You can watch me smile at the Neulanders. Claim credit
for it—we don't want them imagining they don't need your
facilitation."

He bowed. A partner probably wouldn't, but she expected
the obeisance. "Sanda," he whispered.

She looked startled. Her face softened into the woman he
knew at night, who didn't think of political necessities.

"I just wanted to say it." He was embarrassed.

She smiled, and he bowed again, feeling foolish.

Talia Kaviscu was much in evidence, commiserating with
the World Delegates, pledging Neuland's help against the
Bril attackers and expressing pity for the absent Andians.
Havic was more circumspect, watching from the outskirts of
the crowd like a probe on duty. He did a creditable job of
circuitously approaching Alexander and seeming surprised
to notice him. "You, probe," he said. "Where can I get
something to drink?"

"I'll show you, Aspirant Havic." Alexander led Havic to an empty refreshment room near the lobby, listening to the echo of Havic's footsteps and the soft thud of his own. Gesturing at the provider, he asked, "What would you prefer?"

Havic glanced around. Alexander shook his head slightly.

"Something warm," Havic said. "This Assembly of yours is full of cold men. You have a drink, too. I insist."

Alexander took two cups from the mechanism and, feeling petty, set the water temperature high enough to burn Havic's mouth, hoping to do damage—though the pain-free Neulander would not feel it. Cradling the other cup in his hands, Alexander smiled as Havic sipped the steaming liquid.

"Ahh," Havic said. With an impressive sleight of hand, he dropped something small and yellow into Alexander's cup.

"Drink up," Havic said. "My mother always said a warm drink was medicinal."

"Yes, Aspirant Havic." The dark liquid in the cup was not obviously changed. Wincing, Alexander drank. For an instant it was bitter, then he didn't taste anything. "Thank you, Aspirant Havic. I'm grateful for your consideration."

"You should be, toolman. Remember it. But we're pleased with your protocol services, so far, and your discretion."

Alexander looked into the Neulander's worm-pale face, wondering how it was that an evil man was saving his life. He smiled at Havic, gulped the hot, healing liquid, and considered what that said about him.

The Andians had arrived by the time Alexander returned to the lobby. They were the focus of solicitous attention. Delegate Huana's shoulders sagged; his eyes were red and too bright. His mouth was set as if he was gritting his teeth and had been for hours. Alexander watched as Elector Brauna went to Huana's side, murmuring comforting banalities. It should have been the worst hypocrisy imaginable and yet Sanda Brauna's attempted solace appeared genuine. It reminded him of her real sorrow at the onset of his flare, and her failure to do anything to cure it. He'd had to help her by helping himself.

"We'll find these Bril and destroy them!" Alexander imagined a glint of amusement in Elector Brauna's eyes. Looking across the intervening space, he saw only her bloodred Elector's robe. Would there be a war against Neuland if the Assembly learned the truth? Alexander told himself that more death would not promote order or justice; war would do nothing for Andia but absorb resources that world needed in order to rebuild. But perhaps Neuland could be forced somehow to make amends? And the perversion of truth that silence meant made him wonder how he would ever face Huana—his one true friend!—again. He remembered Huana's own word: sophistry, Electors' sophistry.

Delegate Huana sighed. "I hope no other world ever bears a tragedy like this. The private report the quickship brought for me gave more information." He made a choked sound, then said, "One-third of our population is gone."

"Your own family?" Elector Brauna asked.

Huana shrugged hopelessly.

Unnoticed by anyone, Alexander shuddered as he imagined Delegate Huana's family among the blackened remnants of scorched and melted bone in that shattered city.

Elector Brauna embraced Huana. He leaned against her for a moment, then stood back. "Thank you. I've learned from a friend that you have a good heart, Elector."

Startled, Alexander recognized the reference to himself. He bit his lip and purposely scanned a wider area. Ting Wheeling, behind Elector Brauna, watched Alexander steadily, as if Ting sensed something amiss.

Talia Kaviscu approached Huana, but stood off to the side, beyond the range at which Elector Brauna would have to choose between rudeness or a public greeting. Elector Brauna turned slowly, and nodded infinitesimally at the Neulander aspirant.

Talia Kaviscu came forward.

Delegate Huana noticed Elector Brauna's attention behind him and turned. "Aspirant," he said, wearily. "Thank you for Neuland's offer of aid. I regret my previous comments. A crisis has shown Neuland's true humanity."

"Against such a threat, we are all united as fellow humans," Kaviscu said.

Elector Brauna seemed to inspect the Neulander woman. "I have recently been made aware," Elector Brauna said carefully, "that Neulanders are capable of becoming human."

Alexander felt an ache that wasn't hunger. In his gut and in his mind there was a physical yearning for truth. He recalled the views of Andia, of burned Ayacho. The anguish in every stooped line of Huana's body was only the smallest echo of what his entire world was experiencing. He recalled Talia Kaviscu's callous curiosity when the medic had hurt him. He imagined Delegate Huana voting in favor of Neuland's admission to the Polite Harmony of Worlds. It could not be right for such a thing to happen.

Talia Kaviscu bowed again. "Thank you, Lady. We had sincerely hoped that such an ecumenical attitude might exist among those for whom the search for knowledge and universal truths demanded of us by Jon Hsu was a paramount concern."

Elector Brauna smiled faintly and turned away from the Neulander woman. As she did so, her eyes met Alexander's, and her smile became genuine and amused.

It had been necessary for him to act once before on her behalf, without instructions. He balanced the value of his life against the many Andian lives already dead for Neuland. If he lived with this lie, he would have had a hand in killing them. Elector Brauna would be besmirched. He stepped forward, knowing true loyalty meant he must save her honor and that of the entire Harmony. "Elector Brauna!"

The men and women in the room blanched at the disrespectful behavior, then froze as they saw it was a probe who had shouted.

Sanda Brauna went rigid. "Probe, go to your quarters," she said. "You are obviously unwell." The room buzzed with low-voiced speculation.

As if he and Sanda were at opposite ends of a long tunnel, Alexander saw only her. He stepped closer. Guardians raised their weapons; he barely noticed. "Elector Brauna, I have a report to make," he said. "It's urgent. Please listen."

She gestured, and Ting Wheeling approached Alexander. "Go with him, Alex," she said. "Go home."

"No! Elector, if you won't listen, then I'll give my report to Delegate Huana."

Huana looked as amazed as the others. "Alex?"

Ting Wheeling moved quickly past Alexander and grappled with Pavel Havic. In the uneven tussle, Havic shouted, "I was trying to help! This probe has gone insane!" Ting held the Neulander tight and looked to Sanda Brauna for orders.

Her face was pale. Elector Lee whispered to her, and she shook her head.

"Delegate Huana," Alexander said grimly, fully aware he

was killing himself. "Your enemy is not the Bril. It is Neuland."

Delegate Huana stared at him without comprehension.

Alexander bowed. "Delegate, I must report that Neuland has rebuilt a Bril ship and used it to attack Andia, to pretend there was a nonhuman threat. They did it to influence the vote of the Grand Assembly. Andia was expendable to them, an easy target."

"No ..." Delegate Huana came a step closer, his fists clenched, then stopped, looking at Havic. "Alex. You must be wrong."

"He's crazy!" Havic shouted. Ting jerked him roughly away.

Alexander surveyed Sanda Brauna. Her eyes were dry and her back was straight, but she stood as though any movement would bring pain. Alexander bowed to her. "I'm just a toolman, Elector. The only necessities I understand are personal ones. I can't go on."

Guardians of the other Electors surrounded him; one took control of Pavel Havic from Ting Wheeling, who then stood indecisively beside Alexander. Delegate Huana looked back and forth between Alexander and Havic, then at the Electors.

Alexander spoke again to Delegate Huana. "I'm sorry Delegate. I've known for several days, but I told *no one*. The Neulanders offered to cure my flare, if I helped them, and kept the truth from the Electors. I wanted to live."

Delegate Huana's expression changed from confusion to horror, and, as realization came that Alexander had known of Neuland's plan before the moment he'd spoken, Huana started at him, lips pulled back from his teeth in a snarl of pure hatred.

Alexander cringed. "No, Delegate! I didn't know *all* their plan! I didn't know about Andia! I swear I didn't know!"

Huana spat at him.

Alexander stumbled backward, but Ting Wheeling caught him.

"You monster! You brutish, lying, imitation man!" Huana screamed. His face was contorted in rage as finally he found a target for the horror of the attack. "When I think that I considered you as good as human, even against all the teachings of the Electors! I was sorry for you! For you!" Huana's red, staring eyes streamed bitterness along with his hot tears.

"For a creature that would set its unnatural life above those of millions of real men! Alexander—the betrayer of Andia!"

Alexander was unable to speak.

Elector Lee pushed through to them. He touched Delegate Huana's shoulder. Huana turned, striking out at the same time. When he realized who had come, he quieted suddenly, almost collapsing against Jeroen Lee.

"Gather up all Neulanders in Center," Elector Lee said, and men rushed to obey. He turned to Alexander. "You've taken a great deal onto yourself, Alexander," he said gently, but others imagined denunciation in the quiet tone.

"Yes, Elector," he said, finding his voice. "I understand. It was entirely my fault for having wanted to live so much." Alexander couldn't look at Delegate Huana, but heard his sobbing. He longed to make the man understand. To do so, though, would betray Sanda Brauna and the other Electors, so he was silent.

Jeroen Lee looked as if he wanted to say more, but instead he turned to Sanda. "This is your probe. Take him for now and see he doesn't escape before we get some answers."

Sanda Brauna clearly understood, as Alexander did, that no questioning could occur. For the first time since Alexander had known her, she seemed dazed. She moved as the powerless do, slowly, head down and shoulders slumped.

Two guardians took hold of him. The one on his left, Elector Rose's, pushed him roughly forward; the other was Ting Wheeling, whose touch was unexpectedly light.

Alexander walked as they directed him, a prisoner, following Elector Brauna. He felt eyes, but kept his head down. Delegate Huana shouted something animal and intense that he refused to let himself hear. Instead he listened to the rumbling of his stomach, finally able to be amused by his hunger.

They went directly to Sanda Brauna's apartment and stopped in the sitting room she'd used earlier. She dismissed the other guardian. Ting took up a position blocking the door. It was funny. Where could a probe run? Alexander wished that they were in the sunroom. He wanted to sit patiently and watch the slow sunset become dark.

"I'm sorry," he said when the silence became painful.

She sat down heavily on the edge of a straight-backed chair.

He memorized her face, though he would not have memory for long. "I couldn't bear to let them succeed, Elector. The Harmony can survive without Neuland, but not without truth. I only hope that I would have spoken even if it had been another world than Andia."

She sighed. "Alex, you are too young." She sank her face into her hands.

He glanced at Ting Wheeling, who stared fixedly through him. Poor guardian, he didn't want to kill.

Sanda looked up, twisting her fingers together in her lap. "Perhaps you can stay in the apartment. The others might agree. Six months isn't long."

"It isn't long to live, but it's much too long to die. Please, Elector. Let it be quick. Do it now."

She didn't answer and only shook her head. She was crying, and he was afraid he would do worse.

"Please, Sanda," he said, summoning all his courage to beg for death.

She looked directly at him, studying his face. Hers seemed finally to have her true age written in her eyes. She straightened in the chair, and without taking her attention from him, signaled Ting Wheeling to obey him, then said, "A human should have a choice."

Ting looked at Alexander, raising the gun. Alexander nodded and closed his eyes.

PART TWO

•

SUCRE

The Evil Twin Story

Chapter 4

August listened with the rapt attention of a predator, although, as the long-dead Alexander's clone, he felt more like prey. He stared at the blank panel of the closed door as though it might become transparent, waiting for the sound of Ting Wheeling's footfalls on the hardwood floor of the hallway beyond the door. His right hand ached as he gripped the beveled crystal doorknob, holding the door from springing open at his touch. Finally, he heard approaching steps, waited for them to arrive, then released the knob, freeing the door. It banged harmlessly against the wall. Ting Wheeling had retreated in time to escape the trap.

He gazed mildly up at August, though his brown hair was slightly mussed. He nodded, then his lips twitched as he was unable to completely contain his amusement.

August entered the long, empty hall. Despite his caution, his footsteps were louder than Ting's. One for the guardian, nothing for August.

Ting waited patiently as August hesitated. He could wait longer than August cared to tease him with inaction, so August took one farther step, to indicate a willingness to proceed, then stopped again.

"Does she want to see me today?" August indicated the rest of the apartment with a brief jerk of his head, though there was no doubt between them as to whom he referred.

"No." Ting turned, ready to escort August to breakfast in the probe common room. The guardian's expression was once again impassive. He looked much like any other toolman/guardian of middle years—plain, rock-solid, and serene—except he waited better than anyone August had ever seen.

"How old are you?" August knew the answer, but Ting would respond to direct questions, and he was one of the few who didn't refuse to talk or belittle August for trying.

Ting observed August, making eye contact rather than his usual sideways, downturned examination of intention through arms or lips or hands. "Forty-five."

"Then you'll live to see me die," August said in probe monotone, in order to appear to be controlling fear.

Ting glanced down the narrow hall. He wanted to end the conversation, seeming almost ashamed that guardians and subs lived as long as standard humans.

Pleased by this success—score one for him—August leaned against the wall so Ting would know he wasn't escaping so easily. He readied his next Ting attack—mention of his predecessor, Alexander Greeneyes—prepared to gather more information from the guardian's reaction.

"So long as I don't have to kill you," Ting said suddenly, and clearly from the heart. He stared at the floor in unTing-like distress.

The comment was replete with buried data, but August focused on the surprised observation that Ting Wheeling liked him. "Today is my nameday," August confided abruptly. He looked down, involuntarily copying Ting. He hadn't intended to mention his nameday like a child hoping for favors.

"You're twenty-one."

It was difficult to determine if Ting was asking or making a statement. "Yes," August said, recalling the gray day he'd received his name. He'd felt triumphant, youngest in the line of eleven probes to have qualified, but Ahman Kiku had stared at him, his revulsion obvious even to the nameless, toddling littles who had gathered to watch the ceremony under the cloudy Sucre sky. "Your existence is unfortunate," Kiku had finally said, loud enough to be heard by everyone gathered in the formal assembly. "Your face is a badge of shame; see you don't add to the misery and disorder your predecessor brought to the Electors." He'd scowled and stalked away, leaving the farm, and it had been Reverend Researcher Shan, the farm's director, who had delivered August's name at the somber meal that had substituted for the usual nameday celebration. Thereafter, no number of excellent work reports had erased the stain through which everyone saw August. He'd even lost his use-name; no one spoke casually with him again, not even jovial marketers unloading supplies at the gate, as if they, too, had finally recognized the great traitor's clone brother. It had been the same when he came up to Center—except with Elector Brauna. She alone cared for him.

August pushed away from the wall. He was two quick strides down the corridor before Ting reacted, but this didn't feel like a victory.

Ting assumed his accustomed position to the left and behind August. "She's in the sunroom, if you need her." His high-pitched voice was strained by the effort of volunteering information, or perhaps from tension at venturing into intimacy.

August stopped at the end of the hall, before it joined the main axis corridor of the apartment, and turned to Ting again. "Let me walk to the common room alone." He asked every morning lately, certain that Elector Brauna's precaution had become unnecessary.

"I can't do that. I'm sorry."

Usually August acquiesced gracefully, but, sensing possibilities, he stared accusingly at Ting.

Ting shifted on his feet, a show of great emotion for phlegmatic Ting. "For your protection," he said earnestly. "You're not registered in Center. I'm *your* guardian, too."

"You're my jailer." August hit the fabric-covered wall. The soft thud was unsatisfying, like the useless banging of his door.

Ting Wheeling only watched and waited. August sighed, then turned into the main corridor of Sanda Brauna's apartment, a wide passageway with thick, pale green carpeting on the floor, which rose halfway up the walls, oppressively muffling every sound. Above the carpet was a long, repetitive mural of stylized garden plants, recently painted and somewhat similar in feeling to the hothouse sunroom—both were funereal. Unrelieved by any liveliness or splash of color, the effect was monotonous and depressing, a poignant reflection of Elector Brauna's grieving heart.

He stopped after only a few steps. Mei Wang, the Elector's secretary, had come out of her office.

He walked forward stiffly and bowed. "Reverend Wang."

Wang's long black hair swirled around her face as she turned to August; her blue robe of office reflected light from the sun-stones, making her skin gray and deepening the circles under her dark eyes. "I've read yesterday's report. I don't trust you," she said. "I think you're a liar and a fraud, just as you were before. I'm watching you. Elector Brauna may lose her ability to reason when it comes to you, but I don't."

"Reverend, I'm not my predecessor."

Ting came to August's side. Wang glanced at Ting, then seemed to dismiss the other toolman from consideration. "You, of all people, have an obligation to be skeptical of Neuland. Instead, you say that the Harmony should send them aid!"

"My report is honest, Reverend." He wet his lips. "If you believe my analysis is incorrect, please show me where I have erred. I only extrapolated trends within the Grand Assembly and noted the likelihood that they will send humanitarian aid. I did not say that the Harmony should. I explicitly stated the improbability of military aid. There is increasing sympathy for Neuland, however, since the Emirates' raids inside their planetary system have become so frequent and severe." Perspiration broke out on his forehead; August thought enviously of Alexander's coolness. Not once in any replay had he seen that bastard flustered.

"Andia will block any aid to Neuland."

He bowed. "That is the conventional wisdom, Reverend Wang, but while Andia hasn't forgotten, it isn't as vehement anymore, either. Delegate Huana realizes that people tire of a perpetual victim, and he chooses his battles carefully. Unless the Electors actively oppose it, I calculate a better than seventy percent chance that the next time Darien's Chief Delegate Wilder introduces a measure granting aid to Neuland, it will pass. The current Marshall is sympathetic, and the Delegates worry more about the uniting of the Emirates under Aleko Bei than they do about something that happened twenty-three years ago."

"And what do you worry about, probe?" She smiled with nasty satisfaction. "You're trembling. Did you know that? You're not even a good probe, however many reports you write. You have no self-control at all. You can barely function, talking with me." She laughed. The sound vanished in the padded corridor.

He tried. "Reverend Wang, I have been watched all my life. I can't leave this apartment without an escort. I've never been allowed to do the work probes are designed for, or to meet people, or to talk to anyone." She continued to stare coldly at him, seeing Alexander's face. "I hate him! I hate Alexander! I hate Neuland! I wrote a report for the Elector. Shouldn't she know the truth? I only do the best I can for her and the Harmony."

Wang put her hands on her hips and shook her head.

"You're useless. No wonder Elector Brauna's only interest in you is nostalgia." She reentered her office, wordlessly dismissing him.

After a moment, Ting cleared his throat. "Breakfast." He gestured ahead.

"I'm not hungry. Just take me to the tape study room." He started down the corridor to the toolman entrance.

"She isn't fair," Ting said from behind.

As lightly as he could force himself to speak, August said, "Reverend Wang hates me."

"Not her."

August froze in mid-step. Sanda Brauna might be watching him. He often daydreamed that she did, so that the monitors became an intimate link between them. It was to her he recited:

> "When, in disgrace with fortune and men's eyes,
> I all alone beweep my outcast state, . . .
> Haply I think on thee— . . .

"Come on," Ting said impatiently.

When, at fifteen, August had been brought up from the farm, the oldest probes still remembered Alexander Greeneyes. They'd shunned August, his clone—conspicuously avoided all contact with him. One by one those old-timers had been put down during the subsequent six years, but the habit of shunning August persisted. It was such routine that a hush no longer fell when he entered the probe dining room. They noted his presence as they would any minor datum and continued their conversations and their meals. Ting Wheeling, having safely delivered August into public custody, nodded briefly and left.

August took one of the pre-apportioned standard breakfasts from the provider and went to his customary table in the back. No one sat with him. No one spoke to him. He ate mechanically and quickly; eating was embarrassing, with all the charm of refueling a vehicle.

When he had finished, Ellen Short came to his table, swinging her hips as she balanced on the red, high-heeled shoes some admiring Ahman must have given her. The shoes did little to ameliorate the handicap of her lack of height— fortunately she had sharp eyes and a strong nose—but they made her walk a splendid show. "Does Elector Brauna need

anything special surveyed today?" Ellen used probe monotone when duty made public conversation with him necessary. Her posture before his table was formal, but even her
formality was laced with humor as she tottered on her garish
shoes.

"Nothing unusual. Thank you," he said, equally formal.
His role as intermediary between Elector Brauna and the
probe—the other probe—in her personal service was one of
August's few specific duties.

Ellen nodded and her demeanor softened, despite the others surveying them who might take offense. "Good. It's our
nameday. I was hoping for time to celebrate." She smiled. It
was not her best smile, but it seemed sincere. She'd been in
line ahead of August that nameday with Ahman Kiku and
was now the closest thing to a friend he had, except possibly
for Ting.

His return smile felt unnatural. He was too aware of Elector Lee's senior probe, Vincent, watching them. "All right,"
he said, "but you've been wandering too much. Twice recently I had no idea where you were. What if the Elector
wanted you?"

She shrugged and looked at her new shoes. "Sorry."

"Sit down."

She hesitated. He'd spoken at normal volume, a clear order, yet he'd said there was no special assignment to discuss.
Glancing at the others, making a subtle show of wishing to
be elsewhere, Ellen took the seat across the table from him.

"Do you know poetry?" This time his voice was pitched
only for her ears.

She shook her head. "Only a few Jonist naturals that we
learned on the farm."

He leaned closer. "Elector Brauna likes poetry a great
deal," he offered. "Especially ancient poetry: Andrew
Marvell and John Keats. Dante, Kyle, and Shakespeare. You
should read some and add appropriate allusions to your reports. She'd notice and enjoy it."

"Is *that* what you do? Read poetry to her?"

August flushed, thinking of the others watching him react.
It was obvious to any probe what he did *not* do with Elector
Brauna. "Sometimes," he admitted.

One night—it had been real night, with Sucre's ponderous
sun going down and a twilight gloominess in the sunroom;
there had been shadows over everything, so much so that

Sanda Brauna's downcast face had been invisible—that night she cried as he read poetry aloud. He had listened to his own recitation of the verse, seeming almost to remember it because the words had become his own. That night the poetry wasn't even sound, it had become meaning, pure and absolute, a resonance in his soul from emotions that had traveled down the centuries and entered him and, through him, had spoken to her. He'd heard subliminally the sound of her breathing, the silence when she'd unconsciously held her breath, needing all her concentration to form the image that his voice created in her mind. When she'd begun to cry, he'd known before he heard the slight sobbing catch, as if he had smelled the fragrance of her salty tears as they dropped from the corners of her eyes. After his voice had drifted into silence, when he'd read all of the poetry she'd set out, she had taken him to her room. She had left the lights off and whispered an order to him not to speak. That night she had removed his clothes, and hers, and held him close. Sex, too, but it had been the holding he most remembered. In the morning she was staring at him when he awakened. She'd quickly left the bed, the room, and not asked for him again for weeks. When she had, it had been a trivial matter, some research to pursue.

"Well, thank you," Ellen said skeptically, "but I'll just do probe work and leave the poetry to you."

He thrust the empty plate away from him. The fork clattered and fell onto the table, startling them both. He stood. The chair's squeak against the tile floor made him shiver, but it seemed exactly how he felt. "I thought you might prefer Elector Brauna's personal service to being returned to general services"—he hesitated—"or the farm." He kept threats too carefully out of his tone so that she shuddered at the implication, imagining he had influence where he did not. He felt dirty, but he felt better. "And change your shoes before you go into the Assembly."

He left the common room and went directly to tape study. If he did not check in quickly enough, Ting Wheeling would come looking.

August replayed the daily political report, including a review of public news and comment on Sucre and the rest of the Harmony, reviewed Ellen's most current on-sites, annotated them for Elector Brauna, then sent them on to her at-

tention through the Elector's private system. Next, he
assessed the public conduct of each of the Electors since the
day before, beginning with Sanda Brauna herself. The frustration of a bad angle and poor coverage of a discussion of
Neuland that had taken place between Elector Lee, Ahman
Hills, and Ahman Penn caused him to stop in the middle of
his work and walk furiously around those areas within which
he was permitted, working off his angry energy in motion.
Then he surveyed the Delegates, always beginning with the
Andian delegation, and last, he surveyed randomly, stopping
at anything that seemed interesting, as found by programs he
had perfected over the years.

He had unlimited access, allegedly the same as an Elector,
since (not having one of his own) it was Elector Brauna's
registration he used to enter the system. Though he suspected there were further code refinements that he did not
have, all of Center's offices and public spaces were available
to him, both in the Elector's wing—which included the
lower school, Ahmen's laboratories, and the Academy, altogether the largest Jonist scientific community in existence—
and in the Harmony's governmental portion of Center—the
Grand Assembly lobby and Great Hall, the delegation offices, the busy corridors and committee rooms. He was allowed to peruse all the old records: replay and writings. He
could, but rarely did, watch the private corridors: access
halls and lifts to residences, as well as internal monitors in
certain guest suites. More often, he randomly surveyed Center's commercial districts for social trends and opinions, and
to get the flavor of life. He was not allowed to do real-time
on-site work, or interact with anyone but toolmen or Elector
Brauna's staff; few others realized he existed. He supposed
he knew as much as anyone about what occurred at Center,
but it was the knowledge of a ghost, or a soul in some
crossman purgatory. Last, he made his own daily report to
Elector Brauna.

Overnight, a quickship had arrived at Sucre, having come
directly from Neuland, which was virtually unheard of. It
was a trader registered from Darien. August inspected the
cargo manifest—medical supplies sent to Jeroen Lee—and
then the news it brought: another raid on Neuland, with
eight thousand killed at the Kay mines on an outer planet in
Neuland's system. About a dozen of the dead were Harmony
citizens on work contracts.

His stomach twisted. There was a crisis coming; he felt it in the pattern of conversations all over Center, in the reported restlessness of the population of Darien, the closest Harmony world to Neuland, in the attitude of public-access commentators discussing Neuland or the Emirates. He had a duty to tell Elector Brauna what he saw, and yet, did he have a moral duty to do what he could to hurt Neuland, the enemy? What did Elector Brauna really want regarding Neuland? She never said.

He decided to do a position report on Neuland, rather than the usual daily Center study, and began indexing the latest raid on Neuland with the others of the past five years, barely conscious of the glances from other probes as he turned from the standard displayer to his screen, picking and choosing among the archives and reports. Only Henry Librarian could do the same, and August had fuller access. He found what he needed with practiced ease, then closed his eyes, outlining the shape of the report in his mind.

Gradually he slipped into the mental dreamworld of the report, where the words he wrote were the sole reality. He always struggled to make his reports not only precise and informative, but clever. The rhythm of the words was important, and the tone. Reports were his only regular contact with Elector Brauna—the brief, occasional meetings at which she gave him orders were inconsequential—and his goal was to cause her to look up from the displayer when she had finished and, perhaps, smile, or nod, or, best of all, be reminded of August himself in an intimacy of the mind.

Others read certain of his reports, not only Reverend Wang, but often Elector Lee, and sometimes other Electors and various Ahmen. With Neuland the topic, that was particularly likely; he strove for clarity and wit, so as not to disgrace her. He utilized text, as usual, disliking the thought of Elector Brauna watching his reports on replay tape, perhaps seeing something awkward in his delivery, or being reminded yet again of Alexander. Also, revision was easier in text. Within the confines of the need for exactitude and speed, he polished his phrases, forcing them to carry the full weight of both succinct communication and elegance, if not beauty. The reports were never perfect, but when he was satisfied this one said all that it should as well as he was able to say it—outlining briefly the history of the Emirates raids, the Neulander responses, Neuland's requests for aid and the likely result of this recent attack both on Neuland's overtures to the Harmony and the reaction of the Grand Assembly—he looked up from the screen for the first time in hours. The tape study room was nearly empty. It was dinnertime. He'd missed lunch, but he didn't want a meal. He positively didn't want to sit with his back against the wall surveying them from isolation. He wasn't hungry enough for that.

He safeguarded and labeled the report, then sent it to Elector Brauna's personal attention. He stood, unkinking his muscles. The room's two guardians watched impassively as he closed the screen and slid it under the carrel he used every day. He walked past them warily, although neither had ever troubled him; he remembered too well those guardians who had. Elector Brauna had discovered the petty torments and intimidation a few guardians were inflicting on Alexander's clone; she'd immediately brought August out of quarters to live with her, protected by her extraordinary favor and by Ting. The two guardians who'd beaten him had vanished—rumor said put down—and Ting's endorsement and defense had gradually won over the others. It was Sanda Brauna's tears, however, the way she'd held him close when he entered her apartment, the first tenderness after years of shame—those were the memories he had of her that could never change.

August paused in the corridor. His choices were limited. He was allowed in all of the toolmen common rooms and quarters but he would be welcome in none of them. He had access to the archive storage facility, the binding room, the exercise calisthenia (which he still avoided, as it was used mostly by guardians), and TMO, the Toolman Medical Office. Or he could wait in tape study for Ting to find him. If he wanted to return early to Sanda's apartment, he would need to summon Ting. If he wanted to go anywhere else, he needed Sanda's prior permission, and that of Ahman Kiku. Alexander had robbed August of physical freedom when he betrayed the Harmony. August sometimes imagined his life was retroactive punishment for Alexander.

TMO was best. It was staffed with real men who would talk to him. He rubbed his forehead to make a record of his pain, and walked slowly through the empty halls.

"Another migraine?" Elena Radcliffe smiled at August in a comfortingly maternal fashion, and winced in sympathy.

He nodded, feigning pain in the movement of his head. "Too much replay tape," he said. TMO was hung with bright blue, pink, and gold fabric, a welcome contrast to the somber richness of Elector Brauna's apartment. Med. Radcliffe's office walls curved, reflecting its position on an outer wall of Center's complex, but the effect was naturalistic, a feeling furthered by the lack of visible medical instruments, except for a sensor array. Patients had a soft chair beside Med. Radcliffe's desk.

She touched his forehead. The cool pressure of her hand was soothing. "You need fresh air," she said. Her tone was scolding, as if he had a choice and had chosen wrongly.

"Give me a prescription for a vacation on Flute. Maybe Elector Brauna will send me on a trip."

She grinned. "You probes are too high-strung."

"That's right, blame the victim." He felt easy here. None of the medics had any power over him, or seemed to mind who he was. It was a wonder he didn't come every day.

"Well, you could exercise in the toolman calisthenia," she lectured, but she also smiled. "It's not just for guardians. Biology doesn't determine everything; you probes could use strength training, too." She called up his chart on a closed view with a deft motion of her fingertips in the air. He saw the wariness as she scanned it even before she spoke, and wondered what it said. "I notice you're here more often than any other probe." That was delay before unpleasant news.

He smiled widely and leaned conspiratorially forward. Before she could speak, he said, "The others are afraid to come. Superstitious. They're all worried about flare." He touched her hand, resting on the desk, an ancient but important technique. "I don't have to worry. I'm a clone; I know when I'll go." He nodded to emphasize truthfulness and the sense of having divulged something important.

She hesitated uncertainly. Even medics disliked mention of flare, and he'd just given her a plausible rationale for his frequent visits. "Still," she said, "we should do a full exam and see what's causing these headaches."

He'd definitely have to decrease his visits to TMO. He looked down at the golden-tiled floor, studying his own soft-soled black slippers resting there like shadows on the sun.

"Maybe I'm under more stress than the others." He let silence say the rest.

She sat back in her chair. "Do you take the tabs, August?"

At least she was human, not a probe. He was certain his expression slipped at her unexpected shrewdness. "Of course. They help a bit."

She stared at him. "All right," she said finally, "but this is absolutely the last time. I'll give you *falfre* for the stress, but I want you to schedule a full exam."

He nodded, wondering if he should have told the truth, that he came because they talked to him. That would almost certainly result in a message to Ahman Kiku, or worse, a message to Sanda Brauna. "I'm sorry if I'm any trouble, Med. Radcliffe," he said.

"You're no trouble, August." She was friendly again and entirely sincere. "I'm just thinking what's best for you. Alexander never complained of headaches."

Ting Wheeling was waiting outside the probe dining room. August was already high from the tabs, which Med. Radcliffe had watched him take. Though he was rarely confused by visual sleight of hand, August couldn't perform it, so he'd been forced to swallow both.

"She wants to see you tomorrow morning," Ting said.

Made self-absorbed by the work of controlling the uninhibiting tendencies induced by the tabs, August's first thought was that Med. Radcliffe had contacted Elector Brauna after all. Then he noticed the satisfaction Ting Wheeling exuded with delivery of the news and realized there could be worse, or at least, more humiliating circumstances than that. He imagined Ting going to Sanda Brauna. "The boy is lonely," he might have said in his stumbling, high-pitched voice. August was always "the boy" in the brief discussions between Elector Brauna and Ting he'd overheard; he'd been "the boy" ever since he'd entered her personal service at the age of fifteen, uniquely, straight from the farm. He supposed Alexander Greeneyes was the man. Or, Ting might not have been so articulate. "The boy said it was his nameday," Ting might have managed, twisting his hands together like a reprimanded sub. Sanda Brauna was sufficiently perspicacious to understand the rest.

"Fine," August said. He began walking quickly toward the apartment, half running through the service corridors they took in an endless succession of nearly identical days. These spaces were used only by toolmen and sub supervisors, so their lighting system did not emulate a standard day. Instead, a steady harsh white glow always illuminated the area. Like a prison or an operating room, the light was depressing.

August mulled over the reason Elector Brauna wanted him, not this evening, when a long amorphous time would extend beyond the meeting, but rather in the morning, at the start of her busy day. Perhaps it was a reprimand, or perhaps she'd give him some slight, hesitant affection. He remembered the pain of waiting for a renewal of her attention.

August spun around to Ting Wheeling. His facial muscles pulled into an angry snarl he couldn't stop. "I don't want your help!" Some part of him was horrified at his loss of composure where everyone would see it. The only privacy a toolman had was that they were seldom important enough to be watched, but the daily report would include a humorous piece about the breakdown of Elector Brauna's probe. Center's security system scanned for such incidents.

Ting Wheeling's mouth dropped, and he stared, dumbfounded, at August.

"Leave me alone!" Ting had done nothing, but August began to run back the way they'd come. Ting came just behind, grabbing August after a short pursuit, pushing him against the corridor wall. August was panting, but Ting was not winded at all. August's face was damp; he shivered as the infinitesimal breeze from the air circulatory system chilled his skin.

Ting put his arms on either side of August, staring up anxiously at him. "Are you all right?"

It was ludicrous. Clearly, August was not, yet that was all Ting Wheeling knew to ask.

"I want dinner. Let me go back," August said belligerently.

They stared at each other. August blinked back tears. Ting clamped his fingers around August's right wrist. "Come on." He tugged, and when August didn't move, he yanked him forward. "Toolmen obey!" His mouth worked with speechless frustration as he pulled August toward Elector Brauna's apartment like a sack of grain.

August's heels screeched on the hard-surfaced floor. He dropped to his knees. "Wait!"

Ting released him and waited.

August got up. He straightened his uniform, shivering, too ashamed to look at Ting. "I was at TMO. They gave me two *falfre* tabs," he whispered. He wiped his forehead with his sleeve, smelling the sour drug stink in his perspiration, then wrapped his arms around his body, having to control an urge to rock back and forth.

Ting grunted. "I've taken them," he said sympathetically. He touched August's shoulder, then dropped his hand.

August was amazed. "When?"

"After I killed Alexander."

"I knew you did it." He had, but August hadn't guessed until that morning that Ting Wheeling might have been disturbed by the killing.

Ting frowned, deliberating. "If you want to go back for dinner, we'll go. Call me when you're ready to come home."

Home. That was a word August didn't use for Sanda Brauna's apartment, but he supposed it was the only home he had, a home Sanda had made for him. The thought was calming. He looked at Ting and saw his unaccustomed anxiety. *So long as I don't have to kill you,* Ting had said that morning, and now he had stepped beyond his proper role, making a decision that Elector Brauna might disapprove, without even asking her permission. August ached to embrace Ting, but couldn't without embarrassing them both. "Thank you," he said. It seemed too little exchange for the strain Ting felt, so he extended his hand.

Ting brushed his hand against August's palm lightly, and nodded in the direction of the toolman areas. August walked quietly back to the common area, a place he didn't want to go, with Ting Wheeling at his side.

The dining room was empty, the provider closed, but Ting had already left and it would be ridiculous to summon him back so soon. Besides, as he composed himself, August realized he was hungry after all. He went into the kitchen, where a dozen subs were chattering nonsense as they washed surfaces and tools, unsupervised. As always, they seemed cheerful, and August wished, for an instant, that he was one of them, despite their limited intelligence and narrow lives. The yeasty smell of baking bread made his mouth water. He looked around. A bowl of sliced fruit sat uncovered on a counter, looking like a still-life painting: ripe red melon, green slivers of moist honeydew, soft yellow nectarine, and round white goro berries, leavened with bits of apple and black raisins. Food rarely looked so pretty. Watching the subs for protests, which didn't come, he leaned against the counter and began to eat.

A short time later the kitchen door opened, and Ellen came in. She surveyed him from the doorway, then walked over. "I heard you went wild," she said in cautious monotone. She sniffed. "You stink."

"Falfre. Not a good nameday."

Ellen smiled in wary sympathy. "Maybe you got the wrong name." There was a hierarchy of toolmen names, from the regal, "good" names awarded special probes, to the mundane or ridiculous ones given others, as well as guardians and subs. Ellen might have intended an insult, except she added, "Hard on you."

He shrugged and slid the bowl of fruit away with his sticky fingers. There was nothing on which to wipe them.

"Come with me to quarters for a shower and fresh clothes before your stench makes me faint."

He stared, frozen by surprise. He hadn't entered probe living quarters in four years. Finally, he nodded, then realized too late that he should have laughed. Probe interactions were layer upon layer of subtle innuendo; they were too alert to the scent, sound, sight, and meaning of every word and gesture to simply talk. "Are you sure you want to be seen with me?"

Her glance at him was oblique. "Some people wonder why he spoke up. I mean, if he knew their plan in advance, then why change his mind just then? Some people think that the entire incident isn't well analyzed and that there might be . . . six powerful reasons for that."

She wanted him to believe this was her notion, but it reeked of another hand. "Some people are absurd," he said firmly. "He realized Neuland's plan would be uncovered, and he tried to save himself."

Ellen laughed as if they were disputing the weather, and put her arm through his, directing him toward the door. He let her lead him through the corridor, enjoying the double takes as they passed two probes.

Her hip brushed his as they walked. "I thought you were celebrating?" August asked.

"I did. My friend had work to do. He gave me a flute, though, for my nameday. I'll show it to you in quarters."

"Who is it? Ahman Penn? Ahman Lakey?"

She smiled coquettishly at August. "Oh, much nicer than either of them!"

She was so cheerful and so false, it hurt August to listen. He guessed she would proposition him and the desire for her, wanting the closeness, however counterfeit, warred against the rational sense that this was a trap. Frustration infuriated him. He grabbed her arm, pulling her to a stop. Her sudden fear was tactile beneath his fingers, the struggle to flee. "Who is it, Ellen?"

She shrank from him. He was larger and stronger. To act so openly and directly was failure for a probe, but he didn't care. Power over another person felt good. He grabbed her other arm and shook. "Who sent you to approach me?"

She gasped. He was hurting her. Shame made him loosen his hold, but he didn't release her; she'd run and this discussion would be caught by monitoring programs. "Who?"

"Some Delegates want to try probe bed partners. I know it's against the Electors' rules, but who's hurt?"

He released her arms. "Huana."

"Yes." She rubbed her arms and looked indignantly at him. "I felt sorry for you. So does he. We just want to help you. Your trouble, August, is you don't know who your real friends are!"

His face burned. "Tell him I won't talk to him," August said through clenched teeth. "Tell him to leave me alone!"

Chapter 5

"I thought he was dead!" The woman—by her staccato accent, the medical condition monitor on her left wrist, and her skintight bodysuit, a Neulander—rose halfway to her feet in apparent alarm as August entered the sunroom's clearing.

"No, this is another," Elector Lee said quickly. "A clone of Alexander."

The Neulander woman sank back into her chair. Her companion, a handsome, red-haired man in a dark blue bodysuit and heavy cloak, another Neulander, shifted position, his blue eyes studying August as his right hand moved casually toward his left shoulder, where the bunched fabric of his cloak was so thick it had caused him to lean slightly forward. "He's younger," the man said.

August was thinner than Alexander had been, and his face in repose fell into a solemn expression, rather than the reserved emptiness proper for a probe, but he had the same face, same green eyes, same body as his traitor twin. He bowed, pointedly excluding the Neulanders from his respectful obeisance, and attempted to quell his profound disappointment that his meeting with Elector Brauna was not private. She was dressed formally in her Elector's robe. Her long, pale hair was elaborately coiffured, up and off her shoulders, exposing her beautiful, slender neck. She stood in a patch of sunlight that made her luminous against the dull green backdrop; her eyes had been on him from the moment he'd entered the sunroom.

"August," she said. "I have an important task for you."

He glanced at the Neulanders. Both were thoroughly alert, but their postures indicated weariness. They smelled indistinctly of the outside, of the sugar-sweet air of Sucre and, more conspicuously, of sweat and travel. They didn't look like monsters.

Elector Lee stepped between Elector Brauna and the two Neulanders. An elegant, aristocratic man, Jeroen Lee rarely donned his Elector's robe except when required by ritual. His well-tailored gray suit gave him the appearance of a successful businessman. It blended into the lush foliage and shadows in the sunroom like camouflage, drab in comparison with Elector Brauna, but his resonant voice captured attention. "I continue to disagree, Sanda. Involving *this* toolman in *this* matter is irresponsible." They exchanged a brief, hard look, during which the Neulanders tensed, then Sanda Brauna turned to August.

He suspected she saw him as Alexander because her expression saddened and she didn't meet his eyes. "I don't trust these two." She pointed bluntly and rudely at the Neulanders. "I don't trust anyone from Neuland since Andia, but I continue to believe that it furthers order and is plain common sense for the Harmony to help Neuland against those superstitious, over-breeding alans in the Emirates. I've read your reports, August. I intend to publicly support aid—including military aid—to the Republic of Neuland. However, I am afraid that these Altered Neulanders will do something outrageous again, though they protest over and over that they will not. If they did, it could taint me."

The Neulanders seemed poised to assert their innocence again, but she stopped them with a hard gesture, cutting through the air, while August absorbed the shock that Neuland was perhaps not the enemy. He wondered what Mei Wang would say, and if she knew Neulanders were present.

Elector Brauna continued. "I want these two constantly observed by someone I trust, someone who can uncover deceit, however it's disguised. You, August. They'll appear before the Grand Assembly as supplicants as soon as Elector Lee is able to arrange it. I want you with them, reporting everything they do, until the vote is taken. Do you understand what I require?"

"Yes, Elector." Suffused with the knowledge that she was entrusting a mission of such delicacy and importance to him, he added, "I would never betray you, Elector!"

Sanda Brauna quickly looked into the space between two overgrown pole plants, the tall, fibrous natives of Sucre that were a substitute for trees. Beyond, the sky was bright, but the garden threw shadows across her face. August wished he hadn't reminded her of Alexander. "I know you won't, August," she said gently, turning back. "Report anything, no matter how inconsequential, indicating they're lying or have secrets."

Jeroen Lee went close to her. His voice was low, but August heard him easily. "Sanda, this probe has never done on-site work. He may as well be a youngster straight up from the farm, however excellent his written reports."

"Alexander was outstanding, and August is Alexander, at least to that extent." She didn't bother keeping her voice down. "There is no one else I'd trust as completely to keep these Neulanders honest; his face will be a perpetual warning to them."

"His face." Elector Lee looked at August, then shook his head. "Be reasonable, Sanda. If testimony regarding Neuland becomes necessary, nothing spoken by a probe with this face would be believed."

"I would believe it. So would you and all the other Electors." Elector Brauna's tone was very hard. "As for anyone else, they are unaware of his existence."

"You are insulting the Republic of Neuland and these individuals, who are my guests," Lee said.

It was clear to August that Elector Brauna would not change her mind, yet Elector Lee, seemingly so perceptive on the replays August observed, a figure respected for his shrewdness and political skill even by his opponents, continued to badger her.

Sanda Brauna laughed unexpectedly, then bowed low to the Neulander supplicants in a parody of courtesy. "Are you insulted, sirs? Perhaps you wish to withdraw your supplication or proceed without my help?"

They did not visibly flinch at her sarcasm, as if inured to scorn. The woman said, "No, of course not. We understand." The man stood and bowed even lower than Elector Brauna. "Lady," he said, refusing even in Center to acknowledge her title as Elector, "we were sent to negotiate any terms that we can obtain that won't destroy our home. Your support is critical to our success in the Grand Assembly. We have nothing to hide, and personal modesty won't prevent us from doing everything possible to obtain it. If you want this boy to watch each time I relieve myself, then he is welcome with me in the can."

"Good," Elector Brauna said, after a moment. "August,

you will accompany them to Elector Lee's apartment and stay with them, as I've said. If you meet with any obstruction, immediately inform me." August finally understood Lee's truculence; he—a probe in service with another Elector—would be inside Lee's residence, observing the intimate details of Lee's life.

Elector Lee bowed, unhappily resigned. "If you insist, Sanda." While all six Electors were equal, with identical power to issue rulings, some were attended more closely than others. From being a liberal, over time Sanda Brauna had become considered a moderate; August was proud that her rulings were usually joined in by a majority of Electors, giving them the full force of Jonist truth. Lee's rulings, on the other hand, were sometimes extreme and many failed to become majority opinion, but he continued to issue them, like challenges to the others, and somehow had gained wide popular support as well as increasing his coterie—Elector Kurioso called them populist radicals—among the Ahmen. Lee glanced in the direction of the door, and the Neulanders stood.

"Elector Brauna," August said, uncomfortably aware of stopping the departure. "There is a matter I must report."

They all waited. "Yes?" Elector Brauna said. "Do we need privacy?"

He briefly considered, then said, "No, Elector Lee ought to hear. Some World Delegates are aware of my existence. I don't know when they learned, but it was possibly through toolmen."

"*Who* knows?" Elector Lee's tone was sharp.

August faced him, glad to turn away from Elector Brauna, whose frowning attention made him feel guilty. "Delegate Huana, certainly. Possibly others."

"This probe has just become a liability," Jeroen Lee said. August could not read his emotions, Lee was so exceedingly still.

"August," Elector Brauna said, clasping her hands together, "Huana may want revenge on you as Alexander's clone—Andians can engage in endless, convoluted feuds. Be especially careful until the vote is over." She turned to Jeroen Lee, while simultaneously signaling the sunroom monitor for security. "I'm sending a guardian with him, too. I don't want you tempted into precipitate action. August's death now would be a mistake."

"And why is that?" Elector Lee asked acidly, frowning as Tane Strong arrived. The guardian stood at ease at the clearing's edge, watching impassively. The male Neulander shifted position so that Tane was within his line of vision.

Sanda went closer to Elector Lee. "It would be too easily unraveled by Huana, first of all, and secondly, it would precipitate the immediate termination of my support for Neuland."

August guessed that even Elector Brauna herself was uncertain how much was posturing and how truly willing she was to put a toolman's life before Harmony interests, but he was overwhelmed that she had said she would, and astounded as Elector Lee showed he considered it a credible threat.

Lee extended his hand to her. "This argument is unnecessary, Sanda. I won't harm your probe, despite the fact I don't want any of your toolmen in my apartment, assessing *me* along with my guests." When she did not grasp his hand, he dropped it to his side and bowed. "You have my word. In fact, since Huana knows he exists, we should make his existence public ourselves. Boldness can be effective at disarming an adversary, and make no mistake, however orthodox he is, Esteban Huana is our adversary in this."

Sanda Brauna ignored Lee. "Is he sincere about your safety, August?"

That was a delicate question to ask a probe about an Elector who was present. Lee observed him with a frightening intensity, and August wasn't certain he could read anything accurately under that stern attention. "Yes, Elector. He never threatened me."

Jeroen Lee laughed, and his demeanor softened. "A good point, Sanda. You were the one to suggest killing August."

"All right. I'll send August alone." She sat down wearily on her lounger, but didn't recline, only stared blankly forward, her hands folded in her lap. August was reminded of her pose at tedious Establishment Day Assembly sessions, or, more precisely, during the annual memorial of the Andian Betrayal. A loose strand of her pale hair lay curled on her shoulder. August longed to touch it, to take her hands in his own and embrace her, to thank her for the trust and concern that left her in such melancholy. He shifted position and accidentally his heel scuffed the dirt floor; Tane and the male Neulander immediately glanced at him.

"Was there anything else, August?" she asked formally, looking up.

He should have volunteered that Ellen Short was connected to Delegate Huana through illicit bodywork and conversation. He thought he would have, but for Ting, who had shown the prior evening that it was possible to balance loyalty to Elector Brauna with trust and friendship for another toolman. August was uncertain of the depth of Ellen's involvement with Delegate Huana; she had meant him well, and certainly intended no harm to Elector Brauna. He could wait to inform on her. After all, Elector Brauna would not want faithlessness, if that was what it was, announced in the presence of strangers, and she had just indicated that she respected his judgment. Even as he made excuses, he squirmed. Was this the measure of his loyalty?

They were waiting for him to speak. There would have been inspections, but he said, "The male Neulander has a weapon concealed under his cloak."

Tane became preternaturally alert, though he didn't move.

"The medic bag," the Neulander said. Moving with extraordinary care, obviously mindful of the guardian, he removed his cloak. A worn shoulder harness held a small bag suspended under his arm. "Your security people have checked and rechecked us, and it's been passed. Neulanders have certain medical fragilities. There are only the two of us, without any aides, so I took responsibility as our medic."

"You don't think of it exclusively as medical." August felt foolish, but knew he was correct.

"Center Security agreed, when they passed them," Tane volunteered, quietly confirming August. "There's an alert."

The Neulander shrugged. "I'm a soldier. That's no secret. There are devices in any medical equipment that can be used to kill." He smiled, trying to relieve the tension. "I am not about to harm anyone inside the Polite Harmony of Worlds." He bowed, again quite low, at the Electors, then faced August. "My name is Evan Kolet. This is Margot Ash." The female Neulander acknowledged August with a brief nod.

The courteous introduction, which neither Elector had thought to make, discomfited August. He bowed infinitesimally at the Neulanders.

"Are we finally able to leave?" Maliciously, Elector Lee turned first to August, then, cordially, to Elector Brauna.

The Neulanders bowed to her. She dismissed them with a curt gesture. "Take care," she said to August.

Elector Lee's apartment shared only two qualities with that of Sanda Brauna: large size and the feeling that most of it was uninhabited. Lee's rooms were fewer and individually larger than hers, but they were overcrowded with objects, as if he had physically displayed every bit of his reputed fortune. Where her rooms were sophisticated and spare, if somber, his were a chaos of random objects, without a clear plan of collection. Wide hallways were narrowed by scattered arrangements of formal chairs and tables laden with bric-a-brac. Background music was playing, a recent composition from Amacuro's Canin family, popular in the Academy. Elector Brauna's rooms were always silent.

Their odd procession halted in a formal office. It had a dry, stuffy scent that hung in the air like suspended dust. Its walls were covered in rich maroon velvet fabric, impressed with an abstract, asymmetrical Rockland design; there were many window screens, but their false, sun-stone-backed views were veiled by heavy draperies that dimmed the room. Two different rugs, both richly woven, lay on the floor. The topmost rug, which matched the velvet walls, had an intricate design August took several minutes to place, then he was scandalized to recognize it as a traditional allegorical pattern of alan rug weavers in the Emirates. While trade was regular and strong with certain non-Harmony worlds—old Earth, for one—still, it took arrogance, and great self-assurance, for an *Elector* to display the work of heathen hands.

The room was cluttered with furniture, much of it antique and imported from old Earth. Everything had a different pattern, and each pattern was elaborate. The most prominent single item was a huge, dark Chanic desk of inlaid red and brown woods, standing in relative isolation at one end of the room. An immense lounger in mottled red-and-black-upholstered fabric dominated the other side. August could not imagine Jeroen Lee ever reclining in it, and the ungainly lounger seemed entirely unused, as did everything except the desk and a few chairs near it. It was as if Lee had bought furniture gleefully, then kept it wherever it was first deposited; Lee clearly didn't care about balance in his interior decoration.

Framed paintings—an archaic affectation, also from old
Earth—hung on several walls, mixed among the window
screens. Behind the Chanic desk was a landscape of wild foliage and a ruined building, well enough done that it took a
second look to notice it wasn't a window screen; nothing
moved and it gave off no light. Surfaces, except the desk,
were crowded with artifacts. Cut-glass candlesticks without
candles, ceramic vases, crystal vases, silver goblets, picture
frames holding smaller flat drawings, books, bowls, and
lamps—it didn't seem to matter. August couldn't discern any
organization to the exuberant jumble, except that everything
seemed valuable, individually beautiful and, often, break-
able. The apartment was opposite to the stern elegance August had expected of Jeroen Lee and, consequently, puzzling.

"Make yourselves at home," Lee said graciously to the
Neulanders. He sat behind his Chanic desk, separating himself from them. "You are my guests. Whatever happens in
the Grand Assembly, here no one will harass you." He didn't
look at August.

Margot Ash gestured around herself. "This isn't much like
Neuland." To August, she sounded amused, not impressed.

On none of the major worlds of the Harmony was such
fussiness currently in style, and—except for the desk—it
was unlike the simple but heavily polished, inlaid wooden
furnishings of Lee's home world of Co-Chan, Chan's bois-
terous satellite. However, while August thought the room
unharmonious, it was an excellent place to be inconspicuous.

"I suppose it isn't like Neuland"—Lee looked with apparent fondness at the clutter—"where you keep everything
curved and soft and open."

"We take precautions," she agreed. "We don't feel pain,
therefore we're more at risk of injury. Prevention is important. Rapid healing isn't proof against everything, and
these," she lifted her left hand, displaying the black medical
condition monitor, "register problems only after the fact, of
course."

Evan Kolet looked at the place where August had been
when they entered the room, but August had already moved.
Kolet surreptitiously scanned until he located August.

Jeroen Lee noticed. "Ignore him, Kolet. He's furniture."
Disregarding his own advice, he said belligerently to August, "I am their host, and I will not let them be disturbed.

You can monitor them, but not in person. They're not accustomed to it."

"A monitor with an alarm hookup will be adequate. In all rooms, of course, and without a lag." He bowed as if Elector Lee's minor intimidation had been the delivery of instructions.

"Let him stay, as Elector Brauna asked. We don't mind," Evan Kolet said quickly. "We expected to be watched inside the Harmony. You people spy on each other rather obsessively, it seems to us." He smiled, however, and pretended the statement was humorous.

"Jon Hsu said *all* knowledge furthers the ability to determine truth and order," Jeroen Lee said firmly, visibly annoyed with Kolet. "We make no secret of our information gathering—we do not spy. Furthermore, I believe I am more qualified than you to interpret Jon Hsu's writings. Your failure to acknowledge the efficacy of Electors to determine the best road to harmony and order, rather than each deciding for yourself, is as much a handicap to you inside the Harmony as your Alteration." The Elector signaled and Ahman Martin Penn, Lee's current assistant from the Academy, entered as if he'd been just outside. Elector Lee rose to his feet. "Martin will show you your rooms and provide whatever you need. I will contact the Marshall regarding your permission to address the Grand Assembly."

They conferred briefly about the best timing of the Neulanders' appeal to the Assembly, then Ahman Penn ushered the Neulanders out of Lee's office, and escorted them, with August, to a small residence within Lee's own. The suite included two separate bedrooms with baths, a study containing an access screen and unlimited entertainment complex, and a central living area. The rooms were furnished in the same cluttered style as the rest of the apartment, but with fewer knickknacks and no old paintings. There also was no background music, but August couldn't hear the usual faint mechanical hum of Center; Lee's rooms were exceedingly well insulated. No one would eavesdrop on him.

As he showed the rooms, Penn avoided close proximity to the Neulanders, as if they smelled of poison, and his attentiveness was tinged with delicate distaste. Like Elector Lee, Penn wore a businessman's suit, but it seemed out of place on his large, bony frame. His big hands especially looked wrong, as if they belonged to a laborer rather than a biologist and medic—

his training was like Lee's own. Martin Penn was popular with probes, although he rarely used anyone for bodywork, and then only women; Ellen called him "an unpretentious bumpkin," and the contrast between his lilting Flute accent and Lee's well-bred Chanic intonation was odd, but on replay the two men seemed to get along. "Is this satisfactory?" Ahman Penn asked in the suite's living room.

Evan Kolet laughed. "Yes, quite satisfactory, especially if you remove some of this debris." He kicked a chair and a stale odor rose into the air.

"Your pardon, sir," Margot Ash said hastily. "The rooms are lovely. Please convey our appreciation to Jeroen Lee."

"Yes, of course," Kolet said. "I was joking. To Neulanders this place seems like a ... treasure castle."

Ahman Penn watched Kolet through narrowed eyes. "With Elector Lee as Blackbeard the Pirate? Who you've come to raid?"

Margot Ash stepped forward. "Evan!" she said.

Kolet looked at her and took a breath. "Of course not," Kolet said. "I meant nothing of the kind, and I believe you know it. However, I apologize for any offense." He bowed.

Penn turned to Margot Ash. "If you need me, just speak the wish aloud. The house system listens, understands, and will call me. I'll leave you to unpack." He indicated their two slim bags, set in the center of the living area by subs. When they didn't object, Ahman Penn nodded and left.

"Well, just us," Evan Kolet told Margot Ash once the door had closed, "and him," he gestured with a thumb at August, "and three dozen or so monitors and sensors." He tossed his cloak on a table and sat down on an overstuffed chair, leaning back with his arms behind his head.

"Watch your mouth, Evan," she said. "There's him and three dozen or so monitors and sensors who don't know yet that sometimes you're an ass."

"Am I an ass or is she a politician?" Kolet straightened and looked at August.

"I wouldn't know, sir," August said.

"Well, what's your opinion?"

"Leave him alone," Margot Ash said testily. "Furniture, remember?"

"If I consider him furniture, then I'll forget he's there, and then where will I be when he attacks? Oh, I know probes don't attack—the stocky ones do that—and I know we're safely among our best friends in the Harmony, but it never pays to underestimate a man. Right, August?"

She sighed and shook her head. "You need to rest. You're too strung out, and so am I." She took her case with her into the right bedroom, closing the door behind herself.

"Well, August," Kolet said. "What do you say?"

It was time to say nothing. To be drawn into a discussion would personalize the situation exactly as Kolet wanted, so that August could never blend into the background and simply absorb information. Still, the urge to reply was strong.

"Ah, you're a bump on the skin of the universe, August." Kolet winked and leaned back again. He kicked off the heavy black boots that, with his dark bodysuit, gave him the look of a mercenary soldier, hooked a nearby armless chair with his foot, dragging it close, and used the chair as an ottoman. "You can watch me take a nap," he said, and closed his eyes.

There had been a time when August obsessively replayed old records of the Neulander aspirants, Kaviscu and Havic, with his fists clenched at his sides. He had reviewed everything available on Neuland and its Altered population. He had hated them his entire life, considering them unfeeling monsters of inhumanity, as well as his particular enemy, but only a few hours after having met his first Neulanders, against his will, August found himself warming to them both, although he recognized Kolet's facilitation. The Neulander was purposely teasing August, ingratiating himself, undoubtedly trying to make his watcher less effective. August felt he was being seduced into betraying his own heart.

To counter it, August imagined Evan Kolet and Margot Ash as members of the Punishers, a Neuland sect that believed standard humans were animals because, like animals, they felt pain. He remembered scarred Andia, and felt renewed aversion. He thought of Reverend Wang's accusations and Elector Brauna's trust, and knew he must be on guard. The fact that Kolet and Ash weren't immediately loathsome didn't mean Neuland had improved, only that Neuland was clever.

After Kolet was truly asleep—he faked it for a while—and Margot Ash was soaking in the deep tub, August examined the surveillance system of the Neulanders' suite, using Elector Brauna's codes to rearrange a few monitors to his satisfaction. His work, done at the screen in the suite's study, created an interference alarm in Elector Lee's house system requiring intervention from Ahman Penn. Penn reviewed August's adjustments without comment and approved them.

August checked on his charges—Ash was now resting in bed—then used the screen to review the Harmony biographies of Margot Ash and Evan Kolet, though he had recognized both names. Ash was, at only fifty-six, Deputy Premier in Neuland's representational democracy, elected directly by the public rather than from an Academy. To a Harmony Jonist, that meant she was a popular figure, not necessarily a competent one, although she impressed August as capable. Kolet was younger; he had been promoted to his present position—a general in Neuland's unified armed forces—by superiors, a more congenial method of advancement to Harmony prejudices. Kolet had been a "special forces" commander originally and was rumored to have led Neuland's raid against the Emirates, which had successfully assassinated the Emir and his entire family. See, August said to himself, this is not a gentle or benign man. But that raid had much reduced the threat Neulanders lived under from the Emirates, until recently, when Aleko Bei had murdered his rivals and become leader of the United Emirates. Kolet's current assignment was to Inner System Defense, a staff position. Both he and Ash were married; both had children on Neuland. Neither had participated in any capacity in the Andian raid.

The warning sounded on August's new array. He closed the screen and returned to the living area.

Kolet stretched, yawned, and stretched again, then finally opened his eyes, looking directly at the place where August was now standing—the place he'd been when the Neulander had fallen asleep. Kolet grinned. "Did I snore?"

August did not reply.

"Where's Margot?"

In probe monotone, August said, "Sleeping in her room."

"Remind me to do the same next time. I've got to stop pretending I can still sleep anywhere, in any position, and not feel it." He stood and did quick calisthenics, then picked up the remaining suitcase. "So, whose room do you plan to decorate, August Furniture? Hers or mine? I know which I would choose, if I were still single and your age." He laughed and walked into the vacant bedroom, then immediately looked out. August hadn't moved. "We do feel muscle aches, you know. I saw the question in your eyes." He winked and returned inside, leaving the door ajar.

August returned to the study and set up the screen again,

splitting the monitor views between the two Neulanders. Kolet showered—efficiently, without making it a treat—dressed in a duplicate blue bodysuit, then walked around his room inspecting the furnishings. He sat on the canopy bed, got up, then sat down again, staring at nothing. He got up, hung his clothes in the armoire, paced, gazed at the false view out a window screen, then opened a portable displayer and watched part of an episode of the popular Harmony serial entertainment, *One Day on Earth,* on one of Sucre's public channels. He seemed bored, except when the heroine seduced a fictional Reverend Researcher at old Earth's First Academy—then Kolet quickly switched to a Rangeball game between Sucre-semp and Norda. Kolet closed the display seven minutes later and paced. He left the room. August waited and was watching the doorway when Kolet appeared outside the study. "Is she still asleep?" he asked.

August glanced at the screen, where the sensors in Ash's room displayed their data on the bottom line, above the real-time image. It was ridiculous not to answer. "Yes."

Kolet leaned against the door frame. "How detailed are those sensors? What does it show?" His staccatto Neulander accent—while not as pronounced as that of most Neulanders—was sufficiently alien that August could focus on it as a reminder.

When August didn't answer, Kolet sighed. "I hate silence, August. It's death, or at least a form of waiting, and I hate to wait. That's always the worst in a battle, in any plan, in life. If there's someone to talk to, I want to talk. Talk to me, toolman. Ask a question, anything you want. Surely there's something you want to ask a Neulander. I promise to answer."

August watched the screen image of Evan Kolet rather than the man standing across the room. Sensor readings, set only on basic, nevertheless showed Kolet's temperature, blood pressure, and heart rhythm as well as certain substance levels. Kolet was becoming angry. August thought of it as a victory and continued to watch the screen.

"I'm a fair observer, too," Kolet said. His quiet voice disguised the rising frustration indicated on the sensor. "I'd guess that all your life you've been made to feel ashamed of being a toolman, and because your predecessor dealt with us. That's why you hate us, isn't it? But it wasn't fair of them, was it, August-Alexander? So why are you doing the same thing to us? Neuland isn't the world it was twenty-three years ago, and even then all Neulanders weren't to blame. Since then we've been raided dozens of times, mostly minor, but we've also fought off a full-scale attempted invasion. Because the Harmony stopped all legal trade with us, our economy was wrecked and still hasn't really recovered; our military couldn't get resupplied, except covertly, at a much higher cost—just when we had no money. After all that, if your Electors are willing to give us another chance, why aren't you?"

August debated, but before consciously deciding he heard himself ask, in a bitter, biting voice, "Have you ever attended a torture party?"

Kolet came into the study. He dragged a chair across the carpeted floor to face August and sat down. "Yes, many. 'Cutters' we call them, because knives are the usual method, although some people prefer fire—burns, that is." He reached into the medic bag and removed a small, steel knife. It gleamed in the light as he held it up, examining the blade.

"What are you doing?" August turned to watch him directly.

Kolet ignored August. He held his left hand up, palm facing August. A patternless network of thin scars from long healed wounds crisscrossed Kolet's hand. Carefully, like an experienced surgeon, Kolet placed the knife against the flesh of his index finger, just below the fingertip. He pressed, and the blade cut into the skin, leaving a line of red behind it, a trail of blood and open flesh. The oozing blood ran down the sides of Kolet's finger. He stopped cutting when he reached his palm, then turned his hand flat. A drop of blood dripped, bright ruby red, into Kolet's cupped right hand.

August gagged, tasting blood, then realized he'd bitten into his own lip.

A yellow light flashed on Kolet's medical condition monitor. Numbers changed. Kolet glanced at the monitor, touched it with his right hand, and the light stopped flashing, but stayed yellow. Kolet opened and closed his fist several times, the movement causing more blood to flow from the thin cut on his finger. "Nothing," he said. "I didn't feel anything but a slight pressure, not at all unpleasant. I still don't. A Neulander's nerve-endings function, but the brain doesn't register the sensation as pain. A few people feel nothing at all, but most of us experience pressure, light and deep, and can distinguish warm and cool temperatures—but not pain."

He smiled and reached into the medic bag, moving carefully so as not to get blood on the bag or his clothing, but without any obvious concern for possible discomfort. Removing a clean white cloth, he wiped his finger, then, more conscientiously, the knife, which he replaced in the bag. August stared in horrified fascination. The incision welled up with fresh blood, less than before.

"When I was a child, I couldn't understand how we Neulanders were different. Even now, I wonder what you'd feel if you did the same thing. It's difficult to conceive of something you can never experience. Some people even believe pain is a lie, that you're all just faking the phenomenon. We're obsessed with the idea of pain, particularly as adolescents. Torture vids are popular, and we go to parties where we pretend to 'hurt' each other." He sighed. "Other things you may have heard are also true. Sometimes offworlders are hired to ... perform. There are regulations. It's criminal, and considered bad form, to permanently damage a whimper—a standard human, that is—or to continue when they've asked to stop. And yes, I've attended those parties, too. I don't care for them—so much noise, and visible distress is unpleasant to watch, whatever the cause and however exaggerated—but I have friends who've enjoyed them." He glanced at the cut and wiped it again, then extended his hand to August for inspection.

His finger was no longer oozing blood. A thin, crusted scab had already formed.

"RHF makes it difficult to sustain superficial damage," Kolet said, almost apologetically. "It's also difficult for us to avoid scars; we heal too quickly for skinsacks."

August leaned forward, looking at Kolet rather than his hand. "Surely, if your founders managed to design this rapid healing function into your DNA, Neulanders could have been returned to standard human?"

Evan Kolet laughed as he replaced the medic bag in its pouch. "Fanatics! What can I say? It was an eccentric thing to do, something all Neulanders continue to pay for every time the Harmony calls us Altered and says we're not human. Some of our local practices, as I've described, do make other worlds nervous about us. Many Neulanders—not just Punishers—believe that being pain-free makes us superior. It's true that along with the medical disadvantages there are some benefits, including military applications. Also, having seen you people writhe and cry, why would we want to con-

demn our children to it? And being different has given us a
unique identity, formed Neulanders into a cohesive group,
though our original settlers were a mixed lot. Personally, I
think that's what our founders were after. I've never truly
believed in the genetic accident that was supposed to have
occurred during the first generation." Kolet tightened his fist
around the blood-spotted cloth. "They must have been hard
men," he said, "to experiment on their children."

"Evan," Margot Ash said from the doorway. "What are
you doing?" She walked into the study, holding her dressing
robe closed at the neck.

August flushed, abruptly aware that he had neglected his
duties during Kolet's exhibition. He hadn't even known
Margot Ash was awake.

Kolet stood. "Just a demonstration. August asked about
cutters."

"And you showed him? Along with the dozens of monitors!
Just what we need, Evan, in order to gain sympathy. Look at
them, Delegates, they don't feel pain. They're not human! Let
the Altered freaks get wiped out!" She was near tears.

Kolet crossed quickly to her and grabbed her arm. August
saw the power of the grip by the indentation of her flesh
near Kolet's fingers. They don't feel pain, he thought. It's
nothing to her, only pressure. When August had done the
same to Ellen, she had been hurt; she'd winced. Margot Ash
showed nothing. Who was the torturer?

"They know what we are, Margot." Kolet's tone made
August think of Kolet's own words—*hard men*. "They've
weeks of replay tapes of pain-free Neulanders and plenty of
our torture vids if they want to make us look evil. I was trying to explain. Think. If I can make this one boy—who truly
hates us—understand, if I can make him listen and possibly
accept us, then there's hope." He released her arm. "Lee will
be back soon. Get ready." He bowed generously to August.
"We'll talk again." He left the study.

Margot Ash put her hands in the pockets of her robe,
frowning and watching August. "Whatever you think of us,"
she said argumentatively, "we don't manufacture people and
call them toolmen so we can make them into slaves."

August looked back at her, not surveying, only trying to
absorb what he had seen. "No," August said, turning to
his screen. Kolet was in his room, hand-entering text into his
portable displayer. "You only kill people."

Chapter 6

That night Ahman Penn personally showed August to his assigned room—one with two doors, but only a single exit. "Your signal or hand will open this door, but the other opens only for Elector Lee. It leads directly to his bedroom." Penn smiled briefly, then gestured at the barren room. "Is this satisfactory?" he asked in a wry self-satire of his earlier display of the cluttered suite to the Neulanders.

It looked like a prison cell. The room was large but it held only two armless chairs built of fabric-covered mold-foam; August recognized the slight, acrid, chemical scent. A small night table stood beside nothing—there was no bed. A portable access screen lay atop the table.

"Elector Lee's special room," Ahman Penn said. "All his probes come here eventually."

August turned to Penn. "I'm not one of his probes, Ahman."

Penn shrugged. "He said to put you here." He walked to the night table and shifted the screen aside. "Come here."

August went to him. A control board was embedded in the table.

"The bed," Ahman Penn said. "Did you think there wasn't one? An air bed. Extremely expensive; a toy the Elector discovered during his inspection of the newest Academy on Loess. There is no mattress. You float on air in a gravity cushion. It's related to the workings of the quickship generators—you wouldn't understand the principles. I'm told it can be interestingly adjusted. Perhaps you'll have an opportunity to experiment."

"I am not one of his probes," August said stubbornly, wondering if this was something he could rightfully complain of to Sanda Brauna. Would she care? Yes, he decided. "Elector Brauna has not terminated my service with her. She's only temporarily assigned me here."

Ahman Penn straightened, inspecting August critically, amused but not entirely unkind. "Still, you are here. Elector Brauna is not so attached to you as she was to your predecessor. That attachment was a source of disappointment to Elector Lee. He designed you—your original version, Alexander—during his term as Ahman of Sucre. However, by the time he was chosen as an Elector by the Ahmen's vote, Alexander was already in Elector Brauna's personal service. Elector Lee's predecessor lingered longer than most people expected, as I recall, although his successor was never in much doubt. So, here you are. A second opportunity for everyone."

"No," August said. The room's utter silence, without the hum of Center, felt sinister.

Ahman Penn placed his hand on August's shoulder. "Come, probe—who chose that ambiguous name, do you think?—Elector Lee would not have designed a prude. This isn't the Emirates; a Jonist does not deny the importance of pleasure. Do you really want to test Elector Brauna's patience with a complaint she'll laugh at? Your work won't be interfered with—you see a screen has been provided. Enjoy yourself."

This was a trap. Electors did not trade or share toolmen; if he was intimate with Jeroen Lee, then Elector Brauna might not want him back; he couldn't bear such rejection. August placed his hand on the closed screen. The hand trembled. Ahman Penn smiled and August flushed, but he firmly said, "If Elector Lee enters this room, then I will tell him 'no.' If he insists, then I will inform Elector Brauna. It is my judgment as a *probe* that she will not be pleased. I doubt that my unwilling service for Elector Lee is worth his enduring so much inconvenience."

Ahman Penn laughed, the sound entirely free of sarcasm or innuendo. He leaned against the wall beside the night table and surveyed August, still smiling. "I see his handiwork in you. He has no respect for anyone he can push, and he always pushes back when he is pressed." Ahman Penn nodded at August and walked toward the door, the one which did not lead to Lee's bedroom. He stopped there. "You would have been an interesting companion for him, perhaps more than he anticipated. Sleep easy, August. I'll relay your vehement refusal. He'll be disappointed, but I've never known Elector Lee to be interested in rape." He left, chuckling.

August picked up the screen and took it to one of the foam chairs, opened it, and set it to display the Neulander's suite, but his hands were shaking so hard that he closed the screen and placed it on the floor.

They could kill him, any one of them, on a whim.

He rested his head in his hands until the tremors stopped, then he looked up, only then noticing the warmth of the slightly spongy, brown and gold floor tiles and the matching flecks of gold in the creamy weave of the silk-lined walls. The fabric of the chairs was thick and soft to the touch. Inlaid woods in different tones of brown added interest to the simple lines of the night table. The nearly bare room was beautiful, like a woman without her clothes.

He wondered if Jeroen Lee was watching him.

August determinedly brought the screen back to his lap. He watched the Neulanders settle into their dreams, replaying their preparations for bed after the long day of meetings. So far, despite his scrutiny of their every gesture, he had seen no trace of anything covert. He established parameters by which the system would alert him, then set a wake-up that was an hour earlier than the one the Neulanders had requested.

He sat back in the luxurious foam chair, letting it sculpt itself into the new shape, sinuously melting against him, and wondered if it could be forced into some semblance of a bed. He considered returning to the Neulanders' suite—it had the only other doors in Lee's apartment that would open for him—and sleeping on one of their loungers, but to have Evan Kolet tease him about the reason for his reappearance could be more unpleasant than staying here. Kolet had continued to direct comments at August. He seemed to sincerely want August to like him. Horribly, in the fascinated way one can enjoy the exotic company of murderers or thieves—and perhaps because he was lonely and Kolet spoke to him, though he would not admit that reason—August already did like Kolet, and vowed that no one would ever know. Liking was not the same as friendship. He put the screen aside and closed his eyes, letting words and images drift through his mind, hoping to doze.

The door—the other door—opened, and Jeroen Lee, still fully dressed, entered. Beyond was Elector Lee's bedroom, a wide, uncluttered space, austerely furnished except for the warm colors, golden hues, and brown. August's cell might have been a closet, mildly echoing the other. "Did my subs feed you?" Lee asked.

August stood and bowed. "Yes, Elector. Thank you."

"How did you discover that Huana knew about you?"

There it was, the direct question he'd feared. "A probe spoke to me. I recognized that the idea had to have come from Delegate Huana."

Elector Lee turned his head slightly, apparently surprised. "One of my probes?"

"No, Elector."

He nodded. "Tell Sanda about her other probe, August. If anything, she underestimated the danger from Huana. Don't play with secrets the way Alexander did. You're the one who will end up dead."

They looked at each other. Jeroen Lee was a formidable figure, and he was speaking to August as if they were equals, or not quite, as if the Elector was his mentor.

"I thought it would be her guardian," Jeroen Lee said pensively. "The one who killed Alexander. I've suspected him for years of being unreliable. I advised Sanda to get rid of him when he carried on so much back then; I thought it was the guardian you were protecting. So does Sanda, I imagine. You notice that she didn't ask. She has a soft spot for that toolman."

"Ting is completely loyal," August protested.

"Of course. That's how we design toolmen. The question always is, loyal to whom?" Jeroen Lee smiled, studying August, then looked briefly backward, into his room. He indicated the empty space that was the air bed. "This is an acquired taste. There is a real bed in my room, if you would come with me?"

"Sanda Brauna," August said. "Ting is loyal to Elector Brauna."

"How fortunate for Sanda. She has a talent for choosing the best and keeping them. I admire that about her, among other things. Good night, August. A sub will come to show you to another room." Lee turned to leave.

"Elector!"

"Yes?" He looked back, surprised but not annoyed. Perhaps hopeful.

"Why are your toolmen afraid of you?"

Jeroen Lee chuckled. "You're not going to find out;

though if it's any consolation, I doubt you would have been afraid. Interested, perhaps."

"Thank you, Elector Lee." August bowed deeply. "Thank you very much."

"You're welcome," Lee said regally. "Don't give me cause to regret this. You're here to watch Kolet and Ash—not report to Sanda about me." He observed August a moment longer, his brown eyes enigmatic, then he simply left.

A few minutes later a sub escorted August to another room, with one door and one bed, down a short hall from the Neulanders' suite.

Real-time work was tedious. August longed for a speed control to fast-forward through the Neulanders' desultory morning conversation, which he was forced to witness but in which he dared not participate, however much Evan Kolet cajoled him. His former work reviewing replay now seemed efficient and enthralling by comparison.

"If we practice our speeches for the Assembly on you, will you give us the benefit of your wisdom, August?" Kolet asked lazily. He had draped himself across two chairs, rather than use a lounger, and his boots were digging into the wide weave of the second chair's upholstery.

"I still think we should meet with the Andians privately before tomorrow's Assembly session." Margot Ash stood, glanced cautiously at the clutter, then began to pace. "We need to reach an understanding with them. We should make the offer, even though we have the Electors' support."

"Lee, Brauna, and Elector Courane all said it wasn't a good idea to warn Huana." Kolet abstractedly rapped his fingers against the edge of a nearby table in a peculiar rhythm. Perhaps a song? August couldn't believe it was code.

She stopped. "Is their advice entirely objective?"

Kolet looked at August with raised eyebrows. August stared back, blank-faced. He hoped.

Margot Ash sighed. "We tend to think of these six Electors as part of the government. Lee is on our side, and the rest will help because of our concessions, but none of them *represents* anyone. They're not even practicing scientists anymore, they're jumped-up Jonist priests, telling the rest of the Harmony what to do. I think we should talk to Huana. Ultimately our deal is with the Polite Harmony of Worlds, not the Electors' Academies."

Kolet shrugged. "Margot, their system isn't the same as ours. The power to make this work is with the Electors. They substitute for an executive branch on policy decisions because the Assembly is just too diffuse. So, relax." He turned his head, grinning. "Right, August?"

The suite's outer door opened suddenly, without a prior announcement. Kolet sprang to his feet, crouched as if responding to an attack. Ahman Penn entered—he frowned at Kolet—but Penn was bumped aside as Sanda Brauna's assistant, Mei Wang, burst into the room. She stopped just inside the door as she saw August. "Well, probe," she snarled, "I see you're with Neulanders. Appropriate! I've just read your report extolling their virtues. How honest and forthright—how worthy—they are!"

"Mei, I've read it, too," Ahman Penn said sharply. "That's not a fair summary, and this is certainly not the place to discuss it. You said it was an emergency. What is it?"

"Your report was a bit late, though, on one matter, wasn't it, probe?" Wang ignored Ahman Penn and came farther into the room. Kolet and Ash were motionless, watching her. "Or maybe it was right on time, for them." She pointed dramatically at the Neulanders.

"What's going on?" Kolet demanded, looking to Ahman Penn for his answer.

Wang drew back at the sound of Kolet's voice.

"Get out, Mei," Ahman Penn said. "Not here. I'll send August to you in my office."

She disregarded Penn's suggestion. "You bastard probe. I knew it. *This morning* you report that Ellen Short 'may be unreliable,' even now soft-pedaling. But she disappeared *last night*. She left probe quarters and can't be found!"

Like something seen at a great distance, or underwater, August watched Ahman Penn signal for house security. Guilt was ripping his courage to shreds because he knew Mei Wang's charge was justified. He had delayed telling Sanda Brauna the truth. He had—like his brother before him—put his own judgment ahead of that of the Elector, however many times throughout his life he'd sworn he would be loyal. Now Security would interrogate him, dismembering his mind. Toolmen were disposable.

One of Elector Lee's guardians rushed into the suite. August felt the wall at his back and was glad of its support. "Please . . ." he said. His voice was hoarse. He shook his head, unable to say more, hating his loss of dignity.

Evan Kolet walked between August and Mei Wang. "I want to know what's going on."

Margot Ash exchanged a look with Kolet, then she said, "Apparently, this affects us. We need to know what's happened."

"It has nothing to do with you," Ahman Penn said.

"Interesting, who your protectors are, August." Wang nearly spat his name.

"Kern, take them both to my office," Ahman Penn said to the guardian, indicating Mei Wang and August.

"I'll come." August took a breath and concentrated on avoiding obvious distress as he came around Kolet toward the door.

"No toolman takes me anywhere!" Mei Wang tossed her head, furious at Penn's suggestion.

Ahman Penn stared coldly back at her. "Then leave this room on your own. But leave."

"It's you, too, Martin! Toolmen shouldn't exist! You medics think you can do anything, but Jon Hsu said uncurbed experiments with the genome lead to nonhuman creatures. The Andian Betrayal proved him right." She spat at Kolet, the spittle falling on the floor between them.

Kolet, August noted, stifled his first, aggressive, reaction, and remained externally calm at the insult.

"This is an unconscionable disturbance of Elector Lee's household and guests," Penn said sternly, but he did not apologize to Kolet. "If you don't leave, Mei, then I'll have Kern drag you out."

Wang, emboldened by Kolet's lack of response, made a rude, derogatory noise at Margot Ash. "I'll wait outside. Cuff Elector Brauna's toolman immediately and bring him to your door!" As suddenly as she had entered, Mei Wang turned and swept out of the room.

Ahman Penn watched her leave, then looked over at August. "If Brauna's other probe has disappeared, then your situation is not good."

"Yes, Ahman." It hurt to talk, cutting through his rigid self-control.

"Scandal now will be unfortunate." Ahman Penn studied August without enthusiasm. "You are in Elector Brauna's service so I have no choice but to return you at her request.

I will tell Elector Lee, however. It's possible he can intervene. I don't know if he will, of course."

Ahman Penn's small, unnecessary kindness broke through August's incomplete control. He blinked back tears and looked down, hoping they weren't noticed.

"You're saying that August has done something wrong involving us?" Kolet sounded deeply worried. "I don't understand, but if that bitch who just left claims he's working for Neuland, then that is unequivocally not true. We have *no* hidden arrangements."

Ahman Penn shook his head. "It's not so simple. Another probe has disappeared. August knew she was untrustworthy at least as early as yesterday, but he didn't report it until this morning. It makes him appear to have collaborated in whatever scheme she was engaged in, about which we know nothing. This doesn't directly concern you, and I suggest that you dismiss it from your minds." He signaled the guardian.

Recognizing the signal, August stepped forward, then knelt, his head bent forward and to the side. Kolet and Margot Ash stared, but August wouldn't look toward them; his face was burning. He remembered the humiliating trip up from the farm: the reversed scatter-field, so that none of the seven probes could see outside the coach, and their treatment—like a consignment of monkeymen—by the human guards. The forty subs who had been brought to Center with them had been free, but the probes were forced to wear prisoner's cuffs, inserted at the farm by Reverend Shan; losing control of their own bodies had kept them silent and withdrawn throughout the trip.

Lee's guardian removed a cuff from his pouch and shook it once, hard, to start it. The two-inch silver needle glimmered like water in sunlight. Warily, as if August might attack him, he advanced to insert it. Ahman Penn frowned, then glanced away.

"What is it?" Margot Ash asked.

"Some type of control device," Kolet answered, looking for confirmation to the guardian, who naturally said nothing.

August gasped as the thing bit into the back of his neck. Then it merely felt cool. The guardian patted his shoulder, and August rose to his feet. He shook his head and felt the tiny portion of the needle that protruded from his skin catch on his hair, but the area around it felt as numb as August's mind.

Every line of Penn's posture exhibited distaste. "You'd better test it. Wang will complain if he removes it or it doesn't work."

The next thing August knew he was back on the floor, collapsed in an unsightly, undignified heap. Some few seconds seemed to have passed, but he remembered nothing. Kolet and Margot Ash were observing him with great interest. Ahman Penn was at the door.

"Large muscle failure," Kolet announced. He extended a hand to August.

"Next time, Kern, a milder test," Penn told the guardian.

August took Kolet's hand. The Neulander's grip tightened around his wrist, and Kolet pulled, easily hauling August to his unstable feet, holding him a moment while he regained his balance. "Thank you," August whispered, too shamed to look at him.

Kolet squeezed August's hand and released him.

"Take him to Mei Wang," Penn told the guardian.

"Ahman Penn," August began, and wet his lips. If Reverend Wang took him to Security, he might never see Elector Brauna again. She would assume he was a traitor like Alexander. "Please, Ahman, will you tell Elector Brauna that I would never harm her? I protected Ellen because I didn't believe she was dangerous and because she was my friend. I was wrong, Ahman, but I wasn't disloyal. Please tell the Elector."

Penn did not reply, and at his signal the guardian moved into position behind August.

"Please, Ahman," August begged.

"I'll tell her," Kolet said.

Penn turned and glared at the Neulander. "You will do nothing, Kolet. You Neulanders had better not interfere in anything here in the Harmony. Kern"—and he turned to the guardian—"take the probe to Reverend Wang." He left the room, hurrying away deeper into the apartment.

"Go on, then," Lee's guardian ordered August.

August's mind began to clear. The connection Ellen had was with Delegate Huana; why would he take her? The guardian pushed August toward the door. August twisted, and saw Evan Kolet. "Delegate Huana must have Ellen. Something odd is . . ."

Kern did something to the control rod, and August's body lurched forward. "Get going," the guardian said.

Kolet took a step toward August. "Wait!"

August had no choice. He walked forward, mortified at being made into a puppet, and Kern closed the door behind them.

Center had been built piecemeal, and remodeling hadn't entirely erased the transitions between various sections. The small area August knew personally—the Electors' quarters, which included the toolman zone—belonged to an early section, from where Sucre had first been chosen as the location of the Harmony central government. Sucre's old planetary capitol complex (which now formed part of Center's main commercial sector) had been transformed by accretion into a major city; that first super-section addition had been designed with high ceilings and spacious corridors (and also riddled with service passageways) and been built of grand materials, such as real wood from old Earth and Chan, Hellenic gem-marble, Testament hing-skin, and even salvaged Bril circle enamel, not only in the public, governmental areas of the Harmony's Center, but throughout. The later additions to Center for offices, supplementary residences, businesses, and the "soft" manufacturing allowed in the Harmony's Center all lacked the grandeur of that initial construction.

Outside Lee's main door the corridor floor was a mottled red and white marble, worn by centuries of traffic so that there were slight depressions leading in opposite directions: to the Harmony governmental areas and toward the Academy. Mei Wang, standing behind August and holding the control rod in front of her like she was steering a coach, directed August toward the Academy.

"I know where Security is located, Reverend Researcher," August said, surprised that he continued to dislike her and express it under these circumstances.

She didn't answer, and they moved off, alone in the corridor; she had not brought any of Elector Brauna's guardians.

Few people were allowed in the Electors' neighborhood, so the corridor was empty, but when they crossed into the newer section of Center housing the Academy—obvious by the narrowing of the hallways, a mismatching of the marble floor and the subtle sense of greater use—August was surprised that the usual human guard wasn't present. "Turn left at the next intersection," Wang said.

"Isn't there a search for Ellen?" August asked.

"Quiet," Wang snapped.

August hesitated at the intersection, noting the monitors and glad of them. The corridor narrowed again, and became utilitarian, with gray base-stone flooring and painted tile walls. Their footsteps had a different, higher pitch. The sunstones were set too bright. This part of the Academy dated from the Bril wars, when the Harmony, bearing the brunt of the alien attacks, had also done a majority of the research used in the fight against them. The atmospheric poisons that had eliminated Bril on the ground and prevented many human captures had been formulated at the Academy of Co-Chan and at Center's Academy; there still were Academy bubble security zones not integral to the rest of Center. The Academies' discoveries enhanced the Electors' authority and were their major source of income.

"Go!" Wang hissed at his back.

"There's no one here!" Except during an Electors' Council, this area should have been bustling with Ahmen, Reverend Researchers, Reverend Teachers, and their student scholars.

"Do you really want to give me an excuse to use this, August?" Wang asked pleasantly. "I'd be delighted."

Wordlessly, August continued as she directed, following her instructions through several levels and more corridors. Once they passed a scholar—she looked no older than August himself, although appearance was a poor method of estimating age—but on seeing Reverend Wang's blue robe, the girl looked crushed, as if her presence in the corridor was something she had hoped would not be discovered. There must have been a mandatory Academy gathering convened.

"Turn right, ahead," Wang said.

Despite having never been through the area before, August knew Center. That would lead toward the labs, away from the school. Security was in the school. "Why?" he asked. He was increasingly suspicious. If she was not taking him to Elector Brauna's apartment, or Security, then Mei Wang was not acting within her proper authority. He knew of only one conspiracy: Huana's. August stopped at the next intersection, mentally reviewing the placement of monitors in this area, positioning himself so he was easily seen and overheard. The chance this location was being watched real-time was remote, but even if it was not, there would be tracers later. It was to them that he spoke. "Where are you taking me? Will Delegate Huana meet us?"

The left side of his body, from toes to fingertips and up even to his face, fell numb.

"I'm not very experienced with this device, and I haven't much time to learn," Wang said. "I could make a mistake and kill you prematurely. It doesn't worry me particularly. Get moving and keep quiet, or I'll begin to experiment."

It was difficult to force the left side of his body to respond, and August had to half drag his left leg, but he turned as she'd demanded. "Can you stop it? Please?" His speech was slurred and ugly.

Gradually the numbness eased, although she didn't remove it entirely. He talked as he hobbled forward, enunciating as carefully as she'd left to him. "Huana is lying to you," he said. "There is no Neuland plot. Ellen isn't missing; there's no search."

"Quiet."

He'd been blind. Mei Wang had known Ellen wasn't missing all along. He, supposedly so extraordinary, had been self-involved and had failed to spot her lie. It was the worst condemnation of his skills he'd ever had.

"Reverend, my only usefulness is against Neuland, not in its favor," August said, for the monitors. "I'm always watched. You know I'm no traitor. You're taking me to be used by Delegate Huana against Neuland, and therefore against the Electors. *You* are betraying Elector Brauna." But by his failure, he had, too.

"Make all the speeches that you want," she said. "No one is listening; my friends have seen to that. But once we reach the landing field, I'll drop you dead—and laugh about it—if you say or do anything except what I tell you. Now go on, quickly."

She was eager to hurt him. It was kill-fever, the kind chemically encouraged in soldiers preparing for battle, but Mei Wang didn't need drugs to prepare herself to kill a toolman. She only wanted an excuse. August did exactly as she directed.

As they entered the laboratory precincts, there were a few other researchers about; Wang hid the control rod in the folds of her robe. Several passersby glanced curiously at August, since—while subs maintained the Academy areas—probes were rarely seen here, but no one questioned Wang. He tried to speak out, but Wang had done something to prevent speech. He couldn't even raise an arm to signal.

The landing field outside the laboratory was the smallest of three at Center. He hoped that someone there would challenge a Reverend making off with one of the Electors' probes—for once his famous face could be useful—but as they exited the laboratory for the raw sunlight of Sucre's open air, no one was nearby. He hesitated, squinting in the bright light, sensing the differences in color and texture from the homogenized sun-stone light, remembering the half-forgotten light of his childhood, of the farm. He sniffed. Just beyond the door the air still smelled fresh, but as Mei Wang prodded him forward, the filtered Center air sweetened, becoming the cloying, decadent, sugar-scented air of Sucre.

Wang came to his side, closer than he'd been to her before; August felt like an ungainly giant. "Go to the black car," she ordered him. It wasn't height that mattered.

A private car was parked in a loading area. Information about vehicles wasn't relevant inside Center, but August recognized it as a cheaper lifting model, capable of traveling from Sucre's surface to Center, but mostly used on surface roads. There was a dent on the right rear corner that looked several years old, and a general air of neglect, but the engine—which was running—sounded in excellent condition. He went toward it as slowly as he could with her prodding him.

A short, greasy, poorly clothed man emerged from the car, opened the door, and then reentered the front seat. "Get in," Wang said.

August surveyed the field. There was no pursuit. He stood a moment, letting the wind blow his hair against his face, enjoying the temporary and utterly false sense of freedom unexpectedly given him by being outdoors. His arms tingled. "All right," he said, unwilling to suffer stupidly. He lowered his head and stepped inside.

Their driver closed a displayer showing routine Harmony news; the announcer had been talking about a robbery in Sucre-semp, nothing concerning Center. The man showed no urgency as he turned to Wang. "You coming, too?" His accent was of Sucre.

"I wouldn't miss it." She gestured, and August slid along the ripped bench seat, making room.

The car lifted. It was only then that he realized they truly had him. He'd done everything Reverend Wang ordered. He had *let* her make him a puppet. He could have struggled with her for the rod, or done something for himself—and for Elector Brauna—instead of relying on a rescue that never came. He turned to Wang. "Don't bother," she said, bringing the control rod out of her robe, then the sunlight blackened into excruciating pain.

"Extraordinary," Delegate Huana said to Mei Wang. "He looks just as Alexander did when I first met him, so many years ago."

"I'm not Alexander."

"He sounds exactly like him, too." Huana examined August critically, without looking him in the eyes.

August had awakened tied spread-eagled to a cot. His mouth tasted of blood, and his tongue was sore where he'd bitten it. The windowless room was hot and empty, except for the grimy bed and a drain in the mortared stone floor. The place stunk of urine, sweat, and Sucre's stench of candy turned fetid in the sun, the sugar air miasma of the farm. The cell was built of shack-board, flimsy and cheap.

Huana looked odd in a laborer's one-piece outfit instead of his usual mix of colorful Andian and staid Harmony professional clothing. He was sweating and smelled strongly, an individualized aroma made pungent by the perspired spices of regularly eaten, peppery Andian food. He seemed older than on the replays August had studied, more tired.

"Will we be safe from Neuland, now?" Mei Wang asked.

Delegate Huana nodded. "Thanks to you, Mei," he said, "and our other friends. Why don't you go outside? I'm sure you've had your fill of this nasty business."

She blushed, obviously pleased, and handed him the control rod. "Elector Brauna favors military aid to Neuland because of *his* reports," Mei Wang said, shaking her head in disgust. She looked at August with contempt.

"I'll join you in a few minutes," Huana said again.

She took the polite hint and left. The door, swollen by humidity, creaked. She had to pull it several times to shut it tightly in the frame.

When Mei Wang had left, Delegate Huana sat down on

the edge of the thin mattress. August stiffened, but couldn't prevent his body's shift toward Huana. They touched: Huana's thigh against August's chest. Huana hesitated, then reached out and brushed August's hair away from his eyes, where perspiration had made it stick. "You wear it long," he said. "Alex cut his hair short."

August turned his face toward the wall.

"You won't be harmed, and tomorrow you'll be released back at Center." Huana leaned forward. The control rod clicked as it rolled, settling where he'd placed it, at his feet. "I'm sincerely sorry this interference in your life was necessary. You're not going to be tortured for information about the Neulanders or the Electors' plans, or anything like that— and I apologize for Mei's hostility. It's obvious that the Electors intend to announce that helping Neuland's military fight off the alans furthers Jonist order in the universe, or some such orthodox-sounding babble. I don't think they have the nerve yet—except for Jeroen Lee—to proclaim that Neulanders aren't Altered or that Altereds are human. Besides, they want to keep Neuland beholden to them." He sighed. August felt the movement as Huana looked back at him, but he continued to stare at the wall. "I'm going to stop them."

Huana fell silent. August felt foolish, turned away from him like a child trying to punish his teacher by silence. He wanted to see Huana's face, to use his skills to clarify Huana's words, but stubbornness wouldn't release him from his senseless posturing.

"He was my friend," Huana finally said.

August faced him. "Alexander."

Huana nodded, and the bed moved slightly with him. "It took me a long time to remember that, and believe it again. Hate can destroy a man's memory as easily as death. I had plenty of both hate and death back then, and the Electors encouraged the hatred. 'The Andian Betrayal' they call it, blaming Alexander and Neuland, both beyond the Harmony's reach. I suppose I gradually gained perspective; life does go on. Then, approximately a year ago, your existence came to my attention. I couldn't grasp it at first. Why produce a duplicate of a failure, a spectacularly disloyal probe? Hadn't Alexander conspired with Neulanders to betray us? Granted, Elector Brauna had been quite attached to Alexander—she bent more than one rule for him over the

years, not the least of which was allowing his friendship
with me—but the lesson I learned from your existence is
that I didn't know enough, a true Jonist homily, don't you
think?" Huana had a pleasant laugh, low and deep, but it
lacked humor. Heat from his adjacent body was as unpleasant as sitting beside a fire on a summer's day. August's perspiration was soaking the mattress beneath his back and
head; it smelled rank.

"I reviewed the old replay tapes over and over and over
again. There are gaps in the record. I *know* that Alexander
and the Electors were in the lobby when the strike against
Andia was first announced, but they disappear from every
monitor for several minutes. When Alex reappears, he's
talking to Neulanders—speaking ambiguously and oddly
enough, in monotone, which he rarely used. I think that
when the strike was announced, Alex realized *for the first
time* the full extent of the Neulander plan. Moreover, I believe that he immediately and dutifully conveyed that information to the Electors, and they told him to keep quiet. Later
that day, when he publicly denounced Neuland, it was to *me,*
not Brauna. She already knew. Watch that tape closely. At
one point Alex says to her 'The only necessities I understand
are personal ones.' What necessities had they been discussing, to give rise to that? Political necessities, obviously."

"Kaviscu and Havic both admitted Alexander had been
working with them for several days," August said. "He said
so, too."

"Yes, and certainly under Brauna's direction." Huana
sighed sadly and touched August's right cheek with his index finger, tracing a line from eye to lips. He opened his
hand and cupped August's cheek, then put his hand back on
his lap as August shivered. "You need to hate him, don't
you? I know your skill, if you're anything like a match for
Alexander, and you could have figured this out in ten minutes if you'd wanted. Poor boy. If he wasn't a traitor—if
you're not tainted with evil—then someone else *is.* People
you love and trust have been lying to you, and the whole
universe is inside out."

"I don't believe you. I won't let you use me against Elector Brauna." August struggled against the rough bonds, trying to sit up. Huana touched his chest gently. August
stopped and let himself fall back onto the damp bed.

"August, she trusted you alone with the Neulanders. Think about that. She knew she could."

"Yes, because I'm not in flare. Not even close. I'm only twenty-one."

Huana stood up. "Just think about what I've said. I'll talk with you again before I return you to Elector Brauna."

"At the general session, when the Neuland supplicants are scheduled to speak," August said bitterly. "You're going to perpetuate the betrayal story so you can use my face to stop Neuland." August recognized the implication in his statement, that he already believed Huana. What was the use? He did.

"Truth is always better than a lie, August. Alexander knew it, even if the Electors of the Polite Harmony of Worlds did not. I would have let them give Neuland humanitarian supplies, but not this. No Harmony lives will be lost in the defense of Neuland, not if I can help it. Thanks to your existence, I may be able to. I won't let the lie continue; I'm not going to allow the Electors to hide behind a toolman's courage and sacrifice anymore. I'll do that for Alexander, and the Harmony, even if it means bringing the Electors down. I'm declaring a revenge on Neuland."

"They'll know . . ." August stopped, confused, no longer certain which side was his.

Huana bent over him. "I want to be your friend, too. The day the Neuland raid was announced here on Sucre, I had invited Alexander to visit Andia, to stay with my family. They're gone. I've no one left. Perhaps you'd come with me to Andia in Alex's place? I intend to retire shortly." He smiled sadly.

August stared woodenly at the ceiling.

"I'm sorry," Huana said, straightening. "It's much too soon, but it's difficult not to believe you're Alexander. I react as if you are. He was a good man, a loyal friend. Seeing you makes me miss him."

"What about Ellen?"

Huana stepped away from the bed. "A good girl, Ellen. She's fine. She's done nothing that she should suffer for."

"She's a toolman. She can be put down for no reason."

Huana looked at August. "I don't pretend to understand the universe, though Jon Hsu says we should strive for that all our lives. I only know I must be faithful to my people.

I do what I must to see that Neuland does not prosper again at our expense."

"Neulanders are not monsters."

"Perhaps not, but neither are they human." Huana shook his head, watching August, and smiled when their eyes met. "I must leave now. If you'll give me your word not to try to escape, then I'll have you untied."

August didn't speak.

"Please." Huana sighed. "Well, there's nowhere to go from here, anyway. They'll be without transportation until I return, and we're deep in the Green, Sucre's jungle. Even I can smell it. Alex called it sugar air. I think he hated Sucre." Huana stooped and picked up the control rod from the floor. "I'll take this with me," he said. "I'll see that you're untied and treated properly. No one will hurt you."

"You already have hurt me," August whispered.

Huana hesitated, then left August's cell.

Chapter 7

The evil twin story he'd told himself had finally been laid to rest, but the replacement was worse. August lay on the mattress, which had begun to smell of him, as though his imprisonment was a plant that had taken root inside the cell. The idea of leaving traces of himself behind was disgusting. He twisted in his bonds, brooding about a darkling plain swept with alarms. He'd lost faith, and there was "neither joy, nor love, nor light, nor certitude, nor peace, nor help for pain ..." Even his poetic metaphors turned on him. "Ah love, let us be true To one another ..." Matthew Arnold had written long ago, but August had no one by his side.

Not long after he heard a car leave, a guard came in carrying a sharp knife, the cleanest thing in the place. August had expected an Andian, but this man was tall, his missing front teeth obvious against his black skin—not Andian. His face was scarred with pockmarks from the acid of worm spit, so he'd done a turn or two out in Sucre's glades, but plainly hadn't gotten rich. The sour smell from a recent spill of fermented poison poke clung to his worn clothing, but his eyes weren't glazed, so perhaps he supplemented his income not only with holding kidnapped captives, but by a small-scale illicit brewery. He first cut the cords binding August's legs, then waited, watching August flex them. "You got anything?" he asked, clearly not expecting an affirmative. His accent was pure Sucre.

"No," August said, shrugging as well as he could with his arms still bound above his head. "I'm a toolman."

The guard's expression didn't change, as if the word had no meaning to him. Perhaps it didn't if they were far enough from the farm. The Electors treated the several thousand toolmen they kept at Center and their farm as a secret privilege, not widely known outside of Center, and Alexander had always been referred to as a probe.

"I'm a probe," August said, watching.

Slow recognition dawned in the guard's eyes as he examined August's face. "You're him." His tone was flat; he didn't particularly care. The Andian catastrophe, the subsequent deaths, maneuverings and betrayals hadn't touched his life, though he lived much less than a day's ride away from Center. The insularity of the ignorant, Jon Hsu had called it, and August had believed it was eradicated from the Harmony. Apparently it was not, at least among those who struggled on the margins of Extreme worlds, where there was no Reverend to guide them. The man sat on the bed just where Huana had, close enough so the poison poke became a stench, and carelessly cut the cord around August's left wrist. As he freed the right, his knife slipped and gashed August's hand near the knuckles of his index and middle fingers. The shallow, jagged cut immediately welled up with blood. "Sorry," the guard said indifferently, getting up.

August's arms ached as he drew them close to his body. He examined the cut. It stung, but not too badly. He sucked at the blood so that it wouldn't drip onto the mattress, leaving a permanent mark that he'd been in this place. The salty blood was satisfying in the heat.

"He's paying us two thousand counts to treat you good, so don't you make us treat you bad," the guard said, looking down with a shrewd smile.

August slowly sat up on the edge of the bed. His muscles burned. His hands and feet were still asleep.

"Take off your clothes."

The guard was not threatening him, so August asked, "Why?"

"He says to wash them, and keep them until he comes back."

August nodded. "All right. Just a minute." When he could, he removed his black slippers, curling his feet so they didn't touch so much of the gritty floor. He took off the uniform that marked him as a toolman, first the black pants and then the simple black shirt. The dull matte finish—guardians' uniforms were a shiny black material, and subs wore a one-piece outfit reminiscent of a Neulander bodysuit—was stained by his sweat. He stood, wearing only pale gray underpants, general toolman issue. He didn't want to sit down and let his skin directly contact the mattress, but his legs felt wobbly so he did.

"Everything," the guard said grimly, not enjoying his role, but following it to the letter.

August nodded, getting up to comply. "Will you give me something else to wear?" he asked, wondering if it would be an improvement to wear their clothes, or merely like draping himself in the foul ticking of the bed.

"You don't need anything in this heat," the guard replied. "If you're still here for the dark, then you can have my spare."

August nodded and sat down again, cringing slightly from the contact. The farm had been scrupulously clean—sub children kept it so, scrubbing with mad intensity. They all had been well fed, and no one had been purposely hurt by the few human guards and Reverends. Still, three years after gaining his name, August had run away. When they'd found him out in the Green, he'd been grateful. It had been an object lesson in the perfect uselessness of probe abilities without the knowledge to understand what was perceived. Sucre was an Extreme world. He understood the guard's conservation of his human possessions.

"Want anything to eat?" the guard said. It was somewhat of an apology for the matter of clothes.

"Tea?" His stomach was queasy and, at the farm, they said that something hot helped cool the day.

The guard nodded and left, not so careful with the door as Mei Wang and Huana. A line of sunlight fell onto the stone floor, brighter than those from the cracks that otherwise lit the room. August walked to the door and pulled. It opened. Another man, nearly a duplicate of the first except that he had more teeth, was squatting outside in the cleared, bare dirt. "You can come out for a while," he said. "Don't go where you could be hurt or lost, and you can't leave. You need to be here, safe and whole, when he returns. We'll watch."

August smiled. "You're doing my job. Now you're the probe, and I'm a survey object."

The squatting man stared back, uncomprehending and uninterested.

August surveyed the clearing. Besides the hut that was his cell, there were three other structures. Cooking was done in the central building; there was a lingering human aroma emanating from it, like the fragrance of yesterday's bread, which hung over the entire cleared space, about five acres.

Perhaps the smell was a side effect of the scatter-field canopy through which the sunlight filtered down; that scatter-field would prevent casual spotters, although not anything military, from noticing the clearing. With all the Green to search for him, August knew the Electors' searchers would not find him in time.

The central building—August assumed it was the residence—was sturdy, and had the extravagance of sun-in windows, which allowed natural light inside while Sucre's slow sun shone, during which time the windows accumulated power to light miniature sun-stones for use during Sucre's long night. At the farm, sun-in windows had been used only on the training rooms and the human quarters—not for the toolmen children. His captors weren't impoverished.

There was also a mechanical's barn and a storage shed or workshop—a fairly typical Sucre tracker's encampment, except for the scatter-field. If his guards had a still for fermenting poison poke, it wasn't kept in this clearing. Souce bones outlined a garbage heap at one edge of the clearing and drying skins were strung between the house and its outbuildings, but that couldn't fully explain the scatter-field; the ecolaws weren't strictly enforced on Sucre, and any fine could've been paid a hundred times before coming close to the cost of the scatter-field. These were not mere trackers. Of course.

"Good hunting?" August asked companionably of his guard, nodding at the skins. He hunkered down in the dirt, which somehow seemed cleaner than the rough paving of his cell.

The man grunted.

A substantial earthplant garden, though probably Altered to Sucre's leisurely days, grew to the side of the residence, just off center of the clearing. August smelled onions and strawberries, and saw new corn. In one corner someone also grew daisies. Tall post-plants, the supports for Sucre's monotonous vines and creepers, circled the clearing like fortress walls in reverse. It had been the same at the farm; there the cleared area was much larger, nearly four square kilometers, though they'd had to burn out invading creepers' tendrils regularly. He recognized a few species from the farm, and the pole plants and red barrier flower from both farm and Elector Brauna's sunroom. "A touch of home," he muttered to himself. The second guard gaped at him like a child, like any human, seeing very little and understanding less. He frowned.

The first guard came out of the residence carrying a white portable tea service that seemed as out of place in this primitive clearing as Sanda Brauna would have been. Two naked children, a boy and an older girl, followed the man outside, hanging back and staring at August. With a start, he realized this was a family and that probably one of these guards, or both, was married.

The children had tagged along behind August's guard, and he turned to shoo them away as he approached August.

"I won't give you any trouble," August said quickly. He had little experience of families, but he smiled at the children, hoping the guards would be pleased. Marriage was unbreakable in the Harmony and, while encouraged among the general population for its orderliness and stability, it was avoided within the Academies because of its ability to handicap a career. Of the six Electors, only Courane had a spouse and children; Ica Kurioso and Olin had partners. If there had been children produced from the other Electors' liaisons, none had been claimed by them.

"He left a pile of container food for you," the guard said. "Enough for a week. Must be worth eighty, ninety counts."

"Eat it," August said, disgusted by the thought of eating in front of these strangers. "I just want tea. He'll be back for me tomorrow."

The two men exchanged looks. Both warmed toward August. The first squatted down beside his . . . brother? "Here's the portable," he said. "Tea makings are already inside. Just set the temperature however you like it."

The children came around from behind him. The girl looked eight—not old enough to be named, on the farm—and she was pretty in the way a sub might be: strong, but slim, with regular features. The boy, who was plumper than the girl, was carrying a ball made out of gooey pole-sap, not fully hardened by the sun yet, and ready to burst if he threw it.

August took the tea container. It was a standard model and could be drunk from a spigot/straw or poured from the top into a cup. The temperature setting was a small dial inset in the side. He turned it to lukewarm. His hand looked dark against the glare of the sun on the white ceramic. A scab had formed on the cut, and dried blood was smeared across his fingers.

The guard noticed his inspection of the wound. "Sorry," he said, more sincerely than before.

"No matter." August thought of Evan Kolet. He would be healed by now; he wouldn't have felt the pulling pain as the knife nicked him, or the present dull ache. Only pressure. "Wish I was a Neulander," he said. "Pain-free. Nothing ever hurts them."

His brow wrinkled, thinking hard, and the first guard said, "Altered."

"Yes, but so am I. Sort of."

They inspected him, wide-eyed, as if he'd grown gills, as a few people altered themselves to do on Surf, or had grown a filter nose, like the much-maligned inhabitants of Gas. Extreme worlds, too. "You look all right," the first guard said, finally. He clearly was the leader—if that was the proper word when there were only two men—and probably the older brother.

August shrugged. "I see better." He left it at that.

Both men stared. "Go on inside," the first guard ordered his children, "and stay there." They left reluctantly, the girl looking over her shoulder. After a few steps, the boy threw his ball. It missed August, but splattered glop on the ground between them; the boy giggled and ran as the first guard shouted an indulgent reprimand. No one apologized to August.

It was repellent to frighten others by his mere existence; he was no threat to them.

August and the two guards watched the forest wall around them in silence while August sipped his tea from the portable's spigot. He had forgotten the oppressive heaviness of sunlight in a place where noon was as long as a day's work shift and the soil absorbed so much heat that unaltered earthplants burned their roots. Each of Sucre's natural days was like a leisurely sweep by an enemy sun.

The first guard went to the mechanicals' barn after exchanging a few brief remarks with his brother, and soon August heard and smelled a badly tuned liquid-fuel engine start to run.

"Hot in there," the second guard said, nodding in the direction of the barn, sounding pleased not to be inside it.

"Yes." August sipped tea, thinking about the heat,

Neulanders, and loyalty. Twenty-three years earlier, at the time of Neuland's entry petition, when Alexander was in flare, it must have been the Electors' undeclared wish that Neuland join the Harmony, or they would not have directed Alexander to be silent. By speaking, Alexander had—with great success, which continued down to the present—prevented Neuland from entering the Harmony. He had thwarted the Electors. But whatever he had done or betrayed, right or wrong, Alexander had preserved one fundamental loyalty: his services to Elector Brauna. He had maintained her honor, never hinting that the Electors favored Neuland or that they also had known anything of Neuland's plan. He was not a traitor.

"Move into the shade?" the guard asked, interrupting August's thoughts.

August followed the other man to the far side of his cell, where an afternoon shadow was slowly forming. Another clock-day and a half and it would be dark. The family would string their precious lights, ready to blind any of the dangerous nocturnals that might wander here. They would huddle together like punished children in fringe buildings at the farm, listening to shrill wails and thundering shouts made by creatures they didn't want to imagine. Whatever choices these people had made, still, life here was hard. August saw it in the obedient children and in the wary eyes of the adults.

Huana believed, or pretended to believe, that his use of August to prevent Harmony military aid from reaching Neuland was a continuation of Alexander's actions. But it was not. Alexander had told the truth to prevent a miscarriage of justice, but he had preserved the Electors' honor doubly—by speaking and by silence. Huana would dishonor them in Alexander's name.

Some truths were better left unsaid, because they were part of a lesson already learned. Some truths were too old to do anything but harm. There would be no miscarriage of justice if the Electors openly ruled that granting Neuland's supplication was in the Harmony's interest. Huana would destroy the essential quality of what Alexander had achieved if he used August to tardily and vengefully blemish the Electors. This time there were no sordid deals or underhanded maneuvering, just a tired, difficult people who, whatever their faults and many guilts, the Electors believed should not be abandoned to die—and who were willing to grant conces-

sions. Thinking of Evan Kolet and Margot Ash, August did
not believe the Electors were unjustified in their decision.

He looked up at his guard. "What would you do if I tried
to walk?"

The man studied August, then took a dented chrome whis-
tle from a pocket and blew.

August clapped his hands over his ears at the too-close
blare of the high-pitched sound.

The guard noticed. "Altered, for sure," he said worriedly.
"No man can hear that."

August heard the loping run of four dogs, then saw them approach. Mangy animals, marked by hard times, they sniffed him
and alertly watched their master. The guard raised a hand. They
became vigilant and attentive. "This man stays inside the clearing," the guard said, enunciating clearly and pointing at August.
"If he tries to leave, you sound an alarm, but don't bring him
down without an order. Otherwise, only watch him; he's a
visitor-friend. Understand?"

Well trained, they barked almost in unison.

"Altered, too," August remarked. "They understand."

"Level one," the guard said proudly. "Cost a fortune, but
they're worth every bit of it." Their tails wagged at that. He
called them by name, giving each a pat as it came forward.
"Loyalty and intelligence, what you need in a work dog."

"My life as a dog," August said, thinking of Sanda Brauna's
off-and-on affection as he watched their excitement at their
master's favor. He put his head down on his upraised knees.

The guard sent the dogs away. August heard them scatter
into Sucre's underbrush, returning to whatever doggy job
they'd been assigned. He stared into the Green. Maybe loyalty was as bred into him as it was in the dogs, as predeter-
mined as the color of his eyes. Elector Lee had said as
much. Still, it was indelibly *there*. He couldn't avoid it, and
he didn't even want to try. Perhaps that was a measure of its
effectiveness, but his intelligence, which had allowed Alexander to act contrary to Sanda Brauna's wishes even as he
protected her, said that whatever the justice of Delegate
Huana's position, Elector Brauna also was not wrong. He
must not allow himself to be used against her.

She was the meaning in his life. As she had protected him
from harm, so he must be true to her.

He needed to escape from Delegate Huana, or else he
must die. Or would his death stop Huana's plan? Even dead,

his face could make a static display. August sighed. More information about Huana's intentions would be useful, but it was clear enough that mere death would not be sufficient to stop Huana from using him to injure Elector Brauna. August picked up the tea and took a long swig, then set the portable at his feet, staring at it.

"More tea?" he asked the guard much later.

The man nodded and walked back to the house, leaving August alone in the clearing except for the vigilant dogs. From outside, beyond the cleared area, came the sound of skittering, chattering creatures. He didn't want to meet the things that made those sounds, but to test his possibilities, August walked quickly to the nearest edge of Sucre's native growth. He heard four-legged running, but he stayed still, waiting to confirm it, and did his best, despite his tension, to provide an excuse.

The dogs arrived, barking. They circled and growled at his every movement, their sharp fangs glistening with saliva as if they were anticipating him as a meal; he was not human to them. The guard ran back without the portable. "What?" he shouted.

August turned around. "Too much tea. I had to piss," he said mildly and walked back to the shadow.

The guard watched, then signaled the dogs to leave. "Don't do that again," he said, all trace of friendliness gone. "Ask before you move." Suspiciously, he added, "Who knows how you're Altered?"

Clock-night finally came. A woman's voice called out supper, and the guard insisted that August enter his stifling room.

"I'll bring you something to eat," the guard said.

"No, I don't want anything, but could I keep what's left of the tea?" he asked. He hadn't touched it since the last time the portable had been refilled.

"All right. Get inside."

August picked up the container and did as he was told, glad that his knees didn't buckle with the combination of relief and fear that he felt. The guard watched him through narrowed eyes, staring as if, naked and alone, August might somehow have seized a weapon. August smiled to himself, his sweating hands clutching the portable. After all, the guard was right.

The door closed hard, and the man pushed the bolt in place, as they had not bothered to do before. He hoped that meant he was in the room for the night. A dog was called and ordered to keep watch.

August thought with envy of Alexander facing the clean death that Ting Wheeling had given him. This filthy hovel seemed worse than any place he could have chosen for his tomb. He sat down on the floor facing the door, waiting to see if the guard would return. The group—the family—must have some medical treatment available or the means to call for help, so he knew he must not act until they had eaten, relaxed, and fallen fast asleep, with no chance they would check on him again. At least there were no monitors here, no sensors. He was alone.

Alone. As he waited, he wondered what it would be like to have a mother, or any true, reciprocated love. Wasn't love only loyalty taken to its extreme? " 'Ah, love, let us be true To one another!' " he whispered, and then more:

Ah, love, let us be true
To one another! for the world, which seems
To lie before us like a land of dreams,
So various, so beautiful, so new,
Hath really neither joy, nor love, nor light,
Nor certitude, nor peace, nor help for pain;
And we are here as on a darkling plain
Swept with confused alarms of struggle and flight,
Where ignorant armies clash by night.

"Ah, love." When did loyalty require love? Was there more to love than what he felt? What did he feel for Sanda Brauna? "Old woman," he whispered, thinking of her age, but that didn't suit her at all, however many years she had lived. She was beautiful. She was the center of his life. He could never be alone because she was his certitude. She wanted him: *she had caused him to exist,* however much Alexander had hurt her, and she kept him close despite the sadness his presence brought her, a sadness caused by Alexander, who, for all his loyalty, had never loved her. August knew it from the sorrow in Elector Brauna's eyes when she looked at him, and from Alexander's own actions. In that one sense, Alexander had betrayed her.

August would love her.

He took a tiny sip of lukewarm tea, then set it down. He picked it up again and irresolutely shook the container, guess-

ing the weight. Perhaps a half liter of water. Enough delay. He
turned the temperature control to the highest setting, past where
the red line warned of boiling, as far as the dial would move.

He would be true to Sanda Brauna. She would be his love,
his light, his joy, and his peace. She would be his help for
pain. There would be no limit on *his* loyalty.

He would need a steady hand. A half liter of water
wouldn't fall all at once, and he couldn't waste a drop. His
first thought had been to stand up, doing damage all over his
body, but it was impossible to be certain that once the pain
began, he would have the strength of will to continue standing and pouring into his upturned face. It was only his face
that really mattered—the face that Sanda Brauna both craved
and avoided, that Huana touched with affection, that Jeroen
Lee had designed. The face that had marked him all his life,
that wasn't entirely his because it was shared with Alexander. The face that he would purify with water.

He took the portable from the floor and lay down on the bed,
placing the thing on his chest, where he watched the temperature gauge. It already read that it had reached maximum temperature, but he waited anyway, in case there was a lag.

And because he was terrified.

He wished he was a Neulander. It wasn't death he feared,
but failure to die, and the necessity of feeling pain.

He lifted the portable in his two hands and held it outstretched at arm's length until his arms ached. Carefully, using his right thumb, he lifted the cap over the pouring spout.

A cloud of steam rose from the spout. Against the sugar-
scented air of Sucre, the cloud smelled clean. That seemed
right. The water would cleanse him of Alexander's face. If
he survived, he would be reborn a new man. Elector Brauna
would never see Alexander in him again.

He must not delay. Each second the water grew a bit cooler.

He tipped the portable. More steam rose from the opening, then, finally, he saw a mesmerizing drop of water hanging on the tip of the spout. It was beautiful, a rainbow of
colors in the light. He tipped the portable over and watched
as it fell down to him.

He had intended to keep his eyes open. Green eyes were
Alexander's trademark, his use-name, and it would be good
to melt them away, but at the last minute when the heat
rushed at him, August closed his eyelids.

Then the water hit him, and then the pain.

Chapter 8

"For pity's sake," Huana whispered.

The guards had dragged August outside that morning and dressed him in the laundered probe clothes. After their initial shock, they had not spoken to him, as if, faceless, he wasn't real. They shouted at each other, though, arguing over fault and money.

"Why?" Huana asked.

August's sight had burned away along with his eyes. Smell was gone, but he could still hear. He could have spoken, except that thirst was a horrible need, worse than any hunger he could imagine, and his mouth was too parched for speech. Dry breath hissed between his clenched teeth much faster than normal. His tongue felt huge. Whenever he did not consciously prevent it, a low whine came from the back of his throat.

August sensed air movement and the slightly cooler shadow as Huana knelt beside where he was propped against a wall.

"Why did you do this to me?" Huana demanded. "To Andia?"

August tried to beg for water and managed to make a human noise. Huana asked someone, "Did he say something?"

The guard began a rambling, exculpatory speech, and Huana cut him off. "Bring some water."

August felt he waited a very long time before Huana held a cup against the wreckage of his mouth. It clicked against his teeth. August gulped the liquid down, although there was not enough to lessen his thirst or remove the dusty powder he felt coating the inside of his mouth.

"What has he done to himself?" an Andian-accented woman's voice asked, horrified, from some distance away.

Sympathy was unbearable. Sometime during the long night his agony had become, if not manageable, at least something to which his exhausted body had yielded, ceasing to struggle, but now an animal wail began in August's throat. He gasped, trying to keep it down. A rasping sound escaped. It rose in intensity and became a scream, which gave no relief but didn't end. Then, abruptly, he was released. There was nothing at all.

"Can you talk?" Huana asked harshly.

August was free of pain, although immensely thirsty. The dull, vibrating thrum of the car's lifting engine sent waves of distress through his head—not pain, but a hollow coldness. They were aloft; he recognized the gravity flutter. Three other persons were inside the coach, but his own breathing was the loudest, and much too quick.

"I'm using the control rod to cut off sensation from your burn," Huana said.

August's throat ached from the sounds he'd made since his injury. His body felt brittle, ready to break, but the burn pain had vanished into nightmare. He'd considered himself trapped inside a shell that looked like Alexander, but now he knew that shell was integral to the man, as if by destroying Alexander's face, he had immured himself in Alexander's dead body.

Without his senses, he was disoriented and could barely think. He groped near himself with his hands, briefly contacting a slim leg wearing a soft woolen dress—native Andian attire—before the woman seated next to him jerked away. August stopped searching and grasped the seat on which he had been placed, tightening his fingers around its edge to straighten himself.

"Can you talk?" Huana was brusque.

"Yes," August managed, though his voice was husky and distorted.

The woman giggled nervously.

"Good." Huana's voice came from the left, but August was too tired to turn. "You're young," Huana said. "You're not in shock. You'll be all right."

"But can we still use him?" the woman asked doubtfully. August concentrated on identifying her, forcing his mind to think, then had it. The Deputy Delegate, Pilar Macomo. "He doesn't look like Alexander Greeneyes anymore," she said.

"Water?" August asked.

"I would have released you, or kept you with us, safe

from the Electors," Huana reproached him. "How could you betray me, and Andia, and Alexander?"

Thirst was an all-consuming pressure now that the pain was gone. He needed Huana's help to get water; nothing else mattered. He tried to speak again, but the noise he made wasn't right. "Please. More water."

"If Jonism is anything," Huana continued, "it is the search for truth. Alex understood truth. Now you've obscured it. You have badly disappointed me."

August tried to lick his lips, but his tongue found only a crusty surface, like a hard roll, on one side of his upper lip. He shuddered, calm enough to imagine the horror that must be the remnants of his face.

"He wants more water," Pilar said. She moved—he couldn't follow how—and someone steadied him and placed a container in his hands. August's gratitude made him try unsuccessfully to speak again, but only as he opened the spigot. Then he didn't waste time, but put the thing hurriedly between his teeth. It seemed to be a portable much like the one he'd used to burn himself, but this water was cool. He sucked it up. It tasted sweet and oily. He couldn't drink quickly enough to satisfy his thirst. He tried to let the water sit in his mouth, to be absorbed by his dry tongue, but it rolled out and down his chin.

"We'll go on as we intended," Huana said to the others. "Our appeal always was an emotional one, to show the Delegates that the Electors made a duplicate of Alexander, and to explain that Alex didn't betray them, but acted on Electors' orders. To show the entire Harmony that there was another deception, besides Neuland's. His face is still shocking, in a different way. And we can prove he's Alexander. There are records, and besides, having Alex's face is the only reason to have done such a thing."

There was a long silence.

"We could blame this on the Neulanders," another Andian said. Leon, Huana's aide. "Or, at least imply they did it. They don't feel pain . . . their torture parties. It's logical."

"But untrue." August gasped after the effort of speech. They didn't reply.

"The session will have begun before we arrive," Pilar said.

"Then we'll make a grand entrance instead of forestalling the session." Huana dismissed that problem.

August had emptied the portable. He pushed it toward Pilar, asking with a raspy, nearly unintelligible voice, for more. After a moment, she handed him another, without comment.

They all were quiet. August was surprised, since Andians had a tendency to chatter, but his presence and his awful face were apparently inhibiting them. He listened more carefully, trying to form a picture of the coach interior as a distraction from thirst, and thought he heard distant, quavering flutes and high-pitched voices singing. He turned his head to focus. One of the Andians was listening to music, the sound of which was leaking from the personal receiver. He strained to distinguish the words, but Andia had a local language, a mix of old Español and Quechua, and the lyric's meaning was mysterious. It sounded like a lament; at least, that explanation fit with his mood.

Would Huana lie and tell the Grand Assembly that Neulanders had burned August's—Alexander's—face? Or the Electors had? "Delegate," August rasped, pushing himself to speak intelligibly. "Please don't use me against her," August whispered hoarsely.

"They'll let Neuland win if I don't stop them," Huana said. August imagined the wide gesture that must have accompanied Huana's angry reply. "Be quiet, August, and when we arrive at Center, do exactly as I say. If you betray Andia—if you disgrace Alex—I'll have no choice but to hurt you."

August leaned against the back of the seat without trying to hide his horrible face, not caring if they stared. He didn't have to know. The remainder of the ride went slowly, the real-time drag. The Andians' sporadic voices seemed remote. He felt hot, then cold, and always thirsty. Pilar gave him more water. His mind drifted, lost in a haze of overtired speculation, random and sometimes incoherent. He must be loyal to Elector Brauna. Love was an act of will, and he must love her. In his fevered fantasies, she spoke comforting endearments, and he recited poetry to her in the dusky grandeur of the sunroom.

He must not let himself be a tool used against her.

August was being gently shaken. "Wake up. We're here," Pilar repeated.

He had dozed, or blacked out. The car was stopped, its engine off; noise of other vehicles around them established that they were at a landing field, a busier one than where Mei Wang had abducted him. He guessed they were at Center's governmental field, closest to the Grand Assembly.

"He's awake," Huana said.

"How can you tell?" That was Leon, speaking with distaste from outside the car. The door was open. Pilar went out, her long skirt swishing against August's leg.

"Get out of the car, August," Huana ordered. "Do exactly as I say. I don't want to hurt you."

"TMO?" he asked, shivering. He was freezing, despite the sunlight on his arms. He wanted bed and a warm blanket, peace and rest and water. There was no pain, but immense fatigue made him feel heavy and unwell. "The medical office?"

Huana didn't answer, but someone tugged on his arm.

Perplexed by the sounds of activity he couldn't see, by people whom he couldn't observe, slowed by a lassitude so deep that it was difficult to care what occurred, August slowly exited the car. "Please, I . . ."

"Later. You chose this way, not me." Huana prodded August, directing him as he made his way outside. A breeze felt arctic; August whimpered as the air touched his damaged face. Huana took his arm. Much shorter than August, he made a poor crutch.

The walk across the open field was a nightmare. Blind movement was unnerving. August stumbled frequently, disoriented rather than dizzy. There were voices, near and far. He turned his head, straining to see, to smell, to know more than what he only heard, and confused himself.

"Hurry," Huana said. "Leon, help me. Take his other arm."

The few people they encountered stopped, undoubtedly staring, but the Andians never wavered on their way to the Great Hall. More than anything, August wanted to rest, to curl into a warm ball and sleep until this passed, but he thought of Sanda Brauna ahead, of her need for him to protect her, and kept moving toward her, concentrating on keeping on his feet.

"August," Huana murmured close by. "Don't speak, don't do anything but what Leon or I tell you. I'll make it clear to everyone that you're not to blame. The fault is with the Electors. I will personally make certain your medical needs are met, as soon as this is over, and I will protect you from being put down to the best of my ability. I owe that much to Alex."

And what do you owe *me*? But August didn't have the energy to speak. He might have provided the ideal excuse for his own death, but before he died he would do everything in his power to protect Elector Brauna. *Ah love.*

They took him through cold, mostly empty, corridors that he had never before walked. He'd never been inside the governmental portion of Center. It seemed cavernous and endless. Their footsteps echoed on the hard surface. He gathered his strength, letting Leon and Esteban Huana steer him. He knew where they were going.

He didn't know they had arrived, however, until Huana pulled back, stopping him. "Do exactly as Leon tells you!" Huana said, then released his arm. Leon still held onto August's other side, but Huana and Pilar went away. After they had left, Leon whispered, "Come on," and tugged August a short distance forward.

They entered the Great Hall. August knew it by its size, deduced from the coughs and whispers that traveled across the room like a tide of sound, echoing slightly off the walls. He tried to sniff, but there was nothing. His mouth was still dry, but his own sensations seemed remote as he stretched his hearing and tried to create a picture of what he should have been able to see: the center of Center and the Harmony.

Then he realized Sanda Brauna had begun her ruling.

". . . The obligation to make the hard, unpopular, even hateful choice if we determine that objectively it is best— that is, that it advances harmony and order, that it increases the ability of mankind, our species, to which we must be loyal first, to flourish and progress. We Electors cannot think in terms of revenge; our morality cannot be that of an individual, but of mankind. I bear a great and personal shame because the probe who betrayed the Harmony was in my service. I learned twenty-three years ago that the choices we give to others should not be any greater than their personal morality can bear. I trusted a nonhuman, a probe. I believed that in a choice between his own interests and those of the Harmony, Alexander would not betray either the Harmony or me. I was wrong."

"The bitch," Leon whispered. "*She* betrayed Andia."

Elector Brauna's tone was entirely sincere, August

thought, yet wasn't she lying? Alexander never betrayed the Harmony—he had saved *her* from betraying it. Blind, disoriented, the new truths he'd learned were too much for August to assimilate, except to know that Sanda Brauna felt deeply wronged by Alexander. He longed to see her, to let her see him and realize the extent of *his* loyalty and the depth of *his* love.

"Now is the time to make the hard choice," Elector Brauna continued. "To look at the universe clearly, dispassionately, and in the way Jon Hsu directed us: with questions looking for more questions, not only answers. I cannot let my personal inclination to punish those who shamed all mankind, and themselves, by their actions, and who co-opted one who had gained my trust into the great betrayal we all remember, cause me to veer from the clear path of future order. Nor can this Assembly. It is my ruling as an Elector of Order, whether or not prevailing sentiment agrees, that it advances Order if . . ."

"Elector, stop!"

Even having expected the interruption, the strength of Huana's voice sliced through August's attention on Sanda Brauna like an explosion, although the sound system was supposed only to amplify the voice of the designated speaker. Huana had allies.

"Good," Leon whispered.

"Marshall!" Huana shouted. "Marshall, I demand that I be heard!"

There were confused sounds from the podium area and the floor of the Great Hall, then finally the Marshall spoke. "Delegate Huana, Andia's delegation has a place. The podium is taken."

Elector Brauna said, "Esteban, please allow me to continue."

"The matter is urgent, Marshall. I have new information concerning the destruction of so much of my world." Huana was in motion. August guessed from his voice that he was walking to the raised podium.

There was more confusion, then Margot Ash, in a soft tone that lessened her Neulander accent, spoke from the speaker's podium, directly ahead of August's position. "That was twenty-three years ago, Delegate. I am sorry, but it is over."

"No!" Huana shouted. "Lives are over and time passes, but truth is never *over*. Truth remains."

"You'll have a turn, Esteban," the Marshall said in the placating tone often directed at Andians when talk of the Betrayal occurred. "We'll set aside time for your protest."

"I want it now!' Huana shouted. "If you won't hear me, Marshall, then I'll tell the Assembly from the floor!"

There were shouts of "Let him speak!" To August, they sounded orchestrated. People were moving about, and there was scraping, perhaps a tussle. August wanted badly to sit down.

"All right," the Marshall said finally. "Please, Elector, let him get this over with, then we'll proceed."

Hands were clapped, drowning out any objection Elector Brauna made, then the noise abruptly ceased, as if at Huana's signal.

Huana had reached the podium. "Some of you sympathize with the current situation these Altered murderers find themselves in," he began. "You meet two pleasant enough individuals who tell you of their difficulties with alans and crossmen out beyond our frontier, and you forget this same world once sent another seemingly pleasant pair to deceive us. I won't reiterate the story you all know; I won't remind you that all of my family are dead along with one-third of my people. I have only one question to pose to this Assembly: How was it that these killers managed to gain entry into this room to address us?"

Huana paused. Leon began to pull August forward, down the aisle.

"Why is it that these Neulanders"—Huana spat after the word—"come here to such a helpful reception? It's obvious: the Electors intend to give Neuland their joint, favorable ruling. Neuland has friends in the Harmony, six powerful ones." He stopped dramatically, holding the crowd. "The same friends they had twenty-three years ago."

"That's enough!" the Marshall said. "Esteban, I won't allow these aspersions on our Electors."

A few delegates had noticed the man in probe uniform with a grotesquely damaged face—August heard their gasps—but the bulk of the room was muttering over Huana's accusation.

"Marshall, listen now or listen later, but you all will listen." Huana had triumph in his tone. "The Electors knew about the false Bril ship, and they conspired with Neuland to protect Neuland's attack on Andia."

"No!" August whispered, hearing the lie. Voices all around were raised in denial.

"They knew!" Huana screamed over the increasing noise, aided by the sound system. "And when one toolman had the courage to tell the truth about Neuland, they killed Alexander before he could implicate them. Alexander was no traitor!" The room had become silent once again. "Alexander was no traitor," Huana repeated more softly. "He was the Electors' scapegoat. He was Andia's friend and the Harmony's savior. And here's the proof: they knew Alex was honest, not disloyal, and so they made another probe, a *clone of Alexander*. And look what they've done this time to hide the truth!"

Huana must have pointed at August. A woman screamed. People shouted. August strained to distinguish Sanda Brauna's voice—to know what to do, to know if she recognized his love and loyalty—but without the focusing guidance of sight, there were no individual voices, only wild babble.

"They did this!" Huana turned as he spoke, because his voice changed. August guessed he had pointed at the Neulanders. Or worse, at the Electors.

"No," August whispered, the sound tiny and lost in the Great Hall. He lowered his head but it didn't matter, they all had seen and would suppose the Electors had burned his face. Esteban Huana was out of control, consumed by his vendetta against Neuland.

"Examine this man; you'll find Alexander. Yes! A clone of the very probe Elector Brauna mentioned just now with such feigned remorse. They were afraid you'd misunderstand—or understand too well!—so they've hidden him for years, but the truth is as plain as his face. This hideous face—plain as the face that they've hidden. The Electors wronged Andia. By their ruling for Neuland today, they would wrong us all again!"

Confused shouting filled the Assembly Hall. The noise was too loud for there to be any direction in the voices, but August wondered what, from the podium, Elector Brauna saw when she looked at him. Another traitor? Huana had twisted August's attempt to remain loyal to her into the reverse, making the Electors seem evil by the very act August had taken to protect Elector Brauna. In his single-minded devotion to his cause, Huana was making the Electors the scapegoat of his revenge.

August jerked his arm away from Leon, then hesitated, unsure where to go. He pulled air into his lungs and then expelled it in one shout, disregarding his fear and pain. *"No!"*

Someone grabbed his sleeve, and he swung that arm wildly, escaping and running forward until he bumped hard into something, then he turned, his hand trailing along the cool surface of the unknown obstacle, and ran again.

Bodies pressed away from him. He stumbled, righted himself and ran incautiously in the direction from which Huana's voice sounded most natural, hoping it was toward the podium and not a virtual speaker. The attention around him, their revulsion, was almost a physical attack.

"No!" he screamed, dazed by the motion and emotion. His raw throat burned with the word. He stopped like a cornered animal, although he wasn't even sure he had been chased. He raised his voice, forced his body to do what was necessary to be heard, ignoring the difficulty. "I'm August, not Alexander. Huana wants revenge, not truth. I did this—not the Electors! Not Neuland! It's all Huana's fault! He had me! The Electors didn't know!" He couldn't say more. Although he had shouted with the entire remaining ability of his voice, he wasn't certain how far he had been heard. He leaned against something, probably the wooden half wall around a World Delegation's box, trying not to sink, exhausted, to the floor.

A scuffle began nearby. August was too tired to listen over the general commotion, though he heard Leon call his name. Then August was pushed and would have fallen, except another man grabbed and held him, pulling him away from the melee. His rescuer was taller than the Andians, and stronger—able to support August's weight—but without sight or scent, August didn't know his rescuer's identity. Or care. The stranger put his arm around August's shoulder, holding tight against the trembling, and didn't draw back at sight of the grisly face when August turned automatically, unaccustomed to his inability to see.

"I did nothing. I have nothing to hide," Huana bellowed from the podium. The Hall's sound system had finally been turned off, eliminating Huana's vocal advantage. While loud, his voice was only naturally amplified, and was quite close. "Not like Neuland! Not like the Electors! Not like their probe!"

"Leave him alone. This man requires medical attention." It was Evan Kolet's staccato-accented, foreign voice; it was his strength holding August on his feet.

Above them, on the podium, Jeroen Lee said, "Delegate Huana, this bizarre, revolting, sensationalist display must end. Whoever you have dressed in probe clothing and dragged here—and that is a matter into which we must make serious inquiry—he does indeed require immediate treatment. General Kolet, thank you for your compassionate aid. Please, bring this poor fellow behind the speaker's area. I've already called a medical team."

"Lean on me," Evan Kolet whispered.

August did as he was told, grateful for orders. Kolet supported him as August sagged, and he drew them both forward through the crowd. "Those burns are deep. You, guard, help me."

"Yes, sir." It was Ting Wheeling. The familiarity was overwhelming. August sobbed tearlessly as Ting went to his other side. Though they had rarely touched before, contact with Ting was comforting. August listened for Sanda Brauna, who must have sent him.

"You think I'm lying?" Huana shouted, as, with Ting's help, Evan Kolet moved August rapidly through the disorienting press of curious people. "I'm not," Huana said. "He has been a captive of the Electors for years. This is a cuff, a control rod, which only the Electors use, and only on their toolmen. Do you all see it? Who wears the needle? Who was in the Elector's hands until I freed him? I'll show you!"

The pain returned all at once, a weight dropped from a huge height, crushing him. August screamed and collapsed on the floor, clutching at his face. He screamed because he was unable to stop, and because it was all that he could do against the pain, though screams did nothing to help. There were others around him, shouting voices, men trying to move him, talk to him, but none of it mattered to the pain.

August lay on the bed, listless, shivering under the covers, his head held steady with braces inside a cylinder filled with pressurized gases that were supposed to heal him. He absorbed more medicine and fluids through the arm wrap on his left arm, a warm, wet unsatisfying replenishment of what he had lost. Despite his begging, they refused to give him anything to drink, saying it would disturb his recovery to remove the cylinder.

The burn pain was gone; so was the controller. He didn't know how they were managing the pain, but he felt at peace for the first time since meeting the Neulanders in Elector Brauna's sunroom. "Is Med. Radcliffe on duty?" August roused himself to ask, unable to recognize any of these voices.

The medics whispered together across the room; he didn't bother to listen over the faint sibilance of the escaping gas. "She's assigned in the toolman facility," one of the strangers said eventually, a man apparently of average height. The soft inflections of a Windfall accent made him seem kindly. "You are in Center's general hospital, intensive facility."

Someone checked the wrap around his arm. "Is this too tight?" the same male voice asked.

"No, fine," August answered.

The man loosened it anyway. Movement of the wrap temporarily cooled his arm, increasing his trembling, but the physical contact was pleasant. "I'm Med. Jon Kiani," the man said, "in charge of this facility. I've taken your case."

"I'm a toolman." August recalled the confusion over his identity in the Grand Assembly. "Can you move me?"

"No." Med. Kiani lifted August's right wrist and felt his pulse, as though the medic didn't trust his own sensor array. His hand was impersonally gentle. "Not in your present condition. Standard procedure in TMO would be to put down a toolman injured this seriously. They don't have our equipment. Even if they did try, I doubt those people could bring your infection under control, or reconstruct your face."

August heard Med. Kiani's distaste for TMO. "I don't want that face again," August said.

Med. Kiani didn't speak. His fingers tightened on August's wrist, then he carefully returned August's arm to the bed, moving slowly, as if speed could hurt him. August sensed that Med. Kiani had turned toward the door. There were steps as someone left and someone else entered, then the room was silent, except for the sound of the medical equipment. Someone important was there.

"Elector?" August whispered.

No one answered, but August was sure Elector Brauna had come.

"Elector, Huana already knew about Alexander. I didn't tell him anything," August said. "Was I able to stop him? Did I do right?"

"He's becoming distressed," Med. Kiani said, directing his words toward the reticent visitor while lightly touching August's arm again. "He can be questioned tomorrow, unless it's truly urgent."

"No," Jeroen Lee said quietly. "I only wanted to see him. Jon, August will be treated as well as if I were the patient. I will review every aspect of this case personally. I don't expect to find any deficiencies because he is a toolman."

"He'll have the best care I can provide, Elector," Med. Kiani said firmly.

Sure footsteps approached the bed. "You did as well as it was possible to do, August. You confused them. There was no vote." To Med. Kiani, Elector Lee said, "Let me see his chart."

The two men moved to the foot of the bed. "We can replace his eyes within two weeks, if he heals well," Med. Kiani said.

"Not green." August didn't want to look like Alexander, ever again.

Jeroen Lee chuckled. "You're beyond hiding."

Lee didn't understand. Sanda Brauna would never see him clearly, without sorrow, until she didn't see Alexander in him. "Did she send you? Elector Brauna? Is she here?" August strained to see, and tried to rise from the bed, struggling with disappointment. He was certain Lee had entered alone, but perhaps, blind, he was wrong and Sanda Brauna was there.

"You should leave, Elector," Med. Kiani said. "He needs to rest."

Elector Lee returned to August's side. A strong hand firmly restrained August. The shape was different from that of Med. Kiani. The fingers were longer, thinner, and lingered on August, as he lay back heavily on the bed, frustrated. "Sanda was disturbed," Lee said softly. "She is unable to visit you at present. She asked me to thank you for your sacrifice."

August felt the lie in the pressure of Lee's hand.

"Rest," Elector Lee said. "You deserve it." He touched August's hand in farewell, then walked quickly out of the room.

Chapter 9

"Definitely hideous." Evan Kolet leaned back in the reclining armchair—August had groped for it the day before, then sat awkwardly alert, listening to a placid string serenade that was as boring as a musical still life but which Med. Kiani had deemed suitable accompaniment for his recovery—and rested his heavy boots on the side of August's bed. "I've seen men as damaged, and they all recovered." Kolet straightened in the chair, leaned forward, and winked at August; he seemed too energetic for a hospital room. "But that was on Neuland."

"August is healing very well," Med. Kiani said stiffly. "The facial sack is necessary, whatever procedures you people use on Neuland, and the eyes I've installed are only temporaries. His recovery is so quick that we haven't grown eyes to his genetic specifications yet."

"Thank you for giving me these," August said, ill at ease being the patient of an important man. He'd wondered wryly if having human eyes meant he was temporarily closer to human. Certainly, his stay in the hospital hadn't made him feel that he was. The medics and techs spoke to each other, not to August, except for questions relating directly to his condition.

Med. Kiani studied a readout on his sensor array. "His eyes are integrating well," he told Kolet. "He's a good patient."

August felt alive again, now that he could see, albeit with the blurred sight of standard human eyes rather than enhanced probe vision, but there wasn't much inside the room to look at. The decorative touches—a standard window screen that only the medics could program; a displayer set just for entertainment; and wooden shelves inset into a wall, awaiting the traditional gifts of aromatic rose boxes containing Jon Hsu's writings in hard copy, which in August's case, never came—were eclipsed by the medical equipment, which hissed, hummed, and sometimes clicked, altogether isolating him from the sounds outside the room. Each time a piece of equipment was detached, it was placed against a wall, as if it must be kept ready should he relapse. The dominant machine, however, was the sensor array, more complex than any August had seen, and built with four available screens, so several medics could use it at once. Beside it, Kolet's medical condition monitor was a toy.

The Neulander had arrived while August was dully watching an Academy broadcast about the giant burrowers native to Loess. The human soldier stationed outside his door by the Grand Assembly—to what purpose, August wasn't sure—had stopped Kolet, but, interestingly, Med. Kiani had approved the visit, coming inside for a moment, too.

"Don't stay too long," Med. Kiani told Kolet as, apparently satisfied with what the sensor told him, he went to the door. "August will be discharged today."

"Thank you!" August exclaimed, but Kiani smiled impersonally, nodded, and left them alone together.

"Come on, August. He's gone, and you're off duty. You can talk to me." Kolet's tone held too much repressed tension—and his timing was odd—for a mere social visit, but he smiled effortlessly and didn't flinch at August's face.

The window screen was playing late morning sun over a broad, blue ocean and the faint call of gulls. Kolet stood and walked to it. "I miss real sunshine and waves," he said, then glanced at the open door. The guard had moved out of sight. "Center is a sterile place. There's no outdoors, just atriums and gardens, and few enough of them. Don't you wish you were on the surface instead of in this ... facsimile of a quickship, suspended in Sucre's atmosphere?"

August tightened the loose folds of his shirt; he'd lost weight. He moved slowly; pain wasn't far beneath the surface, but the medics had stopped giving him so many drugs. He missed them for the passivity they'd produced. "No, I don't miss Sucre. It's Extreme. But I've read that Neuland is beautiful," August ventured, willing to accept even suspect companionship from anyone who could ignore his face with sincerity. He'd had no other visitor in the six days he'd been hospitalized. "At least your day is close to standard—a clock-day—at only twenty-three hours long."

Kolet looked back and smiled. "That's the spirit, August.

You'll learn to make conversation yet." He came closer and glanced toward the door, though he didn't seem to want to leave. "Yes, Neuland is beautiful. It's all islands. Skimmers—solar powered, oceangoing ships—make a great circle route among the archipelagos. The largest landmass is no more than fifteen hundred kilometers across. We call that one a continent." He spoke distractedly, a tour guide absorbed in other thoughts. "The days are a convenient length, but our year is short. Still, Neuland is a Virtual Earth compared to Sucre, although we're only registered as a Familiar. My family lives in Romoa—city people—but my grandparents still farm."

"The Kolets? Or your grandfather Kaviscu?" Delegate Huana stood at the door, his hand grasping the door frame. He wore a black armband, as he had done in recent years only on the anniversary of the Andian Betrayal. His clothing was a somber, non-Andian suit. "What are you doing here, Neulander?"

"Would you have met me anywhere else?" Evan Kolet asked. He held his hands out, empty palms up in the traditional pleading gesture of a supplicant. The medical condition monitor gleamed at his wrist. August noticed the fully healed finger he had watched Kolet cut, then looked down and searched for the gash he'd received from the guard on Sucre. It had also healed.

Huana glanced at August, then averted his eyes. "The message was from you, not August?"

"Yes, but don't leave, please, Delegate Huana," Kolet said, walking determinedly closer. "I need to speak with you."

Huana's back was rigid. He turned to August, though he seemed to need to force himself to look. "In spite of everything you did to stop me, I didn't believe you sided with Neuland against Andia, only tried to protect Elector Brauna. I'm disappointed you let yourself be part of his ruse."

August supposed it was true. He'd been so eager for company that he hadn't tried to penetrate Kolet's concealed purpose. He looked down, so Huana wouldn't be disturbed by his face, then the spontaneous, self-effacing gesture angered him. His seemed, after all, a little enough fault against what Huana had done. August straightened, and looked back at Huana. "Neither Andia nor Neuland has ever done me any good."

Kolet frowned. "August didn't know the motive for my visit. Delegate, Neuland is desperate. Here. I'll get on my knees if that will convince you to stay." He knelt on the floor near Huana, smiling slightly with embarrassment but no mockery.

Huana stared at Kolet, then came farther into the room. "I never expected to have Talia Kaviscu's grandson kneel to me. Neuland's danger must be worse than I'd guessed."

"You're right, she was my grandmother. Does that make a difference? You hate all Neulanders. Anyway, she's dead. The Harmony executed her, though the proceeding had questionable legitimacy. She was a diplomat."

Huana shook his head. "There's no satisfaction in this. You're posturing, not humbled. Neulanders are incapable of feeling more. Get up." He glanced sideways at August. "I'll listen."

Expressionlessly, Kolet rose to his feet. He bowed to Delegate Huana, then went to the door and tried to close it. The human guard rushed forward to prevent it.

"It's all right," Huana said, motioning the guard away. "This Neulander won't dare harm me."

The guard hesitated, assessing Kolet with a cool look, then he nodded at Delegate Huana and left.

Kolet immediately closed the door. "Psychological privacy, anyway," he said. "I suppose your Electors monitor this room, and it's obviously filled with sensors." He flashed August a reassuring smile.

"Get to the point, Kolet, or I will leave."

Briefly, Kolet's distaste for the Andian showed in the set of his shoulders and compressed line of his lips, then his expression smoothed. "The point is that without help Neuland will be overrun by the United Emirates within the next five, possibly ten years, depending on their luck and our fortitude. We're one world to their eight, and *they* have friends. This matter you've resurrected—that your Electors knew of Neuland's involvement in the sweeps of Andia before Alexander spoke—has nothing to do with Neuland today. It only revives old passions and hurts your own Electors, a very roundabout way to attack us. Military assistance, which the Electors *openly* favor, is life or death to us. I've come to ask on what terms—anything—you'll withdraw your objections to military aid to Neuland."

"Give me my family back, and the eighteen million others

on Andia who already died for Neuland, then we'll talk."
Huana was grim, not enjoying his power, despite his undisguised loathing of Kolet. He looked at the door, but his glance fell on August and he hesitated.

"What happened to Andia was unforgivable," Kolet said soberly. "I don't expect you to believe that the cobbled together Bril ship was out of control during its second sweep or that the extent of the destruction was unintentional. Neuland was wrong, incredibly wrong, to do what we did. There is no excuse, and I don't ask for your pardon. But be reasonable, Delegate. Be compassionate. Killing all the men, women, and children on Neuland won't bring your people back. We're prepared to offer Andia one-third of the total economic production of Neuland for the next twenty years as reparations if you'll only withdraw your objection to . . ."

"No," Huana said, interrupting. "You can offer Andia the entire economic output of Neuland for the next two hundred years, and 'no' will continue to be our answer."

"Andia's or yours, Delegate?" Kolet scowled; he walked to the window screen, staring out at the tranquil image of an ocean as if it was real, then he turned back to Huana. "I intend to make this offer public. You are refusing at least forty billion dollars—twenty-nine billion Harmony counts—each standard year, even at Neuland's current, depressed economic level. I know what that money could do for Andia because I know how we would suffer its loss. But we are willing to do so, Delegate. This would double the size of your economy. Not all Andians prefer revenge to compensation; some might like to put this matter finally behind them."

"You don't care about Andians," Huana said. "Your only concern is recapturing the sympathy of the other World Delegations before tomorrow's vote. You know you're going to lose, despite August's obfuscation, and you're trying to buy Andia the way you bought the Electors."

"We're not 'buying Andia,' Delegate, we're trying to make amends for our acknowledged crime. And our arrangement with your Electors is no secret plot. They've been granted charters to establish an Academy of Neuland, open lower schools and send their Jonist priests—excuse me, Reverend Researchers and Reverend Teachers—to Neuland. Other Harmony Delegates welcome the spread of the Electors' influence. Personally, I dislike being watched and told what to study and how to live, but it's better than becoming alan, or dead. I'll gladly practice your brand of Jonism if it influences even one vote. And you're right—Andians mean less to me than my own people. That's tribal, I suppose, but natural."

Huana was silent, frowning to himself. He went to the door, ready to leave, but then turned back. "You're very good, General Kolet. So rational. A military man. Of course. What else does Neuland know but the gun and the boot?"

Kolet gathered calm about himself like a disguise. "What do you know about Neuland, except that you hate it?"

Huana looked sorrowfully at August, then back at Kolet. "You have no trouble looking at August. I do. Twenty-three years ago the Delegates had the same difficulty watching the replay of your sweeps of Andia. Most left the Great Hall before it was over. Do you know why, Kolet? Of course not." He lowered his voice, and looked again at August. "It's because we feel the pain. We empathize with the suffering. You can't. Your kind are not human." Huana would have left, but Kolet rushed to the door, reached past Huana, and held it firmly closed.

"I'm very tired of being told I'm not human." Kolet stepped back from the door, but his intense attention on Huana seemed to fix the other man in place. "I can look at August because I feel respect and true compassion for him and his situation. Maybe the reason you can't is guilt. You claim I can't possibly comprehend his sacrifice—as if destroying your face is a daily chore on Neuland, something like shaving—but who put him in a position where burning himself was his best choice for performing his duty? Who, for that matter, first brought him medical help?"

Huana's face had reddened; his expression was furious. He stood with his hands clenched, staring at the larger, younger man, and took a deep breath. "Yes, claim credit for hustling him away. Of course, you had no self-interest in removing Alexander's clone from the vicinity of a discussion of aid to Neuland."

Kolet laughed bitterly, and slapped his open hand against the wall. "Now I understand: I am irrevocably evil, and you are entirely good. Alexander was much more my enemy than your tortured logic ever made him the enemy of Andia, but we Neulanders can understand the simple fact that genetics is not memory, and there is no common identity between clones. What I don't understand is why August feels any loyalty to a group of *humans* who have done nothing but treat him as a pariah because Alexander saved them all—from me!"

Huana came back toward the bed. "Do you blame me?" he asked August.

"Delegate Huana," August said softly, purposely using the affectionate intonation he'd heard on replays of Alexander speaking with Huana. It recalled to mind the younger, cheerful man Alexander had known, but there was little resemblance to that man in the Andian Delegate's dark, bitter eyes. August stood, having to lean slightly against the bed. "If you believe you owe me anything, then end your campaign against the Electors. Find some compromise with Neuland."

Huana hesitated, as if he'd heard a ghost. He bit his lip, moved his arms outward, then brought them close to his sides and shook his head. "I can never compromise with Neuland, but as for you, I regret your injury and your pain. I want to be your friend, as I was a friend to Alex."

"Alexander liked you, Delegate. Very much. I've seen it on replay tapes. But after your accusations of the Electors, the lies, after what has happened to me, I can't."

Huana flinched. "I suppose this Neulander is your friend."

"Not a friend, Delegate," August said quickly. "Only someone who's been unnecessarily pleasant to me. A person without friends appreciates that."

Huana's expression tightened, but he didn't turn away. "I don't enjoy this, but I have no apology to make. Senseless, useless, casually inflicted death has changed me, and I can't put it aside. For you, I have many regrets. As for Neuland, let it make its own way in the universe, without my help. I didn't push for war against them twenty-three years ago." He looked at Kolet. "Don't think I couldn't have. Even now, I don't object to selling you people food and medicine. But I draw the line at military entanglements and military supplies. I don't trust you. Learn to get along with the Emirates, fight them or die. I simply don't care, Kolet. Whatever benefit there may be in aiding you, I see nothing worth losing a single additional life of a Harmony citizen. If the Electors say otherwise, then they are deceiving us or mistaken. I'll listen to an offer of reparations when Neuland suffers and grieves the way you've made Andia suffer and grieve. Until then, I see no reason to help your kind stay alive."

Huana looked back at August, his expression bleak, but

his tone softened. "You are a toolman, August, however strange your life has been, and there are things you can't understand. Someday you'll realize that doesn't lessen my affection or my obligation—to you and to Alex. I hope eventually you'll feel differently about me." He scowled and nodded at Kolet. "And about him. He can't offer true friendship; he doesn't know how. He can never share your pain." Huana opened the door, glanced back at August, then left the room.

Ting Wheeling was waiting outside the hospital room with the human guard. Once Huana was gone, he stepped inside and bowed briskly to Evan Kolet. "The medic said you're free to go," Ting told August, scanning his face and somehow smiling at it.

"I'll return with you," Kolet said.

"It isn't necessary." August was anxious to be rid of him.

Kolet didn't appear to notice. "It's no problem," he said. "I'm returning to Elector Lee's residence now, anyway."

"I'm going to Elector Brauna," August reminded him. August had been reborn in that shack-board hut, given a new face. Elector Brauna would see he was no longer simply Alexander's clone. His life would be different.

Ting stared down at his feet, then straight ahead. "My orders are to take you to Elector Lee." His high, light voice was strained.

"Orders from her?" August was openly incredulous.

Ting nodded unhappily.

Kolet tapped his hand against his leg. "Good," he said with forced cheerfulness, "then we can continue your lessons in the art of conversation."

"Has she dismissed me from her service?" August's voice rose.

"We're to go to Elector Lee's apartment, and I'm to stay with you. That's all I know." Ting's apology and sadness, things he hadn't the words to express, showed in his face.

"Let's go, then." Evan Kolet moved toward the door. "Don't worry, August. You'll never understand the simplest woman, and Sanda Brauna is far from simple."

August nodded, pulling himself into a proper probe reserve with difficulty. She had ordered him to stay with the Neulanders until the vote—that was the reason. Or, she did not want to see his unsightly face. Well, that would mend.

Med. Kiani said his recovery was excellent. He refused to doubt her.

Ting led, taking them through the maze of service passages he used with August rather than the much-monitored main corridors. Kolet examined the route with interest, like a scout learning an adversary's stronghold. August gave monosyllabic answers to Kolet's questions about Center's structure, and Ting said nothing at all.

They approached a cluster of four subs cleaning the airshaft covers by hand, and Kolet nodded at them, almost bowing, which set the subs off into giggles. He inspected the subs as they passed—two men and two women—without aversion, although some probes claimed that subs' quick, darting movements reminded them of cockroaches, and said they were less intelligent even than an individual Bril. These four looked back at Kolet with interest, and whispered comments to each other. "Subs are everywhere," Kolet commented to August.

"There are more subs than there are guardians and probes combined." Subs almost had a real society, separate from standard humans and other toolmen.

Kolet raised an eyebrow. 'Your Electors must like things very clean."

August was unsettled by Kolet's sly derision. "Subs wait on other toolmen, too. They're convenient."

"Not up to your standards, August?" Kolet's smile had a sharp edge.

"I don't think about them much."

"Ah. That makes them even more convenient."

"You are *very* tired of being told that you're not human," August said, and then was shocked that he'd been so rude, even to Kolet, an Altered and a Neulander.

Kolet only smiled, and clapped August on the back. "You're right. I am."

When they reached Lee's apartment, Ahman Penn greeted them at the door. "The Elector is waiting for you both," he said, critically scanning August's face—the masklike facial sack. "Later, I'll take a look at Kiani's work. We trained together before he went into government service. The guardian can stay at the station with ours."

"No," Ting said firmly. "I stay with August."

Ahman Penn looked askance at Ting. Guardians were the

most easily managed, the mildest of the toolmen, and such stubbornness was uncharacteristic.

"Let him come, then," Kolet said impatiently. He started down the corridor without waiting.

Ahman Penn went ahead of Kolet and escorted them through the cluttered apartment to the office where Elector Lee had first brought the Neulanders and August. There Lee sat behind the huge Chanic desk. Vincent, the senior of his two probes, was unobtrusively present. Margot Ash stopped in mid-step, as though she had been pacing between the pieces of heavy furniture. Her face was pale, her brown hair pulled tightly back from her face and pinned up in an unflattering bun. "We watched," she said dismally to Kolet.

He shook his head. "He's a fanatic. We'll have to publicize his refusal of reparations and hope that helps enough."

She hammered her clenched right fist into her left hand, making a cracking sound. "According to this probe, Huana has enough support so that we can't possibly override Andia's veto."

"I didn't think he'd deal." Apparently unperturbed by their dilemma, Jeroen Lee leaned back in his chair. "August, you have brown eyes now, eh?" He chuckled.

"Yes, Elector," August said. "Temporarily."

"Report." Jeroen Lee tapped his fingernails on the desk and didn't look directly at August. "What's Huana thinking?"

Elector Lee had no right to request a report from Elector Brauna's probe, even inside his own apartment. August hesitated, glad of Ting Wheeling at his back, to be a witness, since Sanda Brauna would have no replay from inside another Elector's residence. Ahman Penn was out of sight, behind August. August surveyed Jeroen Lee as well as he could with only limited, human vision, but Lee's intentions were opaque.

Near Elector Lee, Vincent moved just enough to catch August's attention. He signaled, "No," the most communication he'd ever made to August after years of shunning him.

"Yes, sir," August said, bowing to Elector Lee, unsure of his motivation, perversity, or intuition. "Delegate Huana is unhappy with the divisive effect of what he's doing; he has always been orthodox. Reparation money would be useful to Andia, as well. I expect other Andian groups will pressure him, as General Kolet suggested. Unfortunately, he is determined to make Neuland suffer. If there was another factor, or if a third party mediator he trusted was involved—just now, not the Electors—something might be achieved. When I suggested compromise without forwarding a specific proposal, he gave the possibility a moment's actual deliberation. But he isn't ready."

"What is this?" Ash asked.

"This is a probe." Jeroen Lee stood, smiling at August like a proud father. "Alexander always had a flair for extrapolation of individual motivations, which August shares. Vincent here is competent at current trends and crowd analysis—you listened to his vote counting this morning—but he doesn't have August's instinct when it comes to nuances of personality. No one does."

August's legs ached. He rested his hand against a nearby chair to steady himself. He thought he'd been discreet, but Jeroen Lee immediately told him to sit down.

"Thank you, Elector." August sat in the chair he'd held, a stiff-backed, white and green armless one that faced the wrong way, forcing him to sit sideways.

"You get all that from a single discussion?" Kolet asked August. "How reliable is anything you say?"

"I make mistakes. It's like predicting weather. The closer in time, the easier the projection, but I have watched Delegate Huana closely for six years, not just this afternoon. I know when I'm right, and I'm certain Delegate Huana feels trapped in his role; he'd like to reconcile with the Electors. Time, or something dramatic, may move him."

"You personally are pivotal to Huana," Jeroen Lee said. "Even I see that."

August nodded. "It's guilt, just as General Kolet told the Delegate. Not much for this," he said, indicating his face with a brief upward movement of one hand, "but because of his misjudgment of Alexander. He wants to make it up to Alexander, posthumously, through me." Despite his fatigue, August was enjoying this give-and-take. Though not as detailed, it bettered the pleasure of preparing a written report, and Elector Lee's obvious relish of the discussion was gratifying.

"That was elegantly done, when you told him you couldn't like him," Jeroen Lee said enthusiastically. "His jealousy of Evan was exquisite."

Kolet shrugged. "I hadn't noticed."

"The polarity," August said. "I said I can't like him, then he leaps to the belief that a Neulander is my friend."

Margot Ash laughed. "No wonder Kaviscu and Havic were discovered. It's impossible to keep secrets around him."

"Quite," Jeroen Lee agreed, looking pleased. "Although secrets aren't impossible, only very difficult. Alexander was actually better than August. Of course he was older then, with greater experience and not nearly as central to events. What is that rule they drum into you on the farm?"

Vincent quickly answered, "More is observed from the rear than from the center."

"No, the other." Lee looked to August.

"An actor only sees from inside his own role." August was tired. He struggled not to slump in the chair, glad, just then, that there was no need to concentrate on his facial composure. They all were watching him, the two Neulanders uneasily, Jeroen Lee and Martin Penn with approval. Vincent was subtly hostile. Only Ting Wheeling's attitude was constant.

"This is all well and good," Margot Ash said, "but Huana's psyche doesn't matter unless knowing it tells us how to proceed."

"Delay," August said, although he hadn't been asked. He was anxious to end this second difficult interview in as many hours.

"Delay," Evan Kolet agreed. "If conditions for a battle are adverse, *but may improve with time,* postpone the battle."

"Exactly," Lee said. "We need an excuse to defer the vote, something to gain time until the flap over the Electors' role in the 'Andian Betrayal' blows over."

Lee walked to the front of his desk, stopping near August. "A Harmony commission sent to Neuland to investigate the alan threat," Lee said thoughtfully. "If the Emirates are ever at our border, we'd want that information."

"*Invited* to Neuland," Margot Ash said, nodding, "to investigate Neuland's military preparedness, and incidentally, our human qualities, since Andia?" She looked at Kolet; he nodded. "We'll still offer reparations, of course, and publicize his refusal."

August's left hand, holding the back of the chair as if readying him to stand up, trembled. He placed that hand in his lap, clasping it around the other.

Jeroen Lee looked sternly from Evan Kolet to Margot Ash, then walked back to his chair and sat down at his desk. "Is Neuland capable of convincing Delegates—not necessarily Huana himself, but the others—that you're not evil? That you've learned and changed? Will they have a pleasant visit and want to help you when they leave?"

Margot Ash said, "Of course. We'll see they do."

Kolet nodded his agreement. "This will delay aid for quite a while. Can we get any equipment now?"

"No," Lee said. "You heard Vincent. Tempers are high, and the Delegates aren't in a mood to listen to the Electors. Don't push; you'll lose it all."

Kolet picked up an antique blue and white vase, then set it down. "Will this commission come to Neuland on a military ship?"

Margot Ash smiled.

"That could be arranged—for our own protection since your system is raided so often," Lee said. "Be sure to invite Electors to accompany the commission, to see after our new charters. Going ahead with the establishment of an Academy on Neuland will impress most Delegates with your sincerity. August, will Huana force the vote or will he let it be postponed?"

"If it's presented as a semi-adversarial commission, and the idea comes from a neutral source, not the Electors, he'll agree. He'll definitely insist on an Order of Noninterference if an alan raid occurs while the commission is in the Neuland system." August turned to Evan Kolet. "You won't get any help from having a military ship present."

"Right," Kolet said, "except for the impact its presence alone will have." He smiled and bowed deeply at August. "I'm glad you're on our side this time."

August's body ached with fatigue; it was an effort to keep from shivering as he returned the bow. "I'm not on your side, General Kolet. I'm in the service of Elector Brauna."

Jeroen Lee kept August behind when the Neulanders left to refine the details of their invitation. Vincent departed, too, at Elector Lee's crisp signal, then Lee gestured at August to come closer. August hauled himself to his feet and stood directly before the Elector's desk. Ting Wheeling waited patiently by the door.

"Martin, have you examined August?"

"No, sir, not yet. There's been no time."

Displeased, Lee frowned at Ahman Penn, but Penn calmly returned his gaze, and sat down in a comfortable chair closer than he'd been during the discussion with the Neulanders. Lee walked around his desk. August held onto its edge with one hand so he wouldn't tremble while the Elector inspected him. Jeroen Lee noticed, and his frown deepened. He brushed aside the hair August had let fall over the sides of his face to cover the junction of the facial sack with his own skin. The Elector's hand grazed August's shoulder, then he touched the sides of the facial sack as lightly as had Med. Kiani, checking the fit and set. Not as tall as August, Lee still looked into his eyes without difficulty, but he didn't see August, only the eyes. "Good fit," he told Penn.

"Jon is excellent with details," Penn replied.

August was relieved, instinctively sensing Lee would be a rigorous critic. After all, this was Alexander's designer, checking the damage to Alexander's latest incarnation. Perhaps that explained the possessiveness in Lee's intent survey.

"How's your appetite?" Elector Lee sounded more concerned than Med. Kiani.

"Fine." Med. Kiani had encouraged him to eat, and he'd had no trouble after the cylinder's removal.

Elector Lee nodded. He palpated August's wrists, held them, then felt the side of his neck. His hands were warm and light against August's skin, but August shivered. "Sit down," Lee said. August obeyed. Looking up at Elector Lee, he caught a fleeting smile. Unreasonably, that made him feel better.

Lee returned to his chair and reviewed the room sensor data he surfaced on his desk. From what August could see, upside down and with merely human eyes, the sensor array seemed as complex as any, except the hospital monitor. Lee liked information.

"Any sign of metabolic dysfunction?" Ahman Penn asked.

Jeroen Lee glanced coolly at him and lowered the display. "No," he said, giving August the impression that Ahman Penn had spoken out of turn. "You have a slight fever, August. Too much excitement and activity, too soon. Also a racing pulse. Martin, take him to his room and monitor his case. I'd rather not send him back to the hospital; we should be able to do as well here."

"Elector, my order from Elector Brauna was to watch the Neulanders. It still stands. I should go to their suite." He suppressed a sigh. The thought of rest was a balm. "Also, I need to bring myself up-to-date. Med. Kiani wouldn't allow me to listen to news reports, even the public ones from Sucre."

"The restriction was my order." Elector Lee waved a hand. "I didn't want you made anxious during your recovery. This business Huana has brought up falls most heavily on Elector Brauna. Alexander was in her personal service, and Huana's evidence—such as it is, and entirely circumstantial—really only implicates Sanda. Elector Kin has implied that Sanda was the only one who could have known about Neuland's plan, and rather maliciously insinuated that she did know. Courane and Olin, of course, are new since the Andian Betrayal, and they are vocally disassociating themselves from the entire incident. Ica Kurioso has been very quiet. For that matter, so have I.

"Sanda realizes it would be best for her not to be seen in association with you at the present. Your existence was never formally registered in Center anyway, so we're creating the fiction that you have been in my service all along. Only toolmen and reliable Academicians know differently. Also Huana and his partisans, but he'll be circumspect regarding you. There is too much sympathy aroused by your situation that doesn't help him—and he feels that sympathy, too."

August wished for better eyes, to catch the tiny, involuntary movements of Elector Lee's face. He felt handicapped and leaned forward, straining to understand the truth. Why would Lee help Elector Brauna in such a risky way? By keeping August, he portrayed himself as privy to Alexander's secret. Lee and Brauna cooperated and often voted together, but there was no personal rapport to explain it.

"So, this will pass. Huana's evidence consists only of your existence—which is ambiguous—and his subjective interpretation of those old replay tapes. But for now, as I'm pleased you intuited already, you are for practical purposes in my service."

August looked pointedly at Ting Wheeling.

"Yes," Elector Lee said sourly, "Sanda's little condition. She still thinks I might have you put down, not realizing I find you quite as valuable as she does, in my own way.

You've become a player in the game, one Huana esteems. Nevertheless, you are here. Will you consider yourself entered into my service?"

Lee confused and intimidated August with his sometimes kind, even considerate, moments scattered against an autocratic background. August turned to Ahman Penn, whom he barely knew, but hours of replay had imparted a sense that this was a man who could be trusted. Penn inclined his head slightly toward Elector Lee. "Yes, sir," August said. "Temporarily."

"Good." Lee stood. "I have a great deal to do. You'll have complete news access again, and your prior ability to review replay—although under my code. Later, you can watch Evan and Margot real-time, but for now you are ordered to your room to rest."

"Do I send reports to Elector Brauna?" August spoke softly, staring down at his hands. They still wouldn't come clear. Nothing was distinct when he looked through these human eyes, and it made him feel stupid. "Will I have any contact with her?"

"Only through me," Elector Lee said firmly. He gestured at Ahman Penn peremptorily and walked to the door. "Martin, take care of him."

"Yes, sir."

August bowed at Elector Lee, who failed to respond. When he was gone, Ahman Penn rose to his feet and said, "I'm going to put a medical condition monitor on you with a tap-in so I'll have constant, detailed information on your condition."

"Like the Neulanders wear? That might be suggestive to some people, Ahman Penn."

Penn stood still. If he was annoyed at having an order questioned, he was honest enough to consider the objection. "You may be right," he said finally. "I'll make do with sensors. Come with me to your room."

"I can find it, Ahman, if it's the same one." Just as in the hospital, August was embarrassed by the attention from a superior.

"Elector Lee said to escort you. Follow me." Penn glanced at Ting Wheeling. "The guardian can go to his quarters."

"No," Ting said again. Period.

"After I'm settled in the room, Ting, you can leave, like when you took me to tape study. I'll call if I need you."

Ting hesitated, then nodded.

"Ahman. One question, please." August used probe monotone. "What did you mean, 'metabolic dysfunction'?"

Martin Penn looked at August for long seconds. August didn't move or turn away.

"Flare," he said finally, "and I think you knew it. It can be brought on early if there's sufficient stress. The answer, you'll recall, was no."

August had watched Jeroen Lee. His immediate emotional response had been muddy, perhaps closer to "not so far," than to a definitive denial. "Thank you, Ahman," August said, following him out of the room. At his back came Ting Wheeling, the sole evidence of Sanda Brauna's continued interest in his existence.

Chapter 10

"Now you've done it," an angry voice said, awakening August from troubled sleep. Aching, disoriented, his heart pounding and his body slick with perspiration, August thought he was back in the tracker clearing, tied to the filthy cot. He gasped, looked wildly around, only then recognizing the room he'd been assigned in Elector Lee's apartment. Vincent was there, alone, watching with a narrow smile. He was the one who had spoken.

"I'm too tired for games, Vincent." August ordered on light to aid his blurry vision.

Vincent stood, arms crossed against his chest, observing August with a stance that said August was a fool. He sauntered over to the bed, his step as arrogant as August remembered, and wrinkled his nose, looking down. "You *are* repulsive," he said.

Although the majority of standard humans were brown-haired and brown-eyed, with a medium beige or brown complexion, toolmen were a rainbow of available human pigments. On that spectrum, Vincent was ivory. His black uniform set off his white-blond hair—fairer even than Sanda Brauna's—and his blanched complexion. His eyes were a blue so pale they made him appear blind. His lips provided the only color; they were full and red, like a woman's, and Vincent accentuated them with a waxy gloss. He was taller than August, and seven years older, with a confident air to his large, graceful movements that was belied by the tension in the small muscles of his face and hands. He wasn't well liked; his only confidant was Lee's other probe, Beatrice, who was herself considered gauche and inept, but on that same color spectrum, Beatrice was midnight black; she and Vincent made a physical polar set. Jeroen Lee had little to do with his inadequate junior probe, beyond his occasional enjoyment of a female companion.

August brushed his long hair back with his fingers, wetting them. The damp sheets were unpleasant; he supposed there was an odor of sweat and fever in the room. "All right," he said. "Say what you want and get out."

Vincent gazed about the room. Though it had considerable heavy furniture, August's room wasn't cluttered, and there was a symmetry to the arrangement that Lee's public rooms lacked. Vincent dragged a contoured desk chair through the thick pile of the cream-colored carpet to the side of the bed, and sat down with his legs casually crossed. "He wants you. You've made him think he can have you. Very risky, August-Alexander."

"I'm not in his service." The covers fell away as he sat up, exposing his sticky upper body to the cool air, giving himself goose bumps. His head hurt, and his throat was dry.

Vincent laughed, naked derision made into sound, displaying vocal control a singer would covet. "How stupid are you? She doesn't want you back."

August shivered and pulled the covers up around his shoulders. "She sent Ting Wheeling. She wants me." He shook his head. His mind was foggy, and the lack of sensation from his face was irritating. "Get out, or I'll signal him. He's tied in to this room."

Vincent leaned forward. "Just you keep saying no to the Elector, or you'll never see Brauna again. I'm giving you fair warning, though you've never done anything so marvelous that I've seen. An animal can cut off its leg to get away from a trap; it's the same thing as that sensational burn of yours. As for your spectacle today, about Delegate Huana, it was all hot air. I know the difference between extrapolation and glib guesswork. You couldn't read Huana so deep. All you did was make the Elector want you more."

"Elector Lee knows I'm loyal to Elector Brauna. There's no conflict between us."

Vincent leaned back in his chair, shaking his head, his expression one of perfect sardonic disbelief in another's naïveté. "He has watched you for years, and now you're in his service."

"It's only a formality." August wanted to get up, wash, and dress, but didn't want this man looking at him.

"He knows you're not loyal to him, but the Elector enjoys a challenge." Vincent leaned close, and sniggered when August drew back. "I'm warning you—he gambles, but never past a certain point. Elector Lee has no patience when something becomes hazardous, and he can always have you put down. So just keep saying no, August-Alexander. Maybe you'll be safe."

Everything Vincent said only told August that he had influence with Elector Lee. He wanted to wipe the sneer from Vincent's face, wanted to redress all those years of being shunned, mocked, and disdained. "How safe are you, Vincent?" he asked. "How close are you to the farm?"

Vincent smiled and shook his head disgustedly. "I knew I shouldn't have bothered, but Ellen insisted."

August reached out and clutched Vincent's arm. "Is Ellen all right? She wasn't put down or punished?"

Vincent seemed puzzled. "She's fine, except she's had her wandering curtailed. She's stuck in tape study like you used to be. Elector Brauna's new probe does most work in the Assembly."

August lay back on the bed, his dignity shattered.

Vincent clapped his hands together. "Didn't he tell you? I was sure he would. Well, let me be the first, August-Alexander. Elector Brauna has a new probe, Charles. Remember Charles? Dark and gorgeous and only nineteen?" He laughed. "Still think she wants you back?"

"It doesn't matter . . ." August's voice trailed off. *Ah, love, let us be true / To one another!*

Vincent hesitated, and his voice lost its sharpness. "It's hard, I know, to be so little to them. Just don't do it to me. Say no as long as Elector Brauna gives you that option." He stood and surveyed the room again, then pulled the chair back to its proper place. He stood with both hands on its back. "This was my room. He let me choose the furnishings, and their arrangement. If it was late, and he didn't want me with him anymore, he let me stay here instead of going to quarters."

August responded to the pain in Vincent's voice, not to the man. "You'll have it back."

Vincent scowled, and walked to the door. "I don't think so," he said quietly before leaving.

Restless after Vincent's visit, August bathed and dressed. He opened his screen, indexed through the routine news, then, unnerved by Vincent's transient sympathy, he backtracked through the listings to a replay of his appearance in the Great Hall with the Andians.

Although most probes saw themselves in the periphery of great events quite often, this was August's first replay of himself. It was unpleasant to view himself from outside, as if he was watching Alexander. The thought made him look away. Everyone wanted Alexander: Sanda Brauna. Esteban Huana. Even Jeroen Lee.

His injuries weren't obvious from a distance, back in the shadows with Leon, but his stance showed blindness to events in the room. He didn't react properly to sound or motion. Slowly, curious but repulsed, he brought the view closer. His face was a red and gray wreckage that oozed at the edges; the eyes were gone and, though his mouth and chin were intact, there was a shallow pink indentation where his nose had been. His cheeks were mottled gray plains with rivulets where flesh had melted and flowed down the sides of his face. It was in every way horrible, so horrible that August turned away, walking to a gilt-framed mirror that hung above a desk. In comparison with that past horror, his mirror image looked passable. The facial sack was a loose-fitting mask, but it had a nose and normal color. His eyes were set deep in the folds between his missing eyebrows and his cheeks, but they were better than empty holes. Even so, Sanda Brauna couldn't be expected to visit anyone so ugly.

He went back to the screen and watched himself stumble up the aisle, held and directed with aversion by Leon, but he didn't bother to listen. He focused instead on Elector Brauna. At first she stared stonily at Delegate Huana, but the moment she saw August, dismay was etched on her face.

Whatever confusion there'd been concerning his identity, she hadn't shared it. She raised her right hand to press it against her mouth, but in the moment before the gesture was completed, she'd spoken. None of the monitors recorded the sound, but there was no mistaking what she'd said. Two syllables, not four, enunciated with shocked intensity. She had known who he was. "August," she'd said. Not Alex. Not Alexander. Then she bit into her hand, turned to Jeroen Lee, and spoke again from behind that hand, impossible to overhear or see. Lee nodded and joined her at the center of the podium. As events progressed, she moved more into the background while he came forward, but throughout the ensuing commotion she often looked at August.

He stilled the screen and enlarged her image as she watched him, about the time Kolet had offered his support. Why was her mouth so grim? Were there tears in her eyes?

The bedroom door opened. Ahman Penn entered the room. August swiftly closed the screen, but Elector Brauna's image seemed to fade rather than vanish. Penn glanced at it distractedly as he came in, walking with his hands thrust into the pockets of his wide-cut, informal pants. "Don't pay attention to Vincent," he said.

August bowed low, warned by the Ahman's voice that he was irritable. "No, Ahman Penn, I don't."

"Good. They're back from a round of meetings. You're invited to join them for an informal dinner before Kolet and Ash set off again tonight."

"To eat with them?" He didn't want them to watch him eat; he didn't want to see them at it: the opening and shutting of mouths, like fish; the gnashing of teeth as the process of garbage disposal was begun and the rest of the body prepared to treat, like sewage, whatever was entered at the mouth; the stench of food and bodies mixed into an unappetizing olfactory slop—at least he wouldn't be able to smell it. Food was fuel. Meals meant bleak isolation. There was no elegance in either end of the digestive process, and nothing friendly about being watched. "Ahman, I can't do my work if I'm included in such things."

Martin Penn frowned. "Your work has changed. This may sound like an invitation, but consider it an order. Your work is to obey." He thumped his hand against his side. "Come here."

Head slightly down to hide his face, August went to Penn.

"Did you rest? Your fever has lifted." Ahman Penn was clinical rather than sympathetic. "Look at me!"

"Yes, Ahman. Thank you. I rested well."

Penn placed his hands on August's shoulders while he studied the facial sack. Unlike Lee, he didn't touch it, but his grip gradually relaxed as it met with his approval. "You'll be all right, August."

Fear at the combined thought of food and infirmity made August reluctant to ask more about flare. Impulsively, instead he asked, "Sir? Have they located Mei Wang?"

"Do you want to punish her, August? Are you a secret crossman?" Penn's tone was gentle, but amused. "What does revenge accomplish?"

"What's the good of letting her go free? It diminishes the authority of the Electors."

Penn smiled. "An eye for an eye?" With one finger, he pulled at the outer edge of the sack, checking its adhesion to August's skin. It set off a wave of itching along the border, but after Med. Kiani's warnings, August didn't dare scratch. He grimaced, though, through the sack, and Penn stopped.

August hadn't recognized the reference, but he understood the sentiment. "The blindness was my own doing and not permanent, but there should be something done. I know I'm not human."

"*Do* you?" Penn touched August's back in a friendly, if condescending, gesture. "Well, since you are so concerned for the Electors' authority, Mei Wang went to Andia—that is punishment enough if you're not Andian, I understand—and she's been banned from work in any school or Academy under the leadership of the Electors as a result of her theft of you. Delegate Huana's role in the theft is being ignored."

Theft. Not kidnapping. August was jolted by the word, and knew from Penn's expression that he had noticed. "I understand," August said.

"Really? On what do you base that judgment?" Penn gestured at the door. "Come with me, August. The Elector is waiting."

August followed Ahman Penn to a small dining room, wishing with each step that he had an excuse for refusing. Like the rest of the apartment, except Lee's private rooms, it could have been a storage facility for a museum.

The dining room was oval. A gilt fretwork of abstract intertwining shapes encircled the ceiling, and a crystal and gold chandelier hung above the oval table in the room's center. Real flames, partially enclosed behind frosted glass, cast as much shadow as light. Open flame worried August, but no one else—Elector Lee, Margot Ash, and Evan Kolet were already present—seemed concerned. A large side table, bowed to follow the shape of the wall, was on one side of the room, with a chair at either end of it. The curved walls were banded by a continuous window screen. It showed well-crafted images of lush countryside: From one direction a canal, bordered by low grasses and wide trees, extended into the distance. Blending gradually into the canal scene were fields of wheat or corn or some other tall crop— August didn't know the difference. As one turned, it gradu-

ally became apparent that the fields were on a high plateau
and the screen changed to a vista of snowcapped mountains
with a tiny, colorful village perched in the foreground, flags
waving in the bright air, before returning seamlessly to the
canal scene.

Evan Kolet was gazing at the screen view while speaking
in a low voice—August heard mention of Delegate Tana—to
Margot Ash. Elector Lee was on a closed call, but faced into
the room. From what he lip-read, August guessed the Elector's discussion was with Elector Kurioso. Including August
himself, there were four people. Four places were set at the
table, thus Ahman Penn had not been invited. That explained
why he'd been testy.

Kolet noticed August. "Good," he said, smiling easily. "I
hoped you could join us."

Kolet's friendliness was a burden. This was a *Neulander*,
and that name was synonymous with evil. Thickheaded from
his interrupted sleep, confused by Ahman Penn's cryptic remarks, August spoke incautiously. "I would rather have
not."

Jeroen Lee gazed coldly at him. August thought of the
toolmen who disappeared after a word spoken by an Ahman
or Elector; he bowed.

"I told you to ignore Vincent," Ahman Penn said, pitching
his voice toward the others. "I'll change house security, to
keep him out of your room." Lee's attention moved over August's shoulder to Penn, and he frowned—not at Penn but at
the image Penn had conjured, saving August from Elector
Lee's disapproval.

Although grateful, August remembered Vincent, slipping
ever further into disfavor. Toolmen had no families, yet
weren't he and Vincent a kind of relation simply by their or-
igin on the farm? "I apologize. I'm uncomfortable in this situation," he admitted to excuse his impudence, and bowed
generally at them.

"Do you want a drink?" Evan Kolet asked, accepting the
apology nonchalantly. He gestured at eight cut-crystal decanters arranged on the side table. Their contents were a variety of colors from clear, through yellow to brown,
sparkling with rose highlights in the flickering light.

"Is it alcohol?" August asked, stepping forward, reluctantly intrigued. He wished he could smell.

Margot Ash laughed gaily. She and Evan Kolet exchanged amused looks. "Yes," Kolet said. "A little won't hurt you."

"He's medicated. There may be chemical interactions." Ahman Penn put a hand on August's shoulder and drew him farther from Kolet.

Elector Lee stood. "There's no problem, Martin, if August wants a drink."

"What did Kurioso say?" Margot Ash asked Lee.

"He finally agreed. There will be a united front from the Electors after all. August, come here. Thank you, Martin." Lee joined Kolet at the side table, casually dismissing Penn.

Ahman Penn patted August's back gently. "Don't overdo it," he said. "Enjoy yourself." He sounded sincere and unexpectedly affectionate, but there was a brief hesitation before Penn closed the door, as if he hoped to be recalled. It seemed unfair that someone who wanted to be present couldn't exchange places with someone who decidedly did not.

"What would you like?" Kolet was playing host to August. "Margot has wine. Elector Lee and I have been working on the imported whiskey."

August knew about wine. It was contraband for toolmen but of the type probes frequently received as gifts and that Ahman Kiku overlooked—in fact, he had even given wine to his favorite probe bed partner, Claire. "Whiskey," August said, to try something exotic.

Evan Kolet raised an eyebrow. "A man with taste." He poured a golden-brown liquid into a short glass and handed it to August. "Be careful."

August took a sip and didn't taste anything at all. He took another.

"Elector Lee says this is from old Earth," Kolet said. "I've heard that before, but this time I'm inclined to believe it. Smooth."

"It's wasted on August." Elector Lee sipped his own drink, watching August over the rim of his glass. "He can't smell anything or taste much at the moment. Just as well; it would probably be too vivid for him under normal circumstances."

August drank and let the warm sensation envelop his throat. It was soothing. He could follow it as it moved into his stomach and spread over his body, easing the aches and providing an alternative to joining in the conversation.

Kolet leaned slightly against the side table. "Well?"

"It's easy to absorb," August said, which made them laugh. They were ready to indulge him, like a favored pet. All three were in good humor, relaxed in the way of people with work ahead that they anticipated accomplishing easily. August drank down his glass of whiskey. Elector Lee gazed at him like a connoisseur, ready to buy. *You've made him think he can have you,* Vincent had warned. "Elector Brauna rarely drinks alcoholic beverages," August said.

"She wouldn't." Margot Ash swirled the wine in her glass as she spoke the closest thing to criticism he'd heard from her. She was *that* confident. Jeroen Lee glanced at her.

There was subtle music in the room, nearly subliminal. August listened, hearing strings and a low, slow horn. The piece was restful, but intricate, in the elaborate style of Chan. Elector Lee stood. August thought he was going to come over, so August turned to Kolet, extending his glass. "May I have more?"

Kolet turned to Elector Lee. "Is it all right for him?"

The Elector nodded, turning to Margot Ash. Kolet poured a second whiskey for August. "Take this one slower," he advised.

A sub entered through a back door, slicing temporarily through the canal. He carried a beautifully arranged tray of appetizers over his head. There were tiny pieces of cold meats arranged like petals on panels of rice, puffs of moussed vegetables or meat set into tiny shells made of bread, and hard-cooked, multicolored eggs with various fillings. The sub displayed the tray first to Elector Lee, then to the Neulanders before setting it down near the decanters.

"Liang-ban?" Elector Lee offered.

"Beautiful," Ash said to Elector Lee. "This is the style on Chan?" She picked up a small shell.

Lee nodded. "I understand your tastes on Neuland are for a . . . heartier presentation."

"Yes, we're a bit cruder." They laughed together.

"Thank the chef for us," Kolet told the sub, who promptly blushed and fled, closing the door silently behind himself.

August watched the three of them use their fingers to pick up the food, tossing pieces into their open mouths like birds being fed, while commenting on the delicacy of the tastes.

"Try some," Lee ordered when he became aware that August was not eating. The two Neulanders made encouraging comments.

August swallowed bile. "No, thank you," he said. He raised his nearly empty glass. "I'm not hungry."

Jeroen Lee placed a blue egg with a yellow filling, flecked by bits of red, on a cloth napkin and extended it to August. "You don't have to hide hunger. You're not in flare." He turned to Margot Ash. "Probe manners," he said. "They try to outdo each other in lack of interest in food. It becomes more pronounced as they age, but even the children would starve themselves if their food intake wasn't monitored. And August had a nasty shock today. Martin alluded to the possibility of early onset of flare because of the stress created by his injury."

"How likely is that?" Kolet asked sharply.

August took the napkin from the Elector, knowing he would have to eat, distracted by the topic and the need to balance his drink in his other hand. It was difficult to concentrate on so many things occurring all at once.

Lee touched August's arm, steadying him. The contact was delicate, rather than firm, and the combination of power and gentleness sent a tremor through August. "Not terribly," Elector Lee said, "but it's not impossible. Martin was mistaken to mention it. Probes have a tendency toward hypochondria. They'll overanalyze every ache and pain, calculate every morsel they eat. Left alone, August would certainly convince himself that he's in flare." Lee watched as August bit into the egg. "Ramanoot," he said, like an instructor.

The name meant nothing to August, and the pasty filling was gritty between his teeth, the flavor unexpectedly piquant. He ate the remainder, forcing himself to chew when he would rather have spat it out. Lee smiled. August stared into his drink. As soon as they weren't watching, he slipped away to a distance where they couldn't conveniently offer him more food.

"Why do you make toolmen?" Evan Kolet asked, seemingly indifferent, except for the stillness of his posture. "I can see some usefulness, but nothing worth the institutional complexities you've built around no more than a few thousand toolmen of all three kinds—why bother?"

Jeroen Lee sat down at a small side—the head—of the oval table. He sipped his drink. Kolet watched. Lee glanced at August then back to Kolet. "History. Genetic research on human beings has been forbidden ever since the first Electors interpreted Hsu's *General Principles* to mean that the standard human genome was an adequate and proper vehicle through which mankind could explore and understand the universe. I know, Kolet, you Neulanders give the *Principles* a different reading and, frankly, so do I, but until the Bril Wars, biologists had less influence than other scientific disciplines. However, a few Electors have always had some interest in these issues. Toolmen—legal nonhumans—are a compromise solution. If we only wanted services performed, we could clone a few successful types. We use toolmen to test the effect of our genetic tampering on aptitudes, abilities, health—in the case of subs and guardians, since probes are not long-lived—for a variety of purposes. A few select changes have been introduced into our general population, which is one reason the Harmony does so well against outsiders. We're healthier, much longer-lived and more intelligent, on average, than unchanged populations, like those in the Emirates. Neuland does the same, though your testing is open."

"Causing us to be called Altered and not human." Kolet grimaced.

"Yes." Elector Lee watched as a different sub entered. She placed a basket of flat bread and rolls and a plate holding two soft spreads on the table. Her movements were efficient. She seemed oblivious of them, and she left without having spoken or looked up. "Then, too, there are benefits to having personnel in close proximity who are completely loyal—that's a fundamental modification in every toolman—and completely dependent. I keep no one in my household who would do me the slightest harm." He smiled. "Except, at the moment, August. With all probes, of course, the balance between such considerations and their high intelligence and access to information is delicate."

"Ergo, flare," August said, grabbing the back of a chair as he stumbled. He was both appalled and satisfied at having spoken.

Jeroen Lee glanced coolly at him from across the table. "Obviously. Sit down, August, you're drunk."

Margot Ash tittered nervously, despite the Elector's genial tone. Evan Kolet pressed his lips together and looked away.

August wanted to hit someone, hard, but there were no targets that he was capable of striking. Frustrated, he yanked out the chair and sat down. His movements felt loose and wide, but he had no grave difficulty. "Flare made Alexander angry," he said. "Hunger was the starting point for everything he did."

Jeroen Lee had brought several of his liang-ban to the table on a plate. He ate a miniature shell while they waited. "Sanda acted irrationally when she kept Alexander after she knew he was in flare," Lee said. "A probe in flare, particularly an extremely intelligent one with a history of indulgence, is unpredictable and dangerous, though I can understand her reluctance to give up Alexander's work." He nodded in August's direction.

"Do you think that was her reason, Elector?" August leaned forward across the table, unaccountably aggressive. And getting away with it, he noted with satisfaction.

Elector Lee smiled. "You don't. You know them both better than I do. But I believe that Sanda has learned her lesson. What do you think, August?"

August stared like a child at the farm brought up short by some new lesson of his teachers. Lee was far ahead of him. "I don't know," he mumbled, turning away. "It doesn't matter."

Jeroen Lee gestured graciously at the Neulanders. "Be seated Evan, Margot. I know you have work ahead of you tonight, unlike August and me, who can indulge ourselves a bit."

Like wards separating two Rangeball captains, though they were the only vacant places, Evan Kolet and Margot Ash took the chairs between August and Jeroen Lee. Immediately the second sub reappeared with a soup tureen and bowls. She ladled a thick, green soup to each of them, beginning with Elector Lee and ending with August. It was full of brown lumps.

"Neuland hummer soup," Ash said, inhaling. "How thoughtful."

August stared down at it, then pushed it away, toward the center of the table, inadvertently spilling some on the white linen. The sub hesitated—she'd been on her way out the door—and looked at Jeroen Lee for orders.

"I'll throw it up," August said, glad he couldn't smell it.

"Remove it," Jeroen Lee directed her. To August, in precisely the same tone, he said, "Eat some bread."

Mechanically, August reached for a roll and took a bite,

then recognized his automatic response. Dog training. "What world is that?" he asked, to change the subject, and inclined his head toward the window screen canal.

"Darien, isn't it?" Margot Ash answered quickly. "They were our largest trading partner in the Harmony twenty-three years ago."

"They still are." Kolet sounded eager to talk. "I've visited, more or less incognito, recruiting workers. We have an understanding with Darien's government: As long as we're circumspect, they leave us alone to make what deals we can. After all, a good percentage of Darien's population has relatives on Neuland." He glanced at the window screen as a green and blue bat-shaped creature flew across the canal. "That's an excellent simulation of the Lake Daniel uplands, but then, all your window screens are extraordinary. Our artists have to concentrate on single frame, or static displays. No one can afford to hire them for a project that will take months to complete."

"Yes, it's Darien, though I've never been there." Elector Lee looked displeased with the conversation. "One of my toolmen chose the screen; he has a knack for it. Toolmen rarely leave Sucre," Elector Lee continued, "but this commission will be a major event. Perhaps I'll take August with me to Neuland. Would you like that, August?"

August looked down. "You mean, will I truly enter your service?" He took another bite of the chewy bread. "Dogs don't change masters very easily. Nor guinea pigs."

"You don't really have a choice." Elector Lee frowned at Evan Kolet, then turned back to August. "I've been gentle with you on the subject. I recognize that you've been hurt in more ways than that burn, and I prefer your willing cooperation. However, the longer you are in my household—I objected to your original presence, after all—the less likely that I will let you leave it. One way or another."

"You wanted me drunk." August pointed a finger at Jeroen Lee. The broad gesture seemed funny, something Huana would do.

"I wanted to give you a decent meal. You began the rest of this." Elector Lee spooned soup to his mouth, clearly pleased as he watched August.

Kolet stood. "August will be my guest if he comes to Neuland," he said. "Whatever his motives, if he had walked into the Grand Assembly with his own face, the emotional impact would have been quite different. There would have been a vote, and Margot and I would be on our way home empty-handed."

"Don't interfere, Evan." Ash stared down at the table.

Kolet hesitated, then sighed. "I apologize sir," he said. "I appreciate that you are a great supporter of Neuland, one we could not do without, but I find this discussion offensive. I consider August something of an ally. I dislike death threats, however veiled, however softly spoken, when directed so . . . inequitably." He bowed at Elector Lee and avoided looking at August. "Perhaps it would be best if we left."

"No, please stay," August said hastily, not relishing being alone with Jeroen Lee. He held his head in his hands, his elbows resting on the table, careful not to touch his face. His mind had become as fuzzy as his eyesight. If drink hadn't insulated him, he would have been terrified. "Elector Lee has only stated the obvious. He needs to be certain I won't disturb the Electors' plans, as Alexander did, or use my presence here to his disadvantage." August looked at Elector Lee, not Kolet. "I'm a toolman, and not accustomed to making promises or arrangements for myself, but as long as Elector Brauna doesn't directly order it, I pledge that I will not act against your personal interests. Can that be enough?" His face throbbed, the most sensation he'd felt in it since awakening in the hospital.

"For now, that will be enough," Jeroen Lee said simply. He smiled broadly, almost grinning, with pride as well as triumph in his eyes, then, like a curtain dropping, he was the stern Elector Lee again.

Kolet resumed his seat without speaking as the female serving sub entered and cleared away the soup. Only Jeroen Lee had eaten much. Another sub brought plates of steaming meat in a red berry sauce, with squash that had the consistency of pudding. Cut fruit artfully arranged into a garden picture, with birds and a bright orange sun was the only item reflecting Lee's apparent sensibilities, and not the Neulander's. August ate nothing, and only stared down at the plate.

"You'll feel better soon," Lee said, breaking the silence. Lee signaled the sub, and she removed August's plate.

"I designed him," Lee told Kolet. "I am less interested in strict obedience than others who tinker with probes; that should tell you something. However, I can't afford to be a fool; neither can Neuland. August is no ally. He's a tool, and it's vital to know who is wielding him. Unfortunately, at the moment no one is. Sanda is afraid, and I don't have his allegiance."

"Elector," August said, then stopped, uncertain what he wanted to say. They were waiting. "I won't put you at risk. Thank you."

Jeroen Lee nodded gravely. "That's the second time I've acted against my own interests regarding you, August. See that you remember it."

Ting Wheeling was outside the dining room. "You didn't call," he said dolefully as August followed the others from the room.

"There was no need." August sat on a handy chair, one of several interspersed along the wide hallway, and watched Jeroen Lee stride toward his office. The Neulanders—Evan Kolet glanced backward and winked—were leaving the apartment to visit more World Delegations.

"I can't keep you safe if I'm not with you," Ting complained.

August pressed his hands against his knees. His head was clearing, but his body ached and his face throbbed. Lee intended to keep him. Vincent had warned him; Ahman Penn knew it, and August was a fool to think otherwise. The dinner proved it. Jeroen Lee was a fisherman, reeling in his catch with care. If she never saw him again, Sanda Brauna would believe she'd been correct to give him to Elector Lee. Ting would eventually be withdrawn. There was even his own suspect gratitude to Lee to consider. He must act now or allow it to happen. "Can you open this apartment's door by yourself?" he asked Ting. "It's urgent that I see her." Recklessness was the hallmark of his line.

Ting didn't hesitate. "I can get us out."

Not by his handprint, then. Probably with alarms sent to Elector Lee. If August was going to prevent a second "theft" of Elector Brauna's property then he'd best act now, when the Elector expected him to be lulled by drink, conversation, and his own promises. "Let's go!" He stood, motioned Ting ahead, and followed the swift pace Ting set.

How did this conform to the pledge he'd just given Elector Lee? That troubled him, but he had to be faithful to Sanda Brauna above all else. Uneasy with the rationalization, August told himself that, while contrary to Lee's orders, escape wouldn't harm Elector Lee's legitimate interests.

He had to act. Lee was convinced of the inevitability of August's entry into his service, and August respected that man's opinions. Elector Brauna had to be reminded of August's loyalty. *Ah love.* August hurried to keep pace with Ting.

They went through an enamel-walled kitchen as large as the entire toolman kitchen, but this was only for one man. It was busy, with eight subs and a human chef cleaning and eating leftovers. The female sub of a few minutes earlier looked up from scraping a pan and bobbed her head at August. The chef stared, but did nothing. Ting led August through a back door into a narrow hall lined with shelves of supplies. "Through here," Ting said. "Service door."

Behind them, someone was running.

A small door, scuffed where boxes had bumped it over years of use, was set into the wall. August signaled it open, but it was secure; Ting put a hand on it, and it swung wide. Such a simple thing.

Shouting came from the kitchen. "Go!" Ting said, looking over his shoulder.

August hunched over—he was too tall for the door—and went through, entering a brightly lit service corridor. Ting came behind.

"Stop!" someone shouted from inside Elector Lee's apartment. August's heart quickened; he was committed to the plan.

"Go left, left, right, and to the third door," Ting said. His voice was calm. "I'll catch up."

August ran. The service door closed, cutting off the sound of pursuit, but Ting stood outside it, waiting for Elector Lee's guardians, his body the only barrier between August and capture as a traitor to both Elector Brauna and Elector Lee—because unless Elector Brauna claimed him and ratified his actions, that was what he had become.

The corridor was low, more of a tunnel than the routes Ting usually took, and August couldn't stand without scraping his head. He ran hunched over, listening for noises of a struggle and hearing nothing but his own footsteps. The place was a honeycomb of doors and passages, a second city where subs made their lives like mice within Center's walls.

August turned left at the first passage. He recognized nothing, and there were no signs. He turned at the next intersection. A sub was up the side passage, carrying something small. When she saw August, she stared and dropped her bundle, or rather, it leaped out of her hands—a kitten, either a mouser or a pet.

August strained but, unusually for a probe, was uncertain if the shouting behind him was real or his imagination. He pushed himself, panting, to run faster, but it was hard in a crouch.

There was a right turn. He took it. One door. Two. Just as he reached the third door he became positive that the pounding was not his heart, that someone moving more quickly than he could was coming after him and gaining. He hesitated a fraction of an instant, wondering if it was Ting, then his hand closed on the doorknob. It twirled uselessly in his hand, not opening. He yanked on it. It moved again, but the door did not. Had he made a wrong turn? He pounded with his free hand, screaming for help as he tugged on the useless knob. They would drag him back in disgrace. He wished he had never begun.

Ting rounded the corner. "Move!"

August jumped out of the way. Ting ran to the door, grabbed the knob, and in one easy motion opened the door. Another toolman guardian came around the corner, limping.

Ting grabbed August's shoulder and shoved him through. August fell into a narrow hallway virtually identical with the one they'd left behind in Jeroen Lee's apartment. Ting rushed inside after him and swung around, pushing at the door, hurrying it closed. The beat of unbalanced footsteps rang behind them, then cut off as the door snapped shut just before Lee's guardian arrived.

August scrambled to his feet and backed away from the door.

Ting extended his hand and made the signal "wait," then squeezed August's arm. "Service doors open *out* to all guardians and subs, but no door opens *in* except with proper security. We're home safe." He grinned like a boy. "Fun."

Home.

Tane Strong sprinted into the narrow hallway. "Sunroom," he said. "Now!"

Chapter 11

Mei Wang's utility desk had been removed from the sunroom; a hole like an eyeless socket gaped where it had been. Just there stood Sanda Brauna, feet planted apart like on a ship at sea. "Why are you here? You knew he was to stay away." She spoke only to Ting Wheeling.

August almost knelt to her. The gesture seemed right—*Ah, love*—it had been so long since he had seen her, and so much had occurred, that he yearned to display his feelings, but Evan Kolet had knelt to Huana too recently and made the gesture hollow. August bowed instead, though that was painfully formal. Beside him, Ting copied the obeisance, then stared down at the dirt floor, clasping his hands together, visibly frightened. He had displeased the Elector by obeying August. "Elector Brauna, please let me explain," August said, a bit unsettled by the depth of hostility in their reception.

"You! Be quiet unless I speak to you!" She didn't look at him. "Ting Wheeling! I expected better service from you."

Inarticulate Ting could never answer her. August stepped forward despite her order. "Ting has guarded me continuously, every day for six years, Elector. I told him to bring me to you."

She whirled on August, then hesitated, glancing at Ting. Time passed without another outbreak of her temper. Finally she went to her usual lounging chair and sat down on its edge. "You mean he guards you. He doesn't obey me."

August shook his head, but made the denial a submissive one. "I only mean that Ting believes I am loyal exclusively to you, Elector, as I surely am. He knows I would never harm you, and he assumes that when I say I need to see you, then it is true."

Her fingertips were white as she gripped the arm of the lounger; her lips were a thin red line; her eyes were hidden by a slender band of shadow cast by a pole plant. Other shadows fell like bars around the clearing, or like ribs encasing Sanda Brauna's human heart. Dressed in her bloodred Electors' robe, the image seemed apt. "Well?" she said. "Why did you run from Elector Lee's apartment like a criminal escaping jail?"

He swallowed hard, fearful of claiming an undue intimacy with her. "Elector Lee intended to keep me, Elector Brauna. I believed I had some value to you and that this was the last opportunity you would have to prevent my . . . loss."

She raised her eyes to study his ruined face, frowning, not meeting his eyes. "Inconsequential. I'm appalled at your poor judgment. Alex never miscalculated so badly."

He remembered that first drop of boiling water, balanced, waiting to fall. Love was a decision he had made, an unswerving, limitless loyalty. August gathered in his fear, silenced all doubts. He would go beyond Alexander. "I love you, Elector. Perhaps that affects my judgment. I would do anything for you."

"Stop! I can recognize a facilitation."

"But do you recognize me? Have you ever? I'm not Alexander."

'I know that." Her hands chopped the air, agitated, in a wild version of the basic negation signal. "Don't you think it's obvious enough?"

Just as Huana had lifted the fog from August's mind regarding Alexander, so Sanda Brauna's terse question cleared his thoughts of the cloud of misinterpretation—of wishful thinking—that years of loneliness had wrought. The boldness that had been the last manifestation of Elector Lee's alcohol vanished as he realized for the first time in his life that the reason for her melancholy regarding him might not be that she saw Alexander in his face, but that she did not. It took great effort to speak. "If you don't want me, why did you have me made?"

She looked at Ting, as if the explanation was for him. "I didn't. Twenty-two years ago Jeroen Lee commissioned a clone of Alexander. He's on his way here to collect you now."

August stood in a classic, motionless probe pose, trying to absorb the changed foundation of his universe. His one comfort—that she wanted him; that she had brought him into being—was gone, and the base cut from the entire edifice of loyalty and love he'd built.

"Once you were here," she continued, "I couldn't bear the thought of not having you. Jeroen found it convenient to indulge my weakness. Perhaps the expectation of it is why you exist; that would be in character for him." She stood up, smoothing her robe with her hands. "But you have never been Alexander. It was obvious from your first days in Center; you were so serious and sad. Alex smiled and teased, he was lively and took liberties as though they were his right, but he never overstepped himself with these . . . theatrics, as you have." She paused, reminiscing, then sighed. "But you are so nearly Alex . . . I refused to let Jeroen take you; besides, it's always good to own something that man wants." She turned away, looking out at the patches of Sucre's gray-blue sky—it was either dawn or dusk—visible through the foliage. "It would be so easy, but I refuse to let myself be hurt again. I refuse to care, then watch you die."

"I'm not dying, Elector! I have twelve years." He moved tentatively closer. Her straight back concealed the loss and pain he'd seen so many times in her lovely, youthful face. Perhaps all that she had said was an excuse for mitigating her own pain. "Please don't send me away from you."

She didn't turn. "You're in flare."

"No! Elector Lee said I wasn't. I'm a probe. I would have known if he had lied." August grimaced, though, as he remembered Lee's comments: *Secrets aren't impossible, only very difficult.* And: *Alexander was actually better than August.*

Sanda Brauna turned back to him. "He did? He lied to me?"

Confused and uncertain, August didn't answer.

"That bastard!" she exclaimed, without noticing August's hesitation. Her hands clenched into tight balls. "He said you were dying. He convinced me we should use you against Huana. He claimed I'd inadvertently let you know about the flare, and that we shouldn't meet." She laughed gaily. "As if *he* is more experienced at keeping secrets! And since when do I take orders from Jeroen Lee? What was I thinking?" She smiled at August, but he was uncertain she saw him. "He won't get away with this."

August wet his lips. "Elector, perhaps he was able to fool me. I can't be sure."

She shook her head. "Well, I am. He's wanted you for years—he wanted Alex!—and this is his plan because I re-

fused to let him have you. No! I should have known he's
never generous without a reason."

Was everything so calculated? The catastrophe of learning
that Elector Brauna hadn't created him, and didn't truly want
him, was lost in this confusion of motivation and method.

Her expression briefly changed as she concentrated on
something the house system sent her. "He's arrived," she
said. "Tane is bringing Jeroen here now." She gestured.
"Move away."

August bowed, then went to where Ting still stood, a
properly subordinate toolman. What did he think of all this?

Very shortly, Tane announced Elector Lee and walked be-
hind him down the dirt path and into the sunroom clearing.
Lee passed August with a brief glance and went to Sanda
Brauna. "What was his excuse?"

"He had something important to tell me about you." She
signaled, and Tane left the sunroom. Ting became more
alert.

"What did he say?" Elector Lee sounded more angry than
concerned, but August suspected Lee was an excellent actor.

"Elector Lee has secrets," August said, wondering about
Jeroen Lee's family. Every human had some relative: surviv-
ing parents, siblings, cousins, children, a partner, or, unusually inside the Academies, since divorce was so exceptional,
a spouse. Elector Brauna had a brother she rarely saw. Lee
had no one.

Elector Brauna frowned, but Lee looked at August and
chuckled. "So do we all."

"What secrets?" Sanda turned to August for an answer.

He bowed at Elector Lee. "I have tried not to know."

"That must have been difficult for you." Jeroen Lee
tapped the toe of his right shoe against the dusty soil floor,
then stopped and looked at Sanda Brauna. "I'll take him
now and deal with this myself."

"You lied to me," she accused Lee. "If he was in flare,
you couldn't have kept it a secret from him during a direct
discussion. I remember Alex."

Lee looked from Sanda to August and back to Sanda. He
shook his head. "You never learn. This isn't Alexander, and
yes, I managed to keep the secret. Ten minutes alone together, and you've undone all my work of disguising his
symptoms from him. Alexander proved that a probe who
knows he's in flare can be the most dangerous force in Cen-

ter. If anything, August is less controllable than Alexander ever was and infinitely less predictable. He's been alone too much, and thanks to your mismanagement he thinks like a human, not a toolman. Now that you've told him, August must be put down."

"No!" Ting spoke so unexpectedly, even August was startled. "I won't do it!"

Jeroen Lee stared at Ting, then turned to Sanda, looking grimly amused. "This is a madhouse. And *I'm* called liberal. Toolmen obey or they're useless. If August is in flare, he's worse than useless, he's a hazard."

"If?" August walked back toward the center of the clearing.

"Which is it, Jeroen?" Sanda had venom in her voice. "I have much less interest in this Neuland matter than you seem to have. I want the truth about August, or I will immediately and publicly withdraw my support for the Commission to Investigate Neuland. I think that would cause some confusion during the vote tomorrow."

Lee made a conciliatory gesture, extending his hands. "I'm honestly not yet certain, Sanda. I suspect flare. There is a strong likelihood after such a trauma, but it's too early to be sure the stress-induced changes—which *do* exist—are permanent." He looked regretfully at August. "Now that he knows, there is no possibility of a covert cure. I've hoped to avoid it, but he should be put down."

"You won't touch him!"

"He's in *my* service. Be reasonable. You'll overcome whatever attachment you feel. You did the other time, and you had fifteen years with that one."

Sanda Brauna's face was red. "Get out, Jeroen."

"With my property. August is registered to me."

They glared at each other in wordless dueling in which August was a pawn or a prize, but in any case, not real. He couldn't watch silently while others decided his fate, so he said, "I give you my word, Elector Lee, never to use anything I might have learned in your apartment to your disadvantage."

Lee turned slowly to him, breaking the deadlock with Brauna. "Your word? I've seen what that's worth."

"I ran away. I didn't harm you."

Lee indicated Sanda Brauna. "The harm occurred."

"Because you were not honest with me or Elector Bra-

una." August bowed, to give himself a moment. He was
trembling. His body ached, and he wanted to have this done
so he could rest. In the moment Lee had turned to him, August knew the scene was acting, something to be gotten
through. Jeroen Lee didn't truly want August put down, and
he wouldn't remove August from Sanda Brauna's service if
he felt safe. Lee only needed to preserve his privacy and his
dignity. "I respect you, Elector Lee. I will not act against
your interests willingly. I will not act against you at all unless you harm Elector Brauna." After speaking, August realized it was a larger promise than he had made before; it
implied he would disregard Elector Brauna's orders.

Sanda Brauna scowled at August, but was silent.

Jeroen Lee grinned. He looked like a different man then,
reckless and young. He bowed, perhaps mockingly, at August.
"All right, Sanda, you and your . . . colleague win. Based on
these assurances, I won't demand the return of my difficult
property, and I won't insist that he be put down. But be careful, this isn't a tame toolman you have here; August isn't
Alexander. Alexander had an easy life, respected as the best
probe we had, and treated accordingly. Thanks to you, August
has lived quite differently. And as for you, August, don't think
I'll hesitate if I consider my interests are in any jeopardy whatsoever. See that you continue 'not to know.'"

"Ting will see you out, Jeroen."

Lee laughed. "And I'll be sure to tell the Neuland supplicants of your continuing support." He nodded at August as
if he were human, even nodded at Ting, then turned on his
heel and left, still smiling.

Sanda Brauna signaled Ting to leave, then looked doubtfully at August once they were alone. "From now on, don't
speak so freely."

"Yes, Elector." It was a fundamental probe rule, to avoid interactions, but the circumstances had demanded he do more. He
bowed, though, and didn't explain, wanting to appease her.

She exhaled heavily. "If Jeroen Lee has important secrets,
then I want to know them."

August felt a tightening of his stomach. He had no rights,
no ability to deny her anything. There was always Security
ready to cut into his mind. His only safety lay in her personal morality and his ignorance. Elector Lee had known

that, and he had left. August's fear receded. "I don't know any of Elector Lee's secrets."

"You know that they exist, and that's more than sufficient for someone of your ability to ferret them out; I knew Alex. Don't believe Lee won't act against you as soon as Neuland's aid is established. Your only safety is in telling me what he doesn't want me to know. I'll use it to protect you."

"Elector Lee said I'd be safe as long as I was ignorant."

"Nonsense. We are Jonists. Knowledge is always more valuable than faith."

She was sincere. His promise, a toolman's word, to Elector Lee meant nothing to her or anyone, except to Lee himself. Still, there seemed no reason to argue. He *didn't* know anything, and he would try not to seek the knowledge out. He bowed low and said, "You're correct, of course, Elector."

For the first time since he'd entered the sunroom, she smiled. "Good, August. I worried that Jeroen had undermined your loyalty to me." She walked to where he stood, near the center of the clearing, and touched his arm, her fingers pressing into his flesh more aggressively than affectionately, although her hand was warm. She released him. "I've missed having a companion who thinks. Alex was the same, forthright. I've missed . . . Well . . . You must learn when to be silent."

"I haven't had an opportunity to spend time among others." His tone was self-deprecating, so she wouldn't interpret the comment as criticism, but he wanted, once, to say it.

She nodded. Looking at his hands rather than his face, she said, "Is Jeroen sleeping with that Neulander general, Kolet, or with the woman?"

August laughed at the unexpectedness of the image, then stopped at Sanda's frown. This didn't seem to fall into the category of a secret. "No. Neither. In fact, although they work well together, Kolet and the Elector dislike each other. Kolet is too blunt, often flippant and, I'd guess, inflexibly heterosexual. Margot Ash is prim and an ascetic. For their part, both Neulanders react as if they think Elector Lee is arrogant and secretive."

"Which he is," she said, smiling. "Does he have a private arrangement with Neuland?"

August wanted to sit down. "Not that I'm aware of, Elector," he said, letting fatigue into his voice since he didn't have a facial expression with which to cue her. "Like you, Elector Lee worries that Neuland will do something to jeopardize their request for aid. The Neulanders don't understand his motives for helping them. They're extremely wary. They definitely don't act as if they have any hold over the Elector. I don't believe there's a secret."

"Interesting." She went to her lounger and sat down, motioning August to come to her and making room for him at its foot. He sat heavily, his legs aching. "Do you need a medic?" she asked, drawing away slightly.

He straightened his back from its slump. "I'm just tired." So close, human eyes were not much of a disadvantage. He studied her without seeming to do so, since she disliked being surveyed. Her white hair was beautiful, juxtaposed against her dark skin. The ends curled at her shoulders, where they came loose from her workaday bun. Her smile could be warm and lovely. He wished he could smell her. During their occasional interviews, she'd had a violet fragrance that hadn't seemed entirely a perfume.

"Why *does* Jeroen favor Neuland?"

He wished she'd stop testing the limits of his promise to Elector Lee, but he knew nothing confidential and so he answered. "I'm not certain, but his support of Altereds is well-known and goes back to the very beginning of his career. I think, Elector Brauna, he simply believes Neulanders are human and an asset to the Harmony, all things considered."

Her expression turned sour. "A pure motive from him? Jeroen is too intelligent to be that virtuous."

Now that he was free of Jeroen Lee, August was also free to acknowledge that he liked him. Elector Lee had treated him as a definite inferior, but no more so than he treated everyone, and without condescension. For all that Lee spoke of putting him down and called August "difficult property," Lee always behaved as if August was worthy of respect.

August looked out at the sky. It was unchanged, as if the sun had been made to stand still. He tried to smile—grimaced probably—at the fantasy, for that was what it was. "Time's winged chariot" hurried even on Sucre. The long days were an illusion. He was a probe. Twelve years and he would die. Twelve years at best.

"What are you thinking?" she asked, softer voiced than before.

He looked back at her, embarrassed, but quoted,

"Thus, though we cannot make our sun
Stand still, yet we will make him run."

She smiled and took his hand. "Quite a different attitude from Alexander's. He spoke of raging against the dying of the light."

"It's precisely the same attitude, Elector," he unthinkingly corrected her, feeling a moment's elusive kinship with Alexander.

She tilted her head slightly to one side and studied his grotesque face. "Perhaps."

The scene was becoming unreal. The shadows of the pole plants, reduced by their loss of color in the weak light to an abstraction of shape, encircled the clearing. They framed a barrier between the two of them and the vastness of Sucre. The garden's stillness—he remembered the skittering of Sucre's creatures and the sound of dogs in that other clearing—added to the sense of the fantastic. "Elector, is it dawn or dusk?"

She smiled. "Dusk. But dawn always follows." More briskly she said, "Charles calculates that the Assembly will approve this commission to Neuland."

That reference was purposeful. "Yes, I agree," he said mildly, bracing himself for a new despair.

"He does good work," she said, "but I don't need three probes in my service, and you work well with Ellen. I'll keep her, rather than Charles, if you wish. Her misbehavior with Huana is at an end." Sanda's smile included him.

"Elector! Yes—I would prefer Ellen. Thank you!"

She hugged him lightly, careful of his face. "Good. Go rest, August. Go to my room." She looked down the path Jeroen Lee had taken. "I intend to keep you close from now on."

"I can't believe I'm still here," Ellen said, "and that you are." She studied his face dispassionately, as one more bit of data to record, then suddenly grinned. "Poor Charles! What a comedown. Ahman Kiku assigned him to research."

"Charles didn't do anything wrong." August felt compelled to defend Charles, who from being congratulated as among the luckiest of toolmen, to have entered an Elector's personal service, was now uniformly regarded as a failure. "She only said she didn't need three probes."

Across the dining room, Vincent whispered with Beatrice, Lee's junior probe, but didn't take his eyes away from August. Apparently August's departure hadn't ended the problems Vincent had with Elector Lee. For the first time in his life, other probes had begun to interact with August, but Vincent's grudge against him was making everyone choose sides.

"Thank you," Ellen said earnestly. "I thought I was farm bait for sure." She politely averted her eyes as August took another sausage from the provider, but Vincent did not. August tried not to let the observation embarrass him.

"It doesn't matter what we do." August spoke his sedition softly, only for Ellen, and he lowered his face so no one could lip-read without a monitor close-up. "We aren't human, so we have no responsibility for our actions." Or credit either. August was exactly where he'd always wanted to be—close to Sanda Brauna and accepted by other toolmen— but being there was elusively unsatisfying.

Ellen, a skillful probe, showed nothing of what she felt, but leaned to whisper in his ear. "Don't say things like that! Vincent would love to report something to Ahman Kiku."

"Let him." August sat back in the chair and glared at Vincent, annoyed by his fuzzy vision, which seemed to reduce the intensity of his glower. Med. Kiani had promised that his eyes would be ready before August left for Neuland with Elector Brauna. He raised his voice. "If Vincent so much as touches me, Elector Lee would put him down."

Vincent stood. From across the room, he said, "Elector Lee let you return to Elector Brauna. He doesn't give a crossman's prayer about what happens to you, Greeneyes. Oh, excuse me. Yours are still shit-brown."

August tried to smirk. This facial sack had some movement in it, unlike the first one, but not enough for scorn. The "Greeneyes" annoyed him—Alexander's nickname. He pretended to speak to Ellen. "If his mind was as well designed as his pretty face, Vincent might realize it's Elector Brauna who would care, and that she would blame Elector Lee. Lee would send him to the farm just to mollify her; he's tired of Vincent, anyway."

"You're right," Ellen said, her eyes twinkling. She'd chosen her side. "I bet Elector Brauna would even insist on sending him to Security first."

Someone laughed.

"I'll outlive you, Shit-Eyes, without doing a thing. You're hungry, aren't you? It's going to get worse." He chuckled, his voice much too loud in the dead silence that fell in the room.

"Shut up, Vincent, and sit down," said James Reader finally. He was in general service and over thirty.

August was frozen, staring at his plate. It was empty, except for half of the sausage he'd just taken, his third. How had he failed to notice his hunger? Had he suppressed acknowledgment of it? Or was it just chance that he'd eaten so much?

"They were talking," Vincent taunted him. "Ahman Penn says it's too bad. He predicts you'll go quick."

James Reader stood up, followed by several other probes. "Some things just aren't said," James hissed at Vincent. "Never. You sit and you be quiet, or I'll call Security on you myself!"

August stood, too. He surveyed the room, seeing the other probes' dismay. They understood how he felt from their own long anticipation. August used all his skill, blessing his luck that his face was so inexpressive. "I guess you've forgotten what it's like to have a long night with an Elector, Vincent," he said.

The others hesitated, wanting to believe him. He was *twenty-one*! No one expected flare at twenty-one. He never would have done so, except for Ahman Penn.

"I'm not so insecure that I have to weigh every portion I eat," he continued. "I have twelve years, Vincent. I'm a clone, remember?" He laughed. It sounded completely natural, he thought. "Besides, Med. Kiani *ordered* me to eat like this, to help myself to heal." Around the room the other probes relaxed, but no matter what he said, no matter how skillfully he strained the truth, from now on they'd all be watching. "You're so inept, Vincent, that you misunderstood Ahman Penn. It was you he meant would go quick—straight to the farm if you continue this obsession with me instead of doing your work for your Elector. What's left of it. I hear you're in quarters every night."

Ellen clapped her hands. August couldn't tell if she was convinced or only pretending to be. Others, anxious to believe, followed her lead. Vincent flushed, further demeaning himself. He jerked his head at Beatrice. She glanced back unhappily at the rest of them, but she'd always been more

Vincent's companion than Elector Lee's, so she followed Vincent out.

August sat down and pointedly finished eating the sausage, chatting with Ellen about those chosen to accompany the Electors during the upcoming trip with CIN. His mouth was dry. The sausage tasted like paper, but he ate every bit of it, smiling and apparently at ease. Sanda Brauna hadn't wanted him when she thought he was in flare. She was afraid to watch him die. She hadn't helped Alexander, though he'd spent fifteen years in her service and she loved him. She wouldn't help August. If she was certain now, she'd send him to the farm. He must keep this a secret from her for a few more days, until after they were on their way to Neuland. There was no farm on Neuland.

"Another?" Ellen giggled and offered him a sausage still left untouched on her plate.

August smiled. "I think I've had enough."

It was implicit in the Harmony's condemnation of Alexander that cure was possible; Elector Lee had said as much himself. Certainly, with their medical expertise, Neulanders could cure flare. "I think I'll ask Elector Brauna if I can have my new eyes dyed blue," August said quietly to Ellen. "I'm tired of parallels with Alexander. I would never, ever do what he did, and I want that clear to everyone, since we'll be on Neuland."

Ellen looked at him quizzically, then looked away. "I understand what you mean," she said. She touched his hand, turning back to him. He'd never seen such depth in her eyes before, never noticed her so distinctly as a person. "I'll make my reports as accurate as possible. No hints or innuendo, unless they're completely verified. Come on. Let's get to the Grand Assembly before the Delegates arrive for the session." She wasn't allowed near Huana without supervision.

He had the freedom of movement he'd never had before. He had friends, though he trusted only Ting Wheeling and Ellen. Though he didn't know quite why, Sanda Brauna kept him at her side. He wanted his twelve years, but he was not Alexander. Under no circumstances would he make an illicit pact with Neulanders—or anyone—in exchange for his life. He stood up, put his plate in the disposer, and smiled as he passed the others on his way out of the room, still hungry.

PART THREE
●
NEULAND

A Sufficient Quantity
of Secrets

Chapter 12

Evan Kolet coughed politely as he left the paved path and joined August on the beach, although the sound of pebbles scattered by his footfalls would have alerted August to his arrival anyway. August looked up from watching the tall waves break against the shore and turned around. Since it was Kolet and he was alone, August didn't bother to bow low. "Before coming to Neuland, I thought all beaches were sand."

Kolet smiled. "In Romoa they're stone. The current shifted about ten years ago and washed away the sand. The alans gloat that it's a sign from Allah." He kicked at the pebbles with the toe of his boot, sending some clattering down to splash into the water.

Out to sea, perhaps a kilometer distant, there was another island, much larger than the one containing the Hotel Romoa complex, which had been taken over by the Harmony: the three visiting Electors and, in a separate wing, the five Assembly World Delegates who comprised the Committee to Investigate Neuland, together with their respective entourages and the soldiers from the Harmony battleship *Guide* sent down to guard them all. On that other island, tall blocks of multicolored pastel buildings hugged the long shoreline, except at one end where jagged structures—with no sign of current or even recent work—open to the air and abandoned unfinished, gave the coast a forsaken appearance. Beyond that island, faint even to August's vision, was yet another. Zigzagging bridges linked these and others to form Romoa, the eighteen-island capital city of Neuland. The metal strands of the bridges gleamed in the morning light, reflecting the many, often crowded buildings, and throwing rainbow colors into the sky. The water was a clear, bright, sparkling blue; just beneath the surface, buttercup fish swam and jealson wriggled. A harvester seal lurched ashore and contentedly began to munch the pungy grass growing at the sea's high-water margin.

Wind blew August's hair back from his face. He took a deep breath, smelling the moldering air, with its salty sea tang. The harvester seal's odor was cutting, like lemon. Polish and soap marked Kolet's position. It was wonderful to smell again, wonderful to use his own eyes to see, wonderful to be alive, despite his hunger. He had everything he'd ever wanted, and he refused to resent that hunger or Sanda's disheartening inconsistencies. "You can see forever," he said. "I never visited a glade on Sucre, but in the Green your view is no farther than whatever space has been cleared, and Center is all walls. I never imagined anywhere I'd like this much."

"I'm glad to have your good opinion—don't misunderstand—but the reactions of the five Delegate-Commissioners, at least the four besides Esteban Huana, are more pressing." Kolet crossed the few remaining steps to where August stood. "How are we doing? What will they recommend to the Grand Assembly?"

August moved away from the water to meet Kolet. "You know I won't tell you anything."

"And you know I'll ask." Kolet clasped his hands behind his back and stared out over his city. "Well, inflation has been down since the Commission arrived; people are more confident of survival. The oddsmakers are busy, and the bets are heavy in favor of our getting aid."

"Gambling?" Jon Hsu had frowned on games of chance, although they existed, well regulated, even inside the Harmony.

Kolet shrugged. "Everyone bets on their vision of the future, one way or another. Some of my men are even betting their sledge, their basic wage, on the Harmony. After all, if we lose, we're probably dead anyway. But we think we have the vote of everyone but Huana, and he'll be discounted back at Center. We hope." He smiled a question at August.

August assumed a proper probe pose, motionless, expressionless, a void. Kolet chuckled, glanced at August in the outdoor light, then looked closer at his face. "They did as good a reconstruction as any Neuland medic, and medicine is our specialty—it's our only export item now. You healed fast, too. Longer than one of us, but not by as much as I'd thought."

To change the subject, August said, "I never understood patriotism before, but I think I could love this place."

"A world is more than a landscape, but yes, Neuland is beautiful. I told you so. I never lie to my friends."

A patched, but dainty, fisher's skimmer glided through the strait between the hotel and other islands like a dancer skipping across a watery stage while holding a glistening parasol—the solar collectors. As it passed, a woman on the upper deck waved at them. Kolet lazily returned the wave without apparent recognition, then returned to questioning August. "What about Elector Brauna? Does she like Neuland? Can you tell me anything? We don't have your system of constant spying."

August laughed. Every night when the Neulander servitors were gone, Tane debugged Elector Brauna's suite. There was always something. Whatever Neuland's usual procedure, this was too important to leave to chance. "Last night Elector Brauna said the weather here was good."

Kolet shook his head, grinning. "Every winter it gets cold enough that the sea freezes between several of the islands. We have a local festival called the 'Water-Walk.' Half of Romoa gets frostbite; I lost my nose to it when I was ten. Grandmother Talia wouldn't let my mother punish me. She said the frostbite was mother's fault for not letting me progress into an adult monitor sooner. I'd refused to wear my headband out with friends. You've seen them on young children—the medical condition monitors that wrap around the head so adults can read them easier?"

August nodded, considering this new perspective on Talia Kaviscu. No one in the Harmony thought of her as an indulgent grandmother. He wanted to give Evan Kolet a gift in return. "I'm certain that what's said about Alexander and Talia Kaviscu isn't true. They were never lovers. He was monogamous, because of Elector Brauna, and it's obvious in the replays that Kaviscu had no interest—she despised him."

"She didn't know him well enough," Kolet said uncomfortably. He picked up some stones and pitched them one by one far out into the water, staring at the waves. "I see you standing in the back of rooms during the meetings, but this is the first chance we've had to talk. What happened between you and Jeroen Lee? After that nasty dinner, you disappeared. I asked. He was evasive. Then you surfaced publicly in Brauna's service. We're all worried there'll be a blowup between Lee and Brauna that will endanger CIN's favorable report."

August spoke quietly, almost in probe monotone. "I have always been in Elector Brauna's service."

"At that dinner I received a different impression. Neuland is grateful to Jeroen Lee, but we find him—I'm speaking frankly, August—a touchy friend. I think he would be a dangerous enemy. For your sake, I suggest you try to get along with him." Kolet shaded his eyes against the sun.

August looked out at the warm blue water, trying to imagine ice. How long would Jeroen Lee rely on a dying toolman's discretion? For that matter, how long would Sanda Brauna want a faulty, dying duplicate of Alexander? He started walking along the beach, toward the path leading to the Delegates' wing of the hotel; Kolet fell into step beside him. The meeting with the Emirates plenipotentiary would begin soon. Not wanting to rely exclusively on Ellen's report, he'd been on his way there when he'd noticed Kolet following.

A hummer—a hairless native quadruped the size of a house cat—darted in front of them, making its low, distinctive sound. August stopped; on Sucre one didn't approach strange animals. Kolet kicked stones at the thing. "I thought they'd cleared this island of these pests. We have to every spring; they have no predators anymore, and they'll eat a place clean of vegetation. Don't get close; they scratch and bite. See the markings on its face, the thin scar lines? They slash each other. It's a social behavior, not aggression—a greeting." He picked up a stone, aimed and threw, hitting the hummer on its snout. "Scat!" The humming stopped. Its tongue licked the empty air, tasting the odors.

Kolet waved his arms. The medical condition monitor cuffing his left wrist gleamed like a diamond bracelet. "Scat!" He started forward, stomping hard on the ground. Too tame, the hummer considered and stayed. Kolet sighed and, with a backward glance at August, squatted and extended his left hand to it. The hummer raised a paw, long claws sharply visible. It slashed Kolet's hand, sniffed its paw, then trotted away seaward and disappeared into the waves. Kolet stood.

"RHF," August said, as they started back up the path to the hotel. "That's where it's from—hummers, or some other native animal? I suppose they don't feel pain?"

"Right. A few native animals are pain-free. They were the model for the genetic mechanism involved in RHF. Pain is an adaptation to a relatively slow healing ability, according to our biologists, and unnecessary if you heal quickly." Kolet rubbed blood off the back of his hand. Parallel lines of thin scab had already formed over the shallow wound.

August nodded. "Neuland's founders were adapting you to the local biological environment?"

Kolet shrugged and glanced up the hill at the hotel. "Too bad they didn't alter us for the political environment. I may as well stop here, so your Commission's soldiers don't need to chase me away from the top-secret meeting with the Emir's Janissary. I wish I could see your report afterward, though."

So much for secret meetings. "I'm sure you won't need it." Kolet grinned and August surveyed him, a man well over twice his age and still considered young, liking him and wanting for once to acknowledge that fact. Their eyes met. "I don't know how your people first conceived of sweeping Andia, and it was horrible and wrong, but really, I think it might have been done by any world that was desperate. For whatever it's worth—I'm no one, just a toolman—I believe you're all human, with human strengths and faults."

Evan Kolet embraced August, then he moved awkwardly away. "Don't say 'toolman' like it's a disgrace. You're as important as anyone, as human." He hesitated, then continued. "I'm told—I don't know how we know—that you're in flare. Is it true?"

"Yes." August could barely say the single word. Though everyone knew, he discussed it with no one and anxiously avoided the subject with Sanda.

"I'm sorry. The cure's medically simple and politically impossible." Kolet's tone had all the bitterness August sometimes felt.

August said what was proper. "I don't want to die, but every day now I am as happy as I ever dreamed of being."

"I don't believe that, August, and I doubt you really do, either. Surely . . ." Kolet looked intently at him, then, impulsively, he said, "If there was a political benefit to Neuland, some risks could be taken. I would do my best."

August felt chilled. Anyone could see a replay of this; probably both sides were monitoring the meeting between a Neuland general and Alexander's clone. If Elector Lee saw

Kolet's spontaneous offer, Kolet might just have killed August. He backed away from Kolet. "Don't be stupid, Evan. Don't say another word. I'm not Alexander and Neuland can't afford to make that same mistake. Neither can I."

Kolet looked troubled, and started to speak.

"No," August said. The waves made meaningless noise crashing onto the shore. Gray gulls, their ancestors imported from Earth, wheeled around the sky calling to each other. August forced himself to relax. "I am loyal to the Polite Harmony of Worlds," he said firmly. "I'm sorry, but I can't speak with you again." He walked away.

The five Delegate-Commissioners stood together at one end of the rectangular conference table, except for decrepit Delegate Lun Chin of Amacuro, who was seated. Chin, sufficiently aged to be palsied and wrinkled, didn't appear to notice, but the other four glanced up as August entered. The meeting room had no side door or toolman entrance. August kept his face blank and his eyes superficial as he drifted around the room to a more or less inconspicuous place on the right side wall. The Delegates, accustomed to ignoring the existence of toolmen, looked away.

The room's huge window overlooked the sea and the path August and Kolet had climbed. The other walls were paneled in a light, grainy material, a native fiber, more resilient than wood, less so than furniture foam. The room's focal point was the conference table, made of the same material, highly polished and with a contrasting band of dyed black, hardened leather around its edge. There were six upholstered chairs: five clustered at the end near the Delegates and the sixth on the table's other side.

Ellen was present, but she had positioned herself subjectively, too closely observing Delegate Huana. August supposed she missed him. Vincent was at the best viewing position, near where August came to rest. Zoe, a senior probe in service with Elector Kurioso, had placed herself at the back of the room.

"What are you doing here?" Vincent's voice was almost inaudible, yet the hatred in his whisper made August stiffen.

"Leave me alone. We're on the same side," August said, just as softly as Vincent had spoken.

"Only of this room," Vincent hissed.

August moved father from him. Huana noticed the movement and, after a brief hesitation, he approached August. The other Delegates looked away from Huana's indiscretion, but their desultory conversation died as they tried to listen.

"You seem well healed," Huana said. He raised a hand to touch August's arm, then refrained. "Blue eyes?" His smile was kindly. "And your look is more direct than Alexander's."

"Yes, Delegate," August said in monotone, hoping Huana would go away.

"What do *you* think of Neuland?"

"I think this is paradise."

"You wouldn't like Andia," Huana said after a moment. "Few outsiders do. The atmosphere is thin. Visitors often need inhalers. The land is steep and barren. We live in the valleys. The new capital, Viru, is on a mountainside. It's surrounded by terraced farmland, not islands in an ocean. The buildings are gray granite, raw and recent. Rain is common, to the delight of farmers, I suppose, but not guests. I have a house there, but when I return home I always go first to Ayacho. It still exists, Ayacho, diminished and badly scarred by Neuland. My family home vanished that day; I stay in a hostelry. You should have seen Andia—we all should have—before coming to Neuland. It's too easy to like people who live in paradise."

The room was silent. "We've all seen replay of Andia, Delegate Huana," August said.

"The impact isn't the same. Alex claimed that replays' lack of smell was a significant disadvantage. More than two decades have passed, and Ayacho still stinks of burning." Huana's eyes moved slightly toward the window, then back to August. "Alex and I had many interesting discussions. For too long, I forgot that we were friends. Odd that now your friend is a Neulander."

"They're human," August said, purposely not denying the friendship. He guessed Huana had seen Kolet embrace him. "Your friend Alexander said so, too. I've seen the replay. He said it to you."

Neela Wilder, the Delegate from Darien, and an avid supporter of Neuland, whispered to Derek Jon Montague, Windfall's senior Delegate and CIN's chairman, that the probe was right. Delegate Pana, CIN's junior member, listened.

Huana gestured at the window. "I'm curious. What do you like about that Altered soldier?"

"The way he treats me," August said immediately. "And he doesn't mention Alexander."

Huana flushed. "That would hardly be in his best interest. You must realize that you're drawn to him because he represents Alexander's antagonists. You've spent your life denying that you are Alex, but you don't need to deny it anymore." Delegate Huana nodded courteously, smiled at Ellen, and took the seat at the conference table nearest to her position.

The door burst open. A heavyset man in a Neulander bodysuit and medical condition monitor, but worn subtly wrong—too far up his arm—strode into the room, followed by a uniformed lieutenant from *Guide*. They walked a full circuit of the room, the false Neulander looking carefully at each person there, including the probes, and studying the sensor held in his right hand; the Harmony soldier watched the stranger. They hesitated in front of the window. "It's scattered," the lieutenant said. The stranger frowned, but continued, and when he had returned to the door, he nodded curtly. The two men left and the standing Delegates all took seats.

Next, a swarthy man of less than average height stepped into the room alone. The door closed behind him. He examined the faces of each of the Delegates, then made a cursory bow. "John Reni," he introduced himself, "envoy on Neuland from Aleko Bei, Emir of Qandahar, Urfa, Safi, Kush, Amudjar, Seki, Bralava and Shkodor."

Reni was the only non-Jonist August had seen firsthand and he inspected him carefully. Reni also wore a Neulander-styled bodysuit, solid black, but without a medical condition monitor. He had a tailored jacket, not a Neulander cloak. There were faint lines on his face, like a laborer too long outside under hot ultraviolet sunlight, and he had a thin, faded scar on his right cheek, partially covered by a wide mustache and beard. His odor was no different from anyone's, and he looked clean. It had been a strain to understand him through the unfamiliar, guttural accent, but he seemed to be a normal enough, standard human, except that a cross hung from a gold chain around his neck.

"Esteban Huana," Delegate Huana said into the silence. He stood, nodded, then introduced the others before resuming his seat. Reni glanced once at the four probes standing motionless against the walls, but dismissed them from his consideration with the ease of a man accustomed to live servants.

"You asked to meet with us." Delegate Montague's tone made it clear he found the meeting distasteful.

"Your government and mine have had direct relations only intermittently, and have none now," Reni said. "Aleko Bei regrets the misunderstandings that have prevented an exchange of ambassadors and hopes that this meeting can prevent a gross miscalculation on the part of your rather insular Polite Harmony of Worlds." He smiled and waited, but none of the Delegate-Commissioners spoke. "The Republic of Neuland has repeatedly provoked us, and we will not let these insults pass. Aleko Bei has proclaimed a holy war and has vowed to retake this planetary system."

"Retake!" Neela Wilder snorted, and leaned across the table toward Reni. "Your claim to this system is based on fantasy and a five-hundred-year-old map. When settlers from the Harmony, including settlers from Darien, came here three hundred or so years ago, there was not a single human inhabitant."

Reni waved his hand like a magician making trivia disappear. "We are aware that Neuland obtains material to make war on the Emirates from *some* members of your confederation and have overlooked it in the past." He glanced at Delegate Wilder. "However, if you form a military alliance with these barbarians, do so in the confident expectation of involving yourselves in a war on their behalf. Leave this system as soon as possible. It is not safe. Your diplomatic status will not protect you if you are here when we redress our grievances."

"I personally have no love whatsoever for these Neulanders, as you must be aware," Delegate Huana said, looking from Reni's face to the cross. "However, I advise you to count again and use greater care not to threaten any citizen of the Harmony. We are now thirty-eight worlds, and you are eight. Nothing is likelier to draw your superstitious masses into a conflict they will lose than an attack on us."

Reni smiled yet again. "The enemy of my enemy is my friend. An ancient and wise saying. Aleko Bei does not wish in any way to threaten the Harmony. We wish to be your friend. But do not threaten us."

"We do not consider Neuland to be our enemy," Montague said quickly, "nor are we likely to take any alan despot or his crossman Janissary as our friend."

"How forgiving you are!" Reni looked first at Huana, then at the other Delegates. "And how narrow! In matters of religion the United Emirates are entirely tolerant, while you Jonists barely acknowledge that anyone of an alternate faith to your own is human, and consider overrunning their worlds to be doing them a service. Your faith lacks a moral center—yet even its practitioners are tolerated by Aleko Bei."

"Jonism is not a faith or a superstitious religion," Montague said heatedly. "It is a way of viewing realty with a clear mind, with ideas not colored by fables or wishful thinking. We search for reason and truth, and we find order." All the Delegates nodded.

Absolutely," Pana said.

Reni smirked and was silent.

Delegate Montague looked at the door. "Did you have more to say, besides warning us we would face swarms of alans and crossmen if we help Neuland?"

"I apologize for bringing the difficult topic of religion into what is a clear-cut matter." Reni looked intently at Montague, and straightened in his chair. "I requested this meeting so I might ask you one simple question: What vital interest of yours does it serve to become involved in a war to protect a society that has harmed you terribly and a world which is inhabited by Altered people you do not consider fully human?" Reni paused dramatically, then nodded as if he'd received approval from the stone-faced Delegates. "The conflict you would be entering is real: I leave Neuland tomorrow. Negotiations between these Altered barbarians and the Emirates have broken down—they are quite confident you'll save them and so refuse to submit to Aleko Bei. The Emirates will withhold our fist for only a single additional day; if you stay on Neuland, you will be in danger."

Montague stood, glanced at the other Delegates, then they also stood. Huana was last to rise. "I suggest to you, John Reni, that Aleko Bei reevaluate his situation if the Harmony allies itself with Neuland," Montague said. "Neuland has done nothing but react to your incursions. If we ally with our brother Jonists here, this certainty of war you harp on would have only one conclusion."

Reni stood up. He looked at Montague alone. "So, the

Harmony *does* want this planetary system; that is your interest here. Then be warned that the Harmony of Worlds is not well liked beyond its borders. You have other neighbors who may not wish you to expand. And your worlds are underpopulated. We have nearly half as many people on our eight worlds as you do on your thirty-eight."

"You have too many," Delegate Wilder said, as if unable to contain herself. "You breed and die like animals—and your women suffer humiliations every day."

Huana cleared his throat. Everyone looked at him. "War hasn't been fought hand to hand since mankind learned to think, Mr. Reni. Tell your multitudes that we are not afraid."

"So you want to die for them?" Reni challenged Delegate Huana, but he returned Reni's gaze calmly, with a placid expression. Then Reni looked at each of them, shrugged, and moving with slow dignity, he left the room.

"Thank you, Esteban," Montague said when the crossman was gone.

Delegate Huana sank back into his seat. "We are a unity. I will do everything in my power to prevent this misguided support for these detestable people, but I am a loyal citizen of the Polite Harmony of Worlds, and a Jonist. One thing Reni said is true. There will be a war. Life means nothing to crossmen or alans—most don't live even a hundred years." Huana shook his head and sighed. "I see where your thinking—all of you—is tending and I have one request. Our hosts, our would-be allies, have planned our itineraries, escorted us and filtered what we've seen since we arrived. We haven't visited the real Neuland. We should do so before you finalize your decision to involve us in their war. I've arranged to attend a local party and meet some of the uncensored inhabitants of Neuland. A car will come for us at eighteen. I hope all of you will attend."

"What type of party?" Neela Wilder asked, frowning. "We all know what Neulanders are. The point is that they're Jonists, and a buffer between us and the Emirates. This is a beautiful world, which shouldn't fall to those alans."

"One of their torture parties?" Delegate Pana looked thoughtful. "Huana is right. We should see it. We owe it to our citizens who may be sent here to defend Neuland."

"Good. Then I'll expect you all." Huana rose to his feet. The others looked at each other. "All right," Montague said. "I don't believe it's necessary, but we'll do this for you, Esteban." He glanced out the window. "Remember, there are perversions inside the Harmony, too."

"Of course." Huana was soothing. "But these aren't perverts, just ordinary Neuland citizens."

The Delegate-Commissioners drifted out of the room. Huana was last. He turned, glanced at August, then Ellen. He smiled and nodded at her, just as the door closed.

"What was that?" August asked her immediately.

"How should I know?" Ellen sounded irritated. "Stop ordering me around, August. I'm not in *your* service." She flounced toward the door.

Vincent laughed. Zoe looked away in a display of tact rare among probes, but she didn't leave.

"Since you didn't trust me to be alone at the meeting, you do the on-site report," Ellen continued from the doorway. "You're the one with the personal, private screen that no one else can touch. Just be sure to mention that facilitation you did to Delegate Huana—if that's what it was meant to be. Has Elector Brauna authorized you to play word games with humans? I've never heard of a probe making so free and easy with a Delegate's public dignity—not even Alexander."

Censure from Ellen stung; August started toward her.

"He's not *Alexander,* Ellen." Vincent's tone oozed sarcasm like pus as he walked toward the door. "Don't compare him with that probe. This is *August.* Haven't you heard? He's human. He was just making conversation with a World Delegate. Why, he even hugs Neulanders."

"All right," Zoe said forcefully, facing them all. "Leave it alone. He doesn't answer to you, Vincent. And Ellen, it's not August's fault that you're closely watched."

August had never especially noticed Zoe. She was twenty-six, plain in comparison with most probes, unobtrusive, competent, and unspectacular. She hadn't previously directed any particular kindness to him, but her quiet authority now made him want to know her.

Vincent glared at Zoe, then pushed the door aside and left. Ellen hesitated. She swallowed, looked down, and said, "Are you doing the on-site or am I?"

It was an apology. "I'll do the report, from Elector Brauna's suite," August said. "Ellen, you can use my screen in quarters whenever you want. I just didn't think to offer it."

Ellen nodded, glancing speculatively between Zoe and

August, making her thought clear, once again her irrepressible self. "I'll leave you two together."

Zoe didn't react to Ellen's innuendo. "Thank you," August said to Zoe when Ellen was gone. He bowed.

Zoe nodded and smiled slightly. "You've been incredibly stupid—letting that Neulander touch you, taunting Huana—unless you have some purpose that totally escapes me. Vincent was right. You were holding a conversation, not being a probe. It's obvious, watching you, why they put us down as soon as it's convenient after we enter flare." She went to the door and waited for August to join her. Holding it open, she glanced down the hall. As August passed, she said very low, soft, and quick, inaudible to any nearby monitors, "But we are human. Don't let them convince you otherwise." Then Zoe nodded serenely and walked off down the enclosed corridor to the Electors' area of the hotel.

Early that afternoon, Sanda Brauna met with her three Ahmen and a Neulander professor of xeno-botany. Ting said she didn't want to be disturbed. "Has she read the report I sent her this morning?" August asked.

Ting stared. Stupid question. A guardian wouldn't know unless Elector Brauna commented aloud.

"How long has she been in the meeting?" August asked instead.

"Since Elector Lee and Elector Kurioso left."

The lack of proper monitors and reporting was the one aspect of Neuland that August didn't like. It was nearly impossible to keep consistent track of anyone, especially since he no longer had Elector Brauna's access codes, only those of a probe. He hadn't known the two Electors had visited the suite and wondered uneasily why they had, remembering Kolet's offer.

"She cried this morning, after you went out," Ting said.

"I'm sorry. There's nothing I can do except to die."

"No. That's worse." Ting shook his head, taking August's statement for an offer.

Perhaps it should be, yet he wanted to live. "I'll be in quarters. I want to talk to Ellen," August said, "then I'm going to research the Emirates in the Neuland public database. I'll be at my screen if she wants me."

"She likes you to stay here."

Sometimes he needed to get away from Sanda Brauna,

away from the need for smiles. He was using probe quarters extensively. Perhaps his slightly altered face made the difference, or Ellen's open support, or the partial rehabilitation of Alexander, but he was comfortable there, enjoying the tentative camaraderie that had developed among those few probes chosen to leave Center. "I'll get more done in quarters," he told Ting. "Ben and Cissy can help me sort the data."

Ting hesitated, then agreed. August left the suite alone. The walk through the carpeted hotel corridors was lonely. He missed Ting's escort, but to ask for a guardian's protection now that his existence was public would worsen Sanda's strained relationship with Jeroen Lee.

The hotel walls weren't thin, but neither were they as soundproof as on Center, and August heard bits of unconnected noise that, like animal scratching, made him nervous. His thoughts wandered to Kolet's indiscretion, and his skin prickled like before an electrical storm on Sucre. Surely no one would believe he would accept Kolet's impetuous offer, and besides, what could he provide Neuland in exchange for health? August forced thoughts of Jeroen Lee away.

Neuland hadn't acquired the knack of lighting an enclosed, interior space into a reproduction of daylight; they used lamps, not sun-stones. The corridor was mostly too dim, yet where the lamps shone brightest, the light was harshly white. He felt a chill, then wondered if it was flare fever or merely too much imagination. Planned air circulation was neglected, since the interior space was fairly small, but odors lingered. The cologne Elector Kurioso wore, the crisp, astringent smell of *Guide*'s soldiers passing through on duty, the clean, faintly medicinal aroma of Neulanders and Sanda Brauna's sweet violet scent all mixed into an atmosphere whose overall effect was heavy with anticipation.

Silence, too, was ominous; a sneak attack in these empty, virtually unmonitored hotel corridors would be easy, which was why they were patrolled. August hesitated, looking over his shoulder, frightened into believing he was being stalked.

He turned the corner. A bored human tech from *Guide*, seated at a desk, nodded and smiled at August. Being surrounded by Altered outsiders, even hospitable ones, made everyone more appreciated. "Good health," August said, beginning to relax.

The guard laughed at the Neulander greeting. "Maybe we

should check," he said, holding up a portable sensor, but not bothering to use it.

August smiled, bowed and continued down two flights of stairs and through another quiet corridor. His steps echoed until he was tiptoeing. It was a relief to finally open the door to the cluster of rooms given over to probe quarters and hear the bustle of voices. Twelve probes were in the common room, an informal tape study area, though there was no librarian through whom they could reach archival material from *Guide*. Bess and Cissy were shouting at each other about a missing necklace, a gift to Bess from Ahman Penn.

"Where's Ellen?" August said.

Cissy pointed at the closed door of August's assigned room and continued arguing.

Quarters smelled worse than the hallway. It held too many bodies and stank of sex, sweat, and sickness. He felt hot; perhaps it was the flare. "The windows do open," he said as he walked to his door.

"Vincent ordered them kept shut," Ben Sharp said apologetically.

Protocol demanded that only another probe in personal service to an Elector could countermand the order. August didn't want to engage in an idiotic battle with Vincent over windows, so he shrugged, rolled his eyes at Ben Sharp, who was a competent and earnest general services probe, and tapped on the door to his room, in case Ellen needed privacy. One never knew with her.

She didn't answer. There was no sound, but the faint odor gave him goose bumps.

August glanced at Ben. "Is she alone?"

Ben rapidly surveyed his display, froze it, then turned to August. "Yes," he said. "But Vincent was in your room earlier." He stood up. "That kind of thing is common back at Center," he said in a lower voice, explaining mores August might not know. "Tricks and such . . ."

August grimaced and cautiously opened the door. He gagged, and worked hard not to vomit. The stench was fecal and sour. Probes fell silent, except for coughing, as the smell wafted out to them. From August's room there was no sound at all. He stepped inside.

Ellen sat stiffly at the desk, one arm extended toward the door, the other on the chair, as if she'd tried to stand. The glow of an unset screen illuminated the sharp planes of her face, making her graying skin sallow. Her mouth was open, her eyes wild. She had twisted, turning to the other room, from where she would have heard voices as she died. August stepped closer.

"Don't touch anything!" Ben shouted. "Contact poison!"

"Vincent?" someone whispered and was hushed.

They crowded behind him. August had to clear his throat before he was able to speak. "Where is he?"

No one answered.

August turned around, glad to look away from Ellen's dead face. Probes stared, interested, curious, eagerly excited. Ben surveyed Ellen's body, absorbing the details of her death. He would make a fine report of it—meticulous, objective, and without emotion—while August would be forever haunted by the last panic in Ellen's dead eyes. Still, he was senior of those present, and they were awaiting his orders. "Cissy," August said curtly, "call Security. No, first call Ting Wheeling direct, Elector Brauna's chief guardian, then Security. Ben, you report Ellen's death to Elector Brauna. The rest of you, get out and wait for Security."

They made way as August left the room, then returned to their own places, preparing reports in low voices, watching each other and August for signs of distress, even now competing to show the best self-control, the least emotion. He let them see his anger, a deep-seated rage that burned as his face had burned, but he hid his grief. Ellen had been as nearly frivolous as a toolman could be. She'd been his friend. Death like this, by mistake—because Vincent had certainly intended to kill August—was even worse than flare. It was murder, except toolmen couldn't be murdered, only put down.

Bess quietly closed the door to August's room. The stink hardly diminished.

Vincent would never have taken such a drastic step alone; Elector Lee had decided to kill August because of Kolet's offer.

They all surveyed him. Well, let them. He sat down in front of an empty displayer and called up a status board, scanning the entries that told where each Elector and Delegate-Commissioner was scheduled to be. Lee was supposed to be dining in his suite.

Ting rushed into the room, followed a few seconds later by more guardians and several human soldiers, one a Security Captain, who took charge. As the others hurried toward the closed door to view Ellen's corpse, Ting went to August. "Are you well?" Ting asked, panting. August imagined the exertion that would cause Ting to pant.

"Fine." Probes were listening. "Come with me." He got to his feet, having to steady himself. "Later," he shouted and kept moving when a soldier called out a request for information. Ting seconded the delay, and they accepted it from him.

August hesitated in the hall, then walked to the nearest dead space, unmonitored, just outside a stairwell. He stopped there and faced Ting.

"Elector Lee did that, using Vincent," he said softly, watching Ting's expression. "He meant to kill me, not Ellen. I have to go to him and convince him that my death is not necessary or next time he'll succeed."

"Elector Brauna?"

August spoke simply, not wanting to sway Ting. "Perhaps she could keep me safe, but I'd be a prisoner again. I hated that. And the main reason not to go to her is that she probably agreed to let me be killed. I only have few months; it's nothing to them. This waiting is hard for her. Remember, you told me she cried this morning? And she met with the other two Electors earlier today."

Ting shook his head. "She loves you."

"I love her, whatever she feels or doesn't for me," August said skeptically. "But she did love Alexander." He paused, watching Ting start and realize what he meant. "So I'm asking—will you let me go?"

Ting's distress was painful to observe. "What you said was right—six years with you. But I've been twenty-five with her." He twisted his hands together, staring sightlessly in August's direction. "I've never understood. She told Alexander he was human, then had me kill him. I didn't like him, not much at all. He thought I was nothing. He hardly saw me. I expected not to like you, either, but this time it was you who was invisible."

August touched his arm. Ting grasped August's hand, staring down at it. He sighed, brought it close against his chest, then looked up into August's face. "Sometimes I pretend I made you, like humans do a child. That makes me feel better about killing him. She was wrong, and she knows it. That's why she cries and is afraid of you. If he was human, then he shouldn't have been killed. If he was human, so are you. I won't kill you, and I won't let them do it, either. I'll go with you to Elector Lee and tell him so."

It was the longest speech August had ever heard Ting make, and the most eloquent. He didn't know what to say. "Ting . . ."

"Let's go. Elector Lee is waiting."

"I hope not." August smiled wanly and looked up the corridor. It still was empty. If he let Ting accompany him into Elector Lee's suite, August would be as bad as any human, disregarding the effect on Ting. "Go home. You can't force Elector Lee to let me live."

"No. You can't force me to leave you."

August recognized the stubborn set of Ting's jaw, the way he held himself closed to any contrary idea. "All right, Ting. Thank you. But if you can't stop them from killing me, then don't try. Understand? If I'm going to die anyway, then don't get involved. Promise me that."

"No." Ting said simply. "I do my job. First, always, I protect Elector Brauna. Then I protect you, even against her orders. I do my job the best I can. No conditions." He started off toward the stairway. After a moment, August followed.

Chapter 13

"I protest," August said desperately to Ahman Penn. "I must see Elector Lee."

"He can't be disturbed." Ahman Penn crossed his arms against his chest as a guardian in Elector Lee's service confronted Ting, who had moved forward, covering August.

"Ellen is dead." Despite his memory of her dead face and outstretched arm, it was difficult to believe she was gone.

"The death of a probe is of no consequence to Elector Lee." Less pointedly, Ahman Penn added, "Go away quickly, August. I'll give you that."

"And wait for someone better than Vincent to kill me? I may not have long, but I want every day I have."

Ahman Penn seemed to study the thickly carpeted floor, then he looked up at August. "Enter his service without any reservations on your loyalty or take your chances outside it. I'm doing you a kindness in giving you the choice at this late date, but I believe Elector Lee would want the offer made. Will you stay?"

The entry surely contained a security screen and several internal monitors. Perhaps Elector Lee was watching. August smelled his own fear and hoped Lee couldn't see it. "I made a promise to him. I've kept it, so far. If I leave without seeing him, I will go directly to Delegate Huana."

Ahman Penn laughed and signaled Lee's guardian, who moved to block the closed door. "You are a delight, August. How many opportunities does an Elector have to be threatened by a toolman?"

Ting Wheeling shifted his weight and rested his hand on the weapon at his side. Ahman Penn looked from August to Ting, then back again. He shook his head. "Are you relying on the guardian to get you out of this suite? It's no small feat to have corrupted another toolman."

"Ting hasn't been corrupted," August said.

Penn waved his hand, indicating the issue was unimportant. "Elector Brauna didn't send him. No doubt she's disappointed with this morning's fiasco, but she doesn't want you back. She says the matter is too painful."

"But that's not a problem for Elector Lee."

Ahman Penn looked sharply at him, and nodded at Ting. "How many people do you want dead with you?"

August hesitated. He was a fool. He had nothing with which to bargain for his life, but, reacting impulsively to the horror of Ellen's death, he had delivered himself to Jeroen Lee. Ting was ready to die, to sacrifice his future decades for a man with only months to live. It was ridiculous and horrible. He couldn't let that happen. August was lucky Lee still wanted him. "All right," he said tiredly to Ahman Penn. "Ting, go home. It's over. I'm staying here. Tell Elector Brauna that I understand and still love her."

"Sweet," Ahman Penn said.

August flushed. Ting signaled "no" without taking his attention from the other guardian.

"Ting, I want us both to live," August said. "If you fight, nothing will be accomplished. I . . . made a mistake." Ting didn't stir from his protective pose. "This is the only way for me to stay alive," August pleaded. Ahman Penn coughed impatiently. "Please," August said softly.

"They aren't right on this. I'll tell her." Ting sounded deeply troubled, but he moved his hand off the weapon and his posture relaxed. Like a dance partner, the other guardian eased off and moved a step away from the door. "She'll do something."

"Just go home."

Ting stared into August's face, then spun smartly on his heel and left. When Ting was gone, Penn said, "That's the first intelligent thing you've done since Kolet's offer. Why did you talk with that Neulander at all? Stupid, August. I expected better of you."

Elector Lee entered the hall. August bowed deeply. His fate was entirely in Lee's hands.

Lee nodded a brief acknowledgment. "August will join me for lunch." Abruptly, he grinned, seeming almost boyish. "Good work, Martin. He looks well, doesn't he? No emaciation, and his face is completely healed."

"Yes," August said, allowing his bitterness to show.

"Amazing, isn't it? Med. Kiani was impressed by probe recuperative powers."

Jeroen Lee nodded. "Perhaps flare's increased metabolic rate actually helped in this instance."

August snickered, seeing how easily and well the Elector lied. "This suite is secured. We all know the truth, that I have a modified type of RHF, the Neulander healing ability. That's what guinea pigs are for. I still feel pain, and my version is not as powerful as the Neulanders', but I heal faster than standard humans. Few serious injuries occur at Center, so I took my rapid healing for granted until I healed so quickly from my burn. There must be other toolmen with this modification, or you would be testing me."

"Quite a few subs and guardians," Elector Lee agreed, smiling and nodding at his guardian. "You're the only probe. There is a fundamental philosophical conflict between the genetic predisposition for metabolic disruption and this modified RHF. In any event, a probe's short life span is insufficient to test most health-oriented modifications." He gestured toward the rear of his suite. "Come with me, August. After so much stress, you're certain to be hungry." He started walking away.

Lee's straight, slim back and elegant demeanor mocked August's hostility. Ellen's death was nothing to this man, unworthy of comment. August stood motionless, too outraged to move.

Ahman Penn patted August's shoulder. "You made the right decision."

August twisted around. Penn looked back at him, eyes widening as he saw August's helpless anger. He didn't warn Lee or chastise August; his expression held only compassion. "You must go on," he said.

The very inadequacy of Penn's attempt at comfort cooled August's anger. Penn was right. He had chosen life; therefore, he must go on. He took a step toward Lee.

Jeroen Lee turned and waited patiently for August to come.

"Eat something, August. You'll feel better." Jeroen Lee handed August a celadon bowl containing white rice over which was spooned a vegetable mixture in a thin red sauce. A small plate of skewered meat surrounded by more of Lee's liang-ban was on the table; Lee alone of the Electors had brought his own chef to Neuland. The thin-walled bowl felt uncomfortably hot in August's hand, so he set it on the lacquer table. His stomach growled—the food smelled delicious—but he didn't want to eat.

"I have meetings until late afternoon, but Martin will give you a thorough physical examination. There's no reason for you to become debilitated. You'll get better care with me. Sanda is only a botanist, after all, and she didn't know your physiology."

"You designed Alexander for yourself, expecting RHF would have a practical benefit," August said in monotone.

"What do you think I do? A 'torture party' every night?" Jeroen Lee laughed, gesturing around the gracious room. "Is this really so bad, August?"

Lee's bedroom was essentially identical with the one August had frequently shared with Sanda Brauna, yet its ambience was completely different. Rather than comfortably romantic, the huge bed, draped with thick beige and ivory fabrics, seemed a monument to carnality. The sparse furniture was Neulander made, with rounded corners and heavy upholstered padding artfully designed into the frames. The huge room had uncluttered space for two separate groupings of chairs and tables, one for dining and one fitted for work or entertainment with a standard Harmony screen. In Sanda's room this spaciousness had been subtly feminine. In Jeroen Lee's bedroom the spareness of the furnishings seemed to amplify the sense of Lee's power. The relative emptiness was not peaceful and inviting, as in Sanda's suite, it was dynamic. Surfaces were bare, except for a low vase filled with red and purple fresh flowers on the small dining table, whereas Sanda had scattered possessions about her room like a creature marking its territory. Elector Lee seemed already at home in the Neulander room. In both suites a wide balcony overlooking the sea ran the length of the room. Lee's was furnished with cream-colored upholstered chairs and a round, ceramic table. The glass doors were open at August's request, to diminish the cloying odor of Jeroen Lee's expectations, and a breeze ruffled the pale, thin curtains. They were ten stories high, rather than Sanda's eight, but the view was the same: empty, open sea. This side of the hotel faced away from Romoa's other islands.

"I've acquired a large measure of respect for your abilities, your person, and your discretion," Lee said. "I understand you have a romantic fixation on Sanda, who hardly deserves it, but you wouldn't be here now if you weren't a realist. I would have preferred for you to come more willingly, but I won't hold that against you. I've enjoyed this chase a great deal, particularly winning."

August tasted the food. The sauce was sweet as well as tangy, but the unusual textural combination of soft rice and barely cooked vegetables was a more arresting contrast. With such interesting food, perhaps one could enjoy eating. Lee was watching him. "Will you have me put down?"

"Not now," Elector Lee said softly. "I don't make any promises beyond the present. I do promise I will have you put down if ever you ask me to do so. Whatever you think now, you may change your mind in the later stages of this condition. I won't keep you against your will."

August stared at him, but Jeroen Lee didn't have the grace to blush or look away; in fact, he smiled. August frowned, then ate more of the rice mixture without bothering to survey Lee, or even watch him very closely.

Elector Lee ate only plain rice, but he offered August the plate of meats. August shook his head, and Lee didn't insist, but took several of the liang-ban. "What kept you from telling Sanda about me once you knew? She would have protected you."

Startled, August stopped eating. "You knew I wouldn't, or why did you trust me?"

Lee leaned back in his chair, looking immensely pleased. "I only guessed you felt some nascent loyalty to me. Reckless of me, really. Fortunately, I was correct."

That was disturbing. "It's not loyalty. I gave my word to you. Anyway, it would only have harmed all the Electors if it was known that you're a Neulander." The accusation seemed to hover between them in the air.

Lee ate more rice, then calmly said, "I didn't expect such sloppy thinking from you, August. Being pain-free is a condition as well as a culture. While I have the condition, I'm a native of Co-Chan, not a Neulander."

"I thought about your apartment: the public rooms so cluttered, unlike anything a Neulander would design, and you so proud of them, in contrast with private rooms set up to minimize small injuries to someone who wouldn't feel them, and who couldn't afford to wear a medical condition monitor. I was curious about your family, and before we left Cen-

ter I investigated the archives. Your mother lived on
Co-Chan, but she was born on Darien, and her father was a
Neulander. It took a great deal of work to uncover that
much, since she kept her origins secret and you buried them
further, but I managed. I never learned who your father was,
but it's likely he was also of Neulander descent. And I
watched replay of you that went back fifty years. You moved
more cautiously then than you do now. Were you afraid of
someone noticing the RHF? You can't be hurt. Inside the
Harmony, everywhere but on Darien, being pain-free makes
you Altered and not human. You would be called a
Neulander."

"You take some satisfaction in saying that to an Elector?"
Jeroen Lee smiled, but the smile was rigid and unreal. However he wanted to appear, speaking of these things made him
anxious.

"None. But Elector, if you are human, then so am I. Don't
have me killed."

"That is a difficult request to make without whining, but
you've managed to avoid it while linking our two fates.
Good for you. I notice you haven't asked me to cure the
flare. Don't. I will not. I can only afford so much forbear-
ance. You would be dead if you weren't dying." Lee took a
skewer and removed its meat by pulling it against the side of
the bowl of rice. The meat fell into bite-sized pieces on the
rice, but Lee set his bowl down without eating anything.

"Ahman Penn knows about you," August said. "No doubt
so do others besides your toolmen."

"Then you should ask yourself, clever August, what I
know about them." Jeroen Lee stood up. "You aren't eating,
and I haven't much time. I need to placate Sanda before we
meet with Neuland's university planning board about the location of our Academy in Romoa." He walked around the table to stand behind August and placed his hands on August's
shoulders, beginning an expert massage. "You're tense.
There's no reason for that." He moved August's long hair
from the back of his neck, entangling his fingers in it for a
moment, then kissed August's bare neck. His arms slipped
over August's shoulders, his hands coming to rest lightly on
August's upper chest. The intimacy was comforting rather
than arousing. August felt lulled. What would be the purpose
of resistance? He would only be put down.

He turned slightly, looking up into Jeroen Lee's face. The

Elector moved his hands back onto August's shoulders and tilted his head, studying August. "I still prefer green eyes," he said. "They were beautiful with the auburn highlights in your hair." He stroked August's cheek with the edge of a hand. "Relax," he said, when August trembled. "I won't hurt you, and you can't hurt me."

Ahman Penn looked fleetingly at August as Vincent entered the office where they were working, then told Vincent, "Get out. Stay in quarters."

"Wait," August called. Vincent was already at the door, but he stopped and turned. "I'll direct your work from now on."

"You can't do that. You're only another probe." Vincent looked to Ahman Penn for support, but Penn looked unsmilingly back and said nothing.

"I can't kill you, like you killed Ellen, but I don't think Elector Lee will deny me a certain amount of revenge," August said, keeping his tone detached, professional, like an Ahman lecturing a Researcher who would never be promoted. He sighed with exaggerated patience, inwardly disappointed by Vincent's appearance. A murderer should exude evil, but Vincent was only his usual disagreeable self, not an obvious monster. "Your reports are sloppy, like everything you do, but you're mobile, and I'll be confined to this suite until we return to Center. So you'll go where I tell you and do as I say—and I intend to make your life miserable. I won't forget her face. I won't forget that it could have been me."

"It should have been! It will be, soon enough. The story is that you killed her. Huana is furious."

That worried August, who had actively avoided watching anything to do with the investigation of Ellen's death, but he said, "Everyone who matters knows the truth." Yet he looked questioningly at Penn.

Penn hesitated, then looked at Vincent and answered. "Huana was your best alternative to an accommodation with Elector Lee, but you didn't overcome your reluctance to identify yourself with Alexander. This rumor is to ensure that if you run from here, you have nowhere to go."

"I doubt that Delegate Huana actually believes I murdered Ellen."

"Perhaps not, but he can't be certain. As far as he knows,

no one has a motive for killing either of you." Ahman Penn cleared his screen. "Send over a copy of your revisions of Vincent's report. I'm curious."

"The Elector will get tired of you," Vincent said as August complied with Penn's request. "Then it'll be you they're laughing at in quarters, you who's treated like a ghost."

"For once, time is on my side," August said. "Now, get back to quarters."

Vincent glanced at Penn. "You have your orders," Penn said. Vincent stared, then bowed hurriedly and rushed from the room.

Ahman Penn smiled at August. "Tell me if Vincent gives you any trouble." He drummed his fingers on the arm of his chair. "What were your impressions of the crossman, Reni?"

August hesitated, feeling guilty about Penn's treatment of Vincent, yet hating Vincent, too.

"August." Penn's tone was stern.

There was no reason to refuse; this was his new place. He thought back to the report he'd written for Sanda Brauna. It seemed a lifetime ago. "Reni doesn't understand the Harmony. He meant to show their religious tolerance—a crossman representing the alan Emir—but by wearing a cross he only offended the Delegates, especially Delegate Huana, whom he seemed to expect to have on his side; Andia has no religious minorities. For a crossman to try to separate the situation of Andia from that of the rest of the Harmony was repugnant to Huana. It brought him closer to supporting Neuland than he's ever been. Reni also hinted that Aleko Bei might permit an expansion of Jonism inside the Emirates—that some accommodation is possible—without realizing that was a proposal he should have made privately to the Electors, not the Delegates."

Penn nodded, but his expression was determinedly neutral. "Do you think they'll attack Neuland?"

August preferred the back-and-forth discussions with Elector Lee to Ahman Penn's subdued questions. "Yes," he answered. "They might purposely attack while we're still here, trying to frighten us from helping Neuland. I believe his threat was serious."

Penn turned back to his own screen. "Do a full report on the meeting for the Elector, not just an annotation of Vincent's."

* * *

"Elector Lee is returning," Ahman Penn said early that evening. "Elector Brauna is with him. She insists on seeing that you're all right."

"Not dead, you mean?" Unexpectedly, it had been a pleasant afternoon. After Vincent left, August had worked quietly at the screen Ahman Penn had provided. The routine work—he noticed a bias toward a more impersonal presentation than in the reports he'd done for Elector Brauna, but also more uncorroborated, intuitive speculations—had had a soporific effect, tranquilizing him with its familiarity, but languor was a welcome change from the fear of earlier in the day.

Ahman Penn had remained in the office at his own screen, making sporadic comments on one thing or another, apparently only to be companionable since none had been significant, or perhaps the conversation was part of the chore of minding the Elector's latest acquisition. August's peacefulness ended with Penn's announcement. "What do you want me to say to her?" He closed his screen and stared at the blankness, which reminded him again of Ellen. " 'Yes, Elector, I'm fine. Your conspiracy to kill me failed. So sorry to have disappointed you.' " Ahman Penn watched without comment. "Do I tell her I love her? What good will that do?"

"Is that why you said it before?"

"No," August said less angrily. "I meant it."

Ahman Penn glanced at the door. August didn't hear anyone, but Penn closed his screen, stood, and walked to the door, the house system no doubt apprising him of Elector Lee's approach. "It must be uncomfortable to love someone whom you can't trust," Penn said. He turned away to open the door.

August stared at Penn's back. *Ah, love, let us be true To one another!* Had Elector Brauna betrayed him? Could an Elector ever betray a toolman? What loyalty did he have a right to expect? He stood and waited to see her for the first time from the vantage of a toolman in Elector Lee's service.

Jeroen Lee walked in, followed by Sanda Brauna. She was biting her lower lip, not making any attempt to suppress her distress. Her casual white gown was full and loose below the blue sash that gathered the gauzy material under her breasts. Her hair was down, curling around her shoulders, and she looked as though she was attending an informal garden party, altogether feminine rather than utilitarian attire. She'd never seemed more beautiful. He bowed first to her and then to Elector Lee, who was only wearing one of his usual tailored suits.

"As you see," Lee said, gesturing at August. "He's untouched."

"Hardly that," August said, wanting to hurt her.

She started, then looked sharply at Lee. He smiled, shaking his head, but his tone was acerbic. "What did you expect? Sanda, he's mine now. This meeting is a courtesy."

She went to August, stopping so close he could have taken her in his arms. "This morning Jeroen said you were a danger to the Harmony, that the Neulander offered to cure your flare if you gave him secrets. I saw the replay."

"Yes, Elector Brauna." He surveyed her grave face, sensing her confusion as though it was a pulse under his thumb, wishing he dared touch her. "General Kolet made the offer spontaneously. There was never any danger to the Harmony," he glanced briefly at Lee, "or anyone in it, since I had absolutely no intention of divulging anything."

"You like Kolet."

"I liked Ellen, too."

Sanda Brauna plucked at a fold of her gown. "So did I," she said softly. "Ellen was a good girl, tremendously alive." She studied August's face. "What secrets do you have, August? What have you withheld from me that you might have told to Neuland?"

That explained her severe tone and why Lee had been able to sway her. She had been truly concerned for the Harmony if he, now in flare, went to Kolet and divulged everything he knew about its personalities and workings, but more than that, she was indignant that he had concealed something from her. He bowed low and held the bow for a long moment. "Nothing which would benefit anyone if it were known."

Lee walked to August's side. "Are you satisfied, Sanda?"

"August, does the information concern Elector Lee?" she asked, ignoring Lee. "You didn't tell any of it to me."

"Elector, I am entirely loyal to you." He felt a pang, thinking of Lee, uncertain where his allegiance should be now, or where it really was. Sheepishly, he looked at Jeroen Lee. Lee was smiling.

Sanda, however, despite his assertion of loyalty, was scowling. "*You* decided what I should know. You, probe." She turned on Lee. "I know when I've been tricked, Jeroen. I consented to his death, not his continued life with you."

"You didn't want him because his flare made you uncomfortable. The rest was your rationalization." Lee spread his arms wide. "I have no secrets from you. I have not and will not demand that August tell me any secrets of yours that he may know—I doubt he would, anyway, outside of Security, and I have no intention of sending him there. However, I won't release him from my custody again under any circumstances. If you insist, then I will put him down, but how selfish are you?"

She faced August. "Are you all right?" she asked gently.

"I'm well enough."

"You didn't come to me."

Her feelings were hurt, despite the obvious fact that she wouldn't have done anything to save him. She'd authorized his murder, but her eyes were sad. How could he blame her? He'd run from her, the person to whom he'd pledged himself. "I love you, Elector. I regret that my existence is painful for you. Perhaps this is best."

She stared down, twisting fabric from her dress between her hands. "Ting says I've done wrong. He suggested that I cure your flare. Can you imagine a guardian saying such a thing?" She looked up. There were tears in her eyes. She shook her head, tossing her pale hair like an innocent, young girl, and looked directly at August. Lee came forward, then hesitated at her brisk gesture. "Ting was right. I was weak, too worried about consequences to do what I wanted. I should have helped Alexander, and I should have helped you." She seized August's hands, pressing them hard with an intensity of emotion, and spoke rapidly. "Tell me his secret. Then it will be over, out in the open. I swear I'll get you back, and I'll eliminate this flare."

Elector Lee grabbed Sanda Brauna's arms and roughly yanked her away from August. "That's enough playacting! I know you, Sanda. You'll do no such thing. If you won't be honest, at least don't be cruel. Martin will escort you out. Now."

Ahman Penn, who had come toward them as Elector Brauna made her offer, touched her shoulder, although when she glanced at him, he bowed. His expression, reflecting that of

Jeroen Lee, was cold. Whether or not they believed Sanda
Brauna, they certainly didn't want August to believe in her
offer. For whatever reason, he wasn't sure that he did; he
was confused almost as badly as when he'd been blind, but
he extended his arm to her. Love was a choice. "This living
hand, Elector, be conscience-calmed—see here it is—I hold
it towards you."

She darted away from Penn as if to leave, then, in a single
swift gesture, she touched her fingers to her lips, kissed
them, and extended her hand to August. Lee stepped between Elector Brauna and August. Penn moved menacingly
forward, her rank forgotten. She looked tiny next to them,
and slightly frightened, as if he had entered a new territory,
where physical size was intimidating. August took a step toward her, but Elector Brauna turned and almost ran out of
the room, immediately followed by Martin Penn.

Jeroen Lee smiled and sat down in a wide, upholstered
easy chair, not quite a lounger, that was near the desk
Ahman Penn had used. "Poetry? That's Sanda's affliction. If
a person can act, he does. If not, then he dreams. Poets are
dreamers, not builders. What was it you quoted?"

"John Keats, a fragment scribbled in the margin of a
larger work."

"Recite it. Otherwise, it's code."

August said, in monotone:

> "This living hand, now warm and capable
> Of earnest grasping, would, if it were cold
> And in the icy silence of the tomb,
> So haunt thy days and chill thy dreaming nights
> That thou wouldst wish thine own heart dry of blood
> So in my veins red life might stream again,
> And thou be conscience-calmed—see here it is—
> I hold it towards you."

"Ancient gloominess," Elector Lee said. "I enjoy music,
but poetry is far too gray. Don't bother reciting any for me."
He stretched, kicking off his slippers and wiggling his thin
toes. "All in all, this has been a good afternoon." Lee leaned
back, staring up at the ceiling, eyes half-closed.

August wasn't certain what was expected of him—to continue work, to disappear, or to participate in Lee's plans for
relaxation—so he stood motionless, thinking of Sanda.

"What about you?" the Elector asked, turning his head.

August remembered the water, waiting to fall. "It's not the worst day that I've experienced," he said cautiously, then, with a pang, he thought of Ellen.

The Elector chuckled. "Such gratitude! And I tried so hard to please you." He studied August, his face softening as he did so. "I'm feeling kindly. What would improve your day? Don't ask for the impossible, you'll only lose my goodwill."

Ahman Penn returned, glanced at the two of them, and began to speak—something about Vincent—but Elector Lee raised his hand, directing him to wait for August.

"A walk along the beach," August said.

Jeroen Lee sat up in the chair and nodded. "Possible. If we go for a walk, will you give me your word that there will be no public scenes, no observable oddities in your behavior if we meet anyone? Your intentions aren't entirely opaque."

August heard the 'we' unhappily, but nodded. "Yes, Elector. I wasn't considering running away—how would I hide?—only of exoneration. I dislike being blamed for Ellen's death."

"I can understand that," Lee said judiciously. "She was your friend, and friendship is rare between probes. I don't object to exoneration. What do you recommend, Martin?"

"I suggest that you refuse, Elector. I had understood that August would remain indoors, in this suite, until we return to *Guide*. He's far too dangerous otherwise. He has friends. Brauna has just suggested she'll take him back yet again and, however dubious her sincerity, she also proposed curing his flare, which would give August a compelling reason to tell her anything she wants to know. Huana is a wild card as far as August is concerned, and it's marginally possible that that Neulander, Kolet, might convince his government to grant asylum."

Unreasonably, August felt betrayed by Ahman Penn. He tried to determine if Lee's offer had been a performance designed to make Elector Lee look affable. No, he decided, disappointed nonetheless.

"You've convinced me," Jeroen Lee said, amused. "Perhaps August didn't have all those things in mind, but I'm certain he could capitalize on an opportunity, if one occurred. Anything you'd like instead, August?"

He tried to think of something they might grant him, but

nothing came to mind. Jeroen Lee was waiting. "Do I have another clone, back at the farm?"

Lee and Penn exchanged an enigmatic look. "Yes and no," Elector Lee said. "We've changed the face a bit, having learned our lesson on that score through you. Personality and skills are intact. You should be flattered. The Electors consider your genotype successful enough to replicate once more, despite the complications we've endured because of Alexander and now you."

"How old is he?" August stopped a tremor in his hand. His voice was calm, verging on monotone. The thought of yet another duplicate was disturbing in a visceral way he couldn't analyze.

"Six. You were expected to live another twelve years, you understand. And there are two boys, twins. They are inseparable, I'm told by Ahman Kiku—best friends. A much healthier situation than you endured. It will be interesting to see their differences from you and Alexander."

"One for you and one for Elector Brauna." He felt ill.

The Elector shrugged. "I answered your questions. The answer didn't make your day better, and I'm sorry for that, but now it's your turn to accede to my wishes. Martin, you can leave."

Ahman Penn laughed aloud as he went to the door. "A new toy certainly changes your routine."

"I'm not a toy," August said. But he was. He could be manipulated by them, reproduced in quantity, played with, and then put away—put down—at whim. He felt tears in his eyes. Embarrassed, he turned away from the two older men, though they would see through the flimsy deception.

Ahman Penn said nothing more as he left, closing the door noiselessly behind himself.

"August," Jeroen Lee said then, "I try to be fair whenever possible, wherever it's deserved. I realize—somewhere beneath the convenience of it—that your status as toolman and my 'toy,' as Martin bluntly phrased it, is fundamentally unfair. So I'll make you one other promise: You can say no to me, and it will have no repercussions on your longevity. Now, do you want to come to me, or not?"

Tactically, he should have refused, if only to test the reality of the offer. He preferred Sanda Brauna's soft curves to Jeroen Lee's energy and skill. But, stronger than an inclination for one person over another, more potent even than the need for sincerity or truth, August yearned for the comfort of being touched and talked to, the warmth of another body next to his, the smell of flesh and sweat that belonged to a person other than himself, the sensations of life. He wanted the intimacy of two bodies fusing into one, whoever was beside him. After the ache of all those lonely years, after Ellen's death, he didn't want to be alone. He went to Jeroen Lee and sat on the floor in front of Lee's chair.

Lee reached out and outlined August's features with his index finger, using the edge of his fingernail against August's lips. August rested his head on the Elector's lap. Lee stroked his hair. August shivered, bitterly reminded of the guard patting his dogs in the tracker clearing; he sat up. Lee moved his hands back to his lap, watching and waiting silently for August to decide. August tentatively reached up and diffidently touched Jeroen Lee's cheek. Lee smiled, and when August's hand was close to his lips, Lee turned his head and kissed August's wrist.

Chapter 14

August held his breath, straining to hear and decipher the muffled sounds from beyond the room as he lay motionless in Elector Lee's bed. Lee had met with his late-night visitors—actually early morning, since the status Lee consulted after dressing had shown local three o'clock—in the suite's office, at the far end of the long hall from the bedroom. August thought he heard Evan Kolet's voice.

Martin Penn, yawning but completely dressed, despite the hour, entered the bedroom. Through the now open door, August clearly heard Kolet say, "We need to find them!"

"Get up," Penn said. "The Elector requires your presence."

"Yes, Ahman." August pushed back the covers with his feet and stood, glad of the dimness, so Penn couldn't see August's naked body clearly. He had marks, like brands, along one shoulder. He hadn't minded at the time, but now they stung.

Yesterday's uniform lay discarded on the nightstand. August picked it up, but Penn said impatiently, "No, dressing will take too long. Wear this." He grabbed the Elector's white silk bathrobe from a chair and tossed it to August.

He pulled it on, tying it tightly, feeling the tackiness Elector Lee's sticky body had left. The robe smelled of Jeroen Lee and elusively, perhaps secondhand, of August.

"Don't say a word that isn't approved by the Elector or me," Ahman Penn said. "Don't signal Kolet. Come on."

The luxurious carpeting tickled his bare feet. Air currents inside the robe circulated differently from those moving against a naked body, more sensually, but it felt indecent to be in Elector Lee's clothing. He hesitated at the threshold of the office, ashamed, as if he had stolen a prerogative of power—or had more obviously become one. Ahman Penn had entered the room; he turned and gestured at August to follow.

August went into the office. Neulander artificial lights created pools of darkness in rooms not supplemented by natural sunlight so, seated behind the desk Ahman Penn had used, the strong planes of Elector Lee's face were accentuated by shadows. He was wearing his red Elector's robe like a protest or a warning to the two Neulanders, who turned in their chairs as August entered, looking. One was Evan Kolet, in a military uniform that, except for rank insignia and a shoulder patch, wasn't different from his usual attire. The other, a woman in the maroon uniform of Neuland's federal police, turned away when August bowed.

"Good morning, August." Kolet spoke as though the greeting was a challenge to Lee.

Even so, surely August was not expected to ignore a courtesy. "Good morning, General Kolet."

"Come here." Elector Lee seemed snappish. He had not been asleep for long when the house system had awakened him for this. August smiled. He had expected to be sent away when Lee was through with him—he remembered Vincent's room in Lee's apartment—so when Lee had finally tired, August shyly offered to leave. Lee had covered August's hand with his own and drawn him close before settling down to his rest. As August approached the desk, Elector Lee briefly returned August's smile.

"They have an emergency," Lee said, looking scornfully at Kolet. "Inept of them as it seems, the Neulanders have lost three of our Delegate-Commissioners: Huana, Montague, and Pana. After their visit to a torture party last night, they left the rest of the group, including their guards, and vanished. The police lost them. There have been no ransom demands. Rousse and Kolet suspect foul play. Foul *play,* indeed!"

Kolet moved restlessly, then settled into a position oriented on August, although he worked not to let his eyes stray lower than August's face. "Unfortunately, that's accurate," he said. "The federal police have begun a search using ordinary procedures, and the military is now supplementing their ranks. This is Chief Anya Rousse, the district chief of police for Romoa." Anya Rousse twirled her cap in her plump hands and didn't look directly at anyone as she nodded. Her face and hands were crisscrossed by thin scars, tracks of old wounds, or parties.

Kolet continued, when she did not speak. "The other Delegates, Wilder and Chin, only know that Huana said they were going to another cutter—another torture party. I remembered your skill, so I asked Elector Lee for your help. I first awakened Elector Brauna, I'm afraid."

There was a question in Kolet's final statement, but August said nothing, having been warned not to speak.

"So, what is this magic you do, toolman, that has impressed General Kolet so much?" Anya Rousse's voice was rough, like listening to a vocal scar. "I hear you conjure data out of air."

Kolet rolled his eyes at the ceiling in apology for her prejudice.

Elector Lee smacked his fist hard against the desk. August winced, the gesture was so unmistakably Neulander, but no one else noticed Lee's lapse. Rousse hadn't jumped, but she turned to the Elector. He studied her until, uncomfortable, she began to turn away, then his voice brought her attention back. "This is Neuland's problem. You've requested our help. I expect a respectful attitude toward each of our people involved in this investigation, including my toolman. If the Delegates have been harmed in any way, you may as well learn the *Koran*."

Rousse snorted and looked out the window, although there was only darkness to see. "We've managed this long without you."

"Be quiet, Rousse. You reservists sit in the ground batteries and think you're safe because you haven't had to shoot at an Emirates ship yet. By the time you do, it'll be too late." Kolet stood and bowed to Elector Lee. "Thank you, sir, for lending us August's service. Perhaps he should get dressed?"

"He can't view the replays here?" Elector Lee was startled.

"No," Chief Rousse said, also getting to her feet. "It hasn't all been loaded, and we're still doing integration analysis. He'll come to our station. It's not far."

"You didn't mention this." Elector Lee turned to Penn. "Martin, call Vincent. He can go."

Ahman Penn shook his head. "Elector, speed is critical. I think, given the situation, August would be all right. His skills are better suited to this circumstance."

They all watched Lee, whose face was in shadows. "What

do you think?" he finally asked August. "Will you be . . . all right with General Kolet?"

"Elector, you can depend on me, as you have before," August said, startled to realize it was true. Despite the events of the previous day and the long night, or because of them, he felt a bond to Jeroen Lee that was impossible to justify rationally. "I am in your service," he said bluntly, a bit bewildered.

The Elector nodded, pleased. "Martin will also accompany you to this police station, Kolet," Elector Lee said. It was an order. "August is much too valuable to me to risk his being injured or lost if I send him off with you alone."

August was almost happy to have been given a jailer, to know Lee did not entirely trust in August's conversion.

"Fine," Kolet said, turning away when Elector Lee stood and went to August, touching his cheek. "Be careful," the Elector said softly. Rousse asked something, and Kolet went to her.

"Get ready as quickly as possible," Ahman Penn whispered to August, "then wait for me. I'll insert a cuff before we go." He walked over to Kolet and Rousse.

August bowed, though only Jeroen Lee was watching. "Find them, or all our work will have been useless," Lee said, in the vulnerable tone of someone asking a favor. August nodded and hurried to Lee's room to wash and dress. Jeroen Lee needed the alliance with Neuland, needed the recognition of Neulanders as human, for his safety and for his pride.

Romoa's darkness was less menacing than Sucre's night, perhaps because of the pallid glow of Neuland's three small moons, or the awareness that night would end in only a few hours, but it still was full of black, unlighted places where anything might lurk. Much of that empty space was ocean, and dark was the time Neuland's amphibious beasts, the bloodsucking hoppers and the toothed sharkins, entered an anxious stranger's mind. August looked down as their roadway car crossed a bridge. It was like staring into an endless pit.

On the islands the streetlights lit ahead of them and went off behind as if they were the moving head of an arrow that never reached its goal. The light gave snapshot glimpses of the city—a blanched facade of a pastel building, a darkened park—but no one else was out. Most of what August saw in the window was his own reflection and that of the others in the coach.

"When we arrive, I'll stay on as liaison between you and the police," Kolet told Ahman Penn, but he looked at Anya Rousse.

August leaned back, forcing the protruding needle of the cuff into the upholstered seat and moving his neck until the skin around the insertion point ached despite the numbness induced by the needle's anesthetizing compound. Ahman Penn had inserted the cuff himself; he had the control rod, concealed, in his possession. "I won't use it unless there's no choice," Penn had said. He hadn't tested the device, nor had he informed Kolet that August was wearing one, for which August was grateful. The cuff shamed him.

Kolet repeatedly turned to August, but didn't ask what was clearly on his mind, and August, staring out the window, didn't provide a smooth opening. Kolet had, indirectly, caused Ellen's death.

To take his mind off that subject, August studied Rousse. The faint ridges of her facial scars were made obvious by the poor, unidirectional light inside the car. To a citizen of the Harmony, they were ugly and exotic. August wondered how they would feel if he could trace them. He remembered reading that some Neulanders found scars erotic. "Are you a Punisher?" he asked. "I understand that while they're a tiny segment of the population, they're concentrated in the police."

She jerked forward in her seat. "No! All Punishers were transferred or dismissed from the force in Romoa when your visit was announced." She settled back, scowling at Kolet.

"You made some enemies for the Harmony doing that," Penn observed quietly.

She shrugged. "The Punishers already hated whimpers—non-Neulanders. They say you prevent extrication of the animal from human beings by inhibiting self-evolution of our species." She herself seemed half-convinced of that.

Kolet observed Rousse steadily, then said, "Police tend to be fascists who think they know what's best for everyone—the natural attitude of Punishers—but generally Punishers and their ideas are in decline."

"What about military attitudes, General Kolet?" Penn asked.

Chief Rousse chuckled softly and gave Penn her first friendly look of the night.

Kolet hesitated. "Absolutely the same." He turned to the darkness out the window, his eyes meeting August's in the reflection.

What had Kolet done but offer August help? The rest had been Lee's doing, not Kolet's, and August had done nothing to hurt Jeroen Lee. Just the opposite, in fact. August turned to face directly into the coach. "Except when there really is a threat, I imagine," he said.

Kolet bent forward and touched August's knee, then leaned back, covering a yawn with the back of his hand.

The vehicle interior felt cold, damp and hollow against the expanse of night. August twisted, unsuccessfully seeking some physical comfort for his aches. He was tired and increasingly hungry, though Penn had given him a cheese roll before they left.

"Yesterday morning you were in Elector Brauna's service." Kolet's voice was loud in the small compartment. "What happened to change that, August?"

"Perhaps you just talk too much, Kolet," Ahman Penn said.

The light made Kolet's face look sickly. "Was it by choice, August?" Kolet asked, more softly, as if dreading the answer.

"Yes." August turned back to the window, thinking of the things Ahman Penn could do with the control rod. Kolet was watching him, unconvinced. I'm reckless, too, he thought proudly, and imagined himself clipping puppet strings. "I chose to go to Elector Lee. I could have been dead instead."

Nothing happened, except no one spoke until they arrived at police headquarters.

"August, how are you doing?" Kolet asked several hours later. "Have you found anything at all?" He peered in from the corridor outside the office that Chief Rousse had assigned August and Penn.

August looked up from the displayer, shook his head "no" while freezing the scene of a ballroom filled with smiling, dancing men and women, some of whom occasionally turned a blade or flame upon themselves. He rubbed his gritty eyes, glad of the relief from the tunnel vision of watching uninterrupted replay.

"Need more caffeine?" Kolet came into the room.

"No," Ahman Penn said. He had dragged two guest chairs behind August's place at the desk—the only desk in the room, although from the room's condition and size, the ousted occupant was one of Rousse's minor subordinates—and sat in one chair with his feet resting across the other. He'd reclined with his eyes half-closed as August worked, yet his occasional comments had been helpful.

"Breakfast?" August asked hopefully. Although he'd decided to ask for food at six-thirty and it was only six o'clock, with his concentration broken, August's stomach ached, his hands shook, and he felt light-headed and edgy; he didn't want to prolong the wait. Never before had he felt hunger like an enemy growling inside his gut. First Elector Brauna and then Elector Lee had kept food constantly available to him: a tray of pastries, a plate of cheese, a box of candy; something was always nearby. He was a fool not to have realized the care they'd taken.

Ahman Penn sat up, his feet banging against the institutional brown and white tile floor. "Bring us fruit, or something with a high sugar content, then a protein."

Kolet glared at Martin Penn—quick anger laced with accusation and frustrated shame that made him immediately turn away. "I'm sorry, August," Kolet said. "I'll get something." He left.

August stretched, enjoying the tension as he extended his arms and back, and surveyed the room to let his eyes adjust to a different distance than the displayer. The plaster walls had hairline cracks that had been painted over repeatedly; the room was now a dreary beige. In front of him the only brightness was an oversized red and blue Republic of Neuland official seal. A glamorized portrait of Neuland's founders hung on the wall behind the desk: two women and two men in a heroic pose beside an endless ocean. The four wore medical condition monitors, although the Neulander affliction had not occurred until the following generation. The office's usual occupant was a patriot, August supposed, or else the two objects were regular issue for federal police; Rousse's office had them, too. Without opening the desk drawers, the only personal memento in the room was a mini display of three shaven-head, laughing children. The two youngest wore headband monitors of the type Kolet had described. August picked up the mini, and the children waved while their three young voices chorused, "We love you, Dad. Happy Birthday!"

Penn said, "Get back to work. The longer the Delegates are missing, the worse their chances."

August set the mini down and swiveled the chair to look at Ahman Penn. "Why do they shave children's heads?"

Penn frowned but answered. "Some Neulanders believe hair conceals bacteria that cause infections. It's ridiculous, but they go overboard with their precautions here. Child mortality is relatively high, because of their condition."

Odd, to hear Martin Penn sound even partially sympathetic. August returned to the replay. The police displayers had none of the sophisticated security or detection programs August was accustomed to using. He'd watched the torture party at the quickest fast-forward setting from arrival of the Delegate-Commissioners through their departure and then replayed portions at only double speed. Throughout the room, usually with some joking beforehand, a party goer would cut or burn his or her arm, hand or face. One giggling woman burned her knee. When Evan Kolet had cut himself—one man and a single, superficial cut—August had been shocked. This cutter was nothing, rather innocent and boring. People didn't even appear to have enjoyed themselves. Some looked frequently at the status to tell the time, or their eyes followed a Delegate as if willing him to leave. "This doesn't make sense, Ahman."

"What?"

"The coverage is too good and too bad." At August's command the displayer outlined the five Delegate-Commissioners in brilliant green. "Look, visual coverage is so good that I can do this: here are the people who spoke with more than one of the Delegates." Figures outlined in red filled the picture. "Here are the ones who spoke with each of the three missing Delegates." The red vanished, and eight blue figures appeared. "But about a sixth of the conversations are inaudible. That's very unlikely, given the almost total visual coverage."

"Suspicious, you mean."

"Well, novices care most for setting visuals, but these weren't set by beginners, but by police." August ran the image forward at double speed. An extremely pretty blond girl sitting near the entrance laughed at something Huana said, raised her hand, then cut herself across the palm while

Huana and Chin watched. Huana frowned. Then August froze the scene.

"Can't the signal be filtered?" Penn asked.

"I've tried, but the transcription is too poor. Old equipment." August returned to work. He chose the nearest monitor positions and looked at one still view after another of the blond. She had no other visible scars. "Vanity?" he muttered, then continued the replay from the primary position. The blond girl tossed her head at Huana, seeming to enjoy his reaction, and said something inaudible. August lip-read it as, "Now, go away," and whispered it aloud as she spoke it on replay. Huana nodded and walked across the room, directly to Delegate Pana.

"Wherever the Delegates disappeared, they probably left at Huana's urging," Ahman Penn said. "Concentrate on him."

"I have been. I've traced his path, listening, although a good portion of the time I can't hear him. Ahman, look at this girl."

Penn stood and leaned over August's shoulder. "Pretty."

August nodded. "No scars. She's also one of the very few people at the party who seemed genuinely to enjoy being there. There's a man—these two look at each other but never talk—he's tense at first. His body's rigid, but look at him here, near the party's end." August outlined a tall, heavyset man, who nodded at something a companion said and laughed, giving every evidence of having a good time. "He looks at the Delegates often—everyone does that—but he never speaks with any of them except Huana, and only at the end, just before he leaves. I can't hear that conversation, and the angle's wrong for lip-reading." He outlined three other men. "These three are having a good time, too, but they're drunk. The first man isn't."

A uniformed woman entered the office carrying a plate containing a few pieces of fried, frosted circles of bread, clearly the remains of a larger portion. She set the plate down next to August's displayer and his empty cup of maté and stepped back, smiling at August. "Real food is coming. We had this in the wardroom, and General Kolet said to bring it to you."

August turned from the displayer, inhaling the sweet smell of the cinnamon mixed into the sugar frosting, and looked at the policewoman. She had dark circles under her brown eyes and smudged cosmetic color on her face, inexpertly applied. Her uniform was fresh.

"Get back to work, August," Penn said sharply.

The woman stiffened, but didn't leave.

August turned back to the displayer, but not before snatching a piece of fried bread and eating it.

"So you're a made-man, like that Alexander," she said, leaning across the desk. Her staccato Neuland accent was strong. "I overheard the General say . . ."

"Get out," Ahman Penn said. "Let him do his work."

She closed her mouth into a tight line, glared at Penn, then turned on her heel and left.

August looked up from the displayer, nodding and grabbing another piece of bread. "They were police." He gestured at the scene.

"At the torture party?"

"Yes. Huana may have thought it was real, but it wasn't. We already knew that, but I assumed they were military." August rushed through static views, chasing from monitor to monitor, then stopped. "There." On the replay was the policewoman who'd brought in the bread, but she was wearing a low-cut white dress and engaging in some desultory flirting with an inattentive man.

August looked up as Kolet walked into the office and placed a bag on the table in front of August. "Breakfast."

"How many of the people at the torture party were real?" August asked, absently opening the bag and reaching in. The escaping aroma of the food made his mouth water.

"Real? How do you mean?" Kolet sat down on the edge of the desk, his back to Ahman Penn.

August bit into the item he'd withdrawn from the bag, one of several, a warm, thin pancake filled with cool fruit in a sweet creamy sauce. He was so hungry he didn't mind that he was observed. The taste was wonderful, and he quickly took several more bites before answering. "Real. Not policemen. I recognized the woman who just came in." He pointed to her on the display with the remains of the pancake, then took another bite, speaking through his full mouth. "They're not spontaneous."

"Oh. None of them were real. The cutter was staffed with federal police, once we knew where the Delegates intended to go. Look. They're adults." He gestured at the display. "Cutters are for adolescents. Not many people still attend this kind of party after they're thirty, except Punishers. They use cutters as a ritual."

"I should have noticed! You once told me that torture parties were for the young." August shook his head and put the rest of the pancakes into his mouth.

"You're not a Neulander. You can't expect to know everything about us. At a real cutter, people injure each other, not themselves. We thought that would be too intense—a cutter can get wild—and we didn't want any of the Delegates damaged by mistake."

"Damaged, like produce." Ahman Penn went to Kolet. "You Neulanders have done it again. These were police. Someone there had a hand in the disappearance—abduction, probably—of our Delegates. It looks official."

Kolet jumped off the desk. "No! You know it's not, Penn!"

Penn returned to his chair and didn't answer.

August licked his fingers and returned to his survey of the displayer's image. "Whoever did the layout of the monitors, particularly the sound, must have been part of the conspiracy." He had Kolet's attention. "And I suggest you question them." He outlined the blonde and the heavyset man. "These two act suspiciously; it's somewhere to begin."

Kolet was staring at the two Neulanders.

"They enjoy themselves, you said," Ahman Penn interjected.

"Yes, but more than that. They *must* have known where the dead spots in the auditory pickups were. Otherwise, the coincidence is too much. Every time she speaks with Huana, I can't hear a thing. And watch this." He found the spot where the woman cut her hand and let it run at normal speed, reciting what he could make out of the lost conversation. "See how Huana reacts? He's not angry when she tells him to leave. He accepts it and goes away, even though he doesn't like her. Watch him. Huana's hands are like semaphores."

"She's involved in the disappearance?" Kolet asked, staring as if memorizing her face.

"They're involved in something. I don't know more. If they're police, maybe they're Punishers."

Kolet shook his head. "No scars."

"I don't have any, either, General Kolet. My best guess is

that she told Huana the party was staged and suggested that they go elsewhere to see the real thing."

"If she's police, we can get her." Kolet was already on his way out the door.

August fell asleep in the stuffy office and woke an hour later too warm, with an aching head, a stiff back, and a hunger that surpassed even his earlier need for food.

"Now Kolet's disappeared," Ahman Penn said testily. "I can't convince anyone to take us back to the hotel or even to release a line out of the station so I can call the Elector."

"I'm sorry," August said to soothe Penn. He stretched, but his back didn't feel better. The air inside the office smelled like the training rooms on the farm, of old tensions and bodies; it made his throat ache.

Penn nodded as if accepting a justly deserved apology. "How are you?"

"A little tired."

Ahman Penn grasped his wrist and held it, feeling the pulse, then placed his cool hands against August's forehead, his right cheek, and finally the back of his neck, gently touching the needle and the numb area around it. Then he removed a portable sensor from his bag and reviewed the display. "It's extremely annoying not to be able to rely on your reports. Why do you consistently upgrade your actual condition?"

"I don't know, Ahman."

Ahman Penn returned the sensor to his bag. "Denial won't change your situation."

"I understand, Ahman. But I don't have to focus on it." He glimpsed the crushed, empty bag Kolet had brought, and wished for another breakfast. "Mornings are the worst."

Ahman Penn studied him. "The fever will break soon. You need food, and you didn't get sufficient rest last night, given your condition, but we'll be leaving when Kolet reappears. They said he's on his way. When we're back, remind me to give you something for these symptoms, and a dietary supplement." He walked a few steps away, then returned. "August, I haven't said this before—there are always monitors—but I am sorry for the circumstance in which you find yourself."

A covert apology didn't spark much gratitude in August, particularly while there was a cuff in his neck put there by

Penn. He straightened and looked at Penn directly. "Which one did you mean, Ahman Penn?"

Penn lowered his eyes and went to the door, peered out, then walked into the corridor. August followed him there, sorry to have been so blunt.

Kolet turned down the hall, walking at a quick-march pace that stopped abruptly when he noticed August and Martin Penn. "Punishers. We've got a location, thanks to August. The girl knew, and Rousse's special medics made her talk. The police are assembling a team, and I've called it in, too, so there will be a backup military company from my command. I'd like you to accompany us."

"This is a Neulander situation now." Martin Penn walked up to Kolet. "Take us back to the hotel."

Kolet shook his head. "We need someone from the Polite Harmony present when we bring the Delegates out. They know you, Penn; you're here and we're ready to go. It might help with Huana if August was nearby, too." He looked beyond Penn to August. "What do you say?"

August stared impassively ahead. Martin Penn had not moved. He had not touched the control rod in his bag, but there was menace in the attention he fixed on August.

Kolet slapped the wall beside himself so forcefully it sounded like his hand had broken, but he was oblivious and his medical monitor didn't flash. "Why is it that whenever he goes dumb, I don't believe it's his idea?"

"Don't use August to sidestep me."

"Your Elector wants aid for Neuland. Unless we get help to those Delegates quickly, that may not be possible."

"I'm not a soldier, a policeman, or a Neulander, and August is a very fragile toolman. I refuse to participate in a police raid on a Punisher hideout. Take us back to the hotel."

They glared at each other. Finally, Evan Kolet stepped backward. "Come with me," he said.

At first August was uncertain. His subliminal memory of the track they'd followed from the hotel to police headquarters was difficult to superimpose in reverse over the one Evan Kolet's military driver was now following, because the night passage had not afforded many visual cues for his conscious mind to recall. However, when they crossed a fourth bridge, August was convinced. There had only been three the night before. "Are we taking a different route?"

"Yes." Kolet looked blandly at August, but he had tensed. "This is the morning rush hour, and the more direct route will actually be slower, due to traffic."

There were a considerable number of vehicles on the road, mostly decades-old Harmony models resourcefully repaired, but they had made way on the street for Kolet's car.

"I see," August said, closing his eyes. They were being kidnapped, yet he kept silent, trusting a Neulander. Then he must have dozed because he awakened, cramped and alone in the stopped car. Ahman Penn and Evan Kolet were shouting at each other just outside.

". . . Perfectly safe," Kolet said as August opened the door. "They're a hundred meters up, on the bluff. If there *is* a fight, it won't be anywhere near here, but I'm leaving a few men to ensure your safety." He nodded as August came over.

Penn turned around. "This Altered freak brought us on the raid anyway," he said intemperately. "He says communications may be monitored, so he won't even let me report to the Elector."

The Altered freak Elector. Quietly, staring at Penn's feet, August said, "I remember how thankful I was, in the Grand Assembly, when I heard a familiar voice. The Delegates may be grateful we're here, Ahman." That first voice had been Kolet's. August looked up. Evan Kolet winked at him.

Penn sighed. "Stretch out in the car and rest. Kolet, you're hurting August with this trick."

"I feel better, Ahman Penn," August said in the same submissive tone. It was true, but Penn pulled out his sensor. August surveyed the scene as Penn studied August's condition, ignoring Kolet.

They were parked in a lot which serviced a small, apparently commercial wharf. Above them, on a bluff, were several sizable buildings, like warehouses. August didn't know which belonged to the Punishers; there was no sign of outdoor activity near any of them, but a good scatter-field would explain that. Down below, to one side of the wharf, a link-chained fenced-in yard was bustling with children who were bent over low tubs. Besides their own, only three vehicles were in the wharf's lot, including one truck that pulled away as August watched. It was impossible to see its shape, even so close, because of the military scatter/heat-fix camouflage, but the four soldiers politely ignoring Penn's argu-

ment with their General were an announcement that
something was beyond the broken image of the scatter-field.
The peaceful ocean made those soldiers an incongruous ele-
ment in a greater, gentler scene. The water looked golden
rather than blue in the diffused morning sunlight; the coast-
line of an adjacent island was hazy in the distance. Skimmers out on the water were colorful additions to the view;
several more were docked at the wharf, access to which was
through the parking lot. The solar collectors of the docked
skimmers looked like partially deflated hot air balloons bob-
bing above the water as their distended baskets—the actual
boat—pitched and rolled with the harbor waves.

"The fever's broken," Penn acknowledged grudgingly.

Kolet gestured and one of the soldiers ran to them, a
woman in a major's uniform with a starchy manner and a
crisp, metallic scent.

"This is Major Jennet Tecu," Kolet said. August bowed;
Penn did not. "She and her men will stay with you. Their orders are to protect you both at all costs."

August wondered at the equality of rank that was implied
between a toolman and an Ahman of the Polite Harmony of
Worlds, but Ahman Penn said only, "We'd be perfectly safe
back at the hotel."

Kolet didn't reply to the barb. "Major Tecu will bring you
to the Punisher lodge when this is over, to assist your Delegates. I'm going up to watch the police raid."

August turned away, glancing wistfully at the tranquil sea.
Three men were loading boxes into the largest skimmer
docked at the wharf, a red and black craft that had its solar
collectors fully distended, ready to depart. He imagined a
pleasure trip with no fixed destination, although the men
worked too determinedly for that. In the yard next door the
children—they looked about ten or twelve, old enough for
adult monitors—were also busy, bringing small objects from
one bin to another, entirely intent. August evaluated what he
saw and finally understood. They were sorting bits of discarded mechanisms by hand for recycling. Neuland made do
with what it had.

"When can I contact my people at the hotel, Kolet?"
Ahman Penn asked.

"As soon as the raid's over—it'll begin once all the police
units are in place." Kolet walked away as Ahman Penn began to speak, leaving him fuming. To Major Tecu, Kolet

said, "I'll take this car. Use the shielded one." Kolet signaled and another soldier ran over, entering the driver's seat
as Kolet walked around the car.

Ahman Penn stepped in Kolet's way. "This had better
work out for you Neulanders, Kolet."

Kolet frowned. "If it doesn't, you'll be the least of my
worries." He stepped around Penn, and got into the front
seat, beside the driver. As he looked back, he smiled reassuringly at August.

"Come with me to the shielded car," Major Tecu said,
standing less formally alert as Kolet drove off.

"I thought we were in no danger." Penn moved closer, assessing her.

Major Tecu looked after Kolet's car, uncertainly twisting
the bulky communication device hooked over her medical
condition monitor. "Risk is never zero," she said. She took
a step toward her vehicle, but Ahman Penn didn't move, so
neither did August. "Please, sir," she said to Penn.

He hesitated, then shrugged and nodded.

She smiled with relief and turned to August. "The General
suggested earlier you might be useful. You can watch one of
our sensor arrays trained on the building."

"No," Ahman Penn said angrily. "Enough is enough. Do
your own work."

"Why not, if you're in the car anyway?"

"We won't be," Ahman Penn said. "Kolet said we were
safe here. August and I will walk down to that wharf." He
started in that direction. August joined him, walking by his
side.

"Wait!" the major called. "That isn't a good idea. You'll
be too far if there's trouble."

Ahman Penn stopped and looked back over his shoulder.
"If you interfere with me, I will personally complain to Premier Wren about you, Major Tecu."

"I'll come along." She started running toward them.

"No. You'll stay away. Nothing can happen to us if you
guard the area." Ahman Penn started walking at a quicker
pace.

Major Tecu's footfalls on the soft ground stopped. August
put her out of his mind, instead considering his likely future,
what there was of it. Elector Lee was no monster—was even
interesting—and Martin Penn was basically kind, but would
he ever be alone with Elector Brauna again? If he was, what

would happen? Temporarily, he was free of surveillance. *Guide* wasn't likely to monitor this wharf, and even the Neulanders—except Major Tecu—were busy elsewhere. "Ahman?" August asked, looking sideways at him.

"Yes?"

"How can I stay alive?"

Martin Penn didn't break his stride. "I don't know." He glanced around them, then added, "I believe Elector Lee would make an exception for you and cure the flare, but there is his special concern. Convince him you're safe, and he might."

"Other probes don't deserve flare, either," August said, thinking of Ellen, of Zoe, and Ben—all of them. Alexander.

Ahman Penn chuckled and rested his hand on the gate to the wharf's entrance, facing August. Sunlight in his eyes made him squint. "Then you must all stop being toolmen and become human."

August surveyed Martin Penn, wondering what Jeroen Lee knew that kept him confident of Penn's loyalty and silence. This was no Neulander, and the usual blackmail material—a discarded spouse, money problems, or addictions—did not seem to apply.

A sign warned that the wharf was private. The gate was closed. Ahman Penn looked back to where the military vehicle was lost in its scatter-field, reached through the fence and opened the simple latch. "Let's look at the skimmers."

August stepped reluctantly up onto the heavy planking. Private space, if not privacy, was respected at Center. The wind off the land was strong; he smelled dust and a machine odor from the land, not the scent of the sea. Nerves or fatigue made him stumble. He steadied himself on the fence. "Why are you safe with Elector Lee?" He waited for a guilty reaction or even—given the Ahman's earlier openness—an answer.

Ahman Penn was merely entertained. "Don't you already know a sufficient quantity of secrets?" Ahman Penn chided. "Has learning them been useful to you so far?" He walked farther onto the wharf, paused to look around, then started off toward the far end.

August came after him, avoiding a wet place on the surface, slowed by a creeping, pervasive fatigue that made his legs awkward and the day unreal. He concentrated on the

problem of Martin Penn's secret, as though it was the conclusion to one of his reports.

"It's going to eat at you until you know, isn't it? Probes!
You're the true Jonists. You'll never believe there are impen-
etrable mysteries."

August shrugged, annoyed by Ahman Penn's amusement,
smiling so as not to show it.

"This is not the way to help yourself to live, August."
Ahman Penn set a good pace down the wharf, passing empty
slots and boats bumping against the structure as if they
wanted out of the water. August was considering all he knew
of Martin Penn, and scarcely noticed his surroundings. They
were at the wharf's end, near the red and black ship when
something—a strange scent, or the men's silence—caused
him to look up. The boxes had all been loaded, and there
were two men aboard, watching them.

Ahman Penn stopped as one of the skimmer men from
that ship jumped down from the deck and came to meet
them. The stranger's face was lined with scars and his entire
nose had the shiny, plastic look of scar tissue. He smelled of
sweat and much more faintly, of clinging blood, like a
woman in her menstrual cycle. "Who are you? What do you
want?" the man asked, peering out into the parking lot.
"How did you get here? This is private property."

"Sorry," Penn said, entirely calm. "We were just walking.
Our mistake." He jerked his head toward the shore, signaling August, and they both turned.

The Neulander grabbed Penn's arm. "Wait. I asked you a
question." He seemed to notice their bare arms. "What are
you—whimpers?" He grinned, as if he'd called them fools.

August moved back a step, eager to leave the wharf. The
air over the water was still. The ocean no longer seemed
peaceful, only dangerous and deep. He couldn't swim.

"We're from Darien," Ahman Penn lied. His accent gave
him away as a native of Flute to any Harmony citizen, but
the Neulander hesitated and Penn pulled away. "We just arrived and were looking around. Sorry to bother you. We'll
leave."

The scar-faced man looked up to the second man, still on
the deck of the red and black ship. Penn took a step back, to
where August stood. The second man had lumpy masses of
scar tissue up and down his arms. His shirt, open at the neck,
showed the smooth, pink flesh of recent, untended burn

scars. Punishers, August guessed. They were so identified with scarification that Kolet had rejected the blond woman as a Punisher because her skin wasn't marked. Punishers, so close to where the Delegates were ostensibly held and leaving the area on a skimmer.

"They say they're from Darien, LaFave," the first Neulander called to the other. "No harm done."

"Yeah? On work permits?" LaFave snickered. "Let's see them." His disbelief was obvious.

This second man, LaFave, had no intention of letting them leave. August glanced at the several man-size boxes still on the open deck, and shuddered.

"Let's go, August." Penn's tone was firm. "Sorry to have disturbed you." He turned and took several long steps back toward the parking lot. August quickly followed.

"You better stop right there." The air just ahead of them was suddenly warm.

Penn stopped, extending his arm to stop August. The breeze shifted, coming in off the water. The air felt sticky, much more humid. Slowly, Penn turned back to the two men. His eyes met August's. Infinitesimally he nodded at the parking lot and smiled. They had protection. August turned back to the red and black skimmer, too, but wasn't as frightened as he'd been.

"You're coming with us. We'll sort it out later." LaFave lowered his weapon only slightly. To his companion, down on the wharf, he asked, "So who are they?"

"Pretty boy looks kind of familiar." The first skimmer man studied August's face, then suddenly he swung and punched August, very hard, in the jaw.

August saw it coming late, and was too surprised to avoid it. He grunted and staggered farther back, touching a hand to the side of his face, tasting his own blood and smelling the rank scent of more blood on the Neulander.

"Whimper, for sure," LaFave said. "More meat. Come on, Manley. The feds are almost ready for their big, surprise raid. We've got to be gone when they burst in with only themselves to shoot." He was looking for a reaction from Penn or August.

Penn backed up a step.

LaFave pointed his weapon at Penn. "I don't give a damn," he said, and waited.

August's eyes were stinging with fatigue. The red and

black skimmer had become something horrible, like a stain of blood and decaying flesh marring the beautiful, bright day. He knew precisely what was on that ship, and it was death, immediate and cruel. Manley grabbed August and pushed him toward the ship. It was firm but not particularly hard, humiliation rather than injury. In that off-balance moment of freedom, heedless of consequences, August broke and ran for land.

There was thunder, a scream, and the nearly instantaneous impact of a body onto the dock. Unhurt, but stupidly curious, August turned to look. Manley tackled him.

As August went down, he glimpsed Ahman Penn directly between him and LaFave, the middle of his body red as an Elector's robe, but still alive, since he was moaning.

Chapter 15

Pinned beneath Manley's weight, August twisted, struggling to see. Martin Penn moaned and clutched at his gaping belly with both hands. Blood ran beneath his spread fingers. The Neulanders watched, fascinated as children learning a new game while, prone on the wharf, Penn hunched over his open gut. "Whimper," LaFave whispered, coming down the ramp onto the wharf. He knelt beside Ahman Penn and pushed, rolling him to make the wound more accessible. He rubbed his right hand in it, then extended the hand, staring at the dripping blood, which shone like liquid rubies in the morning sunlight. He licked blood from his fingers. "Warm," he said with satisfaction. He cupped his hand, letting blood from the wound ooze into his palm, while Penn tried ineffectually to stop him, then LaFave drank again.

Manley let August up and stepped toward Ahman Penn like a man hesitatingly straying toward passion.

LaFave looked over to Manley. "We need to get out of here."

"There's time," Manley said lazily. His attention wavered between Martin Penn and August.

LaFave noticed August. "Taste your friend," he ordered. "He saved your life."

Manley giggled.

"No." August thought he would be sick.

"Do it!" Manley shoved August toward Ahman Penn.

Penn's eyes were unfocused. His face had a sheen of perspiration, and his mouth was open with pain and panting. The blood smell burned August's nostrils and cleared his mind. Penn's eyes moved, his chest heaved and fresh blood still oozed between his fingers, but he was dead unless someone helped him. His flesh was graying even as he still breathed. Penn's body made a gurgling sound, almost like hunger. "No," August mumbled.

Martin Penn saw him; their eyes met. Penn grimaced. First his lips moved soundlessly, then he clearly said, "God's caprice."

"A crossman!" LaFave sounded disgusted. He stood and kicked Martin Penn, who groaned. The blood flow from the ugly wound increased momentarily.

"Not military then. That's a relief," Manley said.

Ahman Penn attempted to smile at August. "Not," he said. "Only ..." He tried to rise, then lost his breath in pain.

"It doesn't matter." August knelt where LaFave had been. He touched Ahman Penn's face, to give comfort since there was nothing else he knew how to do. "Will you help him?" he begged LaFave.

LaFave kicked Ahman Penn again. The impact made a sickeningly loud sound. Although Penn didn't respond to the offense, August stared up at LaFave with hatred, seeing evil. LaFave laughed and turned to Manley. "Throw him over the side and let's go. Bring pretty boy for later."

"He'll die in the water! Drown!" August screamed.

"That's the idea, whimper," Manley said. "Get up."

Ahman Penn lifted a hand away from his belly. It was painted with blood. The nails were outlined in red; the faint lines of human skin tissue, like scales, were as clear as the veins on leaves. His head started to fall backward, but August caught him, bracing his back and feeling warmth flow onto him, human blood soaking his clothing. Penn slowly reached up and touched August's forehead. August felt the blood adhere and cool on his flesh, marking him with Penn's life. "Live," Penn whispered.

"Toss him over," LaFave said irritably. "Come on, you! Come here!" He waved the gun, using it as a pointer.

Manley pulled August back and grabbed Penn's arms. Penn made a mewling, animal noise as he was dragged to the edge of the wharf. Blood dripped a trail to the water. August turned away, but couldn't close his ears to the splash as the body hit the sea. Martin Penn had stepped between a gun and a dying toolman; now he was dead. A stupid bargain. God's caprice.

Surely, August thought, he and Ahman Penn had been under surveillance of some kind. Where was Major Tecu, who was to have guarded them "at all costs"? August obeyed LaFave and walked toward the skimmer, but he glanced back at the parking lot. The scatter-field completely hid the military vehicle at this distance, or else it was gone. On the wharf a red stain, already darkening, marked where Martin Penn had lain.

"Stop delaying," LaFave said. "Get aboard. You'll join the other whimpers."

"The Delegate-Commissioners?" He put his foot on the ramp. The engine sound was a low vibration from below and right, but otherwise the skimmer seemed abnormally quiet. There were two smaller decks above, with closed doors to the inner compartments of the ship, and an external stairway—more of a ladder—leading to them, and down to an open hold below. He wondered where the third man he'd seen loading boxes had gone, and how many other Punishers were aboard. "Where are you taking us?"

LaFave gestured with the gun, and August walked up the ramp to the main deck. It was crowded with crates; from the largest box came a foul smell, old blood and the early sweetness of decay. "Are they alive?" August asked, certain they all were not.

"Shut up." Manley had followed LaFave onto the deck and was untying ropes.

"If not, then Neuland is dead."

LaFave poked August's back with the gun. "Turn around so I can see you. Who are you, anyway?"

"No one important." He looked out onto the wharf. The sun shimmered on its surface, reflecting back an image of the next skimmer over at an impossible angle. Quickly, August looked away.

"Manley's right. I know your face."

"Are Paven and Kim still with the whimpers?" Manley asked LaFave. "We're all set."

The ship bobbed in the current and scraped against the wharf, but the power didn't pick up and they didn't leave. The children from the yard next door had noiselessly abandoned their work, but there were no other sounds of men or their machines. August inhaled. A probe sent down to the farm to die, but with enough life left in him to teach a bit, had told August that smell was the sense least susceptible to deception. August smelled bodies, polish, and machines on the slight breeze.

LaFave jerked his head at the stairway. "Get Paven and put this one with the others."

Men exploded from the scenery around them. On the wharf, two dozen armored soldiers leaped out of nowhere, and another dozen ran from the doorways above and on the main deck, all of them difficult and painful to see against the flashing, blinding light of the dissolving scatter-fields. August's eyes teared, blurring his vision. Manley ran and was immediately shot by at least four different soldiers. His head broke apart. The body wavered on its feet, and then the trunk collapsed.

LaFave, wounded in the arm but still holding his gun, had grabbed August, and held him close, with the weapon against August's back. He shifted position, pulling August down, so he had his arm in a choke hold around August's throat. August had to stand with his knees bent. The soldiers stabilized in their positions and didn't shoot.

"We have the ship!" Major Tecu's voice seemed to come from everywhere, without giving away her position. "The Harmony Delegates are free. Throw down your weapon and surrender."

LaFave tightened his painful grip on August's throat. "You move forward, whimper, when I tell you." He raised his voice. "I have another one of them. If he dies, it'll be your fault."

Behind, on the deck above him, August heard movement. LaFave noticed it, and shouted, "Keep back. I'd as soon take him with me as die alone."

"Get him! That's the leader!" Huana shouted from above. His voice was hoarse, weighted with pain and anger.

No one moved.

"Release the Harmony worker, and you'll live," Major Tecu said. "You're not getting out of here with him."

Worker. A kind word for toolman, August thought.

LaFave jerked August. "Forward. One step." Then he shouted, "I'm leaving. You know what will happen if you stop me. You need this whimper alive—you got one dead already." He pushed August.

August took a single step forward with LaFave, toward the ladder. Nothing happened.

"Another." LaFave pushed. They moved forward.

"Don't let him go!" Huana shouted. "That's only a toolman. Stop that man!"

"It's true," August said softly to LaFave. "The Harmony won't care if I'm dead. Surrender."

LaFave grunted. "Then I can kill you." But he pushed and said, "Another." No one stopped them, and they were only a few steps from the ramp.

"You can't let that murderer go!" Huana shouted.

"This is General Kolet. You know me. Release the hostage, and I promise you safe conduct out of the area."

"No!" Huana screamed. "He peeled the skin off Montague's arm!"

"I don't trust you, Kolet!" LaFave shouted back, but he stopped moving forward. "Show yourself!"

There was a long pause and movement above them. LaFave waited.

"Here," Kolet said from the middle deck. LaFave turned, turning August, to face the inner ship, shuffling backward so his back was to the open sea.

Taking his time and studying LaFave, Kolet came down the stairway. He was wearing full body armor, with a handgun in his belt and a rifle over his shoulder. He stopped a few steps away, but didn't glance at August. "Let him go, and I'll let you go. Kill him, and you're dead. There will be no more hostage, one way or another."

"I don't trust any generosity from you," LaFave said. "The Andian says he doesn't want him."

"I don't listen to the Andian."

LaFave laughed. "There's that, at least. Shit, I know who I've got! It's Alexander!"

Kolet shook his head, but his eyes never left LaFave. August had rarely seen a human in such rapt concentration. Kolet was coolly ready to kill LaFave, was manipulating an opportunity to do so in an assassin's style of facilitation. "No. That one's been dead twenty years. This is another of their toolmen. Show them that Neulanders don't make those distinctions between men. Let him go."

"They're all whimpers."

"Exactly."

They stared at each other.

"Let him go. You can keep the gun, but lower your arm. Step to the edge of the deck."

"You're a traitor to your grandmother, Kolet," LaFave said, but the pressure around August's neck lessened. "What assurance do I have you're not going to kill me anyway?"

"My word. Talia Kaviscu's grandson—you Punishers claim to respect her. Now decide, or I'll tell my men to shoot you anyway, since the Harmony doesn't care about the boy."

LaFave stood still. Waves lapped against the skimmer's side. Underfoot, the deck rocked gently. "How do I get out of here?"

August almost cried out in relief, but Kolet didn't react to LaFave's defeated tone.

"Walk off the wharf beside me, then I'll give you my car, or yours. Your choice. But you have to let the boy go first."

"All right." There was a click as LaFave unset the gun while simultaneously releasing August.

August jumped away from LaFave. As he fled, instinctively moving away from the one direction Kolet's eyes seemed to avoid, there was a single shot, loud in the stillness. LaFave crumpled to the deck, dead, shot through the chest.

"Scum." Kolet signaled that all was well, then shouted, "Medic. Check this man." He meant August. Kolet himself went over to LaFave and looked down at his corpse. Movement resumed all over the wharf and the skimmer.

"You lied to him," August said. He hadn't recognized the lie.

Evan Kolet walked back, loosening the neck of his armored jacket and exhaled. "I could never let him go; I didn't want you killed, too."

A soldier with a caduceus on his collar hurried down the steps Kolet had used.

"I'm fine." Then relief hit August. He slumped against the skimmer's wall. The medic had a portable scanner much like the one Penn used. "Ahman Penn! He was shot and thrown in the water!"

Kolet nodded. "We know. Major Tecu had you under surveillance the whole time. She picked up what was going on inside the skimmer shortly after you were on the wharf. Unfortunately, it was too late to stop you without alerting the Punishers, who would have killed the Delegates. I'm sorry, August, but retrieving your missing Delegates came first. After we holed the skimmer and boarded, the amphib's went searching for Penn. The current's strong here, but he can't have drifted far."

"Sir, there's a strange neurological reading," the medic said.

"The cuff," August said. Kolet stared, uncomprehending. "You've seen it." August was embarrassed. "Ahman Penn used one on me back at Center."

Kolet's eyes widened. "Remove it," he ordered the medic. "It's in the neck."

"No—there'll be trouble."

"Do it."

"Neuland's finished, Kolet." Delegate Huana came down the steps slowly, each footfall distinct as the separate tolling of a bell. When he reached the main deck, August surveyed him. He looked drained and bitter, but appeared to be intact. He didn't look at August. "It's over. Pana is dead, tortured. You've seen Montague's arm. No one in the Harmony will lift a finger to help Neuland after this."

"There are fanatics everywhere, Delegate. Police security was lax. That's why I brought my own people here, but . . ."

"Just look at Montague," Huana said sadly, not gloating. "Or what they did to Pana, if you can see it through the eyes of someone who knows pain. I'm whole because they had something special in mind for me. In honor of Andia, they said." He sighed. "I feel sorry for you, Kolet. You're not as bad as these, but you're tied to them and they've brought you down."

"Delegate." Kolet looked uncertain. He wiped his arm across his sweaty forehead. "What can I do?"

Huana studied him. "Suffer. If even once I thought a Neulander was capable of real compassion, and not just the occasional altruistic reflex, then you might be worth saving."

Kolet scowled. "How do you tell the difference, Delegate, between reflex and compassion? Or are you the only person who can recognize the truth?"

Huana walked to the railing and looked out at the sea.

"Sir," the military medic said, "I don't know these things, and it forms a neural connection. Do you want me to cut it out? There could be damage."

Kolet looked at August and shook his head. "No."

Another soldier led Delegate Montague down the stairs. A medical sack was draped over his arm. His eyes were red, and the tracks of tears made his cheeks glisten. He trembled with each step he took and appeared only marginally aware of his surroundings. "I can't work without him flinching. We need some kind of nerve deadener," this soldier/medic said to the medic who'd scanned August.

"Anesthetic," Huana said, supplying the term. "You people didn't come prepared. Perhaps you hoped we would be dead."

"That isn't true," Kolet snapped. "I don't think even you believe it, and I'm tired of hearing that nonsense." Kolet turned his back on Huana. "Medic, get Delegate Montague a sled and take him to the Medical Emergency Mobile. Locate some anesthetics in MEM." He watched them leave. Others came and removed Manley and LaFave's bodies like awkward garbage, while August, Kolet, and Huana watched in silence.

Finally, Huana said, "Of course you killed them all. We'll never know the truth about who arranged this." He started walking toward the ramp.

"Delegate Huana, please be reasonable," Kolet said, blocking the way. "These Punishers don't represent Neuland. What do I need to do to convince you of that?"

"You can't. These people are tolerated here. Most of their activities are legal. They may be a fringe group, but they're on the same spectrum as you, Kolet, and I won't spend a single additional life to protect them or you. I think others finally will see the correctness of that." Huana hesitated. "August, I couldn't let that loathsome Altered creature escape; I apologize if I seemed harsh toward you. Come with me. We're leaving."

August had his own agenda. "Delegate, I'd like to stay until Ahman Penn is found. It's possible—I know the chance is remote—but it's possible he's alive. Please, sir. It is important to me."

"I'll bring August back to the hotel with Penn's body," Kolet quickly offered. "And we still need to locate Delegate Pana's body, if it's aboard."

"A box," August said, remembering the smell. "That one, here on deck." He pointed. Kolet nodded and spoke an order.

"All right, August," Huana said. "I understand the hope a man feels when there is no body. I'll tell Elector Brauna that you're well and on your way." He turned to leave.

"He's owned by Elector Lee now," Evan Kolet said. His voice stopped Huana. "If it's over for my people, I'll call a toolman what he is—a human slave. Some deal was made, and August has a new master, though not for long. He's dying, by this pointless man-made disease your high and mighty Harmony of Worlds created, that your Electors refuse to cure because of its convenience. A disease you triggered by kidnapping August. Think of that next time you're feeling compassionate. Transportation will be provided, Delegate-Commissioner Huana. Go wait on the wharf and spread your bullshit there."

"Margot is right—I'm an ass. I should've held my temper. Or doesn't it matter?" Kolet stood at the skimmer's rope railing with August.

"It doesn't matter. You'd need a miracle to get help from the Harmony now." August leaned tiredly against the railing and looked around. Noise was the dominant impression, the sound of vehicles and men, but August had sorted the strangeness and knew there was no real confusion. The wharf was surrounded by military vehicles in three dimensions: a VTOL hovered overhead, two amphibious vehicles stood off the skimmer's sides in the water, and the shoreline held four military transports. Police cordoned off the area, but Kolet wouldn't allow them inside the perimeter; August had lip-read Kolet's antagonistic conversation with Chief Rousse and the hostile report regarding the police he'd delivered to his military superiors.

"I wish I could blame it all on him," Kolet said, gesturing at Huana, waiting near the mobile medical facility for Montague. "If we could show he planned it as a revenge on Neuland, we might have a chance."

"He didn't. It was Neulanders."

Kolet grunted bleak acquiescence and turned to August. "If it's over for us, at least there's no reason not to take you to a medic and cure this disease."

August imagined a long life as a defector, confined to Neuland. *Ah love.* "No. I couldn't go home."

"Where's that? A clearing on Sucre they call a farm, although its only crop is men?"

That stung. "Home is Sanda Brauna."

"August, I have a son four years younger than you. If he told me he loved any woman—but especially one five or more times his age—enough to die to be with her until his death, I'd take him to a psych, or lock him in his room until the delusion passed."

"Elector Brauna will cure me," August said. "She said she would,"

"She can't be trusted. She thinks toolmen are disposable." Kolet took off his armored jacket and tossed it to the deck. Perspiration stained the back of his bodysuit. He leaned against the railing, looking out over Romoa. "I was about your age—already a lieutenant—when Neuland attacked Andia. My grandmother was vilified by the Harmony, along with Pavel Havic and your clone. Alexander fascinated me. Until then, I'd never heard of toolmen. Toolman. The word's obscene. I thought, during all that soul-searching—and most Neulanders did, believe it or not—that whatever wrong we had done, we had one moral superiority, and at least Grandmother Talia had tried to save one life, the toolman Alexander. I'm not so naive now, but when I met you I was determined to make you understand and like us. And when I learned you were in flare, I . . . ached to complete the job my grandmother, for whatever motives, had begun. I don't want you to die in that stupid, unnecessary way; particularly, I don't want you to die because of Neuland. I have enough authority to do this. As far as anyone in the Harmony need know, you've vanished."

"No. You'll only cause more trouble for Neuland. Elector Lee will be furious, and he's likely to be Neuland's only remaining friend." August lowered his head. How secretly, how intensely humiliated Jeroen Lee must be by Neuland's imperfections.

Kolet had become distantly alert, listening to something August couldn't hear on Neuland's closed military communication system. Kolet gestured, and a soldier ran forward. "Take August to my car and keep him there until my direct order otherwise." The soldier moved toward August as if he was a prisoner, while Kolet turned to leave.

"Someone's coming," August guessed. He looked away from the land, out at the limitless sea beyond the islands. Nothing was visible but a horizon of indeterminate distance. His eyes ached in the bright sunshine, and he rubbed them. It was difficult to think with fatigue numbing his mind. He wanted to lie down in a soft, wide bed. "I'll wait here."

Kolet turned back. "You don't have a choice, August. Go with the sergeant."

A man in a wet suit ran onto the wharf, shouting. "General Kolet! We've found the Jonist priest!" He stopped to catch his breath. "He's alive!"

Martin Penn was wet and ragged, his skin purplish-blue and gray wherever the Neulander medics hadn't covered him in blankets or medical paraphernalia. Breath hissed from his mouth through a tube, but he was alive enough that his eyes widened when he saw August.

"I need to report to Premier Wren," Kolet said. "You see he's alive, now get to my car."

"Do you have anesthesia?" August demanded of the medics. They ignored him. One moved a black box over Penn's wound, like ironing it. August inched closer, appalled by the fishy stench and the wrenching sight of blood and pulsing organs exposed to public view. He worked to avoid gagging on the odor and watched Penn, studying each breath for signs of another.

"*Now*, August!" Kolet nodded impatiently at the sergeant, who had followed them to MEM. "Get him out of sight; they're here." Kolet went out the door.

The sergeant grasped August much as LaFave had, forcefully but without using inflicted pain as a device to move him; however, August knew Kolet's sergeant wouldn't kill him. Martin Penn kept his attention on him, so August felt his presence had purpose. "No. He needs me here."

"The general says you're going, so you go," the sergeant said, grabbing August again.

The door opened. Elector Lee, stately in his red Electors' robe, entered with one toolman guardian and Delegate-Commissioner Wilder of Darien, who had her arm around Esteban Huana. They were trailed by a frowning Evan Kolet. The sergeant stopped levering August forward. Irate medics shouted at everyone to get out of the room.

Instead, Elector Lee pushed aside the clear curtain and went to the table on which Penn lay. "I'll take over his care." He spoke so authoritatively that all of the Neulander medics but the one working over Penn's stomach moved back. Elector Lee reviewed the sensor data displayed above Ahman Penn and inspected the work the medic was performing. He gently took Penn's right hand from beneath a narrow cover and held it. Penn watched Jeroen Lee's face.

Kolet gestured at the sergeant, and he released his grip on August, but remained close.

"Who are you?" a medic asked Lee.

"Martin, I'm pleased by your survival," Lee said firmly, ignoring the Neulander.

Penn gasped, trying to speak. Lee leaned close to Penn's lips, then shook his head and straightened. "It's all right," Lee said. "You'll recover." Penn grimaced in response, trusting Lee's evaluation.

"How is he?" Neela Wilder asked.

Elector Lee gave Penn's hand a light squeeze, carefully placed it back at his side, covering it, then returned to the visitors' side of the curtain. "They've stabilized him; a competent job. Gut wound, with no major organ damage. They're repairing and closing the intestine, using a standard nerve block. He was extremely lucky, but he'll need rest and time to heal." Lee glanced at the Neuland medic. "I'm taking Martin up to *Guide*. We'll leave Neuland immediately after you close."

The medics protested, but Lee turned his back on them.

Delegate-Commissioner Wilder released Huana, patting him absently, like a distracted mother. "That is far from decided, Elector. If you wish to leave with your people, go ahead, but *Guide* will wait in orbit for CIN. Our mission isn't complete."

Elector Lee glanced at Esteban Huana, who had straightened and moved forward, then shook his head. "Neela," Lee said, "no one, not excepting those of you from Darien, has been more vocal than I have been in supporting Neuland. The time has come to recognize that these people are incurably dedicated to wresting defeat from the jaws of victory. This is the second time they have managed to do the unthinkable and unforgivable. The scale, fortunately for the Harmony, is smaller than when they attacked Andia, but the effect is substantially the same. I've finally accepted that Neuland isn't worth the effort of civilizing. There's no reason to stay on this hazardous world any longer."

"That isn't fair," Wilder protested. "We must review the circumstances."

Huana laughed and watched Jeroen Lee.

"Tell me under what circumstances it is proper for a Delegate to be tortured to death?" Lee said. "And we've just seen what happened to Montague." Lee looked at her, at Kolet, then noticed August, and jammed his hands deep into the pockets in the folds of his red robe. "Come here, August."

There was cold, repressed fury in Lee's voice. August bowed warily, but didn't move.

"I'll take August back to Elector Brauna, while you deal with the care of your own people, Jeroen," Huana said unexpectedly. Perhaps he also sensed violence ready to explode through the icy calm demeanor of the Elector.

Lee told Huana, "He's in my service, Esteban," then August's body tingled with sudden pins and needles. Jeroen Lee, hands still in his pockets, watched calmly, testing August, or giving him a choice.

"No." Kolet was loud. "August stays here, free. The Republic of Neuland does not respect or enforce the Harmony's classification system for men." At his signal, the sergeant moved visibly into a guard position with respect to August.

"What is going on?" Neela Wilder asked. "This is a *probe!*"

Elector Lee's smile was hard as stone. He hadn't looked away from August. "Show us in whose service you are, August. General Kolet and Delegate Huana need to know."

Ahman Penn groaned as he struggled unsuccessfully to move, momentarily diverting the attention of everyone but Jeroen Lee. Penn's eyes were fixed on August. Sweat broke out on his face as he tried to speak. There was no sound, but his lips formed the word "safe." Penn had told August to become human, teasing, yet sincere. He had sacrificed himself and had almost died for August. August bore him an immense obligation he had no ability to repay. If he owed obedience to anyone in this nightmare situation, it was to Penn, but with a tired despair, August didn't understand what Penn meant. That August was safe with Lee? Penn didn't like Kolet.

Huana glanced at Jeroen Lee, his unexpected new ally, smiled guiltily at August, and kept quiet. The sergeant put his hand on August's shoulder, an incomplete assurance of protection.

"Go outside to my car," Kolet ordered.

"Whose service?" Lee demanded.

Every chance he'd ever been given had been stacked against him. The choice he'd made for love and Sanda Brauna in the clearing on Sucre was slowly killing him. Kolet offered, Huana offered, and if he accepted either he could die at Jeroen Lee's hand. Lee himself was an enigma. Perhaps he wouldn't kill August, yet could Lee risk the revelation of his genetic heritage at such a time? And what about Lee's emotional state? If ever there was a man hurt and despairing over the actions of others, it must be Lee, however little he revealed. August's risk was too immediate, the threat too direct for his exhausted mind to judge. There was one safe place, one place that offered rest.

Ahman Penn slumped back, his eyes closed. Live, he'd said, and branded his meaning in blood on August's forehead. August bowed, staying low a moment to censor resentment and shame from his expression—and to prevent himself from tumbling to the ground. "I am in the service of Elector Lee," he said, huskily.

"See that you remember it. Now come here," Lee said.

"I forgot that damn thing!" Kolet was both apologetic and furious. He went a step toward Elector Lee. "I won't allow it."

"Aren't the death and injury of Harmony Delegates enough for Neuland today?" Lee asked. "Are you threatening harm to an Elector, too?"

"No," August said. He kept his attention fixed on Jeroen Lee and went to him. The Elector placed an arm around August's shoulders. The intimacy undoubtedly looked shameful, and August felt disgraced by his choice, but there was unforeseen comfort in Lee's touch. When fatigue and humiliation made August tremble and his knees nearly gave way, Elector Lee helped support August on his feet, but without making his consideration visible to their watchers.

"I'll take my *own people* back to the hotel and wait until the rest of you are ready to quit Neuland. Kolet, arrange for Martin's transfer to me." Toolman and Elector walked out of the hospital together.

Chapter 16

Martin Penn sat up as August entered his bedroom. It was the first time he had managed it on his own, so August smiled and said, "You're getting better." He set the tray on the nightstand and helped Penn fix his angled position against the bed pillows.

"Where's the servitor?" Penn asked, gesturing at the tray. He looked thin, and his face was gaunt. Anemic, Elector Lee said, but mending well four days after his injury. Harmony citizens were hardy.

"Elector Lee won't allow Neulanders in the suite anymore, and since we didn't bring any subs . . ." August shrugged, then glanced out the window. It overlooked the empty shore he had walked with Evan Kolet. He imagined two figures there, then sighed, and turned his attention to Ahman Penn.

"So you've become our sub?" Penn spoke lightly, but clearly intended the insult. Martin Penn had saved his life, but August suspected he would not do the same again. "Well, better our own than a Neulander. What's the latest news?"

August extended the tray's frame over Penn's hips and centered the cereal bowl, then hovered at the bed's edge to be available if Penn required help eating. "Punishers are being murdered on the streets by desperate Neulanders. Only Delegate Wilder still favors aid." As he spoke, he handed Penn the spoon and watched him sip the warm, sweet cereal. The rich smell made August's mouth water, though he'd eaten before bringing breakfast to Penn. He bent over the tray and uncovered strained pears, testing himself against his hunger. I eat, therefore I am.

Ahman Penn placed the spoon on the tray and reached up. He grasped August's chin, turning his head slightly. "That's new."

The bruise inflicted by the Punishers was gone, but August had a fresh one purpling his right cheek.

"What happened?" Penn asked without releasing August. "That's not like him at all."

"Premier Wren and Deputy Premier Ash visited last night. The Emirates' raid on the Kay mines frightened them. They assumed there wouldn't be an attack while *Guide* is in the system, or, if there was, that we would rally to Neuland's defense, whatever we've said. Delegate-Commissioner Montague told them there would be no military aid. Period. They begged Elector Lee to intervene. He refused and sent them away."

"So then, knowing how this is for him, you pushed him too hard last night, and he finally lost control. That's a sneaky, dishonest way to attack. How did your victory feel, August?"

August turned his head, unable to meet Penn's eyes.

Penn's hand slipped around to the back of August's neck. The needle was still in place. Ahman Penn released August in a gesture that, had he not been feeble, would have pushed him away. "If he doesn't get that out soon, there'll be permanent damage."

"Does it matter?" August asked quietly.

Ahman Penn glanced at him. "It's difficult to murder a man inside a hospital," he said cryptically.

August moved, inadvertently jostling the bed. Cereal spilled over the side of the bowl. He mopped it with an extra napkin, feeling clumsy. He continually relived that moment in the Neulander medical facility. The long, sleepless night before, the self-sacrifice of Martin Penn, the conversations with Penn and then Kolet had all seemed to be building to an emotional crescendo, and then he'd behaved like a coward. He had refused the chance of freedom out of fear. No wonder Penn was disgusted. "I'm still alive, Ahman." He looked out the window at the clear blue sky. "God's caprice."

Penn grunted and ate strained pear. "Martyrdom is overvalued as a calling. My gut wishes you were dead, August. Perhaps caution is wiser." His tone said otherwise.

August adjusted the bedclothes, smoothing wrinkles in the soft fabric with his hands. Though the question was rude and sounded silly, like asking a man if he believed in ogres and fairies, August asked, "Do you believe in gods, Ahman?"

For the first time Penn looked at August with something of his former enthusiasm. "I believe there are mysteries that men can't fully know. Some men choose to call them gods or God." He held up a trembling hand for a moment, preventing August from interrupting. "My belief isn't irrational, though orthodox Jonists disagree. It's based on intellectual intuition, not faith, and on my experience of events which are more than chaotic disorder or supra-order, but are equally true. I believe the existence of such mysteries is important. Life is more than Jonism's search for rational knowledge and order. There is a higher ethic. What about you, toolman? I used to think you might understand."

"The Sea of Faith," August said. "No. You think in larger terms than I do, Ahman. My belief is simpler. People should be true to one another. Honest and fair. Respect, I suppose. Without that"—He struck a pose to clarify that he was quoting—"there is no joy, no love, no light, no certitude, no peace, no help for pain." *Ah, love. Are you listening? Will you be true to* me?

"Is that more of Brauna's poetry? It's beautiful, but you hide behind it, August. To whom should you be true? A human chooses for himself; he doesn't choose among masters." Penn waved a hand. "You're tiring me. I want to be alone. Come back for the tray later."

Elector Lee summoned August. "If I removed it, would you run?" On his desk was a tray with a medical setup: a cylindrical instrument, spray antibacterial/coagulant and bandages.

There was no preamble or pretense August had any privacy, but Lee's calm attention warmed into a smile. August bit his lip to keep from returning it, doubting everything about himself. "I don't know."

"Honest, anyway." Lee looked briefly at the work on his open screen. "Convince me that you'll be true to me, entirely loyal, and the reason for having you put down disappears—as does the reason to let your flare continue. I won't give you more than a probe's normal span—at least, not yet—but I can end this current episode and you'll have what you expected, twelve or thirteen years."

August guessed that he would live. "I don't know how to convince you, Elector. I have never acted against you, except I admit I ran away to Elector Brauna."

"Come here." Lee turned his chair to face away from the desk.

August stood in front of the Elector and, at a gesture, knelt. Their eyes were level. He suppressed a smile as he imagined being knighted by some antique feudal lord. *I dub thee human.*

Elector Lee touched the bruise he'd made, but so lightly it felt the same as touching any other place. "I am sorry," he said. After Penn's disdain, Lee's gentle touch, sincere apology and clear self-doubt made August ashamed that he had actively incited Lee to hit him. "I said I wouldn't hurt you, and I have," Lee said. "I promised you the option to refuse, and last night I nearly didn't keep my word. Neither will ever happen again." He studied August. "Martin is a romantic. He's disappointed because he believes you've lost your independence, which he admired. I think otherwise, that in compelling your obedience and hurting your pride I might have lost you. My only excuse is that my own pride was hurt." He leaned forward and kissed August's lips.

August's response was automatic rather than heartfelt, but Elector Lee smiled and touched his cheek again. "I've spent my life trying to make Neulanders and other Altered peoples human in the eyes of the Harmony of Worlds. It seems right to me. Martin's metaphysics aside, the only important distinction between men of human ancestry is legal status. Biologically, the variations are insignificant. However, I've made enough excuses for Neulanders. They simply aren't worth the effort."

"I don't think that's true, Elector."

Their physical proximity made the comment seem intimate. "Thank you for that, August, but Huana's right. Something is missing from them." More softly, looking at August's bruise, he said, "And perhaps from me."

"Sympathy," August said. "No matter what happens to Neulanders, no matter what their danger, they don't evoke sympathy in others. We assume they can't suffer, so people don't care."

Elector Lee looked at his hands. "Unprovoked, and solely for political advantage, they swept Andia and killed eighteen million people."

"But that's hardly the only atrocity humans have ever committed on other humans, Elector. It was evil, but not unhuman."

Jeroen Lee had used the same argument himself, but he stared at August as though believing it for the first time.

August nodded. "General Kolet once told me that it's difficult for Neulanders to believe in pain—and yet they do. You do. It's the standard humans who don't recognize suffering in Neulanders." He took a breath, feeling better than he had since leaving the medical facility with Elector Lee.

Jeroen Lee tapped the medical cylinder against his desk, glancing occasionally at August. "I want you with me," he said eventually. "I'm afraid you won't stay, if you have a choice, and yet I dislike not giving you a choice. Guilt, perhaps, or vanity. Why do you prefer her to me? I know it isn't a question of male or female, not for you."

"To make amends for Alexander," August said quickly.

Lee looked startled. "But what do you believe he did wrong?"

August hesitated, confused. Despite the revelations, he supposed that emotionally he did still blame Alexander. "He never loved her. She's afraid because of that. And all my life I've wanted her to want me."

"Those seem poor arguments for love to me. For all your repetitions that you're not Alexander, it appears to me you're still trying to be him, only better." Elector Lee closed his screen. He picked up the antibacterial spray from the medical tray. "Turn around and bend your neck."

August did, staring at the pale carpeting, trying to concentrate on seeing individual fibers rather than feeling Lee's fingers on his neck. There was coolness, then pressure, tugging, but no pain. Just then, August wished for pain. Did he prefer Sanda Brauna only because of Alexander?

Elector Lee cast the device back onto the tray, but kept a hand on August's head so that he didn't raise it. Lee deftly reached for spray and bandage, and applied both with his free hand, only then allowing August to straighten his neck. "All right. Of course you'll heal quickly, but there'll be a slight all-body soreness for a few days. It was in contact too long to avoid a reaction."

August gingerly felt the back of his neck, but the bandage covered the spot where the needle had been. The medical instrument on the tray now held the thin, bloody needle clasped within it. "Thank you, Elector."

Jeroen Lee frowned. "The situation is no worse than before Kolet asked for your help. My guardians still have orders not to let you pass. I think you will eventually prefer honesty and my steady, true regard over Sanda's erratic passions. I will give you a choice, but not yet. Here"—he reached into his pocket and handed August a tiny, red foil-wrapped pellet. "I've been carrying this since I warned you not to ask. I'm as inconsistent as Sanda, I suppose. I planned to kill you, then made this after the other probe died instead. Take it."

August unwound the wrapper, exposing a pale green tab. Except for color, it seemed identical to *falfre*. The scratched surface of the hard gel showed Jeroen Lee had indeed carried it for days. "What will it do?"

"Reestablish your normal metabolic rhythms. This is a symptomatic treatment. You'll enter flare again, but not until you're older. We'll see, then." He smiled and leaned back in his chair. "Aren't you going to thank me?"

An end to hunger. August stood up. His fingers closed tightly around the tab, but suddenly he remembered Ellen and couldn't thank Elector Lee. "This will help you deal with Elector Brauna. Maybe others—Huana."

Lee shrugged. "You know me well enough to understand I do very little for a single reason. However I view her personal failings, Sanda is extremely effective as an Elector. Nevertheless, there are ways to pacify her that wouldn't involve a potential long-term conflict over you. Frankly, August, if you were dead, this matter would adequately resolve itself in a week. Be glad I don't want to lose you."

August put the tab in his mouth. Its edges melted as they contacted saliva. A medicinal taste, slightly bitter, was released, followed by a surge of artificial sweetness, then only aftertaste. The tab was gone. Jeroen Lee awaited his comment, so August said, "It seems anticlimactic."

"Life generally is." He hesitated, turned his chair back to face the desk, then said, "What can we do before our departure in two days to save Neuland from destruction by the Emirates?"

"Your personal prestige is the greatest of any Elector. I'm virtually certain that Huana would reconsider his position on Neulanders' lack of humanity if you told the Delegates about yourself."

Lee interrupted. "Think again."

August stared at the floor. "Neuland would need to suffer so obviously that the Harmony couldn't ignore the fact that they hurt. It would have to be physical suffering, because it's too easy to dismiss emotional distress. In lieu of that, we might lure the Emirates flight group that's been hiding in-system since the attack on the Kay mines into an attack on *Guide*. Anger at the Emirates could substitute for sympathy for Neuland."

"That's treason, August. *Guide* is a battleship, but lives might still be lost. It's no different conceptually from Neuland's original scheme against Andia. Besides, I doubt that it's feasible. These Emirates raiders would have to be insane to attack *Guide*. And Neuland had better not try any such thing, either." He stood. "You're no strategist—perhaps that's best. I have a few ideas, though I'd rather not have had to use them. Huana is the key. If he's convinced, then even now, everyone will follow." He went around the desk, then looked back at August, grinning in an uncharacteristically mischievous way. "I'm meeting with Sanda and Ica Kurioso. Any messages?"

August smiled, willing to be teased. Not once during the discussion had he felt like a dog, a puppet or a tool. "If Zoe is there, Elector Kurioso's probe, tell her that she was right."

"About?"

"Toolmen are human."

Jeroen Lee laughed without his usual reserve. "I will, and see what Ica thinks of that."

"I was approached by Elector Brauna," Vincent said from the office doorway. His tone shrieked innuendo.

August glanced up from his solitary work sorting through the few Harmony news reports of the attack on the Delegate-Commissioners that had reached Neuland; he was looking for any positive angle Elector Lee could exploit. Vincent leaned—draped himself, actually—against the doorway. As August watched, he slunk into the room. August shook his head in disbelief and returned to work.

"She doesn't have a probe in personal service now." Vincent twitched his hips.

"Is Elector Lee that anxious to get rid of you, that he can't wait for Sucre and the farm?" August scoffed.

"I see how well you're doing," Vincent retorted, eyeing the bruise.

August smiled at the untouched bowl of sornuts on his desk. He was slightly hungry, but he could wait; soon he wouldn't be hungry at all. He had intended to boast of his cure to Vincent, but it didn't seem right.

Vincent laughed and sauntered closer. "Poor August, no one likes him anymore. Elector Brauna says it's best she's rid of you."

Sanda Brauna wouldn't speak so freely, nor would she purposely hurt him so grievously, therefore, he wasn't hurt. August forced a miserable expression and looked up at Vincent. "What did she say?"

Vincent observed him, then answered slowly. "She called herself a bright star, and said you would be her death." Suspiciously, he added, "That was obscure. What did she mean?"

August said nothing and pretended anguish. It was Keats again: "Bright star! would I were steadfast as thou art," a poem acknowledging steadfast love, even to death. "Tell her she is a beautiful lady without mercy," he said in a choked voice, the first thing that came to mind, yet appropriate. Perhaps too much so, he thought, then recognized Jeroen Lee's infiltration of doubts into his mind.

Vincent was motionless. "Do you think I'm a fool? Does she? I should have known better." He turned to leave.

"Wait! Vincent, please!" August stood to stop him, then imagined Elector Lee watching this. Lee had cured August's flare; he would feel betrayed. Sanda Brauna had nothing to lose, but August's life could be jeopardized by her flirtatious game. What could he say to convince Vincent and be innocuous to Elector Lee? Impossible. Anything at all would be suspect.

Vincent looked back. His pale face had reddened—bad self-control. "You take my place, then sneer at me. I wish I had managed to kill you!"

This was real hatred, a heat that filled the room, not probe posturing. August didn't hate Vincent half as much, despite his having killed Ellen. Or Elector Lee had, and August didn't hate Jeroen Lee. "Do you ever think of Ellen?" he asked, sitting heavily down in the chair.

Vincent took one step back toward August. "I never guessed she'd touch your screen. No one dared, with you so solid with *two* Electors. She must have been furious with you."

August gaped at Vincent, noticing the dark circles under his eyes, the lack of his usual lip gloss and his carelessly combed hair. "I told her to use it. I never cared about it as a privilege. I just hadn't thought to make the offer." They looked uneasily at each other. "You shouldn't have done it, Vincent," August said, looking at the full bowl of nuts. "I'm sure the Elector would have let you refuse."

"I thought he'd be pleased with me." Vincent sat down at the empty desk Ahman Penn had formerly used, staring into the blank displayer. "I liked Ellen." He sighed. "I have my on-site report to do," he told August, without looking up.

August turned to his screen. "You might as well do it here," he said.

Elector Lee returned to the suite late, bringing Delegate-Commissioner Huana with him. August stayed in the back rooms, but the Elector immediately sent a guardian to fetch him to the sitting room.

"I'm pleased you're well, August," Huana said. He didn't appear to notice the new bruise.

August bowed to both men. "As well as any probe, Delegate."

Huana was startled. "Of course."

Elector Lee laughed. "August is extremely independent," he said as he ushered Huana to an easy chair across a low, round table from another, where Lee then sat. "You knew Alexander better than I, Delegate. Was he this free-spoken?"

Huana smiled, looking fondly at August. "No, Alex was circumspect in public. Privately, he was now and then quite bold, but he censored himself much more than August does."

"Better trained," Jeroen Lee said. "The ideal probe."

Huana gestured, his hands cutting space. "I met Alex when he was about August's age. He'd been assigned a special duty as my protocol aide. I was flattered to be assigned a probe in personal service with an Elector, since, even then, Andia was neither rich nor populous. It meant the Electors had a particular interest in me. Alexander was withdrawn, I thought, not knowing probes. I interpreted his silence as loneliness. I think I was right. Over the years I've realized probes rarely have close friendships with each other. They compete. They're dependent on the Electors—or Ahmen and Reverends, for the lesser probes—for affection. I've wondered if that's planned." Huana glanced astutely at Jeroen Lee. August wondered about Huana's affair with Ellen.

"I made the assignment," Elector Lee said.

Huana looked puzzled.

"I was Ahman of Sucre—in charge of probes—until I became elected about five years later. Perhaps you knew, I designed Alexander and took a continuing interest in him. I saw the intimacy between Alexander and Sanda Brauna. It seemed excessive and unhealthy. I tried to give him other relationships. A bluff, friendly, intelligent man such as yourself seemed ideal. I was right, wasn't I?"

"In what sense?" Huana stretched his legs and glanced up at August, standing inconspicuously nearby. "What do you think, August?"

"I wonder why you are discussing Alexander."

The two men laughed. Jeroen Lee offered Huana maté or coffee, both of which were declined. He motioned August closer. August came, taking care not to stand within Elector Lee's reach.

"Esteban, we have been on opposite sides of this Neuland issue for decades, since before the Andian Betrayal," Jeroen Lee said. "Despite that, I have always respected you. I hope you feel the same." Huana nodded, and Elector Lee continued, leaning toward Huana and speaking in a lower voice. "When you, Montague, and Pana were taken, I realized that I . . . may have been mistaken." He stopped. His hands were clutching the chair arms as though the chair could throw him. He loosened his grip and went on. "This is difficult for me. The Ahmen don't elect a man who's often wrong to guide our Harmony. I am a biologist who began in the Academy as a medic and researcher on human genetic material, yet one of my deepest beliefs has been the humanity of Altereds. My position on Neuland arose from that, and that the people here are Jonist."

Huana nodded, his expression neutral.

Jeroen Lee stood, went to a window, then came back. "Was Alexander human, Esteban?"

Huana sighed and shook his head. "I see your point. If he was, why not Neulanders? We all draw lines, Elector. They are not within my definition of humanity."

"I agree. My point is other than you've stated it."

Huana made a surprised, interrogative sound.

Lee returned to his chair. "We have three categories now: human, Altered, and toolman. There is a continuum from human to Altered—we call those men adjusted and consider them human, although not standard—but a gap exists between toolmen and the rest. I say Neulanders fall into that gray area, extending the continuum. They are more changed, if less visibly, than other Altereds. As Alexander did for toolmen, a few may bridge the gulf. Most do not. I propose to you that Neulanders, like toolmen and unlike Altereds, require our direct supervision and protection. They have shown an inability to manage independent civilized behavior. Emirates domination will not improve them, nor will it do us any good to have that superstitious multitude at our border. Neuland needs Harmony administration. Aid which allows them to continue autonomously is improper, because it will not protect us from the ills inherent in this people. I recommend that we give them military assistance, but only if they agree to become a protectorate of the Harmony of Worlds—*not* a member world. There is precedent in the slowboat-settled world, Testament. Finally, I suggest that you be senior on the governing body the Harmony sends here with our ships."

Huana said nothing.

"Properly guided over the years by you and Elector Brauna, Alexander became greater than other toolmen. Unselfish. Moral. Willing to go beyond his orders—let me acknowledge the truth of your accusations against Elector Brauna—on behalf of justice. It is conceivable that he could have lived successfully as an Altered, not a citizen, of course, but free of direct Academy supervision. He could have been spared the probe illness. August might mature sufficiently someday, too."

Both men glanced up at August, who was, for once, properly and falsely impassive.

Elector Lee continued in a less impassioned voice. "Neulanders didn't exist when Jon Hsu wrote his *General Principles* and established our categories. We have already added toolmen to his list. I suggest we need a new category—Adapteds. Look at Neulanders—they aren't like our Altered population who, I must add, I still consider and rule are human. Perhaps Neuland will change, eventually. It has lacked guidance, Esteban. Children don't raise themselves, even when they suppose they can. For now, it needs our management. What do you say?"

Huana straightened and sat forward on the edge of his chair. "I have to think about this. It's interesting, Elector.

Yes. It answers in Jonist terms many questions I've had. Yes, I must think about it."

"There isn't much time, unfortunately," Lee said.

Huana stood, holding excitement in check. "I know. We'll talk early tomorrow, if that's acceptable to you? Eight, local?"

Jeroen Lee also rose. He nodded gravely. "I won't present these new concepts to anyone, not even the other Electors, until I hear from you. I value your contribution, Esteban. I know if you worked with these difficult people, you could do great good. Personally, I am glad the truth about Alexander has come out. I have always been proud of him, and I know that his ethical behavior was attributable to you."

Huana smiled sadly and turned to August. "For Alex's sake, I've taken great interest in your well-being. It's saddened me that you don't understand that. Kolet has said malicious things, most recently about your transfer to Elector Lee. I believe you'll be better guided by Elector Lee than in Elector Brauna's neglectful, then overly indulgent service, but are you content?"

The needle was gone but its effect lingered, or else August simply was unwilling to offend Jeroen Lee. Besides, what would Huana do for him? He'd rationalized kidnapping August and wasn't upset by Ellen's murder. "Delegate, I'm reconciled."

"Good. Good." Huana started to the door, escorted by Lee, then stopped. "What is your opinion of this proposal, August?"

Both men looked at him. August could read little from Jeroen Lee beyond a cautious optimism. Huana seemed genuinely to care for August's opinion, as though it was his friend Alexander's, come from the grave. August bowed. "I believe that Neulanders are human, Delegate, and should be treated as such."

"But August also believes all toolmen are human," Elector Lee said. He chuckled, and Huana probably did not hear the strain. He called one of the guardians to escort Huana to the suite's door.

"This has been interesting, Elector Lee," Huana said bowing formally and low. He glanced at August, nodded amiably, and left.

Jeroen Lee went to a wall cabinet and poured himself a

drink; August now recognized the whiskey stench. "Well, August, will it work?"

August had stayed across the room, and didn't come closer. "I can't imagine Neuland agreeing. They lose their independence, their humanity—lower than Altereds!—and have Delegate Huana, who hates them, named their governor."

"Is that your serious assessment, or just outrage?" Elector Lee returned to the chair he'd used before, and beckoned August to him. "They'll agree if they want to survive. Life comes first. You learned that recently yourself. And as for Huana, his appointment is far from certain, but if he was appointed, I expect he'd do a conscientious, honest job."

"Is this what you want for them?"

Jeroen Lee sighed and sipped his drink. "No, but it's all I can find that will keep them alive. In fact, it's more than these bunglers deserve. Report. What will Huana do?"

"He'll agree, Elector; he's very pleased."

Lee leaned back and stretched. "Excellent. I was afraid the business about Alexander was too much."

August moved in front of Lee, with the table separating them. "Nostalgia, guilt, and affection combined with the intellectual appeal of this plan—it was masterful, Elector."

August hadn't spoken with approval, but Lee smiled and settled into the chair, then abruptly got up again. "I'll tell Martin. He'll enjoy the sheer audacity of it. Come along; you can deliver a verbatim and share your outrage with him, too."

With a pleased excess of energy, Lee hurried toward Penn's room. August followed, staying carefully beyond reach. Just outside Penn's door, Lee grabbed August's arm. "Why are you avoiding me? We're beyond this irritating physical timidity."

"Touch triggers something, doesn't it, Elector? I feel my pulse, every part of me telling me to trust you, to be loyal. That's why you wanted me from the first time I was in your apartment, not just for the body work, but to protect yourself."

"You surprise me once again," Lee said. "Yes, you're right, although the imprinting is more diffuse than you're describing, and your insight is far too late. The damage, as it were, is done. Don't pull away, August. Perhaps the bond is mutual. I enjoy the contact, too, and I've already trusted you more than an entirely prudent man would have done." Lee took his arm and drew him close as they entered Penn's room.

Chapter 17

About five in the morning, in Neuland's curious synchrony of clock-time and daylight, dawn began over the ocean. As light seeped through the glass doors into the dim room, August couldn't endure lying motionless any longer. He slid out of bed, barely disturbing the covers, and watched the sky become gray, then pink and gold. Elector Lee turned in his sleep; his teeth clicked together as he settled into the new position. August smiled, temporarily superior. Careful not to make noise, he opened a balcony door and stepped outside, then closed the door behind himself so the breeze wouldn't awaken the Elector.

The stars had faded, but a small moon was visible just over the horizon. The sea was quiescent in comparison with other times August had seen it, but there was a constant rush and swell that made a restful background murmur, like the heartbeat of the world. August leaned against the high, stone railing. It felt cold against his nakedness, and the light wind made him shiver. He wrapped his arms close against his chest and studied the waves breaking on the shore as if they had an innate meaning that a man, if he watched attentively enough, could uncover. The hint of sea salt and dampness was not so pervasive as when he had walked the beach with Evan Kolet. The air smelled light, fresh, and alive. A cluster of hummers huddled near a pile of jumbled boulders at the shore; they joined voices, and their distinctive sound seemed a living counterpoint to the eternal cadence of the waves.

He was safe. He was not dying. Elector Lee cared for him in a private, sensible way. Lee even tacitly admitted that August was human, yet didn't that make Elector Lee less principled rather than more, a pragmatist without a moral center? The image of Jeroen Lee taking his hand during the night, holding August without demands, as if Lee sensed August's confusion, clashed with the other thought. August wished for certainties. He wished for a child's faith, or a toolman's, that others knew the answers to his questions.

Perhaps Elector Lee did his best to balance competing considerations; perhaps that was all a man could do. Threatened, he himself had chosen life against the chance at freedom. Why was it abhorrent that Elector Lee give the same choice to Neuland?

There was one difference. August had not lost ground—he had been and remained a toolman—but once within the Harmony, not even accorded Altered status, free Neulanders would become glorified toolmen. The Protectorate of Testament kept its natives confined to their world, a cage for human-shaped animals. That was what Jeroen Lee proposed to make of Neuland.

The sun had risen above the horizon while August stood on the balcony; the moon had set. A man in worn work clothes, carrying a bag, came around the side of the hotel, walking across the yard down to the rocks and water. His boots left tracks in the dew-soaked grass. A medical condition monitor glittered on his left wrist. The man whistled, waved in the direction of the hummers, then crouched down as he waited. The pitch of their hum changed as they rushed over. He held out his hand, and the creatures approached. When the hummers' leader had performed the bloody ritual greeting, the man stood and tossed kitchen scraps at them. The hummers ate in complete silence. As the man turned to leave, he glanced up at the tall building. His attention caught on someone below August. The Neulander casually waved, then walked back the way he'd come.

Sanda Brauna could be on her balcony. She might have stood, two levels below him, watching the sunrise in an unconscious communion of their spirits. August went to the railing, leaning over it as far as he dared, peering down. He saw no one. "Elector?" he called, trapped between wanting to catch her attention and fear Elector Lee would overhear. There was no answer.

He looked back toward the bedroom. Jeroen Lee stood at the glass door. He opened it and came outside. August walked away from the railing, but not all the way to Lee.

"You didn't sleep much." Lee wore his white silk robe and looked handsomely urbane.

"No, Elector."

Lee went to the railing, stood where August had stood,

and looked down. He turned, glanced back at August, and went to one of the upholstered chairs.

"They're damp," August warned.

Lee raised an eyebrow, nodded slightly, and returned to the railing, resting an elbow against it. "What is it this time? Dropping poems over the side?" He hadn't mentioned Vincent's inadvertent message service.

"No, Elector. I watched the dawn. I'd never seen the whole thing before, like a quick-time replay." He smiled tentatively.

"Do I need to forbid you to come out here?"

"No, Elector." He felt like a screen stuck in bad command. He took a breath, wondering if Lee would believe anything he said. "There was a worker on the lawn. He waved. I wondered who else was out. That's all, Elector. Truly."

Elector Lee shrugged and glanced at the beach. "Why didn't you sleep?"

"Neuland. Please don't do this to them. Your own people . . ."

"Hush!" He spun around, facing August, and signaled for a security field.

"Elector Lee, please don't make humans into toolmen!"

"Ah," he said. Lee waited until his house system secured the balcony. "The proposal I gave Huana is preliminary. Some aspects are subject to negotiation, once it's presented to Premier Wren. It is the concept itself that I wanted Delegate Huana to hear. Attitudes can be formed initially that continue long after the proposal has . . . mutated into a different structure. The agreement to agree is the crucial one, and its power is seductive."

"The essential feature is repugnant."

"Leave judgments of that variety to those they affect. Neuland can refuse, and after all, who are these people you want to save? The same ones who killed eighteen million Andians."

"Only a few Neulanders were involved in that."

"How few? Thousands? Tens of thousand? Did the others refuse, or not bother to know? Where are they all now?" He gestured broadly across the scene in front of them. "Their spiritual descendants killed Pana and tortured Montague. Don't let affection for one man make you forget the rest."

Jeroen Lee smiled when August failed to answer. "Come here."

August joined him at the railing.

"Do you really believe you'd be happier as a probe in her service, reciting dour poetry, brooding over Alexander, sinking into bed with that unimaginative woman? I speak from practical experience, August. Sanda and I have known each other long enough to have tried even that. If Alexander didn't love her after fifteen years, perhaps you should ask yourself why. Or did you prefer Evan Kolet's offer? Tell me, what would you do as a free, human man on Neuland? What are your skills and training? You would excel as a prostitute, but that's a nasty existence. You have an eidetic memory and an excellent native intelligence, but your education is slight, except in poetry and politics. Oh, you can learn, but it will take years before you perform meaningful work. How will you live? On Kolet's largess?" Lee covered August's hand with his own. "You're cold. We'll go inside." He started to the door.

August caught his arm. "I was happy with her. You took that away."

Jeroen Lee looked squarely at him. "How pleasant to have someone to blame. Tell me, August, wasn't that a fantasy existence? How much reality did you hide to maintain it? How much about Sanda do you refuse to see? If she loved Alexander, she still considered him to be less than herself. And she ordered him killed."

"You . . ."

"Yes. I suggested it. She ordered it done. It was expedient. Perhaps she broods about it. I don't. But I won't kill you."

"You tried. You killed Ellen." August tightened his hands into fists. "She was as human as anyone."

Jeroen Lee reached out and took August's right hand between both of his own. He brought August's closed fist up and kissed the knuckles, then looked again and smiled. "Keep your thumb outside," he said, rearranging and warming August's stiff fingers. "Otherwise, it could break when you punch me." His hands massaged August's fist. "Yes, I tried. Your friend's death brought you to me, for which I am grateful. Your death is not an option to me anymore." He released the hand and went into the bedroom, leaving the door open.

August looked at his hands. He opened the fists and flexed

his fingers. It looked melodramatic, so he didn't repeat the gesture, though they ached. The breeze was strengthening. The hummers had vanished, but seagulls were wheeling through the sky making raucous noise. He walked inside.

Jeroen Lee was seated at the small dining table, faced away from August, but the set of his shoulders and the way his posture tensed indicated he knew August had returned.

"You make me feel ignorant and stupid. Weak."

Jeroen Lee didn't turn around. "You're none of those, just inexperienced. I teach you because I'm confident that you can learn; I never waste time on a weak or stupid student. And don't be fooled, August. Everyone, including me, makes mistakes. An obvious example is that I should never have let Sanda have you when you came up from the farm. We're all three paying for that, although I doubt I could have guided you to be any more interesting—or annoying—than circumstances and Sanda's peculiarities have done."

"Why did you have me made at all?" He waited for another painful lesson.

Jeroen Lee turned around and appeared surprised. "Because I wanted you, of course." He laughed. It sounded self-deprecating. "I designed my ideal companion, not another boring mediocrity, and I was proud of Alexander, even when he thwarted the Electors' plans—just as I'm proud of you. I let Sanda have you in part from concern I would become too attached. And here I am. Attached." Lee smiled as their eyes met. He stood. "It's humbling to admit that I'm not the ideal companion of my ideal companion."

"Elector . . ." August stopped. *Ah, love.* He'd chosen Sanda Brauna.

Jeroen Lee placed his hand lightly on August's back and gently nudged him toward the bathroom. "Go wash and dress. Huana will arrive soon, then we'll be busy. Come with me today, observing everything. I'll want your detailed report. Don't send signals to Elector Brauna. I'll notice." He grinned. "And take it out on you tonight."

"You call yourself Neuland's friend?" asked Orrin Wren, Neuland's Premier, of Elector Lee. Wren's face was gray, and his voice shook. Beside him, Margot Ash's expression was impassive, but her palms bled from tiny cuts etched by her fingernails. She didn't appear to notice. Neuland's military Chief of Staff, Anton Weiss, so old his age showed on his dark, wrinkled face, exchanged a grim, incredulous look with Evan Kolet.

Elector Lee leaned back in his chair and gazed mildly at Wren, then he glanced at Delegate-Commissioner Montague, seated at the far end of the Harmony's side of the long conference table. A skinsack, sturdier than the facial sack August had worn, encircled Montague's arm, which rested prominently on the table. Mottled red and purple, it was healing slowly due to his advanced age and standard physiology. Lee contemplated the empty chair, intentionally placed where Delegate-Commissioner Pana would have sat. Finally, he sighed and looked back at the Neulanders. "This is the best offer you will receive from the Polite Harmony of Worlds. I was asked to present it by the Delegate-Commissioners so you would understand that."

"We may as well invite Aleko Bei to Romoa," Ash said. "At least he'd be honest enough to call his arrival here a conquest."

"And he's vowed to slaughter all of you," Delegate Huana said. "He may also be honest in that." Condescension pulled Huana's round face into something narrower. "You still have no conception of what you did at Andia, or less than a week ago to poor Gregorye Pana and Delegate-Commissioner Montague. You don't suffer, and no one human doesn't."

Kolet reddened. The other Neulanders' reactions ranged from anger to disgust, all kept under strict control. August finally understood why probes craved real-time work. The strong emotions in the room had an immediacy they never did on replay, a kaleidoscope of intense emotional beauty.

Premier Wren turned to Delegate Wilder. "Do you support this mockery of assistance? Is this something Darien would do to its cousins?"

She sighed, then looked past Wren's shoulder as she spoke. "If the full body of Electors rules that the category 'Adapted' is a proper one and that it applies to Neulanders, Darien will have no choice but to follow that ruling." She looked pityingly at Wren. "Naturally, you can reject our aid."

The room was silent. Delegate Chin cleared his throat. Huana had a faint, distant smile, and Delegate Wilder stared down at her reflection in the polished surface of the table.

"No!" Weiss whispered. August remembered Kolet's description of Neuland's founders—hard men—and watched Weiss. Would Neuland agree, or die?

Delegate Montague looked at Elector Lee as if asking permission to leave; Lee turned to Premier Wren.

"How long can you wait for an answer?" Wren asked. "To survive by becoming formally subhuman requires . . . time."

"Not subhuman," Elector Lee said firmly, looking at the two Electors and four Delegate-Commissioners one by one. "Only different. The Harmony of Worlds is a federation of human populations. Neuland is not populated by standard humans. To date, the Harmony has not permitted nonstandard individuals—or worlds—into full membership."

"You have your revenge now, don't you, Huana?" Evan Kolet shifted in his chair like a man restrained from violence only by duress. "A reduction to something less than human—whatever our *great friend* Jeroen Lee pretends—is much more satisfying than a war." The old man, Weiss, placed his veined hand on Kolet's shoulder, and Kolet lowered his voice. "This isn't just, and you know it," Kolet said directly to Elector Lee.

"You're right." Huana leaned across the table toward Kolet. "It isn't just. None of you will die."

Lee stood, ending their useless argument. "There isn't much time for your decision. We plan to leave tomorrow."

"It would be dangerous for your ship to leave before the alan bandits are destroyed." Weiss stood, moving with the hesitations age induced even in the pain-free. "They could mistake you for one of ours and attack. Best you wait. I've just ordered our entire fleet into the outer system to hunt them down. Meanwhile, perhaps we can change your minds about us, now that we understand the seriousness of your doubts." He looked at Huana. "Perhaps you'll have an opportunity to see Neuland mourn, and believe it."

Kolet looked rigidly ahead, scarcely breathing.

Montague said, "We're anxious to leave."

"Surely an additional day or two won't matter?" Elector Lee said pleasantly to Montague. August was relieved. Lee *did* want negotiations. "We'll discuss departure among ourselves and inform you of our decision." He gestured, and the Harmony personnel rose, followed by the remaining Neulanders. The two groups did not exchange even the halting, hollow pleasantries of earlier in the meeting. The Neulanders simply walked out of the room, standing close together and reeling a bit, like drunks struggling to maintain some dignity.

"Good," Lee said quietly, once the Neulanders were gone. "We'll wait for their reply." He looked at the four Delegates, and they nodded, a reflexive acknowledgment of Lee's authority.

Elector Brauna frowned and left the table to stand provocatively near August's post against the rear wall. She came so close he felt her warmth, and her violet fragrance made him tingle, but, remembering Lee's playful warning, he maintained his classic, detached probe pose. Besides, her conduct seemed inappropriate, like bodywork at a funeral. Lee glanced at her and said nothing. Everyone but Elector Brauna started toward the door.

"What about August?" Elector Brauna glared at Lee as she stopped the departure. "You stole him from my service."

Ah, love. She wanted him. Yet August was annoyed that she had chosen this somber occasion to reclaim him.

"More precisely, Sanda, you abandoned August and acquiesced in my assumption of his service, but the issue is trivial." Elector Lee smiled at her. He seemed amused. "Any complaint you have will wait. August is not in flare. I cured him."

Everyone stared, nonplussed, even the other probes, Zoe and Vincent. Esteban Huana began a fresh movement to leave, effectively supporting Elector Lee.

"I need him." Elector Brauna's voice stopped them once again. "I have no other probe."

Elector Kurioso looked first at Brauna and then at Lee; he smiled.

Lee nodded affably. "I'll share his reports with you. August, see to it. And Sanda, we brought along several competent probes from general services."

"You killed one of my probes and stole the other," she said intransigently. "I want August back. This is not subject to delay or negotiation."

"I did nothing that wasn't agreed upon first by you," Lee said reasonably. He turned to Ica Kurioso for confirmation, but Kurioso said nothing, only moved a step toward Sanda Brauna.

"What are you hiding that makes you want August so badly? What does he know?" Brauna asked.

It was a direct attack on Jeroen Lee. The Delegates looked down at the floor, except Neela Wilder, who studied August.

"I'm not hiding anything," Lee said. "We happen to have the same taste in men. Sanda, Neuland is no place for dissension among us; I won't discuss August further." Elector Lee turned toward the door. As his gaze swept over August, he inclined his head, motioning August to follow. He was no longer amused.

Sanda Brauna had flushed, apparently embarrassed by Lee's intimate public disclosure—which was no revelation at all, concerning him—but she extended her arm, preventing August from leaving. "A refusal to discuss this is not good enough, Jeroen. You've interfered in my household. I demand that you return my toolman."

"Give her that one, at least," Kurioso said suddenly, indicating Vincent, "since you like this new boy so much." Kurioso smirked.

"Nonsense," Lee said. "We don't trade toolmen like votes. We each need our privacy, don't we, Ica?" Kurioso had known peccadilloes of a different and violent sort.

"Precisely," Sanda Brauna said. "August was in my service for years, and I want him back."

"No."

Very gently, Delegate Wilder said, "Elector Lee, there are so many more pressing matters?"

"What secret are you hiding, Jeroen?" Sanda Brauna asked. She spun around and spoke to August. "Can you tell me?"

August froze. Elector Lee had not threatened him by word or gesture and still did not. The trust he had in August was more frightening than any threat.

Elector Brauna touched August's arm; he shivered. "It's all right, August," she murmured. "You're not wearing a needle. You can come home."

Kurioso smiled as eagerly as a member of a wolf pack awaiting his share of the kill. "Sanda needs a proper staff," he said. "If you have no secret, then give her your cast-off." Again, he indicated Vincent. "Toolmen are all the same, anyway, not human."

August saw Vincent, rigid against the opposite wall, unaccustomed to attention, blinking too much, his eyes fixed on Elector Lee, and remembered Vincent's brief, miserable expression as Lee announced August's cure. It was only too easy to imagine Vincent revealing Jeroen Lee's secret in a fit of pique if he was given up to Elector Brauna.

"No." Elector Lee studied Vincent, frowning, then he looked at August.

"We need to present a united front, Jeroen," Sanda Brauna said jubilantly. That she took her joy from humbling Jeroen Lee, rather than from happiness at regaining August, was apparent and disquieting. August would be true to her, but he did not want Jeroen Lee hurt on his account. If Vincent went into Elector Brauna's service it could be a disaster for Elector Lee, and Brauna and Kurioso had put Lee into a box.

"Elector Lee," August said, bowing deeply. They were startled, except for Lee himself. "I believe it is best if I go with Elector Brauna." He moved slightly, just enough to indicate he was with Elector Brauna, but his attention was fixed on Lee. Their eyes met; Lee sighed, then looked away.

Gleefully, Sanda Brauna squeezed August's arm.

"Fine." Elector Lee thrust his hands in his pockets and looked down. It troubled August to see him openly discomfited. "I consider this a loan, Sanda. As soon as we return to Center, you'll find a replacement. I want August back. August, do you agree?"

Delegate Montague gasped and everyone stared, including Sanda. "You're asking the *probe*?" Elector Kurioso's voice rose.

"Why not?" Lee's changed tone and posture challenged them; he grinned wickedly at August. "We just gave the Neulanders a choice. Have any of you forgotten August's first appearance in the Grand Assembly? He injured himself rather than be used against Elector Brauna, and was dying as a result. When she discarded him because of his flare, I took him in and cured it. There are exceptional cases, where rules become unjust—would anyone argue that curing this man was wrong?" There was bravura in Lee's manner as he regained control of the situation. Huana nodded at the other Delegates, concurring. "Sanda?" Lee said. "You knew he was dying and didn't help him, though you're eager to benefit from his cure now." She didn't answer. Lee turned to August. "So I ask you to choose, August, will you go with Elector Brauna as a temporary measure, until our return to Center, or shall I send Vincent to serve her?"

August couldn't answer; he wanted to be anywhere else. Sanda Brauna's hand was on his arm; Elector Lee was smiling into his eyes. August swallowed. Lee was pushing him—obviously—and it wasn't a true choice, yet Lee had just given him the dignity toolmen never had. August should have wanted desperately to go with Sanda Brauna, but his emotions were horribly mixed. Jeroen Lee would look foolish if a toolman rejected him, and August couldn't bear that. Why *had* he volunteered to go with Elector Brauna? For himself and for her, or for Elector Lee? *Ah love.* When had his loyalty become cruel?

Lee smiled, waiting. Sanda withdrew her hand.

"Perhaps August's proper place can be determined when we return to Center?" Demure, unobtrusive Zoe spoke so unexpectedly, her words could have come from a disembodied voice.

Jeroen Lee laughed and glanced at August as if sharing his amusement. "Acceptable, Sanda?" Lee asked.

She jerked her head affirmatively.

Zoe's comment and Lee's response released August from his dilemma. He needn't choose. He took a breath.

"It seems exceptional probes are more common than we'd thought, Ica," Lee said, while bowing with excessive depth, but no mockery, to Zoe. Kurioso scowled. Lee nodded generally at the others and signaled Vincent, then he led the way out. August watched him leave and then followed Sanda Brauna away from the hushed room.

August was glad to see Ting Wheeling. Such pure pleasures were rare. They stared awkwardly at each other in the entry of Sanda Brauna's suite, Ting grinning so widely that it must have hurt his face. "I'm not in flare," August said, feeling the full joy of that declaration for the first time as he shared it with Ting.

Ting glanced at Sanda, his smile somehow widening.

"Jeroen Lee did it." Her tone pinched off their happiness. "I was too slow. Come, August. I want to hear everything."

He followed her through a hallway identical to that in Elector Lee's suite, but indefinably altered by her feminine presence, perhaps by the indistinct floral scent, or the atmosphere of brooding. Sanda Brauna herself looked different from his remembered image, too delicate and smooth; her artificial youthfulness seemed an ill-fitting disguise. Jeroen Lee, over thirty years her junior, looked a generation older. August wondered why she, unlike most powerful citizens, including women, had maintained an adolescent exterior rather than the look of competent confidence exuded by human middle age. Was it an archaic vanity, or something else? August frowned. Through whose eyes was he viewing her?

She closed the door to her office—taking a chair placed precisely where, two floors above, Lee had sat while he removed the needle—and watched him until he bowed. His heart went out to her; she'd been alone on that same darkling plain, wondering if he was true to her. "Elector . . ." he began.

She held up her hand. "What is this secret that you and Lee share?" she demanded shrilly.

They had not been alone together for nearly a week. Every fantasy he'd had of their reunion had been intimate, not a professional question delivered in the tone of an indignant superior. Jeroen Lee at his most arrogant would have been more sensitive. "I'm unable to tell you, Elector Brauna."

"Unable? Or unwilling?" She gripped the softly padded chair arms, her fingers digging into the fabric; her legs were tightly crossed. "I'm aware that you failed to assist me just now in dealing with Elector Lee."

August bowed again. Their formal setting was uncomfortably reminiscent of Jeroen Lee, as if Lee was a silent witness. In Sanda Brauna's sunroom, with green shadows all around, the atmosphere would have been charged with sensual excitement. He imagined that room and tried to picture himself with her there, but in his mind's eyes he saw only Sanda, standing alone while he watched from a different perspective, outside. From the blue sky of Sucre, the sunroom was a green cage.

"Well, August?"

What did he feel for Sanda Brauna? It didn't matter. He spoke tenderly. She was the loyalty he'd chosen, his peace, his certitude. "I've longed to be here, Elector, and finally I am, but please forgive me. I owe Elector Lee his privacy."

"All right," she said under her breath, calming herself rather than agreeing. "All right." She looked at him through narrowed eyes. "I am badly disappointed, August. You owe Jeroen Lee nothing; your service is exclusively to me. When I ask, I want an answer. Toolmen obey."

He tried to reason with her. "Elector Lee has been your ally for thirty years. He asked you not to investigate."

She shook her head. "He doesn't dictate to me, and neither does a toolman. I am giving you a direct order, August. What do you know about Jeroen Lee?"

"Elector, please." August knelt beside her chair, but that, too, reminded him of Elector Lee, so he was awkward.

Her attention on him was composed and cold. "Jeroen is ruthless. So tell me, August, since you know his secrets, why aren't you dead?" She crossed her arms and studied August when he had no answer. "How can I trust you? He designed you. He's taken you to his bed." She shuddered slightly.

Boring, Elector Lee had said. Erratic passions. August's attitudes were colored now by Lee. Even that didn't matter if he refused to let it; his love had always been an act of will. "Yes. Immediately, for the same reason that you so rarely did. Elector, you can't know how I respect your refusal to use those tricks."

She frowned. "You've changed."

"Elector, my loyalty hasn't changed, only broadened. You are paramount in my regard, of course."

"You're admitting that you hold some regard for Elector Lee? Some loyalty?"

He didn't answer.

"Get up! Get off your knees." She watched angrily as he complied. "You and your . . . brother." She rested an elbow against the chair arm and supported her head in her hand, facing away from him. "I apologize for leaving it to Jeroen Lee to cure your flare. That was my duty to you. I'm more conservative than Jeroen. I hope you understand."

Duty. That was an ugly word, the cold reverse of loyalty. It meant hierarchy and was the antithesis of love. Not once had Jeroen Lee done anything for August from a sense of duty. He acted for his own advantage, certainly, but he had placed August's well-being within the compass of his personal need. Sanda Brauna had not. She never would. She would never be true to *him;* his protestations of love were tedious to her, perhaps a burden, and a poor excuse for disobedience. She could never forget he was a toolman. Alexander must have known.

"Alex never forgave me for not curing him," she said, their minds following the same track. "But how could I have, then?"

August heard her tears. She was feeling sorry for herself. It was time for a devoted gesture to soothe her doubts, time for a revelation about Jeroen Lee, if he wanted to stay in her service. He realized, with a sharp sense of loss, that he did not, if being true to her meant betraying someone else.

He studied the white hair that had come loose from her tight coiffure and lay against her red robe. He remembered the texture of Jeroen Lee's coarse, dark hair as, helping Lee dress that morning—a light moment after all the tension, Lee claiming he had no future as a valet—August had brushed the hair out of the way of the robe's high collar. Black and white. Against his earlier decision, he reached out and touched the soft hair at the nape of her neck. She turned and smiled, pleased.

He bowed, furious with himself. "There are pressing matters, Elector. Neuland. Based on the conference that just ended, I believe that Neuland has some plan. It's one even they dislike." He recalled Kolet's posture, brittle with dread.

She stood up and walked to the window. "What is it?"

"I believe I will recognize it, Elector Brauna, but at the moment I don't know what it is." She stared oddly at him, but he continued. "It makes the Neulanders grim."

"These people!" She paced, her gait made difficult by the intrusion of furniture, but she kept to a pattern August knew and might have transposed onto the bare earth floor of the clearing in her sunroom. She took her garden with her, a pattern and a trap. "They might feign an Emirates attack on *Guide,*" she said. "All that talk about the Emirates' flight group could be laying a foundation. What do you think?"

"Possible. It's essentially what they did before, with Andia." When he had proposed something similar to Jeroen Lee, Lee joked about his lack of strategy. "However, I think their plan is different, but I don't know what it is. Elector Lee might be able to help."

"You have acquired considerable confidence in him, August."

"Elector, we are all on the same side."

"Not really." She watched for his reaction. "Jeroen's plan suits the Harmony, so it has everyone's support, but it won't be enough for him. I know how he works. Whatever he says now, he'll raise his new category, Adapteds, above Altereds and eventually finagle Neuland's admittance to the Harmony of Worlds. Then he'll argue on that basis that Altereds are human. His goal has always been obvious, to declare everyone of human ancestry to be human as a way of increasing his already too-large popular support. I won't let him get away with it. You must help."

He had to try to make her understand. "Elector, I agree with Elector Lee's goal. I would work for it. I'm human. All toolmen are human."

She paced again, agitated. "You're infected by him."

"I felt it long before I knew him, but I didn't put it into words." He hesitated. "Like Alexander."

She studied him, and he saw deep sorrow in her eyes. It was the same melancholy look he'd seen on replay as she left the Grand Assembly lobby with Alexander for the last time, knowing he had to die. "August, I was once fool enough to believe that a toolman had the ability to become my partner. I will not make that mistake twice. Alex betrayed me. He had only a toolman's morality, one that demands allegiance to an individual, not Jonism's ethic of order. When I refused to cure his flare, Alex turned on me. To say Alex acted for truth is wrong; he spitefully switched loyalties. He acted on behalf of a new loyalty, to Esteban Huana, who had offered him more. You also were in flare. I didn't cure you, and Jeroen did; now you are betraying me for Jeroen Lee."

"That isn't so, Elector. None of it. A lack of blind obedience does not mean I am disloyal to you." He tried to understand her skewed explanation. With such an attitude toward toolmen, she would never believe that Alexander had stayed loyal to her. Once again, Alexander would have a hand in spoiling August's life. "Elector, I'm not Alexander!"

She smiled like a mother comforting a dying child. "Never mind, August. Never mind. I know what I must do. I owe you an opportunity to change your mind, to regain your proper loyalty exclusively to me. You have tonight. Tomorrow you will either report everything you know about Jeroen Lee, or else you will be sent up to *Guide,* to Security. If you survive interrogation, you'll go from Security back to the farm. I will not be a fool twice. I will learn what you know, one way or another. I won't have a toolman with any loyalty but loyalty to me."

"I have never betrayed you, Elector. I don't think I ever could." He reached for her hand.

She pulled away and signaled for Ting. "Don't think Jeroen Lee will rescue you. I've made certain that he can't."

He stared at her, unable to think. *Ah love.* His loyalty to

her was real, if engineered, but it had been misplaced. The
love he'd forced himself to feel was misplaced, too. He felt
as alone as he had in the clearing on Sucre, surrounded by
the Green. The land of dreams was gone; she was and would
always be untrue.

"Ting will guard you," she said when he failed to reply.
"Of course, you are confined to your room. I want you out
of my sight until I summon you tomorrow."

"Elector!" he finally managed.

"Don't bother to protest your loyalty or love, August,"
she said. "If you won't obey, I have no further use for you."

Ting entered, still smiling. She turned to him. "Guard August carefully, Ting. I'm concerned Elector Lee may try to
steal him back again. Watch over him, and in the morning
we're probably sending him to *Guide*."

The room Ting led him to was, in Elector Lee's suite, the
one given to Ahman Penn. August didn't speak to Ting.
What could be said without endangering his friend? August
sat down on the edge of the bed. "If you need anything, just
call," Ting said cheerily and closed the door as he left, shutting August inside.

He turned to the window, watching as the sun went down
and remembering its dawn. He wasn't hungry, so he didn't
ask for supper. *He wasn't hungry.* He lay down on the bed.

He wanted guidance and wondered if that made him less
of a man. Jeroen Lee expected him to stay silent, yet surely
Lee had not anticipated this. What would Martin Penn say?
Or Evan Kolet do? Those two men disliked each other, and
yet August was certain they would agree that he must refuse,
even if it meant Elector Brauna would obtain the information through Security, in an invasive, destructive way. He
wanted to refuse, in fact. Survival in Sanda Brauna's service
after betraying Elector Lee would shame him in the same in-
tolerable way Alexander had known he would be shamed by
silence concerning Andia. Like Alexander, he was forced by
her order to disobey, but Alexander had spoken truth, while
August would have to hide it.

He could not allow Security to pry the knowledge from
his mind. Since he could not escape from Elector Brauna,
just when life had been returned to him, he must die.

He looked around. It wasn't an empty cell, like the shack-
board hut on Sucre, but a Neulander bedroom left fewer op-

portunities than most. There was nothing sharp. The window glass wouldn't break. Sheets. Could he hang himself? A bathroom. Could he force himself to drown? Could he act quickly enough to succeed before Ting stopped him?

August rolled over, facing into the pillows so the monitors that surely watched the room couldn't know if he cried. His life traveled in circles. Finally, imprisoned by Elector Brauna, his eyes opened to reality, he could envision a future and a goal he wanted, one now impossible to obtain. The long night ahead of him would end. Another dawn would come. He would die, destroying Jeroen Lee in the process. Lee had made another mistake. He had believed Sanda Brauna's affection for a toolman was as great as his own.

He lay on the bed, reluctant even to move, and eventually he dozed without having made a decision on how to attempt to die.

Much later, a siren went off, a hair-raising wail that flooded the entire spectrum of sound and seemed to vibrate August's skull. He pressed his hands against his ears, then pulled the pillow over his head. If a message was mixed with the signal, August couldn't hear it through the awful sound. Even if he had, the sound was too loud for rational thought; his head was too painful to allow him to wonder why the alarm had begun. He huddled miserably. It seemed the noise filled the universe, but he hoped for silence outside, and stumbled off the bed to try the locked door, inadvertently dropping his impromptu pillow muffler. The sound was no worse without it, so he left it on the floor.

The sound cut off. It took August a dazed moment to realize the silence was real as the emptiness echoed inside his head, then Ting burst into the room. "It's an attack on Neuland," Ting said. His voice had a shimmering quality, like a poor recording. "The Elector took the emergency lift, then I came back when she was safe. We need to reach the shelter underground."

"We're eight flights up!"

"Let's go." Ting looked out at the dark night, then through the open door, and pushed August in that direction.

August ran into the hallway. Ting fell into step beside him, their footsteps hard impacts into the silence. The rest of the staff had probably gone with Sanda Brauna while he stupidly clutched a pillow to his head. "Thank you, Ting, for coming back."

Ting didn't answer. Outside the suite the alarm was still ringing, worse than before because August's head already was pounding from the dying waves of the previous alarm. He closed his eyes, wanting to rest on the ground inert, but Ting pushed on his back, urging him past the lifts, heading for the stairs, and August concentrated on following Ting's example and moving quickly; Ting would never leave him. Another group of toolmen were trudging down the stairs two flights below. No one was above. Within the confines of the fire walls, the sound of the alarm made August's eyes tear and his teeth rattle in his mouth. Each step sent vibrating shocks down his spine. He couldn't hear anything, but his head felt as though pressure would soon make it explode. Except for Ting, he could have wished for a sweep to come, but he lumbered on, trying not to slow Ting, and was dismally pleased when they caught up with the others who had been below.

A soldier from *Guide* was at the bottom of the stairs. He directed their small cluster of toolmen outside the hotel. Another, waving an intense white light that hurt August's sensitized eyes, ushered them into the mouth of a tunnel that had appeared in the middle of an outdoor walkway; that led back beneath the hotel. The pressure in August's head lessened as the ramp took them down, but he heard nothing, no voices, no footsteps, no sound. It was only marginally less disassociating than blindness had been. Nothing seemed real. They entered a cavernous room.

Ting tugged at his arm. August faced him. Ting spoke without seeming to shout, as if the alarm was gone. August lipread, "Over there." August couldn't hear and said so to Ting. Not to hear his own words was funny, like lip-reading his mind.

August forced himself to scan the cavern shelter. A clear demarcation already existed between a Neulander area—cooks, servitors, cleaners, and some management people, as well as a few military guards—and those from the Harmony of Worlds. The Neulanders lounged, yawning and talking, like children let out of school early. One group was having an impromptu picnic on the cold concrete floor. The Harmony people—the humans—were nervous, milling aimlessly about. The Electors and Delegates were mostly clustered around a communication console in the center of the room, the only area where any chairs had been provided. Their human staffs fluttered about, while *Guide's* soldiers stayed unobtrusively between their people and the Neulanders across the room. The shelter itself was damp and chilly. Breath and body odor from several hundred people was souring the poorly circulated air, but clearly even more people could have been packed into the space. Along the far wall were closed, locked cabinets, presumably of food and supplies. The light was dim for standard humans, but entirely adequate; for August it seemed too bright and hurt his eyes, making them tear more.

Ting touched August's arm and pointed. Toolmen had gathered in a separate area on the far side of the communication console, against the wall nearest the Electors, probes sitting distinct from guardians. Led by Ting, August walked toward the toolmen, his head throbbing with each step. He slowed as they approached. Many probes were doubled over, vomiting. Ben looked up, nodded recognition, clutched his mouth, and looked away. August stopped, afraid he'd worsen if he went closer to them. The smell already was appalling.

Someone put a hand on August's shoulder; August recognized Jeroen Lee by scent and touch. Pleased, relieved, he turned around, moving too suddenly. Dizziness blurred his vision. The weight of Lee's hand helped steady him. Vincent, looking green, stood behind Elector Lee, too ill to be unpleasant. Ting moved closer. Chaperones.

"I called to you just now," Lee said. "I was concerned when you didn't arrive with Sanda. Are you all right?"

"I can't hear," August mouthed.

Lee nodded. "A natural probe reaction to that much noise." He over-enunciated. "It should resolve itself within the hour. If not, see me immediately. Understand?"

"Yes, Elector. Thank you." August wiped his eyes with his fingers and looked for Sanda Brauna in the cavern.

"Good." Lee nodded toward a litter in a secluded area near the communication equipment. "I'll check on Martin; I sedated him for the trip down. Let me know if any probe needs help." He began to move away.

Elector Brauna was observing from across the room. This could be August's only chance. He swallowed hard, which relieved some pressure, and avoided looking toward her.

"Elector," he said, unconsciously reaching out to touch Lee's arm. He hesitated as Lee turned back to him and smiled. After a lifetime of dedication to Sanda Brauna, it was difficult to speak discontent aloud. "Elector, I must return to your service immediately. Please."

Jeroen Lee looked into August's face.

Ting stepped forward of August, poised to attack Elector Lee. "No!" Ting shouted. August signaled, "Wait," and Ting subsided unhappily.

"Elector Brauna is not so attached to me as you think, Ting," August said, but he faced Jeroen Lee. "She wants information more than she wants the service of a toolman with . . . divided loyalties. I don't want to be sent up to *Guide*."

"I see," Lee said, nodding decisively. "Don't worry, August. I will take care of it and have you home for breakfast." He grinned and glanced at Sanda. "It seems this drill came just in time. It is a drill, isn't it? To frighten us into staying longer?"

August surveyed the room, focusing on the bored Neulanders, the workers, but also the shelter warden at the communication console. "Yes, Elector. It's a drill." Abruptly, he doubted his handicapped opinion. A disorienting image of Evan Kolet cutting his own hand and then screaming with pain kept replaying through his mind. "I might be wrong."

"Unlikely." Jeroen Lee smiled, exaggerating that, too. He lifted his hand to touch August, then glanced toward Sanda and clumsily made the gesture into something like a salute. "Vincent, stay with August," he said, then he walked away toward Elector Brauna.

As Lee left, August considered his question. Was it a drill? Almost in a trance as he contemplated their situation—or rather, Neuland's—August followed Ting to the toolman area, trailed by Vincent, a very odd parade.

"Is this shelter safe from a sweep?" August asked Ting when they'd reached the other probes.

Ting Wheeling turned toward August. "Maybe." His expression became worried as he glanced at Sanda Brauna, then looked back. "It's only fifteen meters deep. A direct sweep can burn soil twenty meters down. They depend on the hotel structure as part defense."

August smiled reassuringly, as if he knew about these things. A faint movement of air reminded him that the tunnel entrance, not visible from the shelter room, remained open. He smiled. "It must be a drill. They haven't sealed us in."

"They're waiting for someone," Ting said. "I heard them, anxious about his coming."

August sat down. Vincent knelt on the cold floor, facing the wall like a praying alan pretending to look toward old Earth. So far he hadn't vomited, but that seemed willpower rather than fitness. The shelter warden sent a Neulander reservist medic to administer aid to the probes, but soldiers from *Guide* shooed him away.

Vincent turned his head. "Last night the Elector gave me a tab. He said I'd never go through flare."

"Good," August said, meaning it. Jeroen Lee had ensured Vincent's loyalty and eliminated both a source of friction over August's cure and any temptation to betray Elector Lee's secret. It was a practical if improper solution, yet there had been other choices available to Elector Lee. Lee had cured Vincent at about the time Elector Brauna had threatened August with Security.

"You don't believe me, but I wouldn't have told her, either." Briefly it seemed Ellen looked through Vincent's wistful eyes, then his face hardened again.

Was this a drill? The separation between Neulander and Harmony personnel was complete, except around the communication console. August watched the Neulanders. At first they'd been bored, and the Harmony people had been nervous. Trapped in the close atmosphere of the shelter with nothing happening, the Harmony people were growing bored, but as time passed without an all-clear signal, the Neulanders were becoming increasingly anxious. The Neulander mood was the rational one. The answer to the Elector's question wasn't to be found in this shelter, but in Neuland's leaders. *Hard men.* August had been wrong. The alarm was real. The danger was true. It was Neuland's plan to let themselves be injured. This was a cutter.

Chapter 18

"I need to report," August told Ting, and scrambled to his feet. Elector Lee had to be told. His personal dilemma having been forced from his mind, August was surprised to see Lee in earnest, private conversation with Elector Brauna.

"All right." Ting gracefully stood up.

Vincent turned his head in their direction. August lip-read, "He means to Elector Lee, guardian."

"No!" Ting said. "You're back from him. Home." Ting looked suspiciously at Elector Lee, whose conversation with Elector Brauna was imbued with a muted passion. Fortunately, the probes were all too distant or too ill to listen.

August worked to keep his voice low, although he couldn't be sure of his success. "Ting, Elector Lee is best suited to handle this situation. I trust his ..."

"No!" The surrounding probes turned; Ting must have shouted. August moved to block lip-reading of their conversation.

Vincent pushed August's shoulder. "How steadfast you are in Elector Brauna's service," Vincent said. "Bright star."

August flushed. "I won't distort the truth to make excuses for her, or twist myself to love her anymore. I would have died for her, but I won't kill anyone." Vincent lowered his eyes, but only after he'd spoken did August remember that, like Vincent, Ting had also killed for an Elector.

"So I was right," Vincent said slowly, "she didn't want you back." Unable to hear, August wasn't certain, but he suspected the same transient sympathy in Vincent's tone he'd heard before.

"She never wanted *me* at all," he whispered. Louder, he said, "Let me go, Ting."

"No." Ting stepped between August and the two Electors. "You can report to her when they're not together."

"I hated you," Vincent said. "Ever since you came up

from the farm he's had me watch you. What were your assignments? With whom did you speak? He even ordered me to become your friend. I lied and said I did. Beatrice backed me up, but he always knew. He knew."

"Vincent . . ."

"Don't say a word, August, just go make your report." Vincent turned to Ting. "And you, guardian, you let him."

August faced Ting. It was Ting's job to stop August. They watched one another, both aware that Ting would not, but Ting's expression was sad and sullen.

"Ting, I'm not Alexander. She doesn't want me."

"I do."

Ting had never asked the slightest favor; he had done August only good. August took Ting's hand in his own, feeling the hard muscle beneath the skin. "This is important. I think Neuland is going to be swept by these alan ships, and I must tell Elector Lee."

Ting covered August's hand with his other. "I'm sorry I killed him," Ting said. "I never thought about choosing—toolmen obey—besides, I didn't like him. But I should have said no."

"You are the best person I know, Ting." August embraced him. Ting briefly rested his head against August's chest, then almost fearfully, he moved away, allowing August to pass. August smiled, then turned toward the two Electors, only to be confronted with staring faces and the soundless snickers of an audience of toolmen. His face felt hot, and the angry shame of not so many months past surged into him again.

Vincent stood, confronting the others. August heard nothing of what he said, but the probes and guardians turned shame-faced away. Stolid Ting seemed unperturbed. "Go on, then," he said.

August started toward Elector Lee, but just then Evan Kolet ran into the shelter, alone. Everyone turned to him. Kolet wiped his forehead with a sleeve. His chest heaved with exertion; he bent over, resting his hands against his thighs, then straightened and scanned their faces.

A difference in air currents indicated the shelter's entrance had been closed. The change in pressure as the ventilation pumps finally started caused a sudden pop in August's ears, accompanied by a sharp pain. The ache in his head lessened. He made a low, startled sound and heard it.

Kolet looked directly at Delegate Huana. "This is not a drill," he said.

August believed him.

People shouted questions at Kolet. He held up a hand. "I'll tell you!" He wiped his forehead again and directed his words to the Harmony Delegates, turning only occasionally to his own people. "Three Emirates ships were flushed out earlier—before yesterday's meeting. Two were destroyed about an hour ago, with the loss of one of ours. The third escaped. None of our ships can intercept it before it approaches Neuland. Unless *Guide* helps, it's possible that even with our orbitals and ground batteries, Neuland may be swept."

Not just possible, it was likely. August saw it in Kolet's somber, expectant eyes. August shivered, imagining Kolet cutting himself, screaming as flame-red blood dripped down his burning hand. Neuland was letting itself be hurt so the Harmony—so Huana—would finally "see Neuland mourn and believe it."

August quickly crossed the remaining distance to Jeroen Lee. "Elector, he's telling the truth." He barely noticed Sanda Brauna standing beside Lee.

"Do you have a report for me, August?" She glanced across the room at Ting Wheeling, frowned, then put her hand on August's arm. He tensed and didn't move, as though a venomous creature had lit on him. Against the room's stench, he couldn't smell anything sweet about her. She kept her hand on August until Jeroen Lee noticed, then smoothly removed it.

"Enough of this, Sanda!" Lee glanced slowly around the shelter, intimidating anyone from observing the confrontation between the two Electors, as Vincent had done to the toolmen. "August, what is it?"

August kept his voice low and spoke to the floor to inhibit lipreading. "Yesterday I reported to Elector Brauna that the Neulanders had a plan—other than accepting your proposal. I couldn't identify their plan, except that it was grim. Elector, the Neulanders have their plan *in operation.*"

"Why do you say these things to *him*?" Sanda Brauna's lips puckered as if the words formed a sour taste in her mouth.

August bowed to her, as to a stranger. Still worried about

draining him of another Elector's secrets, she didn't realize
the importance of his report.

"*This* is the plan?" Jeroen Lee had understood immediately. Lee tapped his shoe against the hard floor and glanced
intently at Kolet, who was speaking in a low voice to the
shelter warden.

"Yes, Elector."

Huana, standing near Kolet at the communication console,
crossed his arms and began to laugh. "Really, Kolet! Do you
expect to frighten us?" Huana spoke forcefully enough that
he could be heard throughout the shelter. "*Another* false
ship? The Emirates instead of Bril? Neuland lacks imagination." Huana walked away from the console chuckling, and
extended an arm in a broad gesture that asked help against
such foolishness. Among the Harmony citizens there were
many answering nods and a general sense of relief. "If
Neuland wants our help, you know our terms. Otherwise,
Guide will do nothing."

Elector Brauna drifted slightly toward the communication
console, listening to Huana and Kolet. August surveyed her
with a kind of double vision, seeing first the beautiful object
of his long desire, a mournful woman he'd ached to comfort,
then the vulnerable but unreliable person, bitter and insecure
despite her power, that Elector Lee had made him see.

Huana looked around the shelter and seemed pleased.
"Don't think that all you need to do is convince the other
three Delegates to commit the Harmony to your defense," he
continued. "*Guide's* Captain Sabas has strict Orders of Noninterference that require the unanimous agreement of *all*
Delegates present before undertaking any military action.
So, tell your people to stop this charade."

Seizing the opportunity, while attention was fixed on
Huana and Kolet, August touched Jeroen Lee's hand, turned
his back on the probes lying miserably on the ground,
watched his feet, and mumbled for good measure. "The alan
ship is real, but part of Neuland's plan. They let it escape.
They want Neuland to be swept—or to be in danger of it. A
planetary torture party to impress us."

Lee used the same precautions against eavesdropping,
though clumsily. "How far will they go?"

"Kolet worries—too far. The decision isn't his."

Kolet was examining Huana with loathing. "You'll know

the truth soon enough," he said. "This is your doing, Huana. This time the blood will be on your hands."

Huana turned his back to Kolet and shook his head at the Delegates as if Kolet was an errant child, but his arms were held close to his sides. August guessed that Huana had been discomfited.

"They need sympathy," Lee whispered, standing close to August. "And penitence."

Horror hit August like a sudden increase in gravity. This wasn't a report prepared from the distant safety of Center, it was real life and real death: men, women, and children would be cremated with their world.

"Let them try," Lee murmured. "Their choice. Maybe it will work."

"That ship will sweep Romoa, if it can. Here!"

Elector Lee looked directly at August. "Of course."

Hard men. Jeroen Lee was one of them.

Delegate Huana hailed his new ally, Elector Lee, from across the room. "I'll contact *Guide*. I doubt this is true."

Lee nodded absently at Huana.

The Delegates, with Elector Kuríoso, gathered close to the communication equipment. The shelter warden refused to allow them to use it until Kolet intervened.

Sanda Brauna returned to Elector Lee. "What do you think? Is this real or another Neulander fiction?"

"I think it's real, Sanda," Elector Lee said. "We ignored the Emirates' warning. We'd better hope those defenses we saw these past two weeks are sufficient, or authorize *Guide* to help."

She nodded curtly, controlling her fear. "What's your opinion?" she asked August. "Report."

August looked at Jeroen Lee, though it made her frown, then bowed to her. "I believe Delegate Huana will discover *Guide* is tracking an alan ship, heading inbound to sweep Neuland." They could die, and millions of Neulanders with them, because Neuland hoped the Harmony would relent and save the rest without declaring Neulanders less than human.

Elector Brauna didn't change expression. "So you want to stay with Jeroen."

"I don't want to be sent to *Guide*." He bowed.

She had already turned away, to Elector Lee. "Then take him. Keep your secrets for now—don't bother to insist again that you don't have them. I don't care, Jeroen. I'll know them someday, when he betrays you just as his brother betrayed me."

"Sanda, stop this melodrama."

She waved a hand. "You'll see. They're flawed. Neither of them was loyal." Without another word she turned and joined the others gathered at the shelter warden's post. They'd contacted *Guide*. Captain Sabas's image hung in midair at one-third life-size.

"We have work ahead, convincing Huana to stop this thing in time," Lee said to August.

August grabbed Lee's arm to prevent him from leaving. Lee smiled kindly, perhaps imagining that August needed reassurance.

August whispered, "Elector! Tell Huana about yourself. He admires you. You can do what no one else can. Make him stop his crusade against Neuland. Don't permit another Andia to happen."

"If you say a word, I'm ruined."

Lee didn't threaten August's life. He didn't need threats and must have known it. That damnable loyalty, the gratitude and respect, the other feelings he wouldn't name, even to himself, would keep August silent.

Lee nodded. "Come along."

"I expect they'll aim for the capital. What do you think, Kolet?" Huana sounded jovial, despite *Guide's* professional confirmation of the presence of an inbound Emirates warship.

Evan Kolet was gazing at the shelter's low ceiling. A dark stain, like smoke from ancient fires, disfigured the flat surface. He glanced at Huana. "I hope they hit right here. It's Romoa's periphery. Fewer Neulanders will die."

Huana smiled grimly. "Perhaps you'll learn not to count. I did."

August turned to Jeroen Lee, but he seemed not to be listening. Lee stood in front of the display *Guide* was broadcasting: a blue and green globe of Neuland, slowly rotating, with *Guide's* position above it marked by a yellow circle, and the Emirates intruder indicated with a long, flashing red line. The line extended backward into emptiness and was continued forward with dashes until it intersected the atmosphere of Neuland. Romoa was not on the intruder's direct path, unless it changed direction.

August leaned against the damp shelter wall, recalling visuals of Andia recorded during the two sweeps: radiance like a sun moving directly across the land, as if chaos incarnate scourged the world, tearing at it like a beast breaking into its kill, then scorching the eruptions of molten rock that exploded through the rents. Would a man know if such a thing came after him? Would there be a sensation as it approached, melting soil into putty, fusing flesh with stone, charring mountains and searing them bare of life? Would anyone call such a thing down upon himself?

Huana leaned toward Kolet across the communication console, his tone conspiratorial. "On Andia, there were no shelters. None. We had no enemies. The Bril Wars had been over for a generation. Andia's traffic controllers assumed the ship's communication system was down. They didn't become alarmed until your ship set up its first sweep. By then it was too late for a warning. No one waited to die on Andia."

Kolet pushed himself away from the console. "I'm sorry, Delegate Huana. I truly am. Do you believe me yet?"

They studied each other while the hushed room waited. "I suppose I do, Kolet," Huana said. He sighed, and his attention wandered over the huddled crowd of Neulanders on the far side of the shelter, men and women who looked no different from standard, except for their medical condition monitors. The only sound was the hiss of the circulating air. Huana shook his head. "But it's not enough. Neuland killed my family and half destroyed my world. Those deaths are meaningless if they don't at least warn us of what you are. I won't be tricked by fear of personal danger into providing military aid to Adapteds."

Kolet turned toward the Neulander portion of the room, but didn't leave the communication console.

Elector Lee moved closer to the group of important persons. "Evan," he said, his tone unusually empathetic. "Where are your children?"

Huana looked down, but said nothing.

Kolet looked back at Lee. "In the community shelter on Rose Island, with my wife. I hope." August felt the resonance of Kolet's emotion in his quiet, worried voice. Kolet turned to Huana. "Please, Delegate."

Lee went to Huana, touching his arm and bending close. "Be aware of the consequences of your decision not to help them, Esteban," Lee said. "You are condemning many people to death, possibly including this man's children, and perhaps also us."

Delegate Wilder forced her way through the others to confront Huana. "You might want to die, but the rest of us don't!" she shouted. "Montague, Chin, and I all order *Guide* to destroy this Emirates ship. You must agree."

Captain Sabas, watching from the safety of his ship, spoke through his displayed image. "I am in a good position to intercept the intruder, however the Order of Noninterference explicitly requires unanimity among the Delegate-Commissioners."

"Are you still broadcasting neutral status?" Huana asked.

"Yes, Delegate."

"Don't be fooled by Kolet's acting." Huana looked first to Jeroen Lee, then at the clustered Delegates and Electors, ignoring those few Neulanders around the console. "Maybe he even believes this game himself, but we're in no danger. Neuland is heavily fortified. They'll destroy the ship with the orbital batteries, but they'll wait for the last moment before firing."

"The orbitals will have the range of the intruder within a minute," Captain Sabas said. "That will continue until the ship strikes atmosphere, then the ground batteries will be necessary. They will be less effective, of course."

Most Harmony personnel relaxed after Huana's statement, but the Neulanders did not. Delegate Wilder, who, being from Darien, knew Neuland best, seemed leery of Huana's casual dismissal of their danger. "Evan," she said, "you appear less confident of the orbital weapons than our Captain Sabas."

Kolet nodded at her. "There may be complications."

"Complications!" Montague bellowed. "Neuland should have warned us! We could have sheltered safely in *Guide*."

Kolet bowed. "There was no time." Kolet seemed to withdraw. He stared at the medical condition monitor on his own wrist, then moved out of the press of bodies and stretched, an exercise in tension relief. Once he'd begun, he couldn't seem to stop moving. He stepped farther away from the communication console, then came back, glancing into the Neulander portion of the room. Sweat beaded his forehead. While others voiced their outrage to each other, he was preoccupied and pointlessly astir, a man who didn't like waiting. Once he glanced at Jeroen Lee, and noticed August beside him. "I'm sorry you're here, August," he said. "I'm sorry Neuland is such bad luck for you." He moved on before August could reply.

Elector Lee had meanwhile resumed his passive study of the globe of Neuland. This resigned attitude, as though the problem was not his, was nothing like Jeroen Lee's usual dynamic nature; it alarmed August. Huana had a self-righteousness that only Lee's revelation might puncture.

"The minute has passed," Captain Sabas said, quietly puzzled, his dark eyes searching out Kolet. "Everything we know about your systems says they should have initiated firing. Delay adds risk they'll penetrate."

Kolet did not reply. He gestured, and everyone moved out of his path to the communication console. He opened a line to Neuland's military headquarters—the scrambled code identifications flashed past more rapidly than August could focus—then a uniformed Neulander officer held the display, aligned opposite *Guide's* captain as if for a duel. "The orbitals?" Kolet asked.

The Neulander officer vanished and was replaced by the image of Chief of Staff Weiss. Kolet's face went gray.

"They're off." Weiss scanned the area behind Kolet, seeming to see beyond the Delegates to the distant recesses of the shelter, seeking out Neulanders. "None of the orbitals or ground batteries will fire. I'm sorry, Evan. I know you disagree, but . . ."

Kolet banged his fist against the console. The sound tightened August's stomach; the vibration rippled Weiss's displayed image. "It won't convince them, sir! It will be worse! For pity's sake, this is useless, senseless death. These people won't care!"

Huana stepped forward. "He's right. You won't break our resolve with this game of chicken. *Guide* will destroy this allegedly Emirates ship only if Neuland agrees to become a protectorate of the Harmony, subject to our laws and systems of classification. Do you agree?"

Weiss looked out through the displayer. "No," he said, speaking to Kolet and the other Neulanders. "We can't."

Elector Lee pushed past Huana. "How long? When will you fire back at the alan ship?"

Weiss spoke to Huana, as though Huana had asked. "Two sweeps. We took you at your word, Delegate. You'll see

Neulanders suffer, if you live through the sweeps yourself. Will that convince you?"

Huana laughed sharply. It was loud in the otherwise deep silence of the shelter. "Only that you're worse than I expected."

From the display originating at *Guide,* Captain Sabas said, "Five minutes until earliest entry into atmosphere; a bit longer if they set up a sweep in other than their immediate forward direction." He looked unhappy. The red line approached the displayed globe relentlessly and unopposed. "Neuland's ground defenses should be adequate to handle this ship."

"They won't fire," Kolet said. In the shelter recesses, several Neulanders sobbed; none protested. Others—Harmony and Neulander—whispered, their voices becoming hisses in the hard acoustics of the concrete cavern. Weiss looked at Kolet. Kolet shrugged slightly, a kind of surrender. Weiss said, "Good luck, Evan," and terminated the call.

"You see?" Huana looked around. "They aren't human."

"Is there any message we can broadcast to alert the alan ship to our presence in Romoa?" Elector Brauna asked. "Can we—or can *Guide*—apprise them of our neutral status?" Despite everything, it hurt August to hear her voice tremble as she began to believe in their danger. Across the room, seated next to Vincent, Ting stood and hesitantly came a bit closer.

"No," Kolet said curtly.

"They wouldn't listen, Elector Brauna," Captain Sabas said respectfully. "A neutrality message from the capital city and without a properly registered beacon?" The captain shrugged. "They'd assume it was a trick. Even if they knew it was real, they'd probably ignore it. *Guide* is just too powerful for them to take on, so they respect our neutrality."

"Listen, Esteban," Neela Wilder said. Her eyes were wide with disbelief. "Our lives are at stake! 'Two sweeps,' he said. They'll come to Romoa. Let *Guide* engage that ship!"

Elector Kurioso stepped forward. "Huana's right. No one human would do this to his own world. And no one sane would do this to three Electors and four Delegates of the Harmony. Neuland must be bluffing."

Kolet stared up at the dark spot on the shelter ceiling, his hands in fists.

"Elector!" August spoke under his breath to Lee, who immediately smiled slightly and shook his head. He stepped forward, capturing attention with his air of composed assurance.

"You're wrong, Esteban," Lee said. "And you, Ica, should stay with physics, since you don't understand men. Neuland isn't bluffing, and there is nothing in their actions that makes Neulanders inhuman. They're only desperate, and they've hit upon a risky, rather horrible plan, one which is likely to succeed. Esteban, if we don't intervene now, then the Harmony certainly will do so later. The only difference is that there will be blood on our hands—as General Kolet so aptly phrased it—if we don't act quickly. August, explain."

August nodded earnest confirmation, wetting his lips and willing Huana to believe him. "Yes, Delegate," he began, trying to mimic Alexander in vocabulary and intonation. "If the alan ship destroys a significant fraction of Neuland's population, and especially if Electors and Harmony Delegates are killed, it is a near certainty that Neuland will receive Harmony military assistance against the United Emirates attacks. If we don't assist them now, guilt will be a prime motivation later, as well as compassion, because we had the ability to prevent the tragedy." Every person in the shelter was listening, but August aimed his words at Huana. "Please, Delegate Huana, this is prudent. Delay in giving Neuland assistance it will eventually obtain anyway—killing innocents—only advances the cause of Punishers. Order *Guide* to fire now."

While Huana hesitated, staring into August's face, Jeroen Lee returned to his side. "If *Guide* acts now, there will be a war with the Emirates, but we will dictate our relationship with Neuland. If we let Neuland be swept, whether or not you and I survive, Esteban, the emotional context will be much different. Neulanders may well be declared fully human. Stubbornness now plays into their hands."

The room was quiet, awaiting Huana's decision, but most people were smiling, expecting Lee's logic to have convinced Huana of the futility of his position. Around the console, Kolet alone still looked bleak.

"I don't agree," Huana said. A groan went through the shelter. "Have we all forgotten Pana? Montague, can you forgive what you endured? And what of Andia? My world is forever scarred. Elector, even if your analysis is correct, then let them learn to suffer before they enter the Harmony as human. Besides, it still isn't too late for Neuland's own military to act to save themselves. I'm sure they will."

"The only thing Neuland will learn is that we are equally inhuman," Jeroen Lee said, and shoved Huana against the console. August had never witnessed a physical attack between such important, dignified men. It worried him that Jeroen Lee was angry or frightened enough to lose control; he wondered whether Lee's fear was of death or the increasingly necessary revelation he must make. "I thought better of you, Huana." Lee sounded outraged. Mutters from around the console agreed. "Is revenge what all your talk has really been about? Or is it simply that you want to die?"

"Elector," Huana began.

"No!" Lee said. "You're condemning innocents for no reason—or because of something done by others, decades ago. I, an Elector, tell you to give the order to intervene! To refuse encourages disorder."

Captain Sabas interrupted. "There's been no resistance from Neuland. The Emirates' ship is changing course. My people say the intruder is navigating an interception path to Romoa. Four minutes until they can burn territory. Longer before they sweep Romoa."

"No, Elector," Huana said, shaking his head sadly. "You're mistaken. I've had the Neuland lesson burned into me. *They* are the killers. If they proceed with this inaction, it isn't murder; it's suicide." He reached out both hands to embrace Jeroen Lee, but Lee stepped back, knocking Huana's hand away. "Elector, they aren't human. They have no moral sense. The Assembly will see the truth and keep us out of this monstrous alliance."

Head down, face strained with anger and something else—August saw the reflection of Elector Lee's own insecurities in Lee's eyes, unknowingly provoked by Huana—Lee turned away. Ting Wheeling ran to Sanda Brauna, as if his presence could protect her in the coming battle. People began to shout. Huana ignored them and stared at Lee's back.

August looked up at the dark spot on the ceiling, imagining it was the residue of a fire not from within this room, but from above. Would they survive a sweep of Romoa? And if they did? He imagined walking outside and seeing nothing. The hotel would be melted into a puddled liquid rock that hissed whenever a rivulet flowed into the not-quite boiling sea, or it might be a broiled blackened scab on the burned skin of a world. The air would be wet with steam, so hot it might burn unprotected skin. Hummers would have fused into the stone, their rapid healing insufficient against a sweep's rapid, inexorable death. The fiery atmosphere would stink of the charred detritus of vanished life. No one would ever call Neuland a paradise again.

He had to speak, but if he did, Jeroen Lee might be destroyed. Alexander had not abandoned his essential loyalty to Elector Brauna when he spoke his truth, but the secret August knew went to the essence of Lee's life, though its telling might preserve that life, and millions of others. Alexander had not saved a single person.

Even with the droplet of boiling water poised above his face, August had never felt death so imminent, not just his own, but the weight of many lives resting on his shoulders.

"Elector . . ." August said to Jeroen Lee, then stopped. Lee knew what he meant. Lee smiled and pulled August close, his lean strength a relief, regardless of their troubles. "Tell them," August whispered, "or I *must*."

As if inspired by August's promise of betrayal, Elector Lee released him and turned away. "Huana!" he bellowed. "*You* aren't human! I am an Elector, and I can make that determination. Ica! Sanda! Esteban Huana is not human, is he? He shows no compassion; he's as unfeeling as he alleges Neulanders to be. Altereds are ineligible to be Delegates of the Harmony. The remaining Delegates have given you a unanimous order, Captain Sabas. Go destroy that intruder!"

"Confirm!" Sanda Brauna shouted.

Ica Kurioso hesitated, then said, "There are only three Delegates here. Captain, go!"

The entire shelter, first stunned, began to shout and cheer. Release of tension made August feel weak. The Neulanders laughed; there were joyful tears in Evan Kolet's eyes. Elector Lee had saved them, after all.

"That is not a legal or binding determination," Huana yelled, but only a probe could have heard him over the shouts.

Captain Sabas, looking from Huana to Elector Lee, did nothing. The circle representing *Guide* did not move relative to the globe of Neuland. The red line of the alan ship nearly touched the world in the center of a huge blue ocean dotted with tiny islands of green. As they realized *Guide* had taken no action, the people in the shelter quieted.

"I can't accept any such device," Captain Sabas said when he was able to be heard. "There was no hearing, nothing, and three Electors are not a majority ruling."

"You could accept this determination if you choose to do so, Captain," Lee said with menace in his tone, "or must we *kill* Delegate Huana in order to have only three Delegates?" The threat seemed real. Montague, Wilder, and old Chin, like hungry beasts, moved closer to Huana.

Captain Sabas stood, and the display adjusted automatically to his new, imposing height. "My orders are strict and clear. If the Delegate-Commissioner from Andia is harmed, I will take his vote as a permanent 'no.'"

Huana extended his hand to Jeroen Lee, who ignored it. "I dislike being the focus of so much indignation. I do not want to die, as you suggested, Elector. These Neulanders have trapped even you into misplaced compassion, but you yourself don't believe they're human. Adapteds—you named them."

"I lied," Jeroen Lee said, as if it was nothing. "Naming them Adapteds was the only way to obtain your agreement to military aid and to preserve their lives. You must authorize *Guide's* help, Esteban. Symmetry isn't justice. Don't let these sweeps of Neuland begin. Neulanders are as human as anyone. I am an Elector. They are as human as I am." Lee sounded weary and fatalistic, sure Huana would not be persuaded. There was more he could say to convince Huana, but he didn't say it.

Huana began to answer. August interrupted. "Elector?"

Elector Lee turned to August with death in his eyes, opened his mouth, then shut it. August's chest tightened, and his stomach churned. Lee was not going to speak. August had no real choice: if he was true to himself—in a sense, even if he was true to Jeroen Lee—then he must betray Lee and speak.

"Elector Lee is human," August said, surprised that his voice was so steady and so loud. He understood why Alexander had been unable to keep silent, knew how his twin had felt, and August despised the weakness that had prevented him from beginning sooner—until he looked at Jeroen Lee, standing stoic as a probe waiting to be put down. "He is as human as any Neulander, and has the same genetic modifications. He is pain-free."

August saw their reaction through a glaze of emotion that was part fear and part horror at what he'd done. Kolet gaped at August and then at Jeroen Lee; he laughed without humor, the first to believe. The rest of the shelter did not. Some whispered, some laughed, a few were scandalized. Jeroen Lee was motionless, staring at the globe.

"That's absurd!" Delegate Huana said finally.

From behind, where the toolmen had been listening to their superiors decide their fate, Vincent stood.

"It's started," Captain Sabas said, diverting their attention. "The intruder has slowed; she's entering atmosphere. We see the glow. She went in steeper and earlier than we expected. Hard on the ship structure, and it'll cost them speed. We're moving to pace them, in case my orders change." He hesitated, staring at a monitor they couldn't see, his expression hardening as he watched a world begin to burn. "That isn't a heavily populated area, at least."

"Trieste," Kolet said, after a quick glance at the globe. "Hintersea." He remained impassive, and it was obviously false. "Elector Lee?" he prompted.

"Elector Lee is Altered like a Neulander!" August shouted. "Delegate Huana, you know him. Can you say he's not human?"

Sanda Brauna stared at Lee. Everyone did, perhaps beginning to believe because of Jeroen Lee's lack of a denial.

From the toolman area, Vincent shouted, "It's true. Elector Lee is pain-free. There is no difference; he's human."

"This is idiocy." Huana went to Lee. "I won't let you be dishonored by frightened toolmen! Neulander lives aren't worth your reputation." He signaled a soldier.

Others spoke denials; August didn't bother to listen. There was no time. He imagined screams reverberating through the ground, felt a vibration like an earthquake, the epicenter moving steadily closer, to where there were more lives for it to end. Life was the fundamental choice. More life. "Tell them it's true!" August pleaded with Lee, but Lee did nothing. August raised his hands into fists—as Lee had taught him—and wildly punched Jeroen Lee, who didn't move. There were gasps, but the blow proved nothing; there wasn't even any blood. August was snatched from behind and torn away from Lee just as he formed his fingers into claws, the better to use his nails.

"Alex!" Huana sounded horrified.

Two soldiers from *Guide* shoved August to the floor and kept him down. Ting Wheeling screamed and lunged forward. Sanda Brauna shouted. Another human soldier seized Ting. They tumbled, wrestling on the ground, as Ting attempted to reach August, the whole group of grappling bodies a spectacle for others, accomplishing nothing.

Lee frowned, coming out of his emotional paralysis.

August had been pinned with embarrassing ease, but Ting was stronger than the soldier he was fighting and had slowly overpowered him. Seeing that, one of those who'd attacked August raised a weapon. Ting reached for his own, then hesitated and stumbled forward. The soldier fired. Ting grunted and fell over.

August twisted, trying to see Ting. A soldier kicked him in the groin, and August doubled over from the sudden agony.

"Don't ... hurt him," Lee said. "It's true." He looked at Huana. "It's true. What proof do you need? Give me a knife, someone. Kolet, you like them."

Evan Kolet took a small, thin blade from his boot and handed it to Lee. "Hurry!" First glancing at the soldiers for permission, Kolet drew August to his feet.

August glimpsed Ting, pulling himself to a seated position, but it was Jeroen Lee he watched.

Elector Lee held the knife clumsily, then pushed it into his palm, making a jagged cut, showing no sign of discomfort as blood welled at the cut's edges. He pulled the knife out. Blood obscured the shallow wound. He wiped his hand, streaking his gray suit, then held his palm out to Huana for inspection. There were a few new drops, but it was obvious that the wound was already closing. "Rapid healing. Are you convinced, Esteban? Give the order. Now."

Huana seemed fascinated by Lee's hand. "You're a Neulander!"

"Of course not!" Elector Lee looked around at the gawking faces surrounding him. People had edged away, except for Huana. As he spoke, Lee moved steadily even closer to him. "I am a native of Co-Chan. I am an Elector, and I am human. Neulanders are as human as I am. As you are. In all the years we've known each other, Esteban, you have never had cause to doubt my humanity. Give Captain Sabas the order, or you will be no better than the Neulanders who murdered your family. Do it!"

It was more shock and the force of Jeroen Lee's personality than logic that caused Huana to nod at Captain Sabas. "All right. I agree with the others." He kept his arms crossed against his chest as if protecting himself from cold and moved away from Lee, back toward the others.

"Yes," Delegate Wilder shouted. Chin and Montague quickly agreed.

"We're on our way to intercept," Captain Sabas said. The display from *Guide* vanished, even the globe. Their loss darkened the room. Ting's panting, the smell of his blood, mingled with the close, tense atmosphere. There was no cheering this time, not even from the Neulanders.

Elector Kurioso smiled at Elector Brauna. She took a moment, seeming to catch her breath, while she stared at Jeroen Lee, then she nodded at Kurioso.

The soldiers released Ting at her order. Two guardians went to him immediately after he was freed. A red hole had burned through his right shoulder, but as soon as the soldier's restraint was gone, he tried to stand, to move ponderously forward, trying to reach August. August signaled "All clear. Wait." Ting nodded and sagged back to the support of his friends. Hesitantly, a Neulander medic approached him.

Kolet reopened his channel to Neuland's military headquarters. Weiss appeared so quickly August guessed he'd been waiting. "They've agreed," Kolet said. "*Guide* is on its way."

Weiss smiled. "We saw. They've begun firing." Relief had lightened his expression, but Kolet was somber. "How bad is it?" Kolet asked.

Weiss shook his head. "We can't know, yet. Trieste, Hintersea, the Kells, Henland, and Paulin." He stopped reciting names. "It could have been worse. We thought it would take the full two sweeps. I should thank them."

"Not now," Kolet said. "Let us know when it's over."

People began to speak again, whispering to their close neighbors, but they avoided Jeroen Lee. Sanda went to Ting Wheeling—pure courtesy, since she was not a medic. She glanced at August, who was near, and he dropped his gaze.

"You've told the world what you wouldn't tell me," she said.

She had been right. He had betrayed Jeroen Lee. Perhaps he had betrayed even Neuland, since he'd waited too long to prevent death. Alexander must have felt the sense of failure as Huana spat at him.

"Was it worth it, August?" Her red robe was dull in the dim light; her voice was sad.

Ting winced as the medic worked on him. "Yes," August said, watching the pain on his friend's face. "It was necessary."

August looked around the room. Neulander medics were helping the few probes still in discomfort. *Guide's* soldiers were watching from the border between the two groups, but not preventing movement in either direction.

August walked over to Jeroen Lee, passing the subtle dead zone that already surrounded Lee—Lee pretending that rather than being shunned, he was himself aloof. August remembered doing the same. "Elector Lee?" he said.

Lee grimaced. "I doubt that will be accurate for long."

"You underestimate yourself, Elector."

He smiled slightly. "Is that pity or true extrapolation?"

"Can you forgive me, Elector? I saw no other way."

Elector Lee extended his hand. August grasped it, and Lee shook hands with August formally in the rare gesture of equals. Lee's hand was warm, and there was a stickiness August realized was blood. When August took his own hand away, some remained inside his palm. "Did you do something wrong?" Lee said. "I don't think so. Can you forgive me for depending on you to say what I couldn't? Will Neuland?" His head lowered with each word he said, but at the end, he straightened and smiled. "Go back, make up with Sanda," Lee urged August. "You can do it. She might enjoy a conquering hero rather than a tragic one, for variety."

"Elector . . ."

"Vincent spoke up, also, didn't he? Martin will be pleased. Stay away from Kurioso, however. He's afraid of toolmen who can think."

"I don't want service as a toolman anymore." That seemed too blunt, and Lee was silent for a moment.

"Kolet is not entirely a fool," Lee said. "He'll help. You'll learn quickly. Ignore my earlier comments; you may have noticed that I have a selfish streak." He made a short, hurt sound intended as a laugh, then glanced around the shelter. Huana was watching him. "This is ridiculous. *Guide* will make quick work of that Emirates bandit ship, and it's still several thousand kilometers from Romoa. Why doesn't Kolet allow us to leave?"

August put his hands on Jeroen Lee's arms as though restraining him. "You shouldn't hide, Elector, especially right now. Force them to acknowledge that you're human." He watched Sanda Brauna pat Ting, comforting her favored pet. Jeroen Lee touched in a way that was both more wicked and more real. "Delegate Huana will listen to me if I remind him of his initial reaction to Alexander. I can help, Elector."

"August, you can't return to Center independently. To them, you are a toolman. Someone will order you put down, and no one will protest." Lee spoke as though he was already an outsider, as if revealing himself as Altered had made him less human in his own eyes, too.

"Returning to Center will be a risk, Elector. I've become accustomed to risk in the right cause." August slid his hands down until he held Lee's hands, enjoying the tremor he felt—Lee passively watching—then raised and kissed Lee's bloody hand, with the healing cut. "So you'll know. I want to come with you to Center."

Lee smiled, then began to chuckle. Across the room, Evan Kolet watched, puzzled, his expression identical with that of Esteban Huana, but most people looking at Jeroen Lee were wary. "You're too much like me, August. Tell me *all* the truth," Lee said.

"For Ellen. For Ting Wheeling. For Zoe and even Vincent. For the twins still on the farm. We're all human, Elector. I want to go back to Center for the same reasons you do, to make my people human, and for me, because Center is my home. I admit, if I return there, I need a protector. You are the one I choose."

Lee crossed his arms, examining August in a manner that was both intimate and clinical, already regaining his usual arrogant composure. "Delegates must qualify under a written constitution," he said as if he'd thought it through before, "but Jonism has only a custom against admitting Altered's to the Academies, not an absolute rule, nor any explicit rule against an Altered becoming an Elector." He watched Electors Brauna and Kurioso whispering together. "I do prefer to have you with me. The next several years will be difficult; your work is excellent."

"Elector, no," he said quietly. "I won't be your toolman, either; I'm not in your service at all."

"I apologize," Lee said quickly. "I did not intend to imply you were—you never have been, really." The humor in his voice was also pain. "I won't make that mistake again."

"Jeroen," August said carefully, visceral guilt at what he'd done losing to a deeper pride. The Elector's name felt odd on his tongue; he doubted he would ever be able to say it casually, but he straightened and looked Jeroen Lee in the eyes. "I want to be your student and your ally; I need your protection. Most of all, I would like to be your partner, if you'll have me."

"Stop, August, before you begin reciting poetry at me," Lee said. August had never seen quite that expression of interested pleasure on the Elector's face before. It made him glad.

Lee glanced around the shelter. "Kolet!" he shouted. "Can we leave this cave? I have work to do with my partner."

Kolet walked toward them. "August, are you all right?"

August took a deep breath, savoring the smell of fresh air. Pale shadows formed by a distant, natural light lay upon the tunnel floor, even extending into the room. The shelter's entrance had been opened. It was a new day. August thought he heard the waves outside, breaking against Neuland's unaltered shore. He understood their meaning—at least, he guessed it in his heart. "I will be fine," he said, bowing to Kolet. "Birth is always hard."